THE LIES WE TELL

Small Town Forbidden Romance

A Whiskey Cove Novel

GINA WATSON

Whiskey
Cove
Publishing

The Lies We Tell
Small Town Forbidden Romance

A Whiskey Cove Novel

by

Gina
Watson

Your Brother's Coming

1

The scent of fresh pastries and brewing coffee lingered in the air as Clara bustled around the large plantation-sized kitchen, her mind swirling in a vortex of the double wedding plans of her brother and his BFF Auggie. Plus, never far from her mind was her concern for Jackson, the poor overworked love of her life.

Even with all her responsibilities, it was hard not to smile. Today was the perfect day for a double wedding. The early morning sunlight streamed through the kitchen window, casting a golden halo around her, while the soft rustling of her khaki shorts echoed in the otherwise silent room. The sharp ping of her phone broke the tranquil silence, and she glanced down to see Jackson's name flashing on the screen. His message was simple yet filled with an unspoken tension that tugged at her heartstrings.

Jackson: Where are you?

As she began to type a reply, she couldn't help but reflect on their shared world—a chaotic mix of medical residencies, paramedic shifts, her work and college, and now, wedding preparations.

It was a world spinning too fast for Jackson, yet he refused to slow down.

Today was no different. It was supposed to be a day of celebration with Clay marrying Eve, and Auggie marrying Mia. The two women were sisters so that meant Clay and Auggie would become family—a fact they didn't wax on about but a fact Clara knew meant a lot to both of them. But as Clara stared down at Jackson's text, she knew it was more than just another wedding day—it was a test of strength, love, and patience.

She typed a reply text using just her thumbs.

> Clara: Be there in a bit. Had to get brides b-fast trays.

She'd told him to sleep in. Figured she'd be busy as wedding coordinator extraordinaire—she added the flair to her title.

> Jackson: Hurry, I need you.

She whispered, *Oh Cracker Jack, I need you more.* She smiled at the use of his nickname. He gorged on bags of the stuff while he completed endless mountains of paperwork and reports during his hospital residency.

She'd known he wouldn't stay in bed without her, but he had been behind on sleep and so she'd hoped. She grabbed two mimosas from the kitchen and made her way out to the pool house where the men were staying. She'd done her hair and makeup but hadn't put on her bridesmaid dress yet. There was still a lot of work to be done. After all, the stakes were high: a fancy wedding to organize and a sleep-deprived lover to take care of. And all she had in her arsenal were khaki shorts, a white tank top, two mimosas, and her unyielding spirit.

She opened the door to the pool house and found him slouched on the couch, a frown on his face.

She dangled the breakfast drink in front of him, just beyond his grasp. As she kissed his lips, his pout began to soften. "You can have it," she teased, "if you promise not to be such an Oscar the

Grouch." She mimicked an exaggerated pout herself, her eyes catching the shadows under his and the deeper wrinkles beside them, a little deeper than she'd remembered.

His frown was back with a flicker of something more—impatience and maybe even a little fear.

"Come on Cracker Jack, it's a most glorious day." She presented the mimosa to him.

"I'm on call. I can't have it." His bottom lip jutted out in a pout, though his eyes betrayed the act with their weariness. They held back words he'd rehearsed endlessly. She understood what he longed for, but they had to wait.

"I told you to sleep in. You look tired." She felt her face morph into a little frown of concern.

He traced a hair back behind her ear, his fingertips lingering at the spot where he'd first kissed her when she was seventeen and they'd needed each other more than their next breath. "I missed you, Bug."

The nickname had started as a joke about how she'd gotten under his skin, impossible to extract; now it carried the weight of all they weren't saying.

She giggled. "I think we were apart for about an hour."

"I don't care. I don't like waking without you." His eyes narrowed, jaw tightened, that same muscle twitch she'd noticed the first time they'd discussed telling her brother. "And I'm not happy about today either. It's been two years. We should be the ones getting married."

She took a large sip of the champagne and orange juice before setting the glasses on the couch side table. She kissed him and smiled against his lips. "We will be, baby. Soon."

Marriage to Jackson was the thing she wanted most in the world and so she hoped but wasn't sure herself. "But we can't move forward until we tell my brother and your best friend. We can't do that until you finish your residency." Her fingers found their way into his thick, wavy hair.

"Why not?" His hand covered hers, stilling her anxiousness.

"Because that's what we decided." Their eyes met, and in that moment of silent communication, they both acknowledged what remained unsaid; her fear that her brother would make her choose, and her greater fear that Jackson would push her to choose family. How many times had he said he wouldn't dare come between her and her family?

"I want to revise the decision. Anyway, I'm almost done." The words came out light, but his knuckles whitened as he gripped the couch cushion.

"How about I kiss you here," she nipped at his lips, tasting the salt from his breakfast, "and when we're done with that I'll kiss you down here." She fisted between his legs. "See if we can't turn that frown upside down." Even as she offered the distraction, a sudden raw honesty escaped her: "Sometimes I'm afraid we're waiting for a perfect moment that might never come." She blinked, surprised by her own admission before returning to the safer territory of seduction.

Jackson's lips brushed hers with a tender intensity, their breath mingling as a soft, involuntary sound escaped from the depths of his throat.

One of his hands slid up the back of her neck to grip her hair —always at that same spot where her curls gathered in a whorl— while the other cupped her jaw, his thumb tracing the scars from her accident at sixteen. His kiss was demanding and needy. He explored her deeply and alternated rough and soft strokes, as if he couldn't decide whether to worship or devour her. She loved his kiss, his touch, his everything—even his brooding that cast shadows between them on their brightest days.

He was ten years her senior, but that didn't matter because she'd loved him since she was seven years old. Since that summer afternoon when he'd shown up at their home, moved into the room next to hers, one bathroom between them. Even then, she sensed something broken inside him. He'd lost his parents. Hers pseudo adopted him. In the St. Martin family dynamic, they were connected as siblings, but were anything but.

Her Jackson. As the seasons changed, and the years passed, their connection grew into friendship and then into something more complicated—something that made her heart race with both longing and fear. They'd started getting intimate when she was seventeen and he was twenty-seven. It was part of the reason they hadn't told her family. Sometimes, in moments like these, guilt and desire battled within her—the thrill of his touch against the weight of their secret.

She was now nineteen. Still too young in modern times to marry. But she'd always felt older.

Her hand fiddled with the hardware on his jeans as she made a production of slowly undoing the button and pulling down the zipper. The metal was cool beneath her fingertips, a stark contrast to the heat building between them.

She knew how it sounded—their admission wouldn't paint a nice likeness of Jackson. The world would see predator and prey, not two souls who'd grown together across boundaries of age and propriety. A love born of need, her body broken and scarred, his heart shattered at the loss of so much so young.

She knew Clay had suspicions and had even alluded to their relationship, his sideways glances carrying judgment she pretended not to see. They'd thrown him off the hunt numerous times, each lie another brick in the wall between their private world and everyone else. Luckily, Eve had kept Clay exceedingly distracted.

She pulled his hardness free. He smiled at his readiness, but his eyes held vulnerability she rarely glimpsed—as if even now, after all these years, he feared she might find him wanting. His deep blue eyes shimmered like sunlight on the sea, the same gaze that had held fury when her brother once called him "damaged goods." She shimmied down his legs to kneel on the floor.

He grabbed a pillow, "Here Bug, don't kneel on the hard floor." The childhood nickname slipped from his lips—the one thing he'd carried forward from those early days, a reminder of what they'd been before they became this.

She rose and he slid the cushion under her knees, his calloused fingers lingering at the sensitive spot behind her knee. In that small gesture lay everything unsaid between them—his tenderness, her surrender, and the unspoken question of if what they'd built could survive the storm that was brewing and promised to destroy them.

Grasping his weight in her hands, she placed her tongue on his most sensitive part, and then took him between her lips, her heartbeat quickening in that familiar way that made her feel seventeen again—terrified and invincible all at once. He palmed her head and aided her efforts, his fingertips trembling slightly against her scalp. "God, Bug, I love being in your mouth." The words hung in the air between them.

She couldn't respond, not with words, but her eyes fluttered closed as something tightened in her chest—that old ache of needing too much. She loved it too, perhaps more than she should. Their connection had always been powerful. Their energy had been too potent to ignore. That's what had happened when she was seventeen—the first time his hand had brushed hers. Her skin had remembered it for days afterward. And once they'd connected on a physical level they couldn't stop, like addiction, like gravity, like breathing.

It was as if one could not exist without the other. Sometimes that thought woke her in the night, cold with sweat. She took him deep, loving the feel of him and the groans he made for her, while somewhere in the back of her mind she cataloged this moment—storing it away like all the others, a shield against the times when his job as an EMT and his long hours of residency at the hospital kept him away from her. Her fingers dug into his thighs, leaving half-moon impressions that would fade by the afternoon, unlike the marks he'd left on her that no one could see.

"Christ. Your brother's coming."

Her mind was disoriented, but Jackson pulled her from the floor, the momentum throwing her forward and onto him. Her heartbeat thundered in her chest, a metronome of guilt that seemed to broadcast their deception across the room. His hands at her waist moved her onto the couch. While he fastened his jeans she lifted the pillow from the floor, her fingers trembling slightly against the fabric. He'd barely finished containing himself when they heard the snick of the door opening.

The air in the room seemed to thicken, making it harder to breathe naturally.

Clay's wide ice blue eyes met her own before they narrowed to slits. His gaze migrated to Jackson and back to her.

"Clara." He frowned. "What are you doing out here?" His deep baritone reverberated around the room.

"I was looking for you." Each word of her lie seemed to scrape her throat raw, even as she maintained the bright smile. Jackson's hand started to rub against his denim-clad thigh. She knew he hated the lies they sometimes had to tell to hide their relationship. His smile didn't reach his eyes as they exchanged glances—a silent conversation of panic and reassurance.

"I saw you walking out here fifteen minutes ago. What have you been doing?" His eyes darted between her and Jackson, carrying the same skepticism they'd held since they were children and he'd caught her stealing cookies.

"Been talking with Jackson." His hand rubbed faster against his thigh. "I brought mimosas, but he told me about being on call at the hospital." She jumped up and skipped to Clay with practiced lightness, while inside she was sinking under the weight of her deception. She threw her arms around his neck and kissed him square on the lips. As she wrapped her arms around her brother's neck, she caught Jackson's scent still clinging to her skin and wondered if Clay could smell it too.

"Such a wonderful day. I love you. I'm so happy my big brother is getting married to his one and only love." The words tasted both true and false on her tongue—she loved him completely, which made the betrayal burn all the more. Her cheeks ached from the forced smile—the same smile she'd perfected over months of hiding.

He squeezed her tight. "Love you too, Clara Bear," he said, using the nickname her family had given her.

"Are you being a good boy?" She smiled up at his six-foot-five frame, breathing in the familiar scent of his woodsy cologne. Clay could be intense but nobody beat Jackson in that department. Truth told, Jackson reminded her a lot of her brother. Clay was fiercely loyal and protective, something she sensed Eve needed. They'd be so happy together. She wasn't jealous but it wasn't lost on her that she and Jackson were as equally perfect for one another as Eve and Clay.

"Auggie's the one you should be worried about. He's in Mia's room."

"Are you serious? That's not allowed." Her voice shed exasperation but deep inside she knew if Auggie wanted to be near Mia, nothing would stop him.

"She was crying."

Clara's eyes grew large, her hand instinctively rising to cover her mouth. "Why was she crying?"

Clay shrugged. "Auggie made her cry."

"What?"

"Bug—err—Clara, you better go check on her."

She turned to Jackson on the couch and couldn't help the slight smile that was forming at the corner of her mouth. As an EMT and emergency room doctor, Jackson was good at maintaining a tight control on his words and emotions, except when it came to her.

She kissed Clay's cheek. "Text me if you need anything."

"Will do."

She looked back at Jackson. He was always so serious. She'd seen him laugh just a few times and it was usually at something she'd done or said. She wished she could think of something now that would bring him relief. His downturned eyes and stiff body held so much pain it radiated across the room, coiling in her stomach with the familiar heaviness that had become her constant companion these past months. The weight of his silence pressed against her chest, making each breath a conscious effort.

Clay's head was turned away, so she held up the universal hand sign for *I love you*—three fingers extended, the silent language they'd developed during the days following his parents' death.

His grief had left a dampening effect on her entire family. Those days words had felt too loud, too inadequate for the emotion and pain coursing through him. Then she blew him a kiss. The right side of his mouth lifted ever so slightly—that precious micro-movement that had become her sustenance, the smallest proof that somewhere beneath his grief, her Jackson still lived.

Half-Committed Chuckle

2

Jackson loved the entire clan of St. Martins but was closest with Clay. The thought of Clay turning on him over Clara made his stomach twist into a knot he couldn't unravel. His thumb absently traced the edge of Clara's photograph hidden beneath his phone case—a small rebellion, keeping her close even when he couldn't acknowledge her existence.

And God, it was more than just a relationship—it was a huge whirlwind romance that had rewritten the geography of his heart. He loved her with everything he had.

It wasn't just her beauty, but everything about her. Her laugh, and there was more than one. There was the cute half-committed chuckle she made when she was tired, the one he'd heard last night as she fought sleep while they talked on the phone. There was the short burst of laughter that bubbled out when she got tickled at something she'd read or heard on television. There was the sexy breathless half moan, half giggle she made when he nuzzled behind her ear, her ticklish spot—a sound that replayed in his mind during the longest shifts, keeping him awake when exhaustion threatened to claim him.

Clara was immensely kind to everyone. He loved her spirit.

When the door closed behind her it was like someone shut off the oxygen that kept him alive. The air grew stale and thin without her, the scent of her lavender shampoo fading from his pillows until he had to bury his face in them just to catch the faintest trace—he'd been there before and never wanted to go back. The passing of time could steal a memory faster than ice melted under the Louisiana sun.

"You okay?" Clay took the chair across from him.

Jackson's hand jerked away from the phone, his shoulders straightening as he arranged his features into something resembling normalcy. "Just tired."

"You need to take better care of yourself." Clay leaned forward, eyes narrowing at the shadows beneath Jackson's eyes that had deepened over the past months. "Given your full days at the hospital and the number of hours you work at the station, you're gonna run out of steam."

The concern in Clay's voice—the same tone he'd used when he'd stayed up all night with Jackson after his parents' funeral—made the lie stick in Jackson's throat. For a moment, the truth hovered on his tongue: *I'm in love with your sister. I dream about her every night. I'm saving for a ring I saw in Donovan's window, the one with the sapphire that matches her eyes.*

Instead, he swallowed hard and said, "I'll be okay." The words felt heavy, weighed down by the dual exhaustion of working double shifts and maintaining the armor around his secret. But behind his eyelids flashed the image of that ring, of Clara's face when he'd finally be able to claim her publicly, and somehow, that made the weight bearable.

They lived together, though no one knew. Clara had tried to buy things for their apartment using her father's credit card, but Jackson's throat had constricted at the sight of that platinum rectangle sliding across the counter. His fingers had curled into fists at his sides, nails biting into calloused palms earned from extra shifts. He wasn't about to let that happen, and so he'd had to work overtime to provide for the few things she'd wanted to buy to make the apartment a home—their home.

He would provide for her, wanted to provide for her, even as his back ached each night from the double shifts. He knew she'd sensed his limited budget and lived much more frugally than she had done in the past. He'd caught her once, studying a faded receipt with wide eyes before tucking it quickly away when she noticed him watching.

Sure, things would have been easier if they'd waited until he'd graduated, but it was about survival. Some nights, lying awake beside her sleeping form, a cold sweat would break across his forehead as he calculated bills against his dwindling account balance. But then she would stir, her fingers automatically searching for his in the darkness, and the panic would recede. He couldn't exist without her, and he knew she felt the same about him.

Clay cocked his head. "Still, if you need some vacation time or if you need money let me know."

Jackson nodded, his gaze drifting past Clay to the Italian marble countertops in the pool house kitchenette—probably worth more than six months of his rent. Clay had offered this before. He'd even tried to sneak money into Jackson's possession, but there was no way in hell he'd accept it. He sat up straighter, absently adjusting the band on his watch. He wanted the world to know that he loved Clara for who she was not for her family name and money.

"Big day, huh? I can't imagine how ecstatic I'll be on the day I marry my soul mate."

"You talk as if you've met her." Clay's brow hitched.

He'd met her and he wouldn't deny it. He thought of how Clara had smiled last winter when he'd presented her with hot chocolate in chipped mugs by the space heater, declaring it better than any five-star resort her parents had taken her to. He smiled, fingers brushing against the smooth stone in his pocket—a river pebble she'd given him on his birthday last year, insisting it matched the flecks in his eyes.

Clay watched him intently, his gaze narrowing with every second that passed.

Jackson's throat felt like sandpaper as he cleared it. "I might have met someone," he began.

"Still dreaming about Sister Graham?" Clay teased, referring to their stunning middle school math teacher.

Jackson smirked. "Don't act like you didn't have the same thoughts."

Clay wiped his upper lip with a finger, grinning. "Pretty sure every boy did."

Jackson nodded in agreement. "So, have you been exiled to the pool house all day?"

"Yeah," Clay replied. "Auggie too, but he's breaking every rule."

"And you're sticking to them, as usual," Jackson said with a knowing smile.

Clay chuckled softly, nodding as a small grin played on his lips.

Jackson's eyes burned, the lids dropping like anchors. His limbs felt weighted, as if the marrow in his bones had been replaced with lead. It was true. He'd been behind on sleep for several weeks and hadn't slept well last night because they were apart with Clara staying at Auggie's family estate to assist the girls with the wedding preparations.

He'd worked for the last twenty-four hours, not returning home until around six in the morning yesterday, but when he slid into bed he hadn't slept. He and Clara couldn't be next to each other without touching, and touching led to kissing, kissing led to sex. Totally worth it. He'd rather make love to her than get a wink of sleep. Even now, his skin carried the ghost of her touch, the faint scent of her shampoo clinging to his skin. If it killed him, it'd be a sweet way to go.

"Jackson." Clay's voice seemed to come from far away. "Jackson. You're so exhausted you're not even aware when I call your name. Stay here, get a nap in. I'll see that no one disturbs you."

"Thanks, Clay. And hey, I'm happy for you." Jackson's fingers tapped against his thigh, a nervous rhythm to fill the spaces between words.

"Thanks. You know I couldn't imagine this day without you here. You're family."

Something collapsed inside Jackson's chest. The word "family" struck like a physical blow, sending a metallic taste to the back of his tongue. His throat constricted, the muscles working against each other as he swallowed hard.

"Thanks. That means everything." His voice cracked before he could say all of the words, and he looked away, blinking rapidly, his jaw clenching and unclenching.

Clay squeezed his shoulder once, then left Jackson in the pool house. The silence descended like a weight, pressing against his eardrums until he could hear the blood rush through his veins, a roaring tide that sounded too much like the white noise of falling.

"Damn flying lessons," he whispered to the empty room, the words bitter on his tongue as he thought of his deceased parents. If only his dad hadn't taken up flying—but Dad had logged the requisite number of hours, so his parents had embarked on his inaugural flight. The plane had crashed before they'd made it out of Louisiana.

Seventeen years old, Jackson had been at school. The counselor had brought him into the library where he usually spent lunch period. He remembered the shift in the air when they entered—the usual comforting smell of old paper and furniture polish suddenly suffocating, the filtered sunlight through the high windows too harsh. Usually, he and Mrs. St. Martin, the librarian, would share talk about new and upcoming book releases. He still remembered Mrs. St. Martin and his mother taking him to wait in the long lines for the magical books on release days.

When they entered the library, she looked up, her face changing in a way that made his stomach drop before she'd said a word. He remembered thinking it had been strange to be in the library when everyone else was in class, but he'd chalked it up to good fortune and pulled a Harry Potter book off the shelf, the familiar worn cover rough beneath his fingertips, as if holding onto this small normal thing might keep whatever was coming at bay.

He'd grown up with the St. Martins. After his parents were gone, the family absorbed him like he was one of their own. He'd lived with the St. Martins for a year and a half before he'd graduated high school and moved into the dorms at Louisiana State University. They'd had six children, but Jackson had grown closest with Clay because Clay would just let him be. Most of the children talked quite a bit, but not Clay. They could spend an entire afternoon fishing or hunting and not speak.

Once, when they were out on the lake at sunset, Clay had simply reached over and squeezed his shoulder—just once—as Jackson stared at a pair of mallards that reminded him of how his father used to point out wildlife. That single touch had said more than hours of spoken consolation ever could. Once they were older, Jackson had spent a lot of time at Clay's house, where the walls didn't hold the constant expectation that he would eventually heal.

Every night, Jackson would arrange his father's worn leather wallet and his mother's silver locket on the nightstand of his borrowed room, then put them away just before dawn broke. Some nights he'd hold the locket to his ear, as if its hollow center might still contain the echo of his mother's laugh.

Clara had been a seven-year-old child when Jackson had moved in and every morning she would come into the room where he stayed to announce that breakfast was ready. Every single day. The creak of floorboards in the hallway would herald her arrival, followed by the soft twist of the brass doorknob. She'd become such a colossal nuisance he'd slipped a chair under the door thinking he'd outsmart her but damn it all if she hadn't come in through the bathroom door.

"You can't keep me out," she'd declared one morning, standing triumphantly in the doorway while he groaned into his pillow. "Mama says grief needs company even when it wants to be alone."

And her eyes, those enormous luminescent blue pools would blink down at him as he slowly became coherent from sleep—God, he could get lost in their depths even then. That was all she'd said at first—"Breakfast is ready." To which he'd replied, "I'm not hungry,"—and eventually—"stop coming into my room."

One muggy afternoon, the air heavy with the promise of thunderstorms that matched his mood, she'd appeared at his side while he sat on the porch watching raindrops form. Without preamble, she'd said, "The catfish will bite like crazy tomorrow morning, and

Mama's going to burn the biscuits because she'll be talking on the phone with Aunt Josephine."

The next day, Clay and Jackson had pulled in a record catch before 9 a.m., and the smell of charred dough had greeted them when they returned, Mrs. St. Martin fanning smoke from the kitchen while cradling the phone between ear and shoulder.

One day Clara had simply said, "I'm going to marry you," with the same certainty she'd announced the catfish and the biscuits. She had an uncanny ability to predict future events. A sixth sense. It was almost scary—and somehow, in those moments of her strange certainty, the crushing weight on his chest would lift, just slightly, just enough to draw a full breath.

He'd remembered Christmas week—Clara would have been fifteen—when the youngest St. Martin brother, Briggs, was being an ass to his childhood nemesis, now his wife. The memory still made Jackson's stomach clench, not just because of the confrontation, but because of what it had revealed about all of them that day.

Briggs and Jackson had been hanging Christmas lights on the front porch of the house while Clara had sat on the porch swing and hot-glued bows onto garland that was to go around the door. The sharp, clean scent of pine mingled with the metallic tang of winter air, a combination that would forever remind Jackson of desire tangled with shame.

"Do you like the red velvet bows or these glittery ones?" Clara held each in the air to help them decide, the evergreen needles leaving tiny scratches on her fingertips that she didn't seem to notice.

Jackson pointed and said, "Velvet," his voice catching slightly as Clara's eyes met his.

"Glitter," Briggs said, barely looking up from the string of lights he was untangling with unnecessary force.

Clara harrumphed. "Fat lot of good you two are." She blew a strand of hair from her face, her breath making a small cloud in the December air.

Jackson chuckled, though something twisted inside him as he watched her. One of her legs dangled from the porch swing and gently rocked the seat. She wore an oversized, extremely purple LSU sweatshirt that swallowed her small frame. Occasionally she'd look up and give Jackson a coy smile and he could just barely make out her dimples—those damned dimples that made his chest tighten and his palms sweat despite the cold. He was old enough to know better than to notice the way her eyes brightened when they landed on him.

"I think the velvet is the better choice," she'd said, smiling down at the bows in her hand, her fingers nervously tracing the soft edges.

"Of course, you do—if Jackson suggested it, it must be so." Briggs mocked, the words carrying more weight than they should have.

Clara frowned. "You're just a bully, Briggs." Her shoulders hunched slightly, protective.

Briggs stuck his tongue out at her.

"Real mature. Is that what they're teaching you in Physics 101?" Clara asked.

A white golf cart sputtered toward them, the sound cutting through the tension like a dull knife. Clara set aside her garland and stood to wave, her greeting warm and smile sweet. Lacie parked the cart and joined Clara on the swing, her weathered coat a stark contrast to Clara's pristine sweatshirt, the frayed cuffs betraying frequent mending.

"Merry Christmas," Lacie said cheerfully, though her eyes darted around the grand porch as if she were calculating her own worth against every expensive fixture.

Clara and Jackson returned her joyous offering while Briggs frowned, his body going rigid in a way that only Jackson seemed to notice—the same way he always reacted when Clara appeared, as if bracing himself against something unknown. His mind not at all in keeping with what his body wanted.

Lacie's eyes scanned the porch finally resting on Briggs. She rubbed her arms, "It's really starting to feel like winter." Her thin jacket offered little protection, and Jackson saw Briggs notice this too, his jaw clenching as he fought the urge to offer his own coat.

"Don't you have a better jacket?" Briggs snapped, the question carrying too much concern to match his harsh tone.

"I just came to ask if I could ride with you to the Smith's Christmas party." Lacie's chin lifted slightly, pride overriding the discomfort of cold.

"How do you know I'm going?" Briggs's fingers tightened around the strand of lights until his knuckles whitened.

"You go every year. Mom said I could only go if you would bring me." There was a slight tremor in her voice, betraying how much the answer mattered.

"I'm not interested in babysitting your chastity all night. Plus, there's always a lot of tail there and I plan on getting down in my truck on the way home so unless you want to watch, you're out of luck." The Christmas lights around them seemed to dim as he spoke, or perhaps it was just that the holiday warmth had drained from the moment.

Lacie grimaced. "Great. I'll just tell my mom that you'll give me a ride if I sit third chair in your ménage à trois." Despite her brave words, her shoulders curled inward, a flower closing against frost.

Jackson tugged hard on the string of lights Briggs held and the ladder rocked. Briggs arched a brow at Jackson, a flash of vulnerability crossing his features before the familiar mask of indifference slammed back into place. The only person who didn't know that Briggs was in love with Lacie was Briggs.

"Let me know what dear Mommy says." Briggs climbed from the ladder and continued to speak, each word falling like ice. "A little education may help you." He walked up to Lacie at the swing, and she stood, her back straightening as if preparing for a blow. "It's high time you were deflowered. It's starting to get weird."

Thwack. Lacie's hand connected with his cheek, the sound cracking through the winter air like a branch breaking under ice. The red imprint of her fingers bloomed instantly across his skin, stark against his sudden pallor.

Clara jumped up and Jackson went toward her, instinctively positioning himself between her and the conflict, though his eyes remained fixed on the spectacle before him.

Briggs's hand palmed his cheek, and for a fleeting moment before anger reclaimed his features, Jackson saw it—the wounded eyes of the eight-year-old boy who'd cried when Lacie had left to spend summer at camp in Colorado, who'd kept the seashell she'd given him hidden in his desk drawer.

"What the fuck, Lacie?" The words were harsh, but his voice cracked on her name, the Christmas lights reflecting in the unexpected shine of his eyes.

Lacie's face already looked a mess at the callousness of Briggs's words. "You will remember everything one day, and when you do, I hope it burns like acid in your throat."

And in that moment, as the colored lights blinked around them, Jackson understood something about love and pride that would haunt him for years to come, whenever he looked at Clara's dimples in the glow of Christmas lights.

Tears streamed down Lacie's face. "I hate you," she whispered and then she boarded the golf cart.

Next to him Clara's hands fisted at her sides, and she shot him a loathsome stare. Jackson placed his hand on her shoulder. "You want to go inside? I'll make us some hot chocolate."

"In a minute."

She walked up to Briggs and pointed with her index finger. "One day you'll regret having treated her this way."

"No, I won't."

"Yeah, you will. If you go easy on her now, it'll only help you later when you realize that you love her."

Briggs laughed. "That's hilarious, Clara. And I am helping her. Trust me, she takes herself and that golden twat between her legs way too seriously."

Clara gasped and covered her mouth with her hand while Jackson punched Briggs in the arm.

"What the hell, Jackson? Is this beat on Briggs day? Shit."

"How about going light on the sex talk in front of your *baby* sister. And the expletives for that matter."

"Clara's got six brothers, she's heard it all."

"I've never heard Jackson speak a swear word," Clara said.

Briggs's brow furrowed as he looked from Clara to Jackson. "*I have*, so you can stop acting like he's some kind of god." Briggs huffed off, his booted feet striking the floor with heavy thuds.

"I'd like to apologize for the male population."

Clara shrugged. "He's got some growing pains, but he will end up married to and completely gone on Lacie."

Despite the tension and Brigg's unchecked growing pains, those particular memories with Clara and her family had Jackson smiling as he reclined on the couch in the pool house. He breathed deeply as he felt his eyelids grow heavy.

Clara had known there was a future for them too. One Sunday morning she'd come into Jackson's room with a picture she'd made. Theirs was a large family, even by southern standards. There were seven St. Martin siblings including Clara, but she was the only girl. On her drawing there were eight children, along with her mom and dad. The girl was holding a boy's hand. Above were the names Clara and Jackson.

"See this?" She pointed to the picture. "I'm going to marry." She left the picture and started to walk out. "Breakfast is ready," she called over her shoulder. The scent of her mama's buttermilk biscuits and salty country ham drifted up the stairs, mingling with the sweet-sharp tang of the magnolia blooming outside his window. He followed her down the stairs, careful to skip the third one that groaned like an old man with bad knees. Even back then her magnetism could not be denied—like following the pull of something inevitable.

***

Plush full lips caressed his forehead. "Bug." He smiled, something unfolding in his chest like a fist finally releasing. "What a wonderful way to wake from a nap."

He pulled her hand, forcing her down on top of him, seeking the weight of her to anchor him to something real. His fingers found the small crescent-shaped scar behind her ear—the one she'd gotten when she'd had her horrible accident at sixteen that continued to steal the breath right out of his lungs when he recalled the day. His eyes settled on her form in a vision of lavender satin. "You're beautiful."

"You've been asleep for several hours. Are you feeling okay?" Her palm rested on his forehead, cool and familiar against his skin. A strand of her hair—the one that always escaped any attempt to tame it—fell across her face, catching in the corner of her mouth the way it had since she was a child.

"I'm fine. I just need to spend more time with you." He smiled, but felt the truth of it like an ache spreading beneath his ribs, a hollowness that only her presence seemed to fill. "I miss you even when you're right here."

"I agree." Her brilliant eyes closed as she placed a tender kiss on his lips. "It's time to put on your suit. You and I have a date."

He grumbled and frowned, his jaw tightening as he pictured standing in the church, watching someone else make vows that should be his and hers.

She giggled. "Are you going to harrumph all the way down the aisle?"

"It should be us. Our love burns brighter than any of theirs and yet we can't even profess it." The words came out leaving a sour taste in his mouth. He shouldn't compare the love he had for Clara against anyone else but he was so tired of hiding their love from the world.

"You're right, it should be. You know I want to be yours in name more than anything, but a piece of paper won't change the way I love you." He sucked on her lips, tasting the ghost of promises made under summer stars and autumn rains. She always knew the right things to say to him. His heart rate immediately slowed, his breathing leveled out.

"But I'm much too young for the likes of you." She turned her nose to the air with a flourish, and he caught the flicker of fire in her eyes that said she felt it too. The longing to be free of the chains that trapped their love from the world.

"You're an old soul. Besides, I'm southern. We like our women like we like our beef, fresh and young."

Her brow furrowed. "Hmm, I'm not sure I appreciate being likened to a slab of meat." She traced the line of his collarbone with one finger, hesitating at the place where his heart beat strongest. "When I make plans, I keep them. I will marry you into my family." Her words held determination. "And nobody on this earth can stop me."

He loved her sweetness, but her determination could make him melt in her arms. He grew hard beneath her and wished they were anywhere else so that he could take her the way he wanted, letting her know how much her words meant.

He took her earlobe between his lips and massaged before kissing behind the tender folds of skin. Her shoulders rose, "if you don't stop that, I'll demand that you make love to me." Her voice was breathy and staccato and her chest rose and fell with a quickness born of need.

His hold on her tightened as his lips caressed across the most delicate skin of her neck.

She tugged the fingers she had in his hair. "Let's pretend it's us getting married. After all you are my escort down the aisle."

"We don't have a ring."

"We do." She held up her right hand. "I have your promise ring."

"That's not a suitable wedding ring for the love of my life." He grasped her fingers and brought them to his lips.

When he released her hands, she clasped them over her heart. "I love my ring."

He sighed. "It's a cheap ring. I want you to have a big diamond."

"And I just want you." Her hands went to his neck as she set her wide blue gaze intently on him. "You *are* my big diamond." Their mouths sealed in a kiss. Warm silken lips branded and comforted him.

His hands slid along her sides, feeling the smoothness of the purple gown she wore. The fabric whispered secrets against her skin —too mature for her frame yet somehow making her seem even younger in its elegance.

The color deepened her eyes to an impossible blue, like water off the coast of Sicily that shined like jewels under the noonday sun, another sweet memory he could thank his parents for. In these moments, he always pushed away the voice in his head that counted the years between them, focusing instead on how time seemed to collapse when they touched.

"I like your dress," Jackson murmured, his voice carrying the weight of everything unsaid between them. His fingertips hovered at her waist, simultaneously drawing her closer and holding her at a distance—the contradiction he lived with every day.

He shouldn't be doing this at Clay's wedding, but he couldn't stay away from her. Most of the time he refused to let negative thoughts surface about their intimacy, which was real and sacred to him. A thing so pure nothing could make it ugly. But he knew the real world. Had lost his parents to it. No matter how much something mattered to him it could be gone in an instant. That was life. He'd hated it. That is until he had come together with Clara. She was the reason he could get out of bed every day.

"Thank you." She rained kisses on his lips, cheeks, and nose, each one leaving behind the faint trace of cherry lip gloss. "I have to go help the ladies into their dresses, but I wanted to wake you up. You need to get dressed too." Her fingers lingered on his collar, reluctant to break contact.

You're So Young

3

The sudden opening of the door sliced through their moment. A gasp filled the airwaves, sharp as breaking glass. Eve's palm cupped her mouth, her knuckles whitening with the pressure of containing whatever was about to escape.

Ice crystallized in Jackson's veins, the same paralyzing cold he'd felt at seventeen when he'd sat in that library, holding the worn copy of the third Harry Potter book. His throat constricted, narrowing until each breath became deliberate work. The room's temperature seemed to plummet when the door opened, as if judgment itself had a physical presence.

Clara's heart lurched painfully against her ribs as she jumped from the couch. Jackson's hand twitched involuntarily toward her, then retreated to his side—wanting to shield her but knowing his protection was now the very thing that damned them both. She walked over to Eve, each step measured as though she walked on breaking ice. She pulled Eve inside with trembling fingers and pushed the door closed, leaning against it as if barricading them all from the world outside.

"Please," Clara whispered, her voice catching, "you can't say anything." Her eyes darted to Jackson's, holding a knowledge beyond her years—she understood, as well as Jackson did, what it was they were risking.

Both women glanced at Jackson who was standing near them now. His jaw tightened into a hard line, shoulders drew back in a posture that spoke of defiance even as fear flashed behind his eyes. The familiar tension lines around his mouth deepened—marks carved by months of looking over his shoulder, of calculating risks, of justifying to himself what he refused to justify to anyone else.

"Please," he echoed, the word hanging between them like a confession. His eyes briefly closed, a millisecond of wishing he and Clara could be anywhere but here. Inside, Jackson's mind screamed: *They'll take her away from me.* The thought summoned the hollow ache he'd carried since watching his mother's casket lower into frozen ground, that same feeling of something essential being torn away while he stood helpless.

"Oh my God, I just can't believe it." Eve's head shook like a pendulum of doom. "You're so young," she said while looking at Clara. The clock on the mantel ticked loudly in the silence, counting down to something inevitable.

Eve regarded Jackson, her eyes tightening, pupils contracting as if she now saw him as a threat. "And how old are you?"

Jackson felt sound distort around him, Eve's question stretching and warping as his pulse pounded in his ears. He swallowed hard, the movement visible in his throat, knowing whatever answer he gave would never be enough to bridge the chasm now opening at their feet. "Twenty-nine."

That admission elicited another gasp. "Are you two," Eve swallowed, "intimate?" Clara looked to the floor. The ensuing silence crawled like a living thing between them—thick and suffocating—broken only by the distant splashing of the pool filter and the muted sounds of wedding preparations filtering through the windows.

"Clay is just going to kill you."

"You're going to tell him?" Jackson's jaw twitched as he waited for an answer, a familiar knot forming in his throat—the same one that appeared every time their secret threatened to surface. His fingernails dug half-moons into his palms, the small pain grounding him against the larger one looming.

Clara grasped her hands and pleaded. "Please Eve, I need this. Please." Her voice carried the weight of two years of hiding, of stolen moments and careful exits from family gatherings.

"Clara's not quite ready to tell her family, but we will soon." Jackson felt the practiced words leave his mouth—words they'd rehearsed and repeated like a prayer, though the timeline kept shifting like sand through their fingers.

Eve stared them down preparing to strike, like a countdown for a firing squad. It felt like a decade before she spoke. "I won't say anything, but I hope you won't continue to pursue"—she pointed with her finger from Clara to Jackson—"whatever this is. I don't want to have to lie to Clay."

Jackson shared a knowing look with Clara that was impossible for Eve to miss. In that glance passed the memory of last Christmas, when they'd both reached for the same serving dish and let their fingers linger two seconds too long, then spent the rest of dinner avoiding eye contact while Clay told stories about his college days.

"What's going on?"

"We've been pursuing this for two years and now—"

"Oh my God!" Eve interrupted.

"I love him." Clara said, her voice dropping to that soft, certain tone that Jackson had first heard in a whispered phone call at 3 a.m., when she'd finally said the words they'd been circling for months.

"I love her." Jackson countered, his chest expanding with the truth of it—the one honest thing he could say in a room thick with deception.

Eve's hand formed a fist, and it collided with her forehead. "Jesus." Disbelief etched her face. "Two years?"

Jackson spoke first, his shoulders tensing as they did when he had to explain their timeline, justify their choices. "I'm close to finishing school and we wanted to wait until after graduation before we tell the family." The words tasted stale in his mouth, repeated so many times between him and Clara they'd lost their conviction.

"Two years?"

Clara's gaze landed on Jackson, softening in that way that made his heart both soar and ache. "Two years." In those two words lived hundreds of goodbye kisses that hurt more each time, dozens of near-misses with Clay, and countless text messages that read simply *soon*.

"Is that why you transferred from Tulane to LSU?"

"Yes, it is, but please"—Clara squeezed Eve's hands in hers—"let's focus on your wedding day. It's time to get into your dress and Jackson needs to put on his tux. Shall we leave him to it?"

"Yeah, okay." Shaking her head she said, "If Clay finds out about this you two will have hell to pay." She sighed deeply. "I can't be part of that."

Jackson nodded, absently rubbing the spot over his heart where tension always gathered when Clay's name entered their conversations. "I completely understand. We won't put you in that position."

He watched the women exit the pool house. Clara and Eve exchanged some serious dialogue by the look of it. Clara's fingers nervously twisted the gold ring she wore—the one he'd given her for their first anniversary, which she wore on her right hand where no one would question it. Their situation was getting out of hand and now affected other people. He wouldn't have their love be a lie. Not when it was the most honest thing he'd ever felt—more real than any family allegiance or social expectation that kept them hiding in pool houses and whispering "I love you" only when they were certain no one could hear.

Jackson's head pounded with the rhythm of too many night shifts stacked like unpaid debts—a dull, persistent throbbing that had become the background music of his life. He ran his fingers over the creased lines on his forehead, tracing the throbbing rhythm beneath a façade that had seen an excess of pain in the trauma bay.

He cleared his mind of everything except the night ahead, a small sanctuary of possibility he'd carved out from his chaotic schedule. Other than being on call, he was in the clear until tomorrow. Even the charge nurse promised she wouldn't call him.

Still, the familiar weight of his pager sat in his pocket—a tether he could never fully sever, even on his nights off—but the E.R. would likely be quiet tonight. What mattered was that rare alignment of their free time, a celestial event as uncommon as an eclipse in their busy lives.

As he buttoned his shirt, his fingers remembered the weight of the gift waiting at his apartment—a French-porcelain fluted pie dish the color of a clear winter sky. He'd caught her lingering over it at Williams-Sonoma, her fingertips tracing the ridged edge with such quiet longing that he'd returned alone the next day to purchase it.

Jackson wasn't naturally fluent in the language of gifts; the grammar of giving had always felt foreign on his tongue. But he was learning her syntax of appreciation, cataloging the small things that made her eyes light up when she thought no one was watching.

He methodically reviewed the evening he'd orchestrated, not elaborate by anyone else's standards perhaps, but carefully considered for her. The DVD was wrapped in simple blue paper that matched her eyes. It was the film adaptation of that series she kept on her nightstand, dog-eared and well-loved. They would order from Salvatore's, splitting a margherita pizza the way they always did, her taking the crispier edge pieces, him pretending not to notice how she'd carefully redistribute the basil leaves to his side because she knew he loved them.

By the end of the movie, tears would track down her cheeks, collecting at the corner of her smile. He never fully understood the appeal of stories that pulled such emotion from her, but he understood the beauty of her tears—how they weren't markers of pain but testaments to being deeply moved, how she never brushed them away but let them exist as proof of her capacity to feel.

Jackson smoothed his shirt, a small smile playing at his lips. He loved that in a world that demanded constant stimulation, she found contentment in the quiet spaces between words, in evenings spent with nothing more spectacular than shared silence and borrowed warmth.

The door suddenly crashed open, shattering his contemplation like a stone through glass. Jackson tucked away his tender thoughts with the practiced quickness of a man accustomed to guarding his softer parts, his face automatically rearranging into the wry expression his friends expected. Auggie and Clay barreled in, both dressed in smoke gray tuxedos that transformed them from the rowdy college boys he remembered into something approximating respectable men.

"Cigar?" Auggie held out a polished wooden box to Clay, his movements expansive, taking up space the way he always had—as if the world was his stage and everyone else merely supporting actors.

"No thanks." Clay murmured, adjusting his cufflinks with fingers that betrayed a nervousness his voice did not.

"Jackson?" Auggie's hand shot up displaying a cigar like a trophy. "Cuban?" The familiar scent of tobacco already clung to him, as much a part of Auggie as his booming laugh and unapologetic confidence.

Jackson shook his head, waving away both the offer and the swirl of smoke that had already begun to invade the small room. "Trying to quit." The familiar joke fell from his lips easily, a comfortable exchange they'd performed hundreds of times. Behind his casual response, he wondered if he'd ever stand where they were standing—on the precipice of forever with someone. "So you two bastards finally found women to put up with your shit. Auggie, Mia's cool with your cigarette smoke? Clay, you still tying up your women?"

Clay coughed, his ears reddening slightly at the edges. "Say what?"

"Playing innocent?" Jackson shrugged, the familiar rhythm of their banter a comfortable mask over the raw vulnerability of his earlier thoughts.

Auggie laughed, the sound filling every corner of the room. "Everything okay with Mia?"

"Yeah, she just got a little emotional over the gift I gave her."

Jackson leaned forward slightly, genuinely curious about the man who had once sworn he'd never settle down.

Auggie thrust his hand in the air with theatrical flourish,

preparing for his announcement. "Honeymoon in Bora Bora and her birth certificate."

Jackson frowned, trying to piece together the puzzle. "Bora Bora I get, but gifting a birth certificate?" He shook his head, watching his friend with newfound curiosity, wondering what transformation love had wrought in him.

Auggie hooked his arm around Jackson's shoulders with the easy physicality they'd shared since freshman year dorm rooms and late-night confidences. For just a moment, beneath the smoke and the insults, their eyes met in understanding—all three of them navigating love in their own imperfect ways. "My brother, women are mysterious creatures. You'll learn if you ever find someone to put up with your bitch fits."

"Thanks for the tip, cockwaffle." Jackson fanned the smoke away from his face, smiling despite himself. In the reflection of the mirror across the room, he caught a glimpse of all three of them—the boys they'd been and the men they were becoming, each finding their own path to vulnerability and connection, however clumsily expressed.

They Wed, Finally

4

Tending to two brides at once was proving to be an act of monumental patience. Keeping Auggie and Clay away from their brides was damn near impossible. Auggie had ruined Mia's up-do twice.

Clara was glad when the musical notes of Johann Sebastian Bach lilted in the air—the same piece she'd once mentioned to Jackson during a late-night conversation about their own wedding someday. The melody now hung between them like a promise neither had fulfilled. She took her position in line next to Jackson and linked her arm in his, the sleeve of her bridesmaid's dress catching slightly on his cufflink—connected yet snagging.

His free hand squeezed her fingers and they were lost in each other's eyes. Clara saw the question there, the one that had begun appearing six months ago, lurking behind his irises like a shadow. The couple behind them coughed to signal they should begin the processional.

Slowly they traversed the makeshift aisle. She whispered, "Jackson, I love you," the words both true and a shield against what remained unsaid. His fingers squeezed tighter. She could feel his warmth through the suit he wore as it radiated into her body, heat that reminded her of how he would wrap himself around her on winter mornings, as if trying to keep her from drifting away.

As they reached the end of the walkway his jaw twitched—that same involuntary motion she'd noticed last week when she'd absently mentioned her father's wedding gift to Mia.

His vice-like grip was starting to squeeze off blood flow and her arm tingled toward numbness, mirroring the way she'd grown accustomed to numbing the question hanging between them. Each step closer to the altar seemed to tighten his hold, as though the ceremonial ground ahead was territory he feared entering unprepared.

"It should be us," he whispered, his voice catching on "us" as though the word itself carried the weight of every conversation they'd avoided.

They broke apart at the appointed spot, just as rehearsed, just as they'd learned to do with difficult topics. Clara stood and pivoted on the indicated mark, her body performing the choreography while her heart stumbled.

Even from across the stage Jackson's eyes were intent on her, holding her in place more effectively than any floor marker. She agreed with him, a flutter of longing and panic battling beneath her ribs. It should be them, but they were both still in college and they really didn't have any money—a practical truth that felt like both excuse and protection.

A little sigh escaped her lips at the white lies they had to tell. Her parents lived in Whiskey Cove, and so did Finn and Briggs. Clay lived in Baton Rouge and that was tricky. Because her family supported her well, she had her own apartment near campus, but she'd stayed with Jackson most nights.

Clara remembered how Jackson's shoulders had stiffened when she'd unconsciously reached for her father's credit card during their grocery run last month—how quickly shame had replaced joy in his eyes. He paid for everything now, insisting with a pride that seemed both beautiful and fragile, and she felt a little guilty watching him count pennies for coffee while her father's financial safety net remained invisibly beneath her. However, his joyful demeanor when he provided for them—the way his chest expanded slightly when he handed over his debit card—kept her from feeling too bad about their finances.

Still she wondered if what kept them from the altar wasn't money at all, but the unspoken fear that their love for each other wouldn't be enough to convince the world that they belonged together.

If she married without her family's blessing, and a marriage to Jackson definitely would be without their blessing once they learned of the deception surrounding their clandestine relationship, she had no doubt they'd cut off her funding anyway. She pictured the platinum card sitting at the back of her nightstand in her childhood bedroom. She'd left it there for safekeeping, refusing to use it because if Jackson didn't have an endless spending cap, neither did she. They were two parts of a whole and she wouldn't have money skewing their balance.

She considered a future without the safety net she'd known her entire life. The platinum card—a leash disguised as privilege—had been her father's graduation gift, accompanied by his practiced smile that never quite reached his eyes. But the card wasn't about love or generosity of spirit, it was about control. After all, they'd cut funding to Cash when, after completing four years of college, he'd failed to acquire enough credits to graduate. She still remembered her brother's hollow laugh over the phone that night: "Welcome to conditional love, sis. Hope you never disappoint them."

The loss of her father's support didn't mean much because Jackson had said that he wouldn't accept, use, or even require money from them. He was adamant that he should be the one to take care of them. She believed in him. Yet her stomach tightened whenever she remembered the night he'd come home to their apartment after working a double shift as an EMT, his clothes filthy with mud and blood, his hair wet and skin cold from the drizzling rain.

He'd fallen asleep while she was speaking, exhaustion claiming him mid-sentence, yet the small velvet box containing the silver pendant she'd offhandedly admired weeks earlier was still clutched in his calloused palm.

He was disciplined, dedicated, and unbelievably stubborn, but she'd watched him sacrifice himself for two years in order to provide her with things he thought she needed or wanted. She'd learned not to express interest in merchandise she saw online or in the stores because it would inevitably end up in her possession, Jackson having observed her delight and cataloged in his mind the trinkets for future purchase.

Truth told, she didn't need or want anything when she was with him—not the cashmere sweaters in her closet or the trust fund gathering interest in her name. What she craved was the warmth of his calloused hand against her cheek and the certainty in his voice when he spoke of their future, as if loving her was the simplest decision he'd ever made.

Clara's family possessed old southern values that clung to her like the stiff lace collar that was part of her Catholic school uniform —constricting, impossible to ignore. As the baby girl of the family, she knew what was expected: Jackson would need to ask her father for his blessing, and once he did, questions would unravel their carefully constructed facade.

A knot formed in Clara's stomach as she caught sight of Jackson across the room, his tie ever so slightly askew. Her fingers twitched at her side, yearning to correct the almost imperceptible crooked silk. He shifted subtly in her direction, an unconscious lean towards her that was as familiar to her as the steady thump of her own heart beneath her maid of honor dress.

Ultimately, they would have to tell her father that they'd been intimate for two years. The thought alone made her throat constrict. As the oldest and most protective brother, Clay would freak out and add fuel to her father's anger. She could already see Clay's jaw clenching the way it had when Tommy Wilkins had brought her home late from the freshman dance—only a hundred times worse.

Clara didn't want that for Jackson. He didn't deserve to be treated poorly by her brother and father for something so pure as their love. Her stomach clenched at the thought of her father's dismissive sneer, the same one he'd worn when she'd brought home a B+ instead of an A. She could already hear Clay's cutting words,

"He's sick, Clara, I won't let him use you to heal himself." Those words would slice into Jackson's tender heart like shrapnel.

Her family wouldn't understand, and she knew Jackson would beat himself up afterward, hunched over on the edge of their bed, head in hands, muttering some stupid creed about brotherhood and family loyalty that he'd learned from the brother who had abandoned him.

But Jackson was her brother too, and her family. Not by blood but something even stronger—pain born from loss at such a young age it seems you will never dig out. She still remembered finding him behind the community center, she seventeen, he twenty-seven, both orphaned in different ways, his tears mingling with rain as he clutched his mother's worn silver locket. That night, they'd sat shoulder to shoulder under the building's small awning until sunrise, saying nothing, their breathing eventually synchronizing in the dark.

But they did dig out, and it was because they'd had each other to cling to when the nightmares came, when the anniversaries arrived, within weeks of one another on the calendar, yet years apart, two tragedies different in details but sharing the same ugly undertones of loss and suffocating grief.

That night Jackson told her that watching normal families doing mundane things felt like drowning. In a strange way she could understand that too. She felt the crushing weight of her own loss on her chest when watching her friends try on prom dresses, their skin unmarred from the horrors of her accident. In the dress shop, she'd suffocated in her own body.

At last, the other couples started to file into the church antechamber, their laughter echoing against the vaulted ceiling like bells Clara couldn't join in ringing. And yet, she loved Clay and the woman he'd chosen to live a life by his side. But she deserved happiness too and he was standing in her way. The irritation she felt for him made it hard fto be utterly and completely happy for him on this day.

The huge wedding party comprised her and Jackson, all of her brothers and their wives, plus Auggie's two brothers. Their polished appearances—pressed suits and flowing dresses—stood in stark contrast to the mess she felt inside.

Eve's and Mia's eyes, gray and amethyst, inspired the wedding colors that decorated everything from the ribbons on the pews to the frosting swirls on the five-tiered cake waiting in the reception hall. Clay and Auggie had been enamored by the eye color of their fiancées. *The eyes are the window to the soul.* How many times had she heard her mother reference that cliché?

Jackson's eyes were a haunted deep-ocean blue, a color she remembered three summers ago when she'd found him sitting alone on the dock behind her family's lake house, staring into the water as though it might provide answers to questions he couldn't voice.

Now, across the room, those eyes sought hers, a drowning man looking for shore. He clung to her like a buoy in a storm, and she loved him, wanted to help him, but sometimes she felt the water rising above both their heads. Her lungs ached with the phantom feeling of not enough air, not enough strength to keep them both afloat. She wanted him to come to terms with the troubles that simmered beneath the surface—the nightmares that still woke him sweating at 3 a.m.

Clara watched as a single white rose fell from one of the elaborate arrangements near the altar, landing askew among its perfect companions. No one else seemed to notice. She wondered how long it would take before someone straightened it—or how long before her family's perfect facade would similarly crack under the weight of what she and Jackson had to reveal.

The first chords of Pachelbel's "Canon in D" rang out in the ballroom of the estate, the notes hanging in the air like suspended crystal. The scent of peonies and roses mingled with nervous anticipation as the sisters took their first steps. Eve and Mia sauntered down the makeshift aisle arm in arm, all smiles, a stark contrast to the men who awaited their arrival with intense eyes—almost as if they were trying to ensure the women weren't a mirage. Neither man blinked, maybe afraid that when they opened their eyes, the women would be gone.

Clara had her own version of intense. Jackson still glared at her, unblinking, his gaze a weight against her skin that made her pulse quicken in that familiar way—terrifying and thrilling at once. She smiled at him. Nothing. She winked. Nothing. She put her hand on her waist and tilted her head, cocked a brow at him, and then crossed her eyes. The corner of his mouth lifted ever so slightly and his intense gaze finally broke. He blinked and his banked smile broke free. It hardly ever happened, but when it did, warmth flooded her chest like sunlight finally breaking through storm clouds.

His smile—the one only she could coax out—transformed his face into something so naked with vulnerability that Clara often had to look away, afraid of how much she needed that rare gift.

As the vows were exchanged, Jackson's eyes sparkled a little bit more as she sniffled and wiped her eyes. A few times she saw him look down and wipe away a tear, his thumb brushing it away with the same gentle precision he'd wiped mascara from her cheeks whenever she'd cry at sappy movies. The memory sent a shiver through her—how he'd touched her then as if she might shatter, yet somehow made her feel stronger for being breakable.

Eve caught Clara's eye for just a moment as she said "I do," a flash of understanding passing between them—this strange, beautiful ache of witnessing someone profess to love you completely and for always.

The rings were given and finally the grooms kissed their brides. Each couple was announced. Still, Jackson only had eyes for her. It was as if a magnet drew them together, the space between them charged and unbearable. The instant they reconnected he exhaled long and deep, as though he'd been holding his breath the entire ceremony.

His fingers found hers, thumb pressing against the soft hollow of her palm where her lifeline curved. The contact sent relief coursing through her veins, like coming home after being lost for days. His intensity scared her at times—the way he seemed to need her like oxygen—but it was also the truest thing she'd ever known. In a world of carefully measured affections, his unguarded heart was the bravest thing she'd ever witnessed, and she cherished it unconditionally, even when it terrified her to be loved so completely.

As they walked down the aisle, his fingers grazed the small of her back where the scars still puckered beneath her dress—a touch so light only she could feel it. He leaned close, his stubble brushing her earlobe as he whispered, "Gotta get you home. Need to be inside you... wrapped up in you." His voice had that gravel-soft quality that always made her stomach tighten.

"Cracker Jack." She squeezed him a little tighter. "I need you too." Her voice caught on the last word, betraying the depths she couldn't articulate. And she did. In a world where faces streamed past in watercolor smudges and conversations dissolved into meaningless noise, she always found her focus in him. The tremor in her left hand—a permanent souvenir of the jagged metal that had damaged her nerves—steadied whenever their fingers interlaced.

He'd been there when she needed him most. She blinked away the flash of memory: ceiling tiles sliding past above a gurney, the copper taste of blood in her mouth, his face appearing suddenly in the fluorescent haze, mouthing words she couldn't hear. Her hero, her angel, her Jackson. He was the reason she was alive today—not just breathing, but feeling the rush of air in her lungs that still sometimes surprised her with its sweetness.

Wedding Night Plans

5

Jackson couldn't be happier that Clay and Auggie wanted to get their brides alone sooner, rather than later. As soon as the limos pulled from the curb, Jackson and Clara walked to their car.

On the way home, Jackson stopped at a gas station. As he pumped gas into his old, unreliable Honda—the one with the tear in the passenger seat that Clara had covered with a purple scarf—he watched her walk into the store, her purple dress flowing behind her like a ripple of twilight. The fluorescent lights of the station buzzed overhead, casting everything in that sickly, too-honest glow that made most people look washed out. Not Clara. Never Clara.

She was beautiful, but not in the generic way people toss that word around. Beautiful in how she absently tucked her hair behind her ear when she was thinking. Beautiful in how she could quote Dostoyevsky one minute and laugh at stupid cat videos the next. Though they were ten years apart, he never felt as if she were younger.

She'd always been considerate and altruistic, cultured and sophisticated. But she was more than that—she provided him with a reason to exist when his lungs seemed to forget how to draw air.

They didn't always see eye to eye, but even when they disagreed, she was mature, and they solved problems as a team. More importantly, whenever he felt the walls closing in on him—when his heart raced so hard it hurt and the familiar vice grip tightened around his throat—she was the only thing that could hold them back. She'd place her hand on the back of his neck, her thumb finding that hollow spot at the base of his skull, and suddenly he could breathe again.

And just like that he'd passed several minutes. Thinking of her could do that. He'd tried to deny her. After it was clear they were in danger of breaking so many unsaid rules and laws, God knows he tried to pull away, but she'd draw him back every time. Like the night at the hospital cafeteria when another doctor had mistaken Clara for his daughter, and the hot flush of shame had made him suggest they cool things off. She'd shown up at his apartment at midnight with a carton of ice cream and said, "This is what cooling off looks like to me."

Given their ages, it might seem strange that they were so compatible, but he'd been stuck at age seventeen for ten years. He'd needed her to pull him through the quagmire of pain that had entrapped him when his parents died. His world came crashing down but she'd been there, every morning, demanding, even without words, to come eat breakfast. She'd set a plate in front of him and sometimes he'd just stare at it, the smell of eggs making his stomach lurch with an emptiness that had nothing to do with hunger. But she'd sit there, silent, until he took at least one bite. And so he started there. Breakfast turned into lunch, and then finally dinner.

Seventeen turned to eighteen. Graduation from high school, and then college, med school, and now his residency. He'd been pulled through each stage not feeling anything, but waking up and busying his mind so that his body would be present in this life. It was a useful trick that worked out in his favor. High marks and skills in his education and now his residency came from his need to fill any unoccupied time so that his mind didn't go to the dark place—that chasm where his parents' voices echoed, where the weight of absence sat like a stone in his chest, where breathing hurt so much he sometimes wondered if it was worth the effort.

Then, at twenty-seven, she'd shouldered his loss, and helped him move past it. Not with grand gestures, but by sitting beside him on his parents' anniversary when he couldn't get out of bed. By hanging his mother's old wind chimes outside his window so he could hear them in the morning. By knowing when to talk and when silence was the only answer. For the first time since his parents had died, he was happy, content, in love.

The first time he laughed—really laughed—after they died, it had been because Clara had tried to make his father's signature chili and set off every smoke alarm in the kitchen. The sound of his own laughter had scared the hell out of him. She'd never been scared, and she refused to let him pull away from her. When he tried, she'd called him a coward.

He recalled the billowy summer dress she'd worn, standing on the pier by the lake, telling him that no one decided her future but her. The way sunlight had caught in her hair, turning each strand into a thread of copper. The way her hands had trembled even as her voice remained steady—the only sign this confrontation cost her something too.

He'd tried to explain that they'd never be accepted, people would talk and there would be a scandal. Like the time his attending physician had seen them holding hands and had pulled Jackson aside to "discuss professional boundaries with younger patients' relatives." The humiliation had burned in his gut for days.

She was having none of it. "Real love isn't supposed to be easy. When love gets hard, it makes you feel alive. You need that. I need that." She put those huge blue eyes on him, the ones that always saw right through the careful walls he'd built. A smile on her face that held more determination than joy. "People say in a hundred years who's going to care. I don't know about that, but when you're alone at night, in the dark, haunted by the loneliness that sucks the air right out of your lungs, remember that you made that choice."

She raised her arms to the sky, her head tilted up toward the sun, eyes closed. He remembered how his throat tightened, how his hands shook as he shoved them into his pockets. "This is our precipice, our moment to decide to stay and fight, or cut and run. Love has the power to heal your spirit. As time goes on, things will get better, and it's important to keep in mind that love is the only thing we carry with us beyond this life.

"How dare you take away what is supposed to belong to us. I'm not a doll to take down and play with when it's easy and convenient. I'm worth fighting for. You need to show me that I'm worth the fight."

Man did she have a way of putting things in black and white. With her it was always easy. She made life easier. That day, he'd reached for her hand, his fingers still trembling, and whispered, "I'm terrified I'll lose you too." She'd squeezed back and said, "That's how you know it matters."

Through the gas station window, Clara caught his eye and smiled—that particular smile with the slight crinkle at the corner of her right eye that was only ever for him. She held up a package of those terrible sour candies he secretly loved, raising her eyebrows in question. His heart swelled with a tenderness so acute it was almost pain. *You'd never even see it coming, how completely someone could save you without ever making you feel like you needed saving.*

As she headed back to the car, two men piled out of a truck, eyed her up and down, and whistled. The sound transported Jackson instantly to the hospital, machines whirring and beeping, that awful suspended moment before they told him if she would live. His heart jackhammered against his ribs as he hustled to get to her. Wrapping his arm around her he said, "You're beautiful." She smiled sleepily and sighed into his chest.

"Hey." His voice was harsher than he'd intended, and she turned to him with worried eyes, the slight flinch making him hate himself a little. "You're my beautiful Clara Grace." His hand rubbed her arm, his thumb tracing small circles over the fabric where he knew a thin white line ran underneath.

She stared into his eyes with sincerity. "I'm glad." She held a fountain drink out to him. "Taste it."

He sucked up the sugary substance through a red straw. "It's different. What'd you do?"

"It's a chocolate Coke." She giggled. "A combination of two of my three favorite things."

"You consume too much sugar, Bug." He took another sip from the straw and couldn't deny it was tasty. Sounded gross but tasted pretty good. At the car, he opened her door and with his hand still on her shoulder he bent and kissed the small part of her scar not covered by her dress. The tissue felt different under his lips—smoother, tighter, almost waxy—a topographical map of the day that changed everything. She folded herself into the seat, and then he handed her the drink. "What's your third favorite thing?"

"Cracker Jack,"—she palmed his jaw—"it's you of course. You're my prize at the bottom of the box." Her beautiful smile beaming up at him made his breath hiccup. Pondering, he walked around to the driver's side of the car. He couldn't believe she loved him as much as she did, and he luxuriated in the overwhelming obsession he had for her, even as a quiet voice wondered if he deserved to be anyone's prize when he couldn't even provide her the house she deserved.

"Guess what I got?" She held up a pink striped gift bag that she pulled from her wedding stuff.

"What's that?"

"Some new lingerie." She pulled something transparent from the bag. Her eyes sparkled with mischief, but he caught the slight tremble in her fingers, the almost imperceptible hesitation before she continued. "Sheer baby doll nightie and"—she rummaged some more—"matching thong."

"Christ, Bug." He reached down to adjust his crotch. He loved her in lingerie. Lingerie that he'd bought. He frowned, what the hell? "Why would they give you that?"

"It was purchased for Mia but was too big. Then Eve tried it on, and it was too small. Turns out, I'm just right." She shrugged, her voice confident but her eyes seeking his approval in that way that always made his chest ache.

He was going to have an aneurism before they got home.

"Jackson!"

The scream—so like the one he'd heard that day by the fence—ripped through him. He slammed on the brakes just in time to miss rear-ending the car in front of him. For one terrible second, he was back there, running toward her crumpled form, certain he was too late. He shook his head to clear it, his knuckles white on the steering wheel.

"I'll just put it away." Clara busied herself with the task of hurriedly erasing the evidence of his torment. Somewhat collected, he drove.

He inhaled deeply and squeezed her thigh. "You are just right, absolutely stunning and I can't wait to see you in that thing when we get home." Her radiant smile shot straight to his heart and accelerated its pace.

"Why are you so beautiful?"

"You make me beautiful."

"You give me way too much credit." His hand found hers, their fingers interlacing as they always did, without preamble, never a hesitation. They belonged together, no matter the rules of the society they lived in. He turned into their apartment complex, eyeing the modest buildings with a twinge of dissatisfaction. He wanted her to have a big fine house.

That was why he worked so hard—it was all for her. Soon she'd have a nice home in which to luxuriate. Because sometimes, in the dark quiet of night when she was asleep beside him, he worried his love wasn't enough, that someone younger, someone who hadn't seen her at her most broken might sweep in and offer her more than he could give.

He wanted to give her a home that would protect her and cloak her in love. The thought of her in their home, caring for their possessions and tending to his laundry and the contents of their day-to-day life made him lightheaded. Would he ever have that? It seemed forever in coming.

He pulled under the designated carport and cut the engine. She picked up that damn pink bag and said, "I'm going to go in and slip into something a little more sexy." Her voice was like velvet and her chin rested on her chest—her dramatic blue pools periodically veiled by the rapid blinking of dark lashes.

Something that resembled a growl rose from his throat. "Shall I slip into something more sexy as well?"

Her head cocked as she actively pondered the question from the passenger side of the car. "What do you have?"

"Banana hammock."

"Really?" Her eyes protruded in shock.

His eyebrows waggled and he was rewarded with her flirtatious giggle. She dashed out of the car and ran into the apartment. To give her time to change, he walked down to the end of the complex to retrieve the mail, his footsteps echoing on concrete that reminded him of all the things he couldn't yet fix.

He passed various compact cars and several muddied work trucks, their owners invisible but somehow familiar—the man in 3B who'd been fixing air conditioners for twenty years; the woman across the hall who worked double shifts at the hospital.

Had they once stood where he stood, promising someone they loved a better future? The people that lived here worked hard and were a serious lot as they constantly struggled to make ends meet. The complex was located in the downtown area and was relatively quiet, the silence broken only by the distant wail of a siren and the hum of window air conditioning units laboring against the heat.

He suspected the quietness was because there were not many kids around—another reminder of the life stage he couldn't yet afford to enter.

He unlocked the mailbox and pulled out a stack of envelopes an inch thick. He sighed as he thumbed through the letters, organizing them by due date as he walked—a ritual that gave him the illusion of control when everything else felt so uncertain. He counted several bills: utilities (the power company that didn't care that the apartment was poorly insulated), auto insurance (for the car that sometimes didn't start), medical school (the monthly reminder of his seven-year promise), credit cards (the plastic bridges between paychecks). Each envelope seemed to pulse with its own accusation.

As he walked back to the apartment, the medical school statement made his stomach clench. Three more years of payments before he could even think about a down payment on a house. His shoulders inched toward his ears, the familiar tension headache beginning to pulse at his temples.

He pictured Clara in a sunlit kitchen that didn't have water stains on the ceiling, her laughter echoing in rooms they actually owned. He remembered whispering to her on their third date that someday they'd have a house with a garden. That was before he'd seen his first semester's tuition bill. He wondered, not for the first time, if Clara would wait for him to become the man he'd promised to be. It wasn't really a fair shot at her. She'd never once given any inclination that her love for him was tied up in anything monetary, but still his guilt ate at him.

He waved to his widowed neighbor, Mr. Porter, who was taking out his trash. The older man smiled back, his weathered face crinkling at the corners. Mr. Porter had been there the night Jackson had locked himself out after a particularly grueling day at the hospital, sitting with him on the stoop and sharing his whiskey until Clara came home. They'd invite him over whenever Clara baked, her lemon pound cake his particular favorite.

Once inside, Jackson unloaded the bills onto the console table and dropped his keys into the ceramic bowl Clara had made in that pottery class last spring. The soft glow of candles caught his attention immediately—not the practical tea lights they used during power outages, but the expensive sandalwood ones she saved for special occasions. He followed the low light, his chest tightening with anticipation when Etta James's smoky voice floated through the air. "At Last." the song they'd danced to last summer on the pier of the lake, humid wind making sweat where their bodies connected.

His feet padded over rose petals she'd dropped like breadcrumbs, the velvet softness crushing beneath his steps, releasing their sweet fragrance. He bent to remove his shoes, his fingers trembling slightly. His jacket and tie followed, along with other pieces of clothing until he stood only in his briefs, suddenly aware of the goosebumps rising on his own skin—not from cold, but from the weight of whatever moment awaited him.

Turning into the bedroom, the air changed—warmer, heavier with the mingling scents of candle wax and that jasmine oil she dabbed behind her ears. Then he saw her standing in the sheer material of the baby doll chemise given to her by Mia and Eve. She was seduction personified with her parted lips, sparkling eyes, and the way she held part of the material in her hand, lifting it away from her body.

He could see the lower curve of her breasts and a peek of areola, but a band of lace across her nipples kept them from his view. His throat constricted, his pulse hammering so loudly he wondered if she could hear it. The sight of her took him back to their the first night they'd made love, and he'd thought then as now that he'd never deserve such beauty in his life. He couldn't speak yet, so he walked toward her. His palms on her jaw—feeling the delicate bones beneath her skin—he tilted her face and pressed his lips to hers, exploring her gently at first, then increasing the intensity until they were both gasping.

He broke the kiss so they could breathe. "Show me the back."

She hesitated, a shadow crossing her face. Her blue eyes, usually so open to him, clouded with something deeper than resentment. Fear, perhaps. Shame. The familiar pain he'd seen flickering there since the accident two years ago.

With deliberate care, she gathered her lush, copper locks, the strands slipping like silk through her fingers. Her knuckles blanched with tension as she swept the cascade of hair over her shoulder to place it all at her back. Slowly, she pivoted, revealing a waterfall of fiery tresses that draped to the middle of her back, concealing the sinuous scars etched from her right shoulder blade to her waist. "The curves of your body are exquisite, Clara," he murmured, his voice thick with emotion. "I adore how those sheer thong panties trace the alluring arc of your hips. Let me see more—draw your hair aside so I can admire your skin."

She inhaled sharply. "Jackson, why do you make me do this?" Her voice quivered, stirring his own doubts, the gnawing fear that he might never mend her spirit or help her perceive herself through his eyes.

His hands gently cupped her shoulders, feeling the slight ridge where the scarred skin began. "Every inch of you is beautiful. I don't like you hiding any part of yourself from me." He pressed his lips to the top of the scar, the skin smooth and tight beneath his mouth. "I have my own scars too, Bug. They're just not ones you can see."

"But I want to be perfect for you." Her voice broke on the word *perfect*. "Just for tonight can we pretend it's not there?"

He rested his forehead against her shoulder, breathing in the familiar scent of her skin, sweetness and warmth. "No, Bug." He felt her slight flinch at his unwillingness to give in to her. She was usually more persistent than he, but due to the importance of her accepting herself after her accident, he persisted. On one of the summer days when he'd taken her to the beach, he recalled one particular instance of her showcasing just how determined she could be as she tried repeatedly to rebuild a sandcastle, beating the tide as it came in.

The same determination he needed from her now. "It *is* there and it's as much a part of who you are as the curve of your breasts or the swell of your hips. As much a part of you as those freckles I count when you sleep or the soft melody that escapes your lips when you're lost in kneading dough. And I cherish every single part."

Sluggishly, she pulled her hair over her shoulder. Blistered, puckered, and jagged lines marred her perfect skin. White on the edges, but pink in the center, the skin had been torn and gnawed. The scars were large and long, bringing back all the memories of that day. He slid down the straps of her nightgown and kissed the visible memory of the horrific experience, watching her skin pimple as he did.

"You're beautiful." His tongue traced from the tip down to where the tear culminated at the small of her back. She hated the scars and even though her dress today covered most of them, he knew she'd covered herself with makeup. Not only that, but all of the girls in the wedding party had gone and had their hair done in a style that was pinned up. She'd not gone with them to the salon, choosing instead to wear her hair down. He knew why. She hid behind the veil of her hair, which was beautiful and thick, but she did hide. She even had bangs, bangs he loved, but he didn't like it when they covered her eyes. Her gorgeous, bright eyes that protected him in his dreams.

He slid the straps back in place. Nuzzling behind her ear he whispered, "You're a survivor, an exquisite dark-copper-haired sexy woman with smooth dewy skin and bewitching blue eyes. It's a crime to hide any inch of your beauty. I want all of you."

He turned her and saw her eyes bigger than he'd ever seen them. He'd need a life raft to escape their depths.

"You don't play fair. You've stripped me bare, but you won't confide in me about the death of your parents. I love you, Jackson, but it hurts me when I see you in pain, keeping all your worries and deadlines to yourself. Talk to me."

He wanted to talk to her, but whenever he tried the words wouldn't come. He felt his mouth working, but there was no voice to be had. He wanted to be strong for her. Didn't want to burden her with the stress in his life. It wasn't fair to her. If she weren't with him, she'd be so much better off, but he was selfish and kept her tied to him. Every waking day he was afraid she'd realize he was a disaster and leave him. It was his greatest fear. Greater than the loss of his parents, greater than not being able to pay his bills, greater than failing medical school. "I want to tell you, and I will. Please. Just give me more time."

She nodded and placed her palm to his jaw. "I'll be here when you're ready."

His forehead went down on hers. "That means everything."

The mood was too heavy, and he sought to lighten it. "I don't understand the concept of lingerie."

Her brow furrowed. "What do you mean?"

He bent and kissed the corner of her mouth. "It's designed to be worn, but all I want to do is rip it from your body."

"Oh, don't do that. I want to keep it."

He kissed her shoulder. "I want you to keep it too." Lifting the hem, he pulled the delicate fabric over her head until she stood before him in just a sheer thong, blushing across her cheeks. She was stunning and smiling at him with that dimpled smile that made his breath hitch.

The scar above her hip caught the light—and though she'd hate hearing it, the scars turned her from an innocent little girl into a warrior queen, a goddess who'd fought in battle and who possessed the heart and will to survive. It made her almost immortal. He'd kissed it a hundred times since, wishing his lips could soak up some of her will to survive. "I will never get used to how beautiful you are. It's like I'm seeing you for the first time, every time."

He wasted no time taking his clothes off. He faced her and then leaned in, capturing her lips with a tender urgency. His mouth caressed hers, their warmth mingling as he teased her lower lip. She responded eagerly, parting for him, her tongue dancing with his in a slow, tantalizing rhythm. A soft murmur of pleasure slipped from her throat as her fingers traced the contours of his back, savoring every muscle.

"Jackson," she whispered, "please, I need you."

He guided them down to the bed and slid off the sheer panties. His hands, capable of such force in the outside world, trembled slightly as they traced the arc of her collarbone. Sliding slowly into her soft wet heat had him exhaling deeply. In their chaotic world the only time he was able to fully let go was when he was inside of her. For a man who'd spent years constructing walls around himself, each time she pulled him in felt like dismantling the last of his defenses— terrifying and necessary.

Their connection made it possible for him to feel complete and secure; her fate was his fate. No matter what, in that moment, they were one. She couldn't slip away from him.

He needed to be with her for as long as she would tolerate him, so he set the pace with slow, rhythmic movements. Her fingertips skimmed from his neck down to his back. The light touch captivated him as she moaned and seemed intent on plotting every peak and valley he had. The faint scent of her shampoo—lavender and some-thing uniquely her—mingled with their shared heat, a fragrance he'd recognize blindfolded in a crowd of thousands.

Her eyes closed and he took her in as he did every time. Memorizing her every breath, sound, and motion, he wanted to freeze time so that they could be like this forever. For a split second, as she arched beneath him, he wondered if he could ever truly be enough —then her fingers dug into his shoulders, anchoring him to this truth.

He bent and placed his lips on hers, kissing and gently massaging. He pulled back to observe the effect he had on her—her ice blue eyes darker by a shade and heavily draped by her eyelids and lashes.

"Sometimes I'm afraid I'll wake up and you'll be gone," he whispered against her skin, words he'd never planned to say aloud. He swallowed hard. "Three words... they're not enough to express what I feel for you."

"And three million words"—she gasped a breath into her body —"still wouldn't be enough."

Rain began to tap against the window, nature's applause for what they'd created in this room, this sanctuary from the world.

He took a perfectly formed little nipple into his mouth and pulled, eliciting a deep, throaty moan from her. He released her and rubbed his cheek over the erect tip basking in the sensation.

"No, three million words wouldn't even make a dent." He slowed the rhythm of their connection until beads of sweat popped up on his brow from holding back and she moaned for more.

He didn't know how long it had been, but she'd been content to let him feel her for a while before blue lasers pinned him in place. "I need . . ."

His knee clicked as he shifted position—a reminder of his mortality that somehow made this immortal moment more precious. He placed a sensual kiss on her swollen lips. "I've got you." He knotted their fingers together and rested their hands above her head. Gradually he increased the pace of their love making until they were both ready to come together somewhere in the clouds.

It had been forty-five minutes. His girl was patient with him, and he loved her, irrevocably.

Best Laid Plans

6

In the cozy, cluttered confines of their tiny apartment, Clara perched on a worn barstool, the scent of their shared shower still clinging to her skin. The dim light flickered off the polished countertop, casting soft shadows that danced across the room in a playful rhythm.

Jackson was rummaging through the chaotic junk drawer in search of takeout menus, his movements a familiar symphony of domesticity that made her heart flutter in spite of their financial struggles. The quiet hum of their old refrigerator filled the room with an oddly comforting drone, underscored by the muted sounds of city life seeping through the thin walls.

Suddenly, Jackson paused and turned to her with a grin that promised a surprise. Their world may have been small and fraught with challenges, but it was punctuated by these precious moments of unexpected joy.

"I got you something."

"You did?"

"Yeah, I almost forgot. Let me go get it out of the car." As he walked past her, he kissed her lips and handed her the pizzeria menu.

That familiar tug in her chest became ever present as she admired his moving form—gratitude tangled with worry. Jackson got too much enjoyment out of giving her little surprises. She'd learned to smile through the knot in her stomach, to push down the mental calculation of their checking account balance that automatically flashed through her mind with each gift. Last month's electric bill still sat on her desk with the yellow "FINAL NOTICE" stamp that she'd hidden under a textbook.

She had her job at Moretti's Italian deli and store. It had started off as summer employment only, but when she'd transferred to Louisiana State University, they'd asked her to work thirty-two hours per week. A few weeks later Mrs. Moretti became too sick to make the house mozzarella, and so their son taught Clara the process of making fresh cheese.

The first time her hands had sunk into that warm, yielding curd, something inside her had unlocked. There was magic in the way the cheese stretched between her fingers, the slight resistance before it yielded, the quiet squeak against her palms.

In those predawn hours when she worked alone in the kitchen, the rhythmic pulling and folding of the cheese soothed something in her that lectures and textbooks never touched. Now she was responsible for making all the mozzarella they used in the deli and what was sold in the store. She'd make batches of cheese in the early morning hours before class, her eyes burning from too little sleep, shoulders tight from hunching over steaming pots, and she'd return after class to work the cheese counter in the store.

She loved it, but Mr. Moretti was a tough boss. Jackson had wanted her to quit so many times she'd lost count. "He made you cry last week, Clara," he'd said, holding her as she sobbed against his t-shirt after Moretti had berated her for using too much salt.

It was true, Moretti was not a nice man, but she'd learned to breathe through his outbursts, to focus on the photograph of Mrs. Moretti that hung above the prep table. She saw how his hands trembled when he walked past his wife's old station, how sometimes he'd stand in the doorway of the kitchen and watch Clara work, his face crumpling before he caught himself. The poor man had been in much pain since his wife had died.

"Close your eyes," she heard Jackson yell from the front door.

She pivoted on the bar stool and waited with excitement.

"Keep them closed."

She was smiling and tapped her foot with excitement, her pulse quickening despite her money worries. She could never stay anxious around Jackson.

Cold ceramic was placed in her hands. Her fingers traced the fluted edge, the smooth glaze cool against her calloused fingertips. The weight of it settled against her palms—substantial, like a promise. She squealed, "I know what it is."

"What?"

"The pie dish."

Jackson kissed her nose. "Open your eyes."

"Oh my God, it's pink!" The baby pink color caught the kitchen light, almost the same shade as the scarf Mrs. Moretti had worn every day until the chemo took her hair.

"It's a special edition for breast cancer awareness."

Her throat tightened unexpectedly. Her mother had found a lump last year—benign, thankfully—but the weeks of waiting for results had aged them all. She clutched the dish closer. "Thanks, Cracker Jack. I love it." Her voice wavered slightly.

"Your chicken pot pie deserves a proper dish." His eyes met hers, seeing the emotion she was trying to hide. He squeezed her shoulder, his thumb finding the exact spot where her muscles knotted from bending over the cheese pots.

"I'll make you one soon." She leaned into his touch, letting him take some of her weight, just for a moment.

"Can't wait." His voice was soft, understanding the promise was about more than just pie.

"Order a pizza and I'll cue up *The Last Walk Home* on the DVD player." Their Friday night ritual—the one constant in a week of shifting schedules and obligations. In the flickering blue light of their favorite movies, with takeout pizza between them, she could forget about early mornings and demanding bosses and bills piling up. For those two hours, the world contracted to just this—his arm around her shoulders, the taste of tomato sauce, and the certainty that whatever came next, they would face it together.

Clara ran her fingers along the worn arm of their secondhand couch, tracing the small cigarette burn they'd discovered the day they'd hauled the couch home on top of his little Honda. They'd been too broke to care about the hole, covering it with a throw pillow and laughing about it over boxed wine. Even if they could afford better, some things you kept because they held the shape of your history.

Just as she was about to order pizza for their date night, her phone lit up. It was Mr. Moretti calling.

"Hello." She heard his slurred words but couldn't decipher their meaning. "Mr. Moretti?" His nightly ritual included a few passes at the corner bar. Luckily, he lived in a rental directly above the bar. Her eyes collided with Jackson's smoldering gaze. She mouthed to Jackson, *He's drunk.* He slightly cocked a brow, not even marginally shocked. The line disconnected and she shrugged. "I hope everything's okay."

Her phone rang again. "It's Moretti's son."

"Hello."

"Hey, Clara, I'm so sorry to bother you, but it's somewhat of an emergency. The delivery was delayed. They'd told me the truck would arrive early in the morning, but it's at the store now. It would take me an hour fifteen to get there, but they won't wait. Would it be possible for you to accept the delivery?"

She liked Lucian. He'd had to deal with the slow and agonizing illness that took his mother and then after her death, his father's total desolation.

"I'm sorry, Clara. I would ask my father but he's..."

He didn't finish the sentence so she interjected, "No problem. I'll head over there right now." The words came automatically, the same instinct that had made her bring a personal invitation for breakfast to Jackson each morning because without it she knew he'd never get out of bed.

She watched Jackson's jaw twitch from its tightly fixed position.

He'd give himself a migraine. Her hand hovered between her phone and his arm, caught in the gravity of two different obligations. She hung up the phone, jumped up, and slipped her feet into flip-flops. The smell of Jackson's cologne—sandalwood and something distinctly him—made her hesitate, a physical ache blooming in her chest at the thought of leaving their bubble of warmth.

"Forty minutes tops. Order the pizza, I'll be back in a flash and then we can start the movie." She grabbed her keys, the small brass elephant keychain—a gift from Jackson on their first anniversary— cool against her palm.

"If you think I'm letting you go alone to an empty store at night then you don't know me very well." He stood, his expression softening as he reached for his jacket. His fingers brushed against hers as he took the keys, a silent apology for his frustration wrapped in the familiar calluses of his hand. "I'll drive."

Their eyes met, and Clara saw in his gaze what he wouldn't say aloud: that he understood why she couldn't say no, even as he wished she would, just once. She squeezed his hand back—*thank you for understanding, thank you for coming, thank you for knowing me*—all without a word.

Hands clasped, they rode in silence to the store. The delivery truck was waiting when they got there. They exited the car and Jackson followed her to greet the man in the truck. He stepped down and approached her with a nod.

"How ya doing." He passed her a clipboard and indicated where she needed to sign. His lips formed into a nasty smirk as his eyes traveled over her tank top and down the length of her. She suddenly regretted not throwing on a pair of jeans instead of the short knit shorts she wore. His mouth parted, his tongue tracing his bottom lip as his hand landed on her shoulder.

She crossed her arms over her chest, hating that an instinctive gesture of self-protection felt so necessary in a space that was supposed to be hers—her store and deli, her territory, her safety. She looked around for Jackson, but his hands were already on the creep. He had him pinned against the truck with his hands twisted in the guy's shirt.

"Make the delivery." Jackson slammed the man's body against the truck before releasing him. "Keep your eyes off her if you want to keep your spleen."

When he released him the man huffed out some expletives. Jackson stood by watching every movement, jaw ticking and stance dripping with power and charge. She hated the circumstance, but loved to watch him exert his dominance, especially where she was concerned.

Her skin prickled with goosebumps—not from fear but from witnessing his protection, a sensation both comforting and confusing that stirred something primal she rarely acknowledged. The thought of being alone in that moment opened a familiar void—that ancient human fear of being vulnerable when the predator appears, of calling for help and hearing only echo.

The deli's familiar walls seemed to have shifted when they stepped inside—the space both sanctuary and reminder of how easily boundaries could be crossed. She stood on her tiptoes to whisper in his ear. "How about I prepare a pizza for us." He nodded his assent, but never removed his focus from the deliveryman.

While the pizza baked away in the oven, she prepared a caprese salad using mozzarella she'd made yesterday. She shaped the cheese with gentle hands, reclaiming control through creation, building something beautiful in the wake of ugliness.

She sliced deeply into a tomato, watching the seeds spill out like the jumbled emotions she couldn't quite contain—relief, lingering fear, and the unsettling awareness of her own vulnerability. Outside, the delivery truck's engine faded into distance. She stood motionless for a moment, knife suspended above the cutting board, realizing how quickly safety could become something foreign.

Warm hands caressed her from behind, sliding over her waist and across her stomach to pull her back.

"The delivery is secure." He set the invoice on the counter. His stance exuded power, but she caught the slight tremor in his hands when he finally turned away from the window—strength and fragility existing in the same body. "I got the guy's name and truck number. I was thinking of reporting him, but I'd fear retaliation and, unlike this time, I may not be around."

He turned her around to face him. "Thinking what may have happened had I not been here had me more scared than I've ever been." His voice caught, surprising them both.

She leaned into the temporary shelter of his body, both of them silently acknowledging what they couldn't change—that this moment of protection was just that: a moment.

She kissed his chin. "But you were here." Pushing a stool up to the counter she pointed, indicating he should sit. She put a plate of salad in front of him and handed him a roll of silverware.

With a white towel draped over her arm she presented a large pepper mill. "Care for some freshly cracked pepper, sir?"

A smile erased any leftover traces of his agitation from the delivery ordeal. "Please, miss."

She heard his knife and fork scrape the plate, followed by moans of satisfaction. "Mmm, you're worth so much more than eight dollars per hour. This is the most tender mozzarella I've ever had the pleasure of eating." Using the fork in his hand he gestured at his salad. "Knocks this salad out of the park."

Smiling, she shook her head knowing he was so in love with her. Why else would he go on and on about a simple salad.

"I don't think Mr. Moretti has more than eight dollars to give me."

"No, I don't guess he would if he's drinking it away every night."

"Jackson, his wife died. It hasn't been so long ago." Her throat tightened as she said it, remembering the deep lines and shadows on Mr. Moretti's face when he'd handed her the newspaper. She'd seen that same lost look in Mr. Porter's eyes after his wife passed—that bewildered gaze of someone navigating a world suddenly emptied of its north star.

"I know, baby." His brow creased. "Your altruistic nature is just one of the things I love about you." He kissed her cheek as he patted her butt.

The familiar weight of his hand lingered even after he moved away. She allowed herself to lean into it for a moment—this small, wordless reassurance that they were still solid when so much else was not.

She brought the pizza to the table and they devoured it. Steam rose from the golden crust as she pulled apart her slice, watching the mozzarella stretch in glistening strands. The scent of basil and garlic filled the kitchen.

"Mmm. Superb." He wiped his mouth with a napkin. "You have very talented fingers."

"Just well-practiced," she replied, though inside she treasured the compliment more than she'd admit. These small moments of approval meant everything to her. She suspected Jackson knew it since he never failed to deliver.

They ate until they were full and then she started the cleanup process. The familiar rhythm of stacking plates and wiping counters calmed her mind—this restoration of order, this small control she maintained in their shared space. He watched her as he delighted in a slice of tiramisu. She packed him two leftover slices of pizza for tomorrow's lunch and grabbed a prepackaged side salad from the fridge.

She hollered from her bent over position at the refrigerator, "What dressing do you want for your lunch salad?"

"Whichever one you made."

She pulled a picnic package of utensils and a white sack from beneath the counter. Her fingers hovered over the napkin, pen poised. How could she sum up all they were in one little sentiment? The blank card stared back at her, pristine and demanding. She gripped her pen tighter, her eyes blurring with the tears that always came when emotions overwhelmed her capacity for words.

She hesitated, then wrote: "You make even ordinary days extraordinary." Her pen hovered over the paper. The phrase felt both true and terribly inadequate. She thought of last month when the power had gone out during the storm, how he'd gathered every candle in the apartment and arranged them around the bathtub, how they'd soaked in lukewarm water while sharing whispered confessions until the water grew cold. How could she compress that kind of magic into a greeting card platitude?

She crossed out the sentence, then wrote it again, her handwriting betraying her uncertainty. The paper absorbed a small drop of moisture that had fallen from her eye without her noticing. She touched the tiny warped circle with her fingertip, a physical manifestation of what she couldn't say: that sometimes his kindness made her feel undeserving, that she worried one day he would see through to the broken parts she kept hidden—the scars that marred not only her skin but her heart.

She pulled out a fresh card and wrote, "All my love". She traced her finger over the simple words, knowing they couldn't possibly hold the vastness of all that he meant to her. There were feelings that existed beyond language—the ache in her chest when he smiled at her across a crowded room, the hollow feeling when he was away, the peculiar safety she felt when their breathing synchronized in sleep.

It wasn't enough—it would never be enough—but it was something. Enough to let him know she would be thinking about him. She pressed the card briefly to her lips before sliding it into the envelope, sealing away all the words in her heart that wouldn't fit on the card.

I Aced Female Anatomy

7

"Bug a boo." The hair at the nape of Clara's neck rose and she giggled as he tickled the sensitive skin behind her ear. She turned, looking up into his eyes. "Coffee?" Jackson held a steaming mug hovering just above her. Smiling, she sat up and reached for the cup.

The first sip of the smoky caramel notes awakened her senses and the liquid radiated warmth from her belly. He sat next to her on the bed in their apartment, sipping a mug of his own, already dressed in his paramedic uniform and ready to begin his long grueling day. His hand patted her head. "I gotta go start my shift at the station. Don't forget, I'm on nights this week so I'll be sleeping at the hospital."

She forced a slight smile on her face so he wouldn't clue in to her quickly diminishing mood and set her mug on the bedside table. She didn't know how he kept up with it all. His schedule made her dizzy.

"I'll miss you, Cracker Jack." She leaned into his side, and he kissed her head. They would miss each other in the morning when she left for work. Heck, he was probably going to try to work at the station when he left the hospital in the early morning hours.

He'd been doing that lately—running between the two, racking up as many hours in a week as he could. She worried about his unrelenting schedule and his body's need for sleep and relaxation. Sometimes he didn't even eat. "Don't forget the leftovers I packed for you. You can have them for dinner."

"Oh yeah, almost forgot. Where would I be without my girl?"

Without his girl he'd be a lot better off financially. She was a burden, but he always said she was a burden he didn't want to live without. He stood and she laced her hand through his, not wanting to break their connection.

He kissed her knuckles. "Don't go back to sleep, okay?"

He knew her so well.

"Okay." He attempted to walk away, but she wouldn't release his hand and instead pulled him close to her.

"What is it?"

"I just don't want you to go."

He followed her body down to the bed, one of his legs nestled between hers. His hands framed her face before he went in for a deep kiss. He tasted of coffee and cinnamon and she reveled in it. He pulled away, but hovered close to her face. "I more than love you, Bug. I want to stay here in your warmth, but I also want to provide us with a future and I need you to be proud of me."

God, his words cut her to the bone. "Jackson." Her voice was a whisper. "I've never been more proud of anyone. I sometimes feel inferior to the man you are and strive to be. I should be the one saying I want you to be proud of me."

"Silly girl, shut up. You don't know what you're talking about."

"You shut up too then."

"Gladly." His lips descended on hers again and she wished more than she'd wished for anything that time could be frozen at this moment.

"I've got to go. Need to air up my bicycle tires."

"Why do you have to ride that bike all the time? It's dangerous —especially over the bridge."

"How many times have I told you not to worry? I ride defensively."

"I want to use my dad's credit card to get your car repaired."

"Absolutely not. You know how I feel about that. Now"—he squeezed her thigh—"I would love to stay here and argue with you all day, but I really must go. Remember, I more than love you." He kissed her deeply.

"Be safe, Cracker Jack. If you die, I die. Remember?"

"I remember how crazy you are."

"Crazy in love with you," she whispered and nuzzled behind his ear.

***

At the deli, Mr. Moretti nursed a hangover and was crankier than usual. At six-thirty in the morning, she wasn't in the mood to deal with his nastiness.

"What the fuck is this shit?" He held menus high in the air above her head.

She frowned and snatched them from his grip. "These are the new menus Lucian designed. They turned out so well. You should be happy to have such a talented son." She smiled at the memory of how proud Lucian had been when he'd showed them to her.

"What the fuck was wrong with the old menus? Where is that cocksucker?"

"Stop!" The word tore from Clara's throat before she could think. Her fingers clenched around his sleeve, her knuckles white as she tugged him toward his office. Her heart hammered against her ribs—the same thundering panic she'd felt when Lucian had called her last month, voice breaking. Mr. Moretti reluctantly followed, his cologne a suffocating mix of bergamot and resentment.

Shutting the door with a click that seemed to echo in her chest, she said, "Mr. Moretti, what's wrong with you? Without your son and his skills in the kitchen, you are nothing." Her voice shook slightly, but she forced herself to breathe through the tightness in her lungs. "A new menu was overdue. It's fresh and includes new dishes. Did you even see the scene he drew by hand on the back cover?"

She reached for one of the menus, fingers tracing the delicate lines of the Italian coastline Lucian had rendered in ink—the same coastline Mr. Moretti had described to the staff a hundred times when speaking of his childhood home.

His brow furrowed and he massaged his scalp with stubby fingers. Clara noticed how they were shaped exactly like Lucian's—the same broad nails, the same slight curve to the pinky—though his son's hands created beauty while these seemed only capable of destruction.

She hovered at the office door, pulse still racing, about to leave but then turned back. The framed photo on his desk—Lucian's graduation from culinary school—was now face-down on the mahogany surface. "And one more thing, Mr. Moretti." He looked up at her from his office chair. "The next time I hear you call him that name, I'll be turning in my resignation." Her mouth went dry as the words left her, the reality of what she was risking—her job, her income, her place in this makeshift family—settling heavy in her stomach.

Something flickered across Mr. Moretti's face—a brief crack in the facade, his eyes suddenly lost like a child's. He opened his mouth, closed it, then asked, "He's gay, Clara. What the fuck would you have me call him?" He ran a hand through his greasy sparse hair, and for a moment, his fingers trembled against his scalp.

"Lucian," she said, her voice softening despite herself. "Or son."

"Get out of here and take these with you."

Her lungs finally expanded as she stepped out of the stifling office. She took the menus and placed them at the hostess station, running her thumb over Lucian's signature hidden in the corner of the drawing. She retraced the steps to his office, this time bearing a cup of coffee and a Danish, the sweet scent of almond paste and butter a sharp contrast to the bitterness lingering in the air between them.

He lifted his head when she entered the room with the steaming brew. The pain she saw in his eyes, raw and ancient, the same expression she'd seen in her own father's eyes at her grandmother's funeral, froze her in place. It was the universal look of someone who doesn't know how to love what they don't understand, but beneath it all, still loves.

"Mr. Moretti, I realize it has been hard, but it's been hard for Lucian too. Mrs. Moretti would have wanted to see you two happy and connected. Love him while you are still able. You of all people know how quickly things can change." She placed the breakfast on his desk. "Let me know when you're ready for a second cup." She wrapped her arms around his round form. His arms slowly rationalized they too could reach out to her. Finally, he embraced her.

She left him in his office and wiped the tears from her face before returning to the kitchen to get started on preparing the cheese exactly how Lucian had taught her.

Around eight thirty, she left to attend her philosophy class. It was not a class she enjoyed. Actually, she didn't enjoy any of her classes. She'd much rather be enrolled at some culinary school, but that would have required moving away from Jackson.

It didn't matter anyway because she had specific interests. She liked to talk about food. It may have started at the small cheese counter at the Italian shop, but her culinary interest had grown. In Austin, she'd visited a cheese shop that had varieties of cheese from around the globe. Over one hundred cheeses had been on display and she and Jackson spent an hour in the shop tasting all the different varieties.

She realized she'd been sitting in class for thirty minutes and not heard a word. She felt her phone buzz in her pocket and discretely fished it out.

Jackson: Sunday off from hospital and FD. Calling it National Clara Day.

Clara: Sounds nice. It's Dad's birthday.

Jackson: Right. I'll drive you to the estate.

Clara: Told everybody I'd be there Saturday.

Jackson: I'll make it happen Bug. Love you.

It was around three o'clock when she returned home. She settled in to study for an anatomy exam on the female reproductive system. The birthing videos she'd been subjected to in class had made her stomach turn and she wished she'd taken geology instead.

An hour and a half later she got up to make a glass of chocolate milk and saw Jackson's dinner in the refrigerator. It was nearing five o'clock. The ping of her phone disturbed her thoughts.

Jackson: CODE C

Clara: On my way!! Bringing dinner.

Something must be wrong. Code C was what Jackson called a code Clara, meaning he needed her asap. Recalling that he had a bed to sleep on in his office at the hospital, she thought it would be nice to spend the night in that bed next to him and wondered if such a thing were even possible. She'd been in the little room before when they'd needed privacy to talk. It was quiet and out of the way.

With the tantalizing idea in her mind, she changed into yoga pants and a tank top and pulled on a hoodie in case she became cold. She slid her feet into flip-flops, grabbed his dinner and her books, and left for the hospital.

Once there, she went straight to his office and used the toaster oven to heat the leftover pizza. She went to the soda machine and purchased him a fruit water with electrolytes so at least he'd be well hydrated. On the table in his office, she set out the heated pizza, salad, and love note, and then she texted him.

Clara: In yr office. Dinner is ready.

Jackson: Be there in five.

Clara set out her books and pulled a fresh stack of notecards from her backpack. Upon finishing her fifth notecard she heard the door snick open. She looked up and saw Jackson slumped against the door in his green scrubs.

"What's wrong?" She guided him to the table. He folded into a chair and his hands clasped around her waist as he rubbed his face against her stomach. An agonized moan tore through the room.

"Jackson?" She'd seen him like this before, when he'd lost a patient. Her hand massaged his stiff neck. "What happened?"

"Bug." He whispered as he continued to bury his face in her stomach.

"Talk to me baby."

"There was a pile up on the I-10." His swallow was audible. "Took us five hours to clear. I wanted to be done with the unrelenting death, destruction, and loss, but I couldn't outrun it. When I got to the hospital all the victims were here to haunt me. Their mangled parts, the blood, the families." His haunted eyes pierced her in place. "What if I lose you?" His hold on her was so tight it hurt.

He was frantic. "Hey." She squatted in front of him and took his face in her palms. "Jackson, look at me." His tortured dark blue eyes looked into hers. "I'm right here. I'll always be with you. You won't lose me. I promise." At her reassurance his brow went smooth. "I'm going to stay the night here too, sleep on the cot. When you're able, come to me. I'll be waiting for you."

He took her hand in his. "Thank you." He kissed her palm. "I need you so much."

She leaned in and placed a kiss on his lips. What he saw in a day's work were things no one was meant to see. Any other person would have cracked by now, but not Jackson. He dedicated his life to helping others during their time of need. He knew firsthand what it was like to lose a family member. He'd lost two all at once.

"Can you eat?"

"I don't know. Feeling kind of sick."

"How about some juice and a little salad and bread?" He nodded and let her take care of him. She passed him the love note she'd written on the napkin and his thumb caressed it as he read.

"I'll always love you, Cracker Jack. Thank you for making sacrifices so we can be together. I'm proud to call you my one and only. Can't wait to be your wife."

A lone tear rolled down his cheek. "Bug." He gasped and pulled her into his chest. "I love you."

"I more than love you." As he ate, she massaged his shoulders and neck relieving some of his stiffness. She finally sat next to him and took a few bites of pizza while she worked on her notecards.

Pulling the five-pound book toward him, he read the chapter she studied, "Anatomy of the female reproductive system." His brow knit as he looked at her. "When I get my reporting done, I'm going to assist you with your studies."

"Oh really? Are we going to play doctor?"

"I want you to pass your exam so I'm going to conduct one of my own."

She laughed and he clasped her hand where it rested on top of the table. "Thank you for being here. It makes all the difference."

"I will always come running for a code Clara."

"Code Clara," he whispered.

***

Things finally quieted around eight o'clock and Jackson was able to catch up on his reporting. Seated at the nurses' station he typed away on one of the computers, fueled by what awaited him in his office—a snug Bug. The nicknames were corny, but they always made her smile, and he'd make a fool of himself a million times over for a chance to witness her smile just once.

As he finished his reports, a woman brought in her eight-year-old child who had taken a nasty fall from a bicycle. The skin beneath her chin hung loose and needed to be sewn on by a steady hand. A plastic surgeon would be best, but none had answered the call. Jackson knew he could do it, so he took the child and her mother into one of the curtained exam rooms.

Regarding the room with wide eyes, the child stood wearing a football jersey that functioned more as a dress than a shirt. "What's your name little bit?" He tousled her head.

"April Crawford."

He smiled at her. "I like that name. Are you a Cowboys fan?" She nodded as he injected her chin with a numbing agent. Not a tear was shed. The kid was tough, and with her short hair and denim jeans, had a boyish quality that reminded him of Clara when she was that age. While he patched her up, they spoke about team stats, and she named all of the players. When he finished, he sat back and admired the stitching. The wound would heal without much of a scar, if any.

As he walked toward the back corner of the floor, he felt his burning need for Clara. It scared him how much he needed her. He believed if anybody knew, they would tear her away from him. Without her he would not, could not, survive. He knew it was anything but healthy, but their connection ran deep.

Clara was seven when she'd offered him comfort the first time. How can a seven-year-old comfort a seventeen-year-old? It was difficult to explain, but her determined spirit at that young age had solidified in him that no matter what had happened, this tiny child with the striking blue eyes believed in his future.

Even when he'd bellowed at her to leave him be, sometimes directly in her face, she'd never given up. She'd been the only one he'd confided in about the death of his parents, and though she didn't remember their talk all these years later, it was in that moment when those seven-year-old blue eyes pleaded with him that he'd been saved from self-destruction. For her, he'd give everything.

Walking to the linen closet he snatched an additional pillow for the cot. He hadn't known eleven years ago they'd end up together.

He just thought she'd always be special to him. *How had it even happened?*

It was after her accident, she'd thought she was undesirable. He'd sought to reassure her any man would fall all over himself to be with her. Case in point: he had. Once their bodies connected in a kiss, it had not possible to stop. She was what had been missing from his life, and she was the best thing about his existence. Since that moment, every breath he took, every muscle he flexed was for her.

Finally on the other side of the door, he leaned against the door jamb watching her closely. She had her foot up resting on the edge of the chair. She wrote on a note card crinkling her nose up as she sat back to read what she'd written. He chuckled and she lifted her head. Her blue eyes danced as they rendered him momentarily immobile.

As she walked toward him, he closed the door. She wrapped her arms around his neck and kissed his cheek. "How are you?"

"Better now."

"What were you laughing at?"

"Your face as you read the notecard."

"In class we had to watch a birthing video. It was horrific. Hope you weren't planning on having children because I'm not going through that."

His head went back to accommodate his abrupt release of air from the deep laughter elicited on her behalf. She was the only one who could extract such a reaction from him. "I think it's time for a quiz. Take off your pants and go get under the covers."

"Hmm, that's very clinical talk, doctor."

"Panties too." He gathered her notecards and joined her on the cot.

"Let's see what we have here." He lay above her, resting his weight along his side, and pulled the covers to their neck. "Labia majora." His fingers traced down her thigh until he reached the juncture between her legs. "Labia majora would be here"—he lightly traced the outer flesh—"two cutaneous folds that extend from the mons pubis down to the perineum." His fingers lightly grazed each anatomical point as he spoke.

70

He sat up to his knees. "Here, why don't you hold these." He passed her the note cards. "What's next?"

Breathily she answered, "Clitoral glans."

"Lucky you." He smiled. "That would be here"—he pushed his finger down on the knot between her legs. "It's no larger than a pea and is comparable to the male organ, the glans penis, although much more concentrated and therefore highly stimulable." He massaged the area with light repetitive movements. "During arousal the clitoral glans engorges with blood and will either protrude past or swell under the clitoral hood."

She gasped, "What's mine do?"

"You're a tricky girl because you swell under the hood. Fortunate for you, I aced female anatomy. However, I need more information to make a thorough assessment."

Beneath the soft cocoon of blankets, he nuzzled gently against her skin, drawing forth a cascade of giggles that danced through the air. Her youthful energy was infectious, filling him with a sense of joy. He tenderly explored her body, his lips caressing her most sensitive places with reverence and care. As his mouth found its way to where she was most responsive, he savored the intimate connection between them, feeling her fingers weave into his hair as if anchoring herself to him.

Her thighs closed around him in a tender embrace, enveloping him in warmth and closeness that felt like a sanctuary. As she lifted slightly from the bed, her breath came in soft gasps, each one whispering his name like an incantation. He marveled at how attuned he was to every nuance of her body's response; it was as though they moved in perfect harmony. Her increasing warmth and gentle quivers confirmed what he'd already etched into memory—their shared moments were filled with an unspoken understanding that transcended words.

Needing to be inside her he stood to his knees and pulled the string on his scrubs. He looked down at the contented look on her face while she smiled up at him and mouthed, *I love you.*

Beep, beep, beep.

That pager would be the actual death of him. It always seemed to sense when he was about to escape deep inside her body and taunted him. His head went down to rest on her stomach while he pulled his pants up, tied them off, and willed his erection to stop raging. He sat, hanging his legs off the cot. "I gotta go."

"I'll be here, waiting for you."

He kissed her and then exited the room to head to emergency.

Match Maker

8

By Saturday Clara was packed and waiting for Jackson to return from his shift at the hospital. Her back pocket buzzed. She pulled out her phone and saw a text from Clay.

Clay: Clara Bear, you want to ride with us?

Clara: Gotta go to the deli for a bit. I'll catch a ride with Jackson.

Clay: Be safe. Love you.

Clara: Love you.

She hated lying to her brother, but if he were to find out about Jackson, life as she knew it would crack open, spilling its guts onto the pavement. She wasn't quite ready for that to happen. Not having a family of his own, Jackson spent all holidays with the St. Martins. In addition, he'd attend events like engagements and birthdays, his own included.

For all intents and purposes, he was one of the St. Matin children. Since they were lovers, she assumed others would think it weird that he was part of the family, another brother. However, since she'd first known met him, she'd considered him her one and only so to her it wasn't weird at all.

She started packing a bag for Jackson. For two years they'd been intimate, and their relationship had created an interesting situation when they visited her childhood home. They'd cut eyes to one another from across the room and sneak in and out of bedrooms. She giggled at the memory of almost getting caught. Secretly she wished they would be discovered, so she wouldn't have to lie to her family any longer.

They'd coordinated gifts for her father's birthday. She'd ordered monogrammed golf balls and Jackson had purchased a Honma nine iron to replace the one that Lacie almost beat Briggs in the head with when she'd found out he'd bet his friends that he could score with her in Vegas. As Clara smirked at the memory, her phone rang from the top of the dresser.

Jackson's face filled the screen. "Hey, Cracker Jack."

"I love to hear your voice. Can't wait to spend the weekend with you. I'm pulling in to the complex as we speak. Got you something special."

"You spoil me."

"Always. Come out to the car before it melts all over me."

SHE HUNG up and made her way to the front door. Spotting his old Civic, she walked up to the car. He stepped out looking gloriously disheveled with his day of stubble and his short hair out of place. He bent to take her lips before handing her a chocolate dipped cone. Her favorite. "Thank you for the cone."

"You're welcome. I wish I could buy you so much more. One day."

"But I like dipped cones."

His intense eyes leveled at her. "It's so easy to please you."

She put her arm around him. "I love you, Jackson. I would rather be monetarily poor with you and rich in life."

He chuckled. "Then I think your wish has come true."

"Wanna bite?"

His head came down and he took a bite that demolished half the top.

"Hey!" He pulled her in close and kissed her lips. When she opened her mouth, he shared his prize with her. The chocolate had already started to melt, and she moaned from the delightful sensation.

They waved to Mr. Porter as he parked in his stall and started to unload his groceries. He was in his sixties and worked as an electrician. As Clara licked her ice cream cone, she recalled the day he'd helped them put in a ceiling fan, patiently relating to Jackson the wiring process. They'd offered to pay him, but Mr. Porter had said he'd only accept payment in the form of homemade chocolate chip cookies. Clara made him three dozen and continued to keep him stocked with homemade sweets—a currency she understood when the checking account dipped too low at month's end.

Jackson gave her another quick kiss. "Let me give Mr. Porter a hand with the groceries and then let's get loaded up. I'll need to shower. Any chance you'll join me?"

"Love to."

"We'll need to take your car. I don't have much faith mine will make it. I need to get that oil leak checked out." His fingers drummed against his thigh as he spoke, unconsciously tallying invisible repair costs. That familiar vertical crease appeared between his eyebrows—the one that deepened with each unpaid bill. At least they had her car.

Once the stuff was loaded, they went into the bedroom, and she undressed him while the shower water warmed. When he was naked, she traced the thin, straight scar that ran across his left shoulder blade—a souvenir from a bicycle accident he'd had three years ago, before they'd made promises to one another, when he'd skidded across wet pavement and got caught up in some wire.

She swatted his perky butt and he climbed into the shower; she followed behind. He was slim but had defined muscles from jogging and riding that damn bicycle to work—over the bridge. It was dangerous and she always worried, so he hadn't done it as much as he used to, but with his car on the brink of breaking down, he'd recently taken to riding it more than ever.

She sighed as the hot water pelted around them, the steady drumming against the tile sounding like the summer rain that had kept them in bed all weekend when they'd first met. He loved for her to lather her hands and massage away the workday. She started at the back of his neck, feeling the knots of tension—the physical evidence of what he carried. Moving down to his shoulders and then the muscles of his upper back, she pressed harder than usual, trying to reach whatever lived beneath his skin that he couldn't name.

"You're quiet today," she said, her hands still working.

"Just tired," he replied, but his shoulders remained rigid under her touch.

She loved his butt and could hardly wait to massage farther south. It was the same thing every time. She'd start on her massage and by the time she ended up at his butt he'd turn, just as he was doing now, and offer her a teasing, naughty smirk.

He lifted her and she wrapped her legs around his waist while he rested her back against the tile in their small bathtub shower. She liked the size because there was barely enough room to accommodate them both and they had to remain close. In their passion neither of them could speak, but their communication was strong. His eyes darkened and pleaded for her acceptance, which she gave by roughly pulling him toward her, even as a fleeting thought crossed her mind: *Am I enough to keep whatever haunts him at bay?*

She groaned her impatience as he slowly entered her. Whenever they made love it was like it was their last time. Or their first time. She didn't know, but she felt the intensity and his pinpoint focus. It was like he deliberately tried to make their connection last as long as he could.

She also wanted to be connected to him for all of eternity and even beyond, so she didn't mind that he would get frenzied, but then slow to an almost stop just before she was about to experience bliss. He'd always come back around and work her up again. He kissed her, the shower water mixing with their saliva. His tongue slid down her chin and neck to her breast until he was at her nipple. He loitered, tracing the pebble with his tongue while his pace was steady but slow. She raked her nails across his back and his gaze caught hers.

"I love you," she whispered.

A soul cleansing sigh escaped his lips. "Three little words. Not enough." His pace increased until he was assaulting her and the skin at her back stung from being pulled by the tiles. "You save me from darkness, Clara. You're everything."

A flash of memory hit her—Jackson sitting on the bathroom floor three months ago, head in his hands, breathing so shallow she'd thought he might disappear. She'd sat beside him all night, not understanding but refusing to leave, and in the morning, they'd started this shower ritual. She didn't want him to be even on the precipice of plummeting into the depths of the darkness he spoke about.

"Jackson, I hope you're happy because you make me happier than I've ever been or could imagine being." Her words felt inadequate against whatever demon he wrestled.

"Bug, I'm flipping rapturous. With your love I could hold up the world." He called her Bug for many reasons, one of them because the first night they'd spent together, she'd curled against him so tightly, so desperately—"like a little bug seeking warmth," he'd said —that the name had stuck. She'd never told him she'd been seeking more than warmth that night; she'd been seeking refuge from her own shadows.

They held on to each other with hard unrelenting grips as they came together, like they always did, intense and cleansing, whole and complete. For these moments, at least, the darkness receded for them both.

***

Driving to the estate with her hand entwined in his, listening to her emo music, was the epitome of happiness for Jackson. What she'd given him in the shower was the closest to heaven he knew he'd ever get. Fine with him. Paradise couldn't get any better than Clara naked, sudsy, and writhing under his touch.

Making the turn that placed the car on the estate sent a cold ripple up Jackson's spine, settling like a stone in his throat. The gravel crunched beneath the tires with finality, each pebble marking another second closer to their undoing. He sensed the end of their utopian cocoon—those stolen afternoons when Clara would trace the lines of his palm and whisper "these are all the places we'll go someday"—and the beginning of despair. He pulled up under a pecan tree, its leaves casting dappled shadows that seemed to write warnings across Clara's skin. The air smelled of sweet oak and impending rain, a cruel reminder of their kiss during the first summer storm.

The scariest thing of all was he knew she felt it too. Her eyes turned down and her wringing hands communicated trouble. Given her sixth sense, he was not surprised when he exited the car, inhaling the scent of expensive cologne and horse sweat. Mr. St. Martin sat atop a horse, the animal's hooves cutting divots into the manicured lawn that Jackson imagined were mirroring the gouges being carved into his future. Next to him a stately gentleman rode alongside him.

"This is my boy, Jackson," he announced, his voice carrying the weight of expectations Jackson had never agreed to bear. He loved Mr. St. Martin dearly, but he would only ever have one father and he never wanted his dad's memory diminished. "He's in his final year of residency at Baton Rouge General. Jackson, I want you to meet Warren Granger."

The two of them were a matched set—powerful men sitting on top of majestic animals looking imposing as hell. "His daughter, Veronica, is inside; I'll introduce you to her later. Told him you'd wine and dine her for the weekend. She's got her masters in nursing. She's twenty-seven years old. Do I smell a love connection?"

Jackson's gaze flickered involuntarily toward Clara, still sitting in the passenger seat, before he forced his attention back to the men. His mouth went dry as cotton.

"You always did enjoy playing matchmaker," Warren said, then extended his hand toward Jackson.

Jackson took Warren's hand into his. The man squeezed like he had something to prove. Jackson deliberately relaxed his grip, a small rebellion that no one but he would recognize. Warren's signet ring pressed painfully against Jackson's knuckles as he sized him up like a bull at auction. Jackson stood two inches shorter, aware of how he diminished in their presence while with Clara he always felt ten feet tall.

"I think I'm coming down with something, so I'll be spending this weekend in bed," Jackson offered, hoping to thwart the matchmaker scenario. The lie tasted bitter, another in the growing collection that was eroding not just his grinding teeth but his soul.

"Nonsense. Veronica's little black bag will get you fixed right up and ready for the festivities. Baton Rouge General is an impressive feat. I know Cliff is very proud of you."

Jackson nodded, bearing down on his teeth. Behind his closed lips, he silently recited what he should say: *I love Clara. I've loved her since we were children. I won't be part of your business merger disguised as a marriage.* The lies had to stop before there was nothing left of his enamel—or his integrity.

"We'll just let you get unloaded and then I'll do the introductions." Laughing, Mr. St. Martin strode away alongside Mr. Granger, their shoulders nearly touching while the distance between Jackson and everything he wanted stretched into miles.

Jackson turned and looked across the hood of the car to see Clara, frozen in place. The grief on her face wasn't just etched—it transformed her.

"Bug, it changes nothing. I'll get out of it. No one can compare to you." He walked over to her and took her earlobe between his fingers—the gesture that had always been theirs since the day he'd caught a ladybug there. She didn't respond, but looked to the ground, a single tear tracking down her cheek and disappearing into the dust at their feet.

"Bug?" he whispered, his voice breaking. In that moment, he wasn't just afraid of losing her—he was terrified of becoming the man who wasn't valiant enough to fight for her, but he'd wanted to. She was the one holding him back from professing his undying love to his family. He'd respect her wishes, for a while longer.

Her held breath pushed from her lungs in a painful sounding gasp. "But she's... she's in medicine and she's your age. Veronica's perfect for you." Her fingers twitched against her thigh, betraying the casual tone she was failing to maintain.

She used to ask why he wanted her, a dumb seventeen-year-old girl. Those questions had terrified him once, forcing him to excavate motives he preferred to leave buried. It had taken him a year of uttering reassuring words in her ear for her to start believing him.

He'd finally told her she was everything good and pure he'd ever known. In comparison he was dirt, a black hole—a man who should have known better, who sometimes woke in cold sweats wondering what kind of person crosses such lines. She'd stopped asking after he'd shared those words, which only deepened his shame and his need.

"No." He shook his head. "Bug, I've found my perfection already." He took her hands in his, noticing how they'd grown steadier in the years since they'd met, when they used to tremble at his touch. "Hey, look at me." Her pained eyes scorched something tender behind his ribs, a place he didn't know existed before her. "All that I am, all that I'll ever be is wrapped up in you. You alone make me who I am."

Her smile broke. "That sounded like emo lyrics. I thought you hated emo."

"I could never hate something you love." He kissed her nose, inhaling the faint scent of lavender that always clung to her hair, the same scent that haunted his pillows for days after she'd been in his bed. They shared an intense glance. "Those powder-blue eyes follow me in my sleep. You're all over my dreams. I could never exist apart from you." The words hung between them, and for a moment he glimpsed his greatest fear—that one day she would outgrow him, see him for what he truly was, a man who had claimed her before she'd fully become herself.

Others started to arrive so they broke apart, his hand lingering on her waist a fraction too long before sliding away. He straightened his posture slightly, donning the mask of appropriate family friend as he removed their bags from the car.

"What's this bag with wine and cheese in the backseat?" He held up the bottle, feeling the weight of his hypocrisy—concerned about underage drinking while the memory of her seventeen-year-old self still burned in his conscience.

"Give it to me." She reached for it, that familiar determination hardening her features—the same expression she'd worn when she first told him she wasn't too young to know what she wanted.

"You want to explain why you have a bottle of wine given that you're under age." His voice carried a gentle admonishment that sounded hollow even to his own ears.

"Oh pipe down with the underage speech. I'd not intended for you to see it until tonight. It's from Moretti's. An expiring Manchego cheese and a bottle of petite Syrah that Lucian said would pair nicely with it."

"Mmm." He licked his lips and brushed them together, amazed at how she'd blossomed from the girl who once thought wine only came in red or white.

"And guess what? It's a Viejo, aged two years." She emphasized the time with a knowing look—two years, just like them, as if their relationship could be measured in the same careful aging process.

In the past year, he'd learned so much from her about cheese and wine. He could listen to her talk about it all day, her passion a reminder of all she brought to his life beyond the dangerous thrill of loving someone he shouldn't. "Are we sharing this lone bottle and my Manchego with the rest of your family?"

Her eyes sparkled with that mischief that had first drawn him to her, the spark that made him forget all the reasons they shouldn't be together. "I sure didn't have that in mind when I packed it. Thought you could sneak into my room later tonight, like you did last time."

"You should be a party planner. You'd earn millions." They kissed behind the privacy of the car door, his heart racing with both desire and dread—knowing each stolen moment brought them closer to a reckoning neither was prepared to face.

Inside he greeted most of her brothers and went upstairs to stow the luggage just to get away from the leering eyes and snide comments about the Granger girl. Truthfully, it was hard for him to watch all of her brothers happily married and looking on their wives with utter love and devotion, the way he was free to look at Clara only in the privacy of their apartment.

He knew nobody ever loved anybody the way he loved Clara. Not even her brothers. It made him yearn for the day they'd be accepted as a couple. His gut seized when he realized they probably never would be—a physical pain that spread like ice water through his abdomen, making his fingers tremble against the banister as he climbed the stairs. The familiar sensation of his throat closing up, the same suffocating tightness he felt every time they had to pretend to be just friends, made him pause on the landing to collect himself.

He dropped her bags on the bed in the room that had served her during her childhood years. As he looked around the room with its framed handwritten passages from her favorite poems and colorful Chinese lanterns, he inhaled the lingering scent of lavender and old books that calmed his sole immediately. His fingers traced the edge of a dog-eared journal on the nightstand—the one she'd told him contained her fifteen-year-old dreams. The décor was whimsically original and thoughtful just like her, each element a piece of the story she'd shared with him in whispered conversations late at night.

In the hall he ran into her mother. "Mrs. St. Martin." His hand instinctively moved to his pocket, where his thumb brushed against the smooth river stone Clara had given him on his eighteenth birthday, his private talisman that he carried everywhere.

"Jackson, honey, you look tired." She placed his jaw in her palms and kissed his cheeks. "You don't come around enough. How's your residency going?"

He loved this warm woman that was the only semblance of a mother he had. Her sincerity with him, despite the fact that she had six other children, always boosted his spirits. He liked that she made his time with her special. The memory of her bringing him chicken soup when he'd caught the flu during his first year of med school made the deception between them even more painful.

"The hours are long." He unconsciously rolled his shoulders, trying to release the knot of tension that had taken permanent residence between his shoulder blades from months of vigilance.

"I just read about the huge accident on I-10. They took a lot of the victims to Baton Rouge General. Guess you saw them both going and coming didn't you?"

"Yes ma'am." He felt his eyes go unfocused at the graphic memories. The face of the teenage girl with the shattered windshield embedded in her forehead flashed behind his eyelids—her vacant stare as he'd called time of death haunted him in the quiet hours before dawn.

She clasped his hand in hers. "Will you have coffee with me in the morning? Just you and me."

"I'd love to."

"Great. I'd like to catch up with my favorite son."

He smiled, knowing she said that to each of her children.

"Hope you plan on staying the night."

"Yeah, we thought we'd stay through Monday."

Her brow furrowed and it was then that he realized he'd referred to Clara and himself as a 'we.' His heart stuttered, then raced; sweat beaded instantly at his hairline. His tongue felt swollen in his suddenly dry mouth as he scrambled to recover.

"I mean Clara and me, she rode with me."

She smiled at him, squeezing his forearm. "I'm so grateful she has you to look after her. I don't worry so much about her alone in that big city."

He couldn't say anything at her overt display of trust in him. Through the window behind Mrs. St. Martin, he could see Clara's childhood swing, now hanging from just one chain—broken but still attached, neither fully functional nor completely abandoned. The sight of it sent a wave of shame through him that tasted like copper pennies in his mouth, the weight of their secret pressing down on his shoulders until he had to consciously stop himself from hunching under the invisible burden.

Funny Smelling Cheese

9

Inside, Clara went around and hugged each member of her family —her family that had grown by leaps and bounds. She held Daria in her arms. Isa and Cash's baby was just an infant, but she was the most beautiful baby Clara had ever seen. Cash had a few new tattoos that he was showing to the crowd. Scrawled in beautiful cursive script over his heart were the words, Isabela and Daria. Her eyes filled with tears at the happiness her brother projected. And he wasn't the only one.

They had all found someone and so had she. She just couldn't show any outward signs of it in front of her family, but she longed for the day when that would no longer be the case. She thought maybe they should tell Briggs first since he was pretty easy going, but it was hard to predict how he or any of her brothers would take the news. She was ready to start an honest life with Jackson. There would never be anyone else for her.

"Who have you got there?" The smooth, deep voice that was so familiar to her now almost brought tears to her eyes as she held the babe.

She smiled up at Jackson. "You remember Daria."

"Wow, she's grown since I saw her last."

"Do you want to hold her?"

"Sure." Clara gingerly laid the baby in his arms. Daria cooed and Jackson erupted with the sweetest baby voice she'd ever heard. Watching him with the infant made her heart swell. She didn't want to have kids right away, but she wouldn't want to wait too long after they married. Maybe two years, that way she'd be an official adult. *But there was that video they watched at school.* Jackson's deep sapphire gaze met hers and his eyes held their many secrets in their depths.

A slight smile on his lips was visible to her. Most people probably would have missed it, but she saw it. She knew what his every breath meant. He was imagining their family just as she had been. Video aside, she wanted to make babies with Jackson.

"Clara Grace." Clay was beside her and pulled her into a huge bear hug until her feet no longer touched the ground. "I've missed you coming around the house."

Since the wedding she'd made herself scarce because she was trying to give him and his new bride some privacy. "I miss you too."

"Let's remedy that, shall we? Come with us next weekend. I plan to take Eve to that place you love so much in New Orleans."

"Jackson Square." Clara wasn't doing a good job of concealing her excitement and Eve smiled at her bouncing.

"The French Quarter Festival is next weekend." Clay said.

She turned to Jackson, and he too was smiling at her. "When are you leaving?" Clara asked.

"We thought we'd go up on Friday morning."

"Hmm, well I have to work but I guess I could meet you later."

She heard Jackson's low voice filter over her shoulder. "I was actually going to go up Friday evening after my shift." She knew that was a lie but was grateful he'd interceded.

"Oh, I can ride in with Jackson."

Clay wrapped his arms around both her and Eve. "Great, a weekend with my two favorite ladies. Can't wait. I'll look forward to it all week." He kissed her cheek.

Clara heard the bellow of her father before she actually saw him. "There's my Clara Bear." She went to his open arms. "When did you get in?"

"Dad, I was in the car with Jackson."

"I didn't see you."

No because you were too busy playing matchmaker.

"I rode in with him."

"I'm glad he looks after you if I'm not around to do it. Sure wish you'd move back home, kiddo."

"I know Dad, but I'm okay, really okay." He kissed the top of her head.

Jackson returned Daria to Isa who went to feed and put her to bed. Cash followed behind them.

Clara took the seat perpendicular to the couch where Jackson sat. He told Clara a story about some celebrity chick that had come into the E.R. The set they filmed on collapsed and she sprained her ankle. Clara felt eyes on them and turned to see a busty bottle blond lustfully eyeing Jackson.

Mr. Granger followed behind the woman. Dad joined them from the kitchen holding two glasses filled with ice and an amber liquid.

"Warren, a little aged bourbon." They clinked and toasted to their children.

"Jackson, may I present my daughter, Veronica."

"Nice to meet you." Jackson nodded stoically. He didn't stand, just shook her hand from the couch.

Veronica's voice was high pitched and saccharine sweet. She took up the space next to him on the couch, their thighs touching. Jackson repositioned himself and slid over to reestablish the lost distance. He met Clara's eyes and pleaded, silently saying, *I'm sorry.*

"So, you're at Baton Rouge General."

"That's right."

"I'll be transferring there next week."

Oh, how peachy! She was pretty in a really obvious Dallas-house-wife-reality-TV-show way. She wore a dress that was fancier than any Clara had ever owned and that had her breasts on display. In fact, it was amazing one of the melon shaped mounds hadn't sprouted legs and walked out of her neckline.

Veronica's hair was really long and wavy. So long and perfect it almost didn't seem real. Her nails, long and thick, appeared fake, and possibly her lips, which seemed too puffy to accommodate her face. Out of proportion, her thick lips drew the eye toward their pink, wet surface. Her synthetic tan made her appear a little too bronzed in the low light of the living room.

Her appearance was fussy, but men seemed to like fussy, and Clara wondered if Jackson liked that look. Veronica was a bit of forced sophistication with her sheath dress and platform shoes. Clara wondered if she should purchase shoes like that. How did one even walk around in those things? Maybe she could practice.

Looking down at her own attire, Clara grimaced. She'd worn a blue jean skirt, white T-shirt, and pink flip-flops with big blue bows. She took the shoes off and threw them behind the chair and then she slid her legs beneath her. From the corner of her eye, she saw Jackson watching her every move. *Her* every move. Not the sophisticated woman next to him, but her. He mouthed, *you're beautiful*, and she smiled at him.

Veronica was talking about her new job and relocating to the area from Dallas. *Bingo.* She definitely looked like those women on TV and Clara couldn't figure out how she worked with patients given her long acrylic fingernails. Wouldn't she scratch someone or put an eye out? If Clara were to get Veronica as a nurse, she'd send her back for a real one.

"I'm glad I'll be focusing on case management and won't have to see any actual patients. I never really enjoyed the whole nursing thing."

Yeah, she'd definitely cast her back for a new nurse.

"If you loathe patient care, why'd you become a nurse?"

Good question Cracker Jack.

"I'm not sure. I was going to become a doctor, but then I got bored and wanted to just be done with school. I wanted to do dermatology so that I could use all the skin care products on myself. I love products. Can you imagine how convenient?" Jackson frowned. "Anyway, since I had most of the classes completed, I chose a degree in nursing."

Hmm, Clara smelled a rat. She would bet money the woman chose nursing so that she could meet doctors. It wasn't uncommon and she seemed to fit the bill.

"What branch of medicine are you in?" Veronica asked.

"Emergency."

"Oh, emergency is the worst." Her arms flailed as she talked. "In school we had to do a rotation in emergency. It sucked. Had to be on call and it was just the worst hours and so messy. Yuck. And there's so much paperwork and caregiver counseling. I hate emergency. Where will you specialize?"

"I am specializing in emergency."

"For your career you mean? You actually want to work in emergency."

"I actually do."

A nervous giggle escaped Clara's throat, the sound hanging in the air like something foreign. Heat crept up her neck, and she felt her shoulders inching upward, armor against the judgment lacing Veronica's tone. She twisted the silver ring on her middle finger— her mother's ring—three quick rotations, a habit she'd developed in middle school when the boys at lunch would ask why she didn't have a chest yet.

"You enjoy a fast paced setting."

"Something like that."

Jackson got up and walked from the room, leaving the two of them alone. Clara watched him go, a flicker of betrayal tightening the space between her ribs.

Veronica's nut-brown eyes shot to Clara. "So, you're the sister."

Clara nodded. "I'm the sister." The words felt worn on her tongue, like a path she'd traveled too many times—the constant identifier, the asterisk to her existence.

"What's it like being the only girl in a sea of hot men?"

She crinkled her nose at the woman, the faint scent of Veronica's expensive perfume suddenly cloying. "My brothers, you mean?"

"Well, yeah."

"I hadn't noticed." Clara shifted, the leather of the couch sticking slightly to the backs of her bare thighs. She resisted the urge to peel herself away, to make that embarrassing skin-on-leather sound that would only make her feel more exposed.

"What do you do?"

"I work at an Italian restaurant."

"A waitress." The word dropped like a stone between them.

"I wait tables, but I also make mozzarella cheese and a few of our signature dishes." Clara's fingers flexed against her thigh, remembering the satisfaction of stretching the warm cheese, the way it yielded to her touch, unlike this conversation.

"That sounds interesting. Do you make that funny smelling cheese too?"

"Funny smelling cheese?"

"You know, the moldy one."

"Do you mean blue cheese?"

"Yeah, that one. They should throw it out once it gets moldy. That's disgusting."

"But they add the bacteria to the cheese so that it will age and mold."

"Eww. It's added on purpose?"

"Yes." Clara swallowed the explanation that sat on her tongue about the centuries-old tradition, the craftsmanship. What was the point?

Jackson was back and leaned against the fireplace with a smirk on his face. Evidently, he thought this funny. Clara thought it anything but. A familiar hollowness expanded in her chest—the same one she'd felt at thirteen when her brothers' friends would go silent when she entered a room, the awareness of being both seen and unseen.

She stood, grabbed her juvenile flip-flops, the plastic warm and slightly tacky against her fingers. For a moment, she hated them— these cheap, childish things that somehow confirmed everything Veronica probably thought about her.

Clara walked into the kitchen to sit with the rest of her family. The familiar scent of her brother Briggs's aftershave and the lingering aroma of this morning's coffee wrapped around her like an old blanket. Her brothers discussed plans for the evening that included a dance hall concert by Andres Bellefontaine, one of her favorite zydeco singers.

As they talked, Luca caught her eye across the table and slid his hand across the worn wood to tap her wrist twice—their childhood signal that meant *ignore them, you're fine.* The simple gesture loosened something in her throat.

The women all headed upstairs to get ready and left her surrounded by her brothers. Clara ran her finger along a groove in the kitchen table, thinking about how Bellefontaine's accordion would feel later—like a second heartbeat in her chest, drowning out the echoes of "a waitress" and "that's disgusting" with something that needed no explanation or defense.

Tired of always being left out, Clara decided to voice what was on her mind. After all, she was nineteen now and in the state of Louisiana that meant she was legal. Legal enough to walk into a bar anyway. "I wanna go too."

Clay was the first to answer her. "Clara Bear, you don't belong in a place like that." He cupped her cheek in his hand and kissed the top of her head.

"Why?" She cocked her head at him. "I like Andres. And why don't I belong in a place like that, but your wife does?"

The other brothers laughed at the point she was making, and Clay raised a brow at her. "Did you say you were currently enrolled in philosophy?"

She felt her nose crinkle at his perplexing question. What did that have to do with anything? "Yeah, it's utterly boring and useless."

"Not so useless. You just rendered his logic inadequate," Finn signed.

"I was trying to be nice, but the truth of it is there will be an odd number. I'll be worrying after you all night," Clay grumbled.

"Jackson doesn't have a partner." Briggs retorted.

"He's got Veronica." Cash had returned and laughed as he discussed Jackson's plight.

Her skin grew heavy as if it were being pulled down. She'd been unaware Veronica was going and never dreamed she'd go as Jackson's date, on his arm, in *her* place. There was no way she'd be staying at the house.

Cash placed his arm around her. "Clara Bear, you'll be my date. Isa wants to catch up on some much needed sleep, and if I'm around it doesn't really happen since I can't keep my hands off of her."

"Ugh." Clara cupped her hands over her ears. "Spare me the details." She started to walk from the kitchen but turned back. "I'm going to get ready. Don't leave without me."

She ran up the winding staircase taking the steps two at a time. Rounding the corner for the wing to her room, she ran into Veronica. *Veronica* decked out in a red dress way more revealing than the one she'd worn previously. Clara had not thought that was even possible.

The front of the dress cut deep and all the way down to her navel. *Veronica* whose dress was barely enough to contain her melon sized breasts. *Veronica* who wore a necklace that was so long the dangling jewels dripped down into her cleavage.

"Hello there. You wouldn't happen to have a flat iron, would you?"

Clara shook her head. "No."

"Didn't think so since your hair is"—she regarded her for a moment—"well it's *natural*."

She proceeded down the stairs, the back of the dress as revealing as the front with its low plunge that almost exposed butt crack. Her platform heels were silver and it awed Clara yet again that she could float along as she did in shoes that had her foot at a ninety-degree angle with the floor. The shoes made her butt stick out and the fire engine red lipstick she wore drew attention straight to her mouth.

In her room Clara looked at herself in the mirror. Her lips weren't as thick as Veronica's so outlining them in red lipstick just seemed foolish. She undressed and considered her smaller natural looking breasts. Breasts that would get lost in a dress with a plunging neckline.

Clara turned and looked at her scarred up shoulder and back. Deep jagged rivers meandered down to her lower back. The skin puckered white, but in places was darker than the rest of her pigment. She cringed as a burning sensation radiated through her at the memory of her accident. Being back at the estate made those memories more vivid, but she loved this land and would endure the darkness.

She would never, could never, wear something backless. An A-line dress with a seersucker pattern hung in her closet. It didn't have sleeves but at least two inches of material covered the shoulders. The dress came to her knees and the only heels she had were beige kitten-style pumps. Compared to Veronica it seemed she was headed to a convent to celebrate her celibacy. She wondered if Jackson would even notice her next to the siren in red.

She took a deep breath and brushed her long bangs down across her forehead, almost covering her eyelids. Calling on her philosophy class she mumbled, "It is what it is." She could never be the type of woman who would serve as flashy arm candy and she really didn't want to be, but if Jackson liked that kind of woman, then she would reconsider, for him. She wanted to be what he desired and what he needed.

The best thing about me is you. She pulled a Post-it from the side of her mirror that hadn't been there before. *Jackson.* She'd recognize his barely legible scrawl anywhere. She took the piece of paper in her hands and pulled it close to her heart. "I love you, Cracker Jack." Somehow, he always knew what she needed even before she needed it. It was more than incredible. She retrieved her purse and placed the note in the pocket and patted the outside with her hand.

Back in the living room everyone was paired off. As she entered, Cash opened his arm to her. "Clara Bear, you're beautiful. I'll be the envy of every man." She smiled at Cash while she basked in his adoring words.

Across the room her eyes connected with sizzling sapphire jewels. Dressed in a gray Henley and black jeans that fit his body like a glove highlighting every muscle, Jackson embodied every woman's late night fantasy. Her mouth opened and she breathed out a short shallow breath of air. Standing beside him, also taking him in, was Veronica. Her eyes practically bulged as she scanned down his body and back up, but he didn't connect with her. Instead, he stared into Clara's soul, their connection, even from across the room, unmistakable. She hoped no one else would become aware.

Since there were fourteen in their party they loaded into two SUVs. Cash and Clara rode with Briggs and Lacie, taking the third seat while Veronica and Jackson took the middle.

Jackson turned to face Clara and smiled. "Bellefontaine's playing. You love him."

"I do." She returned his smile. "I like the rubboard the best."

Veronica turned and observed their interaction. After a few beats, she began to twirl her fingers in Jackson's hair. His hand closed over hers as he placed her arm back on her side of the seat. A few minutes later her body inclined toward his and her fingers found their way back into his hair. Her long sculpted nails raked his neck. When he grasped her fingers this time he wasn't as gentle. He tossed her arm down and said, "Stop." Her eyes locked with Clara's and the fire she saw in them made her uneasy. What was she thinking? Was it Jackson's presence that caused her to look so vi

Next to her, Cash was oblivious as Isa texted him pictures of herself and the baby.

The next few hours were an exercise in futility. Veronica started to drink and became even more belligerent with Jackson than she'd been in the car. Around the dance floor her hands were all over him. He tried to keep his distance, but it was useless. As the night wore on, he actually had to hold most of her body weight up to keep her from falling flat on the floor—a sight Clara knew she would enjoy but felt guilty for thinking.

Leaning against the wall, she and Cash were catching their breath when Veronica and Jackson approached, "You wanna give me a break here, Cash?"

Cash exhaled through clenched teeth. "I guess I can do that, but to be fair Dad intended her for you." Cash laughed at his plight. "Probably wouldn't have to work very hard to take advantage of that either."

"Not interested." Jackson's head shook.

"Yeah, that's a high maintenance nightmare." Cash walked over to Veronica who was too drunk to have followed their conversation.

Jackson stood next to Clara and exhaled long and slow. "Bug, you're so beautiful." At his words she sat up a little straighter. His thumb slid under the shoulder strap of her dress. "I love you in this dress. So pretty." He leaned close to her ear and inhaled. "I need you so hard right now. Dance with me."

He led her to the dance floor and when their connection was finally secured, she watched him breathe in deep. "Clara, I can't go so long without touching you. It makes me anxious. I can't explain it, but I'm like a runaway train. The only thing that can stop me from destructing is you." His right hand knotted in her left while his arm slid across her back, pulling her in close—so close they were no longer moving their feet, just swaying in the space as couples swirled around them.

Jackson pulled her to a dark corner and that's when she noticed there were two guys she didn't recognize dancing with Veronica while others watched from the sidelines. She put on quite a show in her red siren's dress. The men cheered and whistled, motivating her to continue. Her dress crept up while her neckline plunged creating an erotic display. She seemed like one of those playboy models. Jackson's face looked pained.

"Jackson?"

"Yeah."

"You don't like her?"

His hands on her tugged her into his side. He kissed the spot behind her ear that made her giggle. "No."

How could he not like her? She was sexy and pretty. "Why not?"

"She's all surface with no deep structure."

He spoke in guy code. She didn't know what he'd meant by that. "Do you like to watch her?"

"The spectacle she's creating? She's making idiots of those men. It's also kind of sad don't you think?"

"She's sophisticated and confident. Kind of sexy." She shrugged.

He pulled back to look down into her eyes. "You know what's special, Bug?"

"What?"

"The way I make you confident in the privacy of our bedroom. That you save it just for my eyes. That's sexy. That's sophisticated."

She smiled and leaned into his neck using her teeth to trace the slightly raised vein.

"Mmm, don't do that here or I just might combust on the hardwood floor."

"I'm not going to stop."

"I DON'T WANT YOU TO."

"What are you going to do with her?"

"I guess I'll see her back to the estate since she's in no shape to see herself back."

"Don't move," Clara whispered, her body tense against Jackson's. Eve froze in the bathroom doorway, eyes widening at the intimate scene illuminated by the light. Clara's warning came too late, she and Jackson were entwined like rose bush canes and had been kissing. What would Eve do now that she'd witnessed their ongoing romance? Clara's heart pounded as she considered her options. Should she confront Eve again? Beg and plead, yet again. Or break down and start crying to make a scene?

You Need A Bang Trim

10

Clara's head popped up from where it rested on Jackson's shoulder, the sudden movement sending a jolt of electricity down her spine that Jackson felt through her skin. "Here comes Eve." Her throat constricted around the words as her gaze darted to the approaching figure. Jackson knew Eve hadn't mentioned a word to Clay about their relationship. If she had, the atmosphere wouldn't have been so festive—it would have been a battlefield with him at the center, exposed and judged.

"So, you two are still together." Eve's voice carried the weight of their secret.

Jackson cleared his throat, his Adam's apple bobbing beneath skin that had grown hot. "It's much more than that." His fingers found Clara's and held tight, tracing the familiar figure eight pattern across her palm that had become their silent language of reassurance.

"Are you deliberately trying to be discovered? Plus, I told you to break it off. I can't keep this from Clay, especially if I keep running into you like this. He's already suspicious."

Jackson shook his head, not knowing how to solve their situation in the moment. "I know he is, but we will tell the family soon. I'm sorry we've put you in this situation."

"What is the tell-the-family-soon-plan then? Honestly, I'm more interested in *when* the plan is."

"They will never understand. They won't accept our relationship." Clara's foot tapped nervously on the dusty floor, sending up tiny clouds that caught in the sporadic light—relics of a hundred forgotten celebrations in this old venue.

"I'm not disagreeing with you. It's going to be a fight." Eve frowned. "Jackson, you're one of their brothers and Clay's best friend. It will be seen as betrayal."

Jackson's stomach knotted, acid rising in his throat. The same sensation he'd felt that Christmas morning when he'd brushed Clara's hair from her face, and Clay had narrowed his eyes from across the room.

"I stayed with them for a while after my parents died. Until I went off to college." Jackson clarified, his voice carrying the echo of nights spent crying silently into his pillow while Clara's father stood awkwardly in the doorway, attempting comfort but never quite being able to cross the threshold. On the other hand, Clara's mom had been exactly like Clara, pushing him to rise up out of bed every morning. Women were so much stronger than men. It was important to make this distinction. "I'm not biological family."

Dawning spread across Eve's face. "I thought you'd been living with them longer than that."

"No, but I am around a lot." He grimaced.

Eve nodded. "Right. To be close to Clara."

"But it's not betrayal; we want to get married." Clara smiled, her fingers tightening around Jackson's with the desperate strength of someone clinging to driftwood in a storm.

Eve gasped. "Clara!" Her hand went to her chest. "You're way too young to get married." She set her intense gray eyes on Jackson. "What are you thinking to allow these fantastic notions to run through her head?"

"Were it up to me, I would have already married her." The

words fell from his lips with the solemnity of a vow, his eyes never leaving Clara's face.

Her head shook. "This is so bad. Clay is just going to kill you."

Jackson grimaced, a flash of memory crossing his face—fourteen years old, bloody-nosed and on the ground after being attacked on his walk home, Clay standing over him with clenched fists, promising the bullies would never touch him again. He didn't like when Eve said that particular phrase. A phrase she was beginning to use a lot lately. Jackson looked up to Clay and the last thing he wanted was to cause a rift between them and lose him as a friend and brother.

"You can help us." Clara said, leaning forward, the scent of stale beer and decades of spilled drinks rising from the floor.

"No." Eve's head shook vigorously, her earrings catching the pulsing lights from the dance floor. "Please don't ask me to do that." The burden of their secret seemed to press down on her shoulders, bending her normally straight posture.

"But he'll listen to you."

"I can't talk about this here." She seemed frayed as she trudged off to link up with Clay on the dance floor, her steps heavy as though wading through invisible quicksand.

"Well, Bug, we're loving on borrowed time." Jackson stared out onto the floor, watching Eve with Clay. His voice caressed the nickname remembering Clara at just thirteen, when she had rescued a praying mantis from her brother's boot, Jackson watching in wonder as she whispered to it, "Fly away, little bug, before they hurt you."

Clara took his hand in hers, feeling the calluses that hadn't been there when they'd first touched—testament to the years that had transformed him from the broken boy her family had taken in to the man who now risked everything to hold her. "No matter what happens we will always be together."

He kissed their connected hands, his lips lingering against her skin, the warmth of his breath a promise more binding than any wedding vow. "Always," he whispered, the word carrying the cadence of their private ritual—the first syllable soft, the second stretched like the endless future they were fighting for.

Given the late hour, the dance hall had emptied by half and some of the brothers had wanted to head back to the house. Jackson tried to pull Veronica away from the dance floor, but he couldn't get through the pack of rabid males. As a result, they'd missed the first SUV back to the estate.

She'd been shoeless for the last hour. The slit in her dress had torn and now was actually revealing things that should not be uncovered in public. When he'd tried to tell her, she cooed in his ear and asked if he liked what he saw. He couldn't be more disgusted with his current predicament. Did her father know she had a drinking problem? He suspected not, but he wasn't very happy at getting stuck with her for the evening. Meanwhile his sweet Clara was back in her room with the pink-canopied bed. A bed he wished he shared with her.

The night wore on and even the youngest St. Martin brothers had had enough. Briggs spoke up from the sidelines where they all currently watched. "Jackson, if you don't go and physically throw her over your shoulder so we can leave I'll fucking do it."

From beneath his arm Lacie spoke up, "Over my dead body. She came with Jackson; he needs to be the one manhandling her."

Exasperated, Jackson exhaled. "She didn't come with me. She was thrown at me by her father." Briggs laughed from his position atop a barstool.

Lacie took a swig from her beer and said, "It's been a while since we've been able to get out. My stamina for this stuff is not what it used to be. I'm beat. If you don't go and fetch her, I'll freaking do it."

They all laughed, and Briggs said, "I think you could take her."

Shit. He headed onto the dance floor to retrieve this privileged daughter of some land tycoon who had an overblown sense of entitlement. What problems did she have that she needed to conduct herself in such a manner? Tomorrow morning when her head was nice and fat because her electrolytes would be out of sync, he'd give her a piece of his mind, and he'd do it loudly.

When he arrived at the center of the wooden floor, she brashly slurred, "Jackson, you super fine man, get that juicy ass over here and let me grab a handful."

He bent and shoved his shoulder into her abdomen and threw her over his shoulder.

"Oomph."

He'd be lucky if she didn't vomit down his back.

"You're a strong man." She squeezed his ass.

"Will you please stop violating me." The brothers howled with laughter. "Let's get the hell out of here."

Back at the estate he carried Veronica up to her designated room and placed her on the bed. She immediately started to gag so he turned her onto her side and held a trashcan beneath her head. Once she was done gagging, he went to the attached bathroom and ran cold water over a rag. On the bed her top had unhooked, and her huge jiggly breasts were exposed. And yeah, they were attractive but there were some problems: A) they were silicon, unnatural; B) She'd gone a few sizes too large, and they exceeded the width of her back. He personally didn't like that look; C) They weren't Clara's.

"Will you help me get this dress off?"

Of course he would. He just felt sorry for her now. He peeled the dress down and since she'd been showing what she had all over the dance floor he wasn't surprised to find her completely naked beneath. He wiped her face with the cold rag and gave her a bottle of water.

"If you stay, I'll fuck you really well."

Her hand grasped his crotch hard, and he instinctively turned and pushed her away. "No thanks."

"You like the daughter."

His head shot up and he looked into her eyes. "What?"

"The daughter, Clara, you like her."

His lips tightened at her expert analysis. What could he say that wouldn't implicate them both?

She leaned forward and placed a chaste kiss on his lips. His spine stiffened. "Don't worry hot guy, I won't say a word." She pinched her fingers together and ran them from one corner of her mouth to the other. "Your secret's safe with me."

"How do you feel now?"

"I'm okay."

"Are you done vomiting? Because if you're not you need to sleep on your side. You've got a trashcan right here. Don't lie on your back." As a nurse, he was sure she knew that but still, the woman was inebriated so he thought she needed the reminder.

"Yes doctor." She giggled and it was a sickeningly sweet sound, high pitched and excessive. Not a breathy and perfect low volume giggle like Clara's. God, he couldn't wait to get to her. "Do you have something you can put on?"

"I sleep nude."

"Fine. But you may get sick all over yourself."

"Maybe I can wear your shirt." She pulled at his shirt, exposing his stomach before he could pull it back down.

"I don't think so."

"My, my, that sister is a lucky lady." She raked her nails over his clothed abdomen.

He stood. "Make sure you stay on your side." He hated to leave her sick as she was, but he wasn't about to play nursemaid to her all night and miss out on Bug's precious promise of wine and cheese and her sweet body.

He left the room and headed straight for Clara's. He twisted the handle ever so slowly to avoid making a sound. Inside he found her sprawled on the bed looking sexier than he thought possible in the white cotton sleeveless gown she wore. On her nightstand the wine was open and about half empty. Had she drunk it?

His hand slid up her thigh, connecting with her hip. "Clara."

"Mmm, Cracker Jack. I've been waiting much too long for you."

"I agree." He took off his shoes and socks and climbed up on the bed next to her.

Pulling her across his lap he bent and kissed her lips confirming that she did in fact drink the wine. "Bug, you drank the wine."

"Mmm, I did." Her eyes were closed, but she had a ridiculous smile on her lips.

"But you're—" Her finger pushed into his lips.

"Spare me, Jackson. I waited for you for three hours. I didn't think you were coming. Where were you?"

"I had to tend to Veronica. She got roaring drunk and puked up her guts."

"Why can't she find her own boyfriend?"

He kissed behind her ear. "Did you eat my cheese too?"

She giggled in delight, the sound so precious to his ears he could cry. "No, I just drank your wine."

She stood on her knees and bent over the edge of the bed, hanging upside down. When she was once again upright, she had a knife and cheese board, along with the brick of cheese.

"Talk to me about the cheese."

While she cut into it, she rattled off the information. "I told you it's aged one year. It's named after the town in Spain—La Mancha. If it reads Manchego, you know it's the real deal." She bopped his nose with her finger and then placed a kiss on his lips before she started up again. He felt his soul turn from dark to light. "The region is located on a vast plateau high above sea level. The sheep endure arid conditions with excessive wind and heat. The winters are quite cold and the summers quite hot, so the best cheese is produced between August and December when the sheep are happy and fat." She placed her arms in a large circle over her puffed up belly and laughed.

He was mesmerized as he watched her relate the information. "I. Love. You."

She smiled, "I'm glad to hear it because I'm in love with you too." She poured wine into a glass she no doubt pilfered from the kitchen. As she passed the glass to him she also placed a piece of cheese in his mouth.

"What do you taste?"

"Mmm, it's nutty. . . and is that caramel?"

Her eyes lit up as she took a bite. "Now sip the wine."

"It's very complex, isn't it?"

She nodded. "Quite intense. I think it's your favorite. You always moan when you eat it."

"I do not moan."

"I hate to break it to you, but yeah, you do."

He finished the cheese she'd cut. "I want more." He also wanted to watch the little show she gave that she wasn't aware of as she bent over the bed.

She went down to the end of the bed again and started to lean over when his hand landed on the back of her thigh and then he bit into the fleshy part of her butt.

She squealed with delight. "Shh. You're gonna get me shot by a firing squad." He drank from the glass in his hand and then flipped her over, kissing her deeply. Dipping his fingers into the glass, he painted her lips with the drops of wine dangling from his fingers. Her pink tongue slid along the slickened surface.

He lay alongside her and played in her beautiful natural waves with his fingers. "You need a bang trim."

"I like to keep them long."

"I don't like it when I can't see your eyes."

She crawled on top of him, straddling him and removed her nightgown. He forgot what they were talking about. She wore a white lace thong and nothing else. "I need you." She pulled at his belt, and he assisted.

"Can you keep it quiet?"

"I'm quiet."

"Not when you're on top."

She smiled shyly and placed the tip of her index finger in her mouth. "I'll be quiet." She slid out of her lace underwear and was completely naked as she set to work on his clothes. First, she pulled his shirt off and then raked her fingers down his chest and torso. Her tongue traced over his abdominal muscles as she sighed sweetly.

This is what he'd been wanting. He needed her sweetness and light to save him from the bitter darkness that awaited his dreams. As she slid his pants and boxers off, he aided her efforts by raising his hips. She started rubbing her wetness over his penis. Her tongue circled his nipples, and it felt better than anything else he'd known in his twenty-eight years.

Except when she put her mouth on him. Everything good started and ended with her.

His hands went to her hips and caressed, helping her slide back and forth until he panted her name. She sat up and gathered his arms, placing them above his head and then traced with a light touch down the underside of his arm to his armpit. "You stay put now or I'll stop." She smiled her shy smile with deep dimples and hooded eyes.

"I need you." His voice was a strained whisper.

"I know what you need." She leaned forward and nibbled on his lips and then slid down his charged body. She bent and grasped his cock in her grip. Her tongue darted out and she tasted the glistening tip. She continued to lick her essence from him.

"Do you like how you taste?"

She nodded but kept sucking him harder and deeper into her mouth.

"I like how you taste too," he said.

She slid a finger through her wetness and reached up to place the finger between his lips, not aware how sexy she was. The moves she made left him breathless as he licked and sucked her finger clean. He made a note to get more wine to leave around the apartment for her to drink.

"More," he simply said. This time she sat up and watched as she brought her fingers to his mouth again and thrust in and out , their eyes never losing contact. His brain sizzled as it committed the hot thrill of the scene to memory.

Slowly, she took him into her warm tight center until he was fully consumed by her. Her movements were rhythmic and hypnotizing. He liked this position because to maintain pace they had to communicate. Not with words, but with their eyes and she never took hers from his gaze.

He watched her hips and abs dance as the shadows in the room played off of their movement. She leaned back, placing her hands on his thighs, and then rode him hard, raising her hips high and slamming back down, her breasts springing up and down. He bit his lip to keep from screaming and he detected the metallic taste of blood in his saliva. Her pace grew less and less steady until she was gasping for breath and collapsed on top of him. He grabbed her hips and continued the motion that brought them to climax together.

As they came down, he gathered her long wavy dark hair and pulled it over her shoulder, his fingers trembling slightly from the enormity of their connection—a detail he hoped she wouldn't notice. He placed his lips on a drop that was sliding down the column of her throat, tasting the salt of her effort, of her trust in him with her body and her scars. Her trust wasn't something he was sure he deserved but desperately wanted to keep.

"I'm in awe of you, Clara," he whispered, the words barely audible, as if speaking them too loudly might break the spell or reveal how utterly disarmed he felt in her presence.

Her smile against his neck—that particular smile he'd come to recognize, the one that acknowledged both his sincerity and his tendency toward reverent overstatement—and something in his chest uncoiled, a tension he'd carry until he could make her utterly and completely his.

"Don't leave," she said.

"I'm not going anywhere." She closed her eyes and then he did the same and they fell asleep in each other's arms, the feeling too good to care about what it meant if they were found.

In a dream someone whispered harshly in his ear. "Mmm, Bug."

"No, it's Veronica."

He jumped up from the bed, realizing too late he was naked.

Morning light streamed through the windows. "What are you doing in here?" he and Clara asked in unison.

"Good morning to you too." She overtly stared at his morning hard on. A pillow came sailing through the air to hit him in the crotch. Given his erection it hurt, but he held it there to cover himself. He looked over at a guilty Clara.

Veronica whispered, "Thought you might want to know the big guy is up and he's looking for you." She pointed to Jackson.

Veronica pulled him along through the bathroom that

connected her room to Clara's. Looking back over her shoulder she addressed Clara, "Gather his clothes and throw them into my room." Clara did as she was told, while Jackson thanked all the deities for Veronica, not something he ever thought he would praise.

Jackson picked up his boxer shorts and put them on faster than he ever had in his life. As soon as Clara shut one door it was as if a pulley system opened the main door.

Veronica was on her knees on the bed, pulling his head to her bosom. "Mmm, Jackson do you have to leave so soon?"

Clay's deep baritone laugh could be heard around the room as it bounced off the walls.

He closed the door leaving Jackson and Veronica staring awkwardly at one another.

She bit into her bottom lip while he finished getting dressed. She cleared her throat, "I wanted to apologize for my behavior last night and to thank you for being so kind and patient with me."

"Don't mention it. And thank you for not ratting me out."

"Clifton speaks highly of you."

Well he wouldn't once he found out what Jackson had been doing with his daughter.

"I'm not going to say I wasn't disappointed to observe that you are in love with Clara."

Jackson froze. "You observed that."

"I did and then felt embarrassed that I'd carried on as I did. She's sweet and too young to be worrying about another woman. She's a lucky girl. For what it's worth, I can tell you two are the real deal. Have you considered telling her family?"

He shrugged, "It's complicated."

"Still, your love for her is honest and pure. You shouldn't have to lie about it."

He moved to walk from the room. "Thanks again."

What she'd said ate at his gut. Their love, even though pure, was surrounded by a web of deceit.

The Bug Cut

11

Since Jackson needed to wash his EMT uniforms and Clara needed to study, they'd left the estate on Sunday evening.

On the drive home, Jackson decided it was time. "I want to tell Clay about us." j

he said.

"I know."

"No, I mean next weekend, when we go to New Orleans. I want to tell him then."

"But it'll ruin everything."

"Clara." His grip on the steering wheel tightened. "We've told so many lies about our relationship I've lost track. And why should we be telling lies when our love for one another is absolute truth? We're lying to your family."

He heard a sniffle and looked over to her side of the car but couldn't see her eyes because her bangs had grown too long. "Clara, look at me." She turned and he pushed the hair out of her eyes. "Baby, why are you crying?"

"Because I don't want our love to be cradled in a lie, but I don't want my family to be mad at us."

"They might be mad at first, but when they see how much we

love each other that will dissolve their anger." He tangled her hand in his. "It's you and me together. We can do this. Okay?"

She nodded her assent. "Okay."

A few minutes more down the road had him turning the car into the mall. It was five-thirty. If they hurried, she could get her bangs trimmed.

"What are we doing here?"

"You need a haircut."

"No, I don't. I like for my bangs to reach my eyes."

"Well, I don't like it."

"I don't care." She folded her arms across her chest.

"I'll buy you a hot pretzel."

She shook her head and kept her eyes forward.

"I'm not going to argue with you—"

"Then drop it and let's get out of here."

He sighed and put the car in reverse. They drove to their apartment in silence.

By the end of the night, they were all in love again and he spooned her as she fell asleep in his arms. He knew she liked to hide behind her hair, but she needed to learn not to do that.

The next morning as he started the coffee, an idea popped into his head. It was a horrible idea, but he thought it too good not to employ. While the coffee brewed, he walked around the apartment gathering scissors, a comb, and a piece of cardboard.

In the bedroom, he found Clara sound asleep on her side. It was too perfect. He lightly combed her bangs, placing the cardboard underneath. He wouldn't want her to wake suddenly and risk stabbing her with the scissors. Once he had the hair lined up, he took the scissors in his grip. Holding his breath, he made the first cut. Then he followed the line across the length of her forehead. She had a ton of thick hair, and he had to make several cuts. He pulled back to look at his work. He couldn't tell if they'd be slightly crooked or if it was just the way her body was positioned in the bed.

He gathered up the cut hair from the bed as best he could without disturbing her. Lucky for his nuts she was a sound sleeper.

Boy, was she going to be hot when she woke to discover what he'd done. He went to the kitchen, disposed of the evidence, and set about his morning ritual of pouring them each a cup of coffee.

Back in the bedroom, he held the smoking coffee cup under her nose, and she slowly came around. When her eyes opened and pinned him in place, he smiled. There she is. His girl with the powder-blue eyes. He needed to see them in all their glory. They grounded him.

"Good morning, Bug." She sat up and he was able to confirm that the haircut was a little crooked, but he thought it was cute.

"What are you smiling so much about?" She patted the sides of her hair down into place. "I must look crazy."

"You're perfect." He kissed her nose and then went to take a shower.

***

Clara woke slowly and opened the chest of drawers to put together an outfit for the day. Catching a glimpse of herself in the mirror, she thought something seemed off. No wonder Jackson had been laughing at her. She even started laughing at her image until she realized she'd been sabotaged.

"Jackson Reid Olivier!" She smoothed her palms against her bangs over and over, but it was no use. Her bangs were as misshapen as a crookneck squash. "I'm going to kill you!"

She stormed into the bathroom where she found him drying off.

"What?"

"Don't play innocent—you know what you've done."

He kissed the top of her head as she pushed him away. "I think it's very original. Come spring everyone will have that cut. Call it the Bug cut."

"Jackson, the only one who thinks this is funny is you."

He frowned. "That's not really a fair assessment. You've only got a sample size of two people."

"I told you I didn't want my bangs cut, but you did it anyway.

My hair is part of my body, you can't just cut it when you feel like it if I don't agree because that feels a lot like violation."

"I'm sorry. You're right. Will you forgive me?"

She didn't answer him but instead started rummaging through the cabinet beneath the bathroom sink, exasperated and whispering under her breath. She finally found what she was looking for and plugged it in. She slid the switch to on and the gadget produced a deep satisfying buzz in her hands. "Get in here now!"

From the door, he watched nervously as she held the electric clippers in her grip. She pointed to the toilet seat. "Sit."

"Now I think you should just calm down. You really are overreacting a bit, don't you think?"

"You scalped my head while I was asleep!"

"It sounds bad, but I only did what I did out of love for you. You're doing this"—he pointed to the clippers in her hand—"out of revenge."

"It's only fair and it's the only way I will forgive you for what you've done."

His lips tightened. "Fine, just don't make my tail too poofy." She bit her lip to keep from laughing at the image his words conjured up.

"I can't believe you did this to me and then you didn't even say you were sorry."

"I'm not sorry. I need to see your bright eyes because they save me from the penetrating darkness."

His words gutted her. With his admission she knew she wouldn't be able to shave a hair on his head. Still, there was no harm in him thinking she would, even if only for a few seconds. She scrunched the hair on top of his head together into a Mohawk pattern. He had a head full of the thickest, waviest brown hair. It really was quite something.

"I still have to treat patients you know."

"And I have to attend work and school with this." She pointed to her forehead.

She held the clippers next to the collection of hair in her hand. "Ready?"

"Do your worst." He squinted in preparation for what was to come.

She turned the clippers on and they buzzed to life. She ran the blunt end across the top of his head and released her hand. She deliberately made her eyes large as she looked at him.

Jumping up, he looked in the mirror, running his fingers through his thick, wavy hair. His laughter was explosive and bigger than she'd ever heard before.

Once he composed himself, he reached for her and pulled her into his chest. "Bug." He kissed the top of her head. "I'm sorry I got them crooked. Can you forgive me?"

"Forgiven. I'll go by and get them evened up. It'll be a funny story to tell Shelly while she cuts my hair."

He placed his hands on her jaw, kissing her lips. "Can I meet you for lunch today at the deli?"

"I'd love that. What time?"

"One."

"You want chicken piccata? It's the special today."

"My favorite."

"Everything's your favorite." She smiled. "I'll have it ready for you at one."

He squeezed her tight. "I more than love you."

"And I love you more than you love me." She ran her fingers through her bangs.

He crossed his hands over his heart. "That hurts."

***

As Clara stocked the case with various Italian cheeses, she couldn't help but feel a sense of pride. This small store and deli had become her pride and joy, a place where she could share her love for all things cheese with the community. She glanced at the cards she had made for each cheese, smiling as she imagined customers reading about their origins and flavor profiles.

The clips she had found at the dollar store were a steal, she thought, turning them over in her hands. They were just the right size and color to complement the cheeses without being too over-powering. She couldn't help but wonder how Jackson would react to them when he came in later.

A quick trip to Shelly's Hair Salon had left her with somewhat of a new 'do' thanks to Jackson's handiwork.

Around twelve forty-five, she ordered two specials, slicing tomatoes and mozzarella for Jackson's favorite salad, excited at the thought of him enjoying it. Her phone buzzed persistently in her pocket, and she silenced it before Mr. Moretti could notice.

Jackson: On the porch.

Balancing the tray with their lunches, she deftly weaved her way through the deli to the back porch. After carefully setting down their meals, she wished him *"Buon appetito."*

He rose to his feet, enveloping her in a hug and planting a gentle kiss on her head. "Your hair looks good." The remark elicited a playful scowl from her. "Too soon?" he teased, earning a nod paired with a grin.

The day was glorious; Clara felt warmth blossom in her chest. With the sun shining and birds chirping, she relished sharing this meal with her beloved—it didn't get much better than this. Next to her, Jackson sat in aviator shades that gave him the air of a dashing soap opera doctor as he cut into his chicken. The moment he tasted it, he dropped his utensils and let out a satisfied moan. "Oh, this is better than it's ever been before," he declared through a mouthful of food.

Her smile was so wide she thought it would crack. "You really think so?"

"No thinking about it; it's a scientific fact." He took another huge bite.

"Guess what?" She almost couldn't wait for him to answer.

"Mmm, what?"

"I made the sauce today."

His hand slapped his thigh. "That's what it is, Bug. Everything is made better by your touch."

She smiled and cut into her own chicken.

"This mozzarella is the best too. It's tender and incredibly full of flavor." He gestured with his fork to the salad she'd made. "They pay you in peanuts even though you provide them with a ton of skill."

He was absolutely right about the pay. Her secret to making mozzarella was that she used the most flavorful sea salt that money could buy. "Fleur de sal. That's the secret to the cheese."

"Like the salt you use at home?"

She didn't have the heart to tell him that they couldn't afford the salt they used in the cheese at the store. "Yes, that is one kind of sea salt but what I use here is from the Isle of Ré. The salt mines there were created in the twelfth and thirteenth centuries."

"Wow. So there were other things going on during the Crusades." He smiled and wiped his mouth with a napkin, looking hotter than a Louisiana summer day in August. She liked how smart he was. She hadn't known the Crusade connection but to her, he knew everything.

"Yep. And I make Mr. Moretti buy the salt or I won't make the cheese. Before I started making it, they used table salt. But this is a much better product. Lucian said the sales have doubled. Not sure if it's the salt or not but I'd like to think it is in some small way the contributions I've made." She savored another piece of fresh mozzarella, tasting the smoky salt on her tongue.

Jackson watched her intently. "Of course the double in sales is because of the salt. You've tweaked the recipe in such a way that the cheese is not just better but irresistible. I don't think you know how talented you are." He laughed lightly, shaking his head.

She felt her face flush with embarrassment. Of course he thought the sales were due to her ingredients, but she didn't like taking credit for something like this if it wasn't certain.

Jackson placed his hand gently on her shoulder, making her look up at him. "Young one." He chuckled again, an amused grin spreading across his weathered face. "You need to start taking more credit where it's due."

He forked his last bite of chicken. "I saw your notecard clips in the case. Turned out nice. I like how you organized the cheese by region."

Of course he'd noticed. He observed her every move. His intensity could be overwhelming at times, but she wouldn't change anything about him. He noticed every little thing, including her too long hair and even her efforts at work. She smiled, "I've moved twenty-three pounds of cheese already today."

"Wow, that's incredible." He ran his finger across his lower lip, something he did when he was thinking. "How many pounds were sold on average per day?"

"Three."

"It's truly astonishing."

"I've also started a cheese log for my regulars so I can keep track of their purchases and reference what they liked. And it'll help me keep the case stocked with favorites."

"You're really happy when you talk about managing the cheese counter."

"I really am. I have something else I'd like to discuss."

"Okay, shoot." He wiped his mouth with a napkin.

She swallowed. "I think I'd like to quit college and work here full time. What do you think of that? Is it crazy? Do you think it's a horrible idea?"

He thought for a moment. "I can't answer that for you." His fingers swept a rogue curl behind her ear. "Feel it in your gut. What's it saying? The answers will come; just keep an open mind."

His forehead creased. He'd removed his sunglasses and his eyes blazed at her like sparkling jewels in the sun. She had no idea how he'd take her news. There was no major at her school that was remotely culinary unless she enrolled in the college of business—and that was a stretch—it was really of no use to her.

"But yeah, I get it."

She exhaled the breath she hadn't known she was holding. She didn't know if he'd be indifferent or even upset. He'd been through so much school, and she didn't want him to think her foolish for not seeing its value.

"I mean I think if I were in medical school or law school, I would be pursuing it with everything I have, but I'm passionate about food and there's no major at the college for me."

He nodded. "It makes sense. People go to school to learn a trade, which you're cultivating here in the deli." His index finger tapped the table. "What do you propose?"

"If I drop by Friday Dad will get eighty percent of his money back for classes."

"You know you're really good at all of this." He waved his finger in a circle in the air. "You need your own place. Imagine what you could do without being held back by an evil dictator."

"He's not that bad. He's had a hard year."

He nodded and placed his hand on hers. "I know." He was sincere and his lips almost curled into a comforting smile. He was so afraid to let himself be happy. She envisioned tickling him to make him less controlled.

"So now you have to tell your father."

She bit her lip. "I guess I'll call him tonight. How do you think he'll take it?"

He leaned back as deep thought settled across his face. "I think the key is to let him know you're happy and that you have a plan."

That made a lot of sense. "How'd you get to be so smart?"

"I've surrounded myself by smart women." She started to lean into him for a kiss. "You're brother's here."

She froze in place, restless as she thought about the day they would no longer have to hide their love. That day would come soon enough. For now, it was best not to ruin everybody's lunch.

"I'm going to go say hi. I'll see you tonight." She squeezed his arm. "I love you."

Claudia The Psychic

12

By Saturday Jackson was ready to get out of town and he sensed Clara was too. This weekend was to be her last hoorah before she joined the full-time work force. She'd spoken with her father and while he was accommodating, he did keep her options open if she ever decided she'd like to return to school.

Glad this weekend was finally here, he was almost euphoric as he thought about not having to hide his love for her any longer. He wouldn't let himself get too hopeful until it was clear her brother would accept them as a couple.

There was a part of him that was held by the gangly wooden and knotted fingers of doubt. Fingers that reached to him and scratched like those of a hundred year old tree. Doubt that once the truth was in the open her family would let him continue to see her. Doubt that she would even want to be with him if her family turned on him. He shook his head to clear it of those unwelcome thoughts that left him breaking out into a cold sweat.

"Cracker Jack, I more than love you."

From the passenger side of the car Clara's sweet voice came to him, soothing and assuaging his mood. He forced a broken smile her way.

"That's just pathetic." She squeezed his free hand in hers. "Stop worrying. No matter what happens it's you and me forever." The smile she offered was far from pathetic. Her eyes sparkled and her deep dimples called to him like a beacon in a storm. More than once he'd thought he'd like to shrink down small enough to live in them.

He wanted, hell he *needed* to be intimate with her in that very moment. Maybe some of her goodness and contentment would rub off onto him.

"How do you want to reveal our relationship to Clay?" Jackson asked.

"I was thinking we wouldn't do anything except be ourselves. No more lies."

"How will that accomplish revealing that we've been together?"

"Trust me, people can tell that we love each other. Hands tangled together, simple but meaningful touches and glances. We just won't hide it. I feel like if we go in with a script, we will make it into something huge. Don't get me wrong, our love is huge, but it's also uncompromising." She shrugged. "There's no need to open the door to conversation about it. Together. Forever. Simple as that."

She was wise beyond her years. He loved how she problem-solved big issues and broke them down into manageable, simplistic parts. In a way she'd done that with him, and it had helped him deal with his trust issues. He'd been afraid to seek solace in another individual—afraid that person would also be violently snatched from his life just as his parents had been. He was afraid to admit to himself that he was extraordinarily happy. It had caused some strife in their relationship early on, but she'd told him to live in the moment and get over himself. Day by day they let things play out. They didn't attempt to quantify what they did: dating, kissing, and loving. It had freed him from worrying about the deep and unrelenting pain born of loss. He knew that pain all too well and never wanted to experience it again.

"Jackson."

"Yeah?"

"I called your name three times before you answered. Tell your brain to stop tormenting my lover. Do we need to pull over?" Her brow rose in question. "Maybe for a kiss?"

"Absolutely for a kiss. There's a Dairy Queen at the next exit. Can I interest you in a chocolate dipped cone?

"As long as it comes after a kiss."

"It will most definitely be after a kiss."

Approaching the restaurant, he searched for the most privacy possible and pulled into a slot, parking in front of a wooden fence. Before he could turn to her, she had crawled over the gearshift and straddled his lap, her hands threaded through his hair as her eyes looked down into his. She smiled her dimpled smile above him. "Hey, you."

He inhaled slowly, taking her scent deep into his lungs. "Hey." She brought her mouth down on his and placed a kiss so sweet on his lips his body grew swimmy at her tender care.

"Why do you stay with me?" he asked.

Her brows furrowed inward as she regarded him with a look of concern. "Jackson," she whispered. "If you don't know the answer then I'm not a very good girlfriend." She lowered her chin to her chest.

"Hey"—he cupped her chin in his grip and tilted her head up—"you're the best. You give me a reason to exist. I just don't know what I give to you that you couldn't get from some fun guy closer to your age. Not some intense old-timer with a ton of unsettled issues and a mountain of responsibilities and debt. How can you even have fun with me?"

"Frankly, given that description I'm amazed we even let you out of the basement. You should remain chained there for all of eternity."

He cracked a smile. "Don't I know it."

"You accept me and affirm my endeavors, but it's more than that even. You make me feel wanted and needed and smart. Beautiful and sexy. You listen and really hear what I have to say. I feel innately connected to you by a bond that comes from something not of this world. Maybe it's astrological." She shrugged. "I don't know, but I *do* know we're supposed to be together. Neither of us could survive without the other. We are two parts of a whole. You push me like only you can"—she pointed at her bangs and smiled—"to be the best person I can in this life. You care about my wellbeing and happiness, and I love your intensity surrounding all things me. I might not always understand what you're doing, or even why you're doing it, but I always know it's going to benefit me and make my life better because you won't stop until I have more than what I need."

She kissed his eyes, nose, and lips. "I hope that gives you a starting place to begin to understand why I love you. I'm a little sad that you don't already know." She stuck her lips out in a pout. He kissed his index finger and pressed it to her mouth.

"I did know all of that, but sometimes it's just nice to hear it out loud. Thank you for sharing your thoughts with me."

***

HE DROVE them to Jackson Square, and they parked on the street. Something was unsettled in the air around them. Clara didn't want to upset Jackson, so she'd kept it to herself, but she was convinced the big reveal wasn't going to go so well. What else was there to do? The family needed to know.

She sighed.

"Everything okay?" Jackson asked.

She nodded and they exited the car.

She stood looking at the St. Louis Cathedral with its triple steeples and thought how lovely it would be to marry there. Great wedding traditions abounded in New Orleans. Entire wedding parties would walk through the French Quarter led by a brass band playing "When the Saints Go Marching In." She wanted that for her wedding. She also wanted to be surrounded by her family as she publicly appointed Jackson her partner for life. The plaque on the front of the church read *1794*. That was a lot of wedded bliss, and she wanted to be part of the rich heritage.

"Bug, what's wrong?"

"I'm just tired."

"Are you sure that's all it is?" He rubbed her back and she leaned into his side.

"Yeah, Cracker Jack." She pulled him along into the middle of the square. All around were performers within every possible genre. A saxophonist belted out bold rough tones while a one man band dueled with him for ownership of the airwaves. A mime enacted a comical scene on the church steps. Hip-hop beats blared from speakers as a group of three men danced in synchronized perfection. Lone ballerinas, twirlers, sculptors, and caricaturists each demonstrated their skills for passersby and hoped for a little coin to be tossed their way. Actors, magicians, and even ministers performed for no one in particular, but orated in clear, deep vocal tones, which echoed across the courtyard. A woman sat in a chair, her shirt and bra pulled to reveal her breast to the air as she benefitted from the skills of a tattoo artist.

It was truly astonishing, and Clara couldn't believe she'd never really noticed it before. The square pulsed with a vibrant energy that seemed to beckon her in a way she'd never felt. Perhaps more in abundance than even the musicians, street performers, and artists selling their wares were the psychics scattered amidst the bustling crowd. A quick survey of the scene revealed their prevalence— Clara counted nine. Any other time, with any other person, she might have scoffed at the spectacle, but today the square comforted her, its colors and clamor a balm. Perhaps it was because it was a place where one could seek answers to life's questions without feeling judged or scrutinized. Perhaps it was because it offered the solace of believing in something greater than oneself. Clara slowly wandered through the noise and vibrancy, feeling the hopeful and wary eyes of the fortune tellers tracking her. But as one drew her in with a nod, she took a seat beneath the umbrella of a tarot card reader.

"Hi," she said, her voice tentative but full of expectation.

"Hello," the reader replied smoothly, "have you chosen me?" Middle-aged, with deep-set and penetrating eyes, she had an abundance of deep mahogany hair that tumbled in loose waves to her waist. Clara felt both exposed and understood beneath her gaze.

"Yes, I have," Clara said, allowing herself a smile.

"Welcome," the woman said as she settled into her seat. "I'm Claudia."

"Clara." She felt a slight tremor in her voice as she introduced herself. She sat in a lawn chair that creaked beneath her, while Jackson stood solidly behind her, a pillar of unspoken support amidst her uncertainty. Claudia gave him a brief glance but focused intently on Clara, her coffee bean eyes filled with an almost other-worldly intensity.

"What are your needs?" Claudia's voice held the kind of patience that suggested she'd heard it all before.

"I need to know everything will be okay." Clara hesitated, her heart pounding as if demanding the answer, her words spilling over in a rush of urgency. "That we will be okay."

"Who?" Claudia asked, though there was a hint of knowing in her question, as if she could already feel the depth of Clara's longing.

"The one I love." Clara's voice faltered slightly, exposing the vulnerability she'd tried to mask. "I need to know."

"Are you entering a new phase in your life?" Claudia's words were deliberate and probing, as though unearthing Clara's fears with a gentle shove.

"I hope to be." Clara swallowed hard, the enormity of her hope and fear caged within that single admission. She wished the answer could burst forth from the cards like a revelation. Her future felt perched upon the cusp of an unknown too large to comprehend.

"You are in pain." Claudia's words were gentle yet unyielding, slicing into Clara with the surgical precision of a truth she'd been trying to ignore. Clara tightened her grip on the armrests of the chair as if bracing herself for what she'd come to hear.

"We'll use the cards to guide you," Claudia continued, a hint of assurance in her tone that suggested Clara was not the first with such questions. She placed a deck on the small table between them. "Shuffle the deck." The cards were old and worn, as if they held the histories of a thousand seekers within their creases and corners.

Clara reached for the deck. It felt unwieldy in her slightly trembling hands, the cards a little too large for her fingers to manage nimbly. She did her best to shuffle, half afraid they might spill across the table and betray her clumsiness. Each movement felt like a struggle between control and chaos, mirroring the turmoil that had settled into her heart.

When she finally finished, Claudia took the cards back with a single, fluid motion and expertly fanned them in her hands. "Choose four," she instructed, her voice calm and steady, a stark contrast to Clara's growing unease.

Clara hovered her fingers above the deck, her hands twitching with the weight of her decision. She could feel Jackson's presence behind her, an unspoken question in the air between them. She pulled one card from each end, hesitated, then worked her way inward until she'd selected four cards. The simple act felt monumental, as if each choice carried with it the trajectory of her entire life.

"Okay, now choose two cards." Claudia laid them out in rows on the table, the colorful images staring up at Clara like taunts or promises.

For several seconds, Claudia studied the cards in silence, her head bopping slightly from one row to the next as she absorbed what they had to reveal. Clara found herself holding her breath, her eyes darting between Claudia's face and the cards. "You're up and down all day, every day," Claudia finally said, her voice more certain now, slicing again with its insistent truth. "Highs and lows. Good and bad." Her eyes flicked toward Clara, seeking confirmation. So far, the reading was uncomfortably accurate.

"You've drawn the three of swords here," Claudia said, indicating the top row with a knowing nod, her hand brushing gently over the card's face. "But then later the ace of swords." Her words danced between promise and caution, leaving Clara to teeter between dread and relief.

"Let's talk about the first one that's going to hit you," Claudia said, her tone now slightly more urgent. "The three of swords:

heartbreak, loneliness, and betrayal." Clara's lips parted as if to form words that would not come. She took a harsh breath, the kind that seemed to echo an ache she hadn't realized was lodged so deeply inside her. The card boasted a giant red heart with three daggers plunged mercilessly through it. Her mind screamed, *No!*

"It's got to come in order to clear out the past and make the path clear for the future," Claudia continued, her voice compassionate yet firm, like that of a doctor announcing a necessary surgery. "When your pain reaches its zenith, the tide will start to turn. You will experience great loss and sorrow."

Clara's eyes widened as she absorbed Claudia's words; she didn't like the suggested path ahead. Her heart raced with a fear that felt both ancient and immediate.

Claudia's hand hovered over another card, almost tenderly. "And then," she said, shifting from the dark tones that seemed to engulf the earlier diagnosis, "a complete change and pursuit of ultimate truth. Ah, we're hatching from the chrysalis, fresh and new. A rebirth."

That sounded much better. Clara exhaled, only now realizing she'd been holding her breath for what felt like an eternity. Hope flared in her chest like a sudden and unexpected light, and she clung to Claudia's words as though they were lifelines thrown into an ocean of doubt.

"You will walk through the fire first," Claudia warned, her eyes still locked onto Clara's with a depth that suggested she saw the whole story laid out like chapters in an unfinished book. "When you do, hold on to what you know to be the facts, dump the rest." Clara nodded, unsure whether she was ready to face what lay ahead, but unwilling to ignore its coming.

"You will suffer," Claudia said, her voice unflinching, as she drew out the last card. "But the ace of swords shows brilliance, clarity. You will have a long and happy life."

Jackson's finger twirled a curl at her nape as she sat and enjoyed that his touch was never far from her.

"It will get you to great love." Her hand rested on a card that resembled Adam and Eve in the Garden of Eden. "Love and sex, a union, and the strongest force of all—a relationship built on deep love, the highest of all unions." Her hand was on the move again and settled over The Empress. "Extravagance, giving and receiving pleasure, health, and harmony." The two of cups next. "Marriage, healing, peace, forgiveness." Finally, she touched the ten of cups. "Joy and family."

She saw Clay and Eve approaching in the distance and Jackson made no effort to remove his hand from massaging her neck. She looked up at him to see if he was paying attention. He was looking directly at Clay. Closing her eyes she took a deep breath and exhaled it slowly. Claudia whispered so only she would hear, "It's going to get rough before it gets better. Don't give up even when he does."

Her jaw fell open and she inhaled a ragged breath. Her gut seized with the thought of Jackson giving up on their love. What else could she mean, it had to be that. Quickly she stood and met his deep blue gaze. "Jackson, promise me now, quickly, that it's you and me together forever against the world."

His forehead creased. "Bug?" His stare was intense. "What's wrong?"

"Please hurry, tell me before they get here. Tell me no matter what happens we will always have each other."

His lips tightened into a thin line as his gaze shifted to Claudia and back to her. "You know how I feel. I can't live apart from you. I'd say that's pretty solidifying." He tangled her fingers in his. "Always and forever. You and me against the world." They walked hand in hand to meet Clay and Eve.

Clay waved and they returned the greeting, each step bringing them closer to their destiny. Toe to toe now, Clay took in the locked fingers between their bodies and raised his brow.

"How was the drive in?" Clay asked.

His voice was low and soft, an unusual attribute for him. Clara tried to remember when he'd ever been so quiet, but she couldn't. He continued to speak softly with Jackson about the traffic. Next to him, Eve toyed with her own confusion at their linked hands. Her gray eyes traveled from their hands to Jackson's face and back to Clara.

Their connection was severed when two kids playing a game of tag around the statue of Andrew Jackson ran through the space that linked their hands. Like magnets they reconnected once the space between them was cleared. All eyes were on their hands.

The tension was getting palpable. Eve spoke up. "Clay is taking me to see the tomb of Marie Laveau."

"Clara, you in? You love that shit," Clay asked with a crease in his brow.

"Oh, yes. The Voodoo Queen. Somebody painted the tomb pink with latex paint, which is not good because it will trap in moisture and cause deterioration."

Clay chuckled. "I really would like to know where you get all this information." He took a few steps forward, leading the way. "Jackson, we'll catch you later. Thanks for safely bringing my baby sister to me."

"He's coming with us." Clara said. Clay shrugged and they all trekked down St. Peter Street.

At the cemetery, they broke away from the intense eyes of Clay and Eve and chased each other up and down the rows of tombs until Jackson caught and tickled her senseless.

It was an overcast afternoon and a storm was approaching. The weather caused the cemetery to appear all the more eerie and gray. The cement was dark with absorbed moisture, adding to the grayish blue hues. Tombs of varying height towered like giant marble gods creating irregular shadows that settled over the cemetery. Few inches separated one above-the-ground tomb from another.

Clara remembered her grandmother telling her when she'd misbehaved that she'd bury her in the St. Louis Cemetery where the dead lie close together, so close there's no peaceful rest to be had and the dead spend eternity in search of higher ground.

"*Il est mort sur le champ d'honneur.*" Jackson read from a crooked epitaph cemented on a rectangular white tomb. "He died on the field of honor." They walked the narrow aisle between the tombs having to turn sideways at times to fit. "*Victime de son honneur.*"

"What does that mean?"

"It means he died because he had too much honor." Jackson stopped in front of a faded red brick tomb encased with a black iron gate. The latch had rusted and the lock no longer worked to keep the gate closed. *"Pour garder intact le nom de famille."* He pushed the gate open but didn't walk through it. "To keep unsullied the name of the family." He stared at the tombs for several minutes. "These men must have died in duels."

"Duels?"

"Back in the day if somebody did you wrong you would challenge them to a duel—set a time and place and show up with your gun. Once the clock struck, you drew. Hopefully your fingers were faster than your opponent's or you'd end up in here before your time with an epitaph such as this."

His story gave Clara a shiver. They walked to the back of the cemetery where a long row of vaults stacked three deep was situated. One person on top of another, on top of another, all the way down. Clara counted at least twenty-two rows in one of the long walls of vaults. "Are these paupers graves?"

"This part of the cemetery is considerably less maintained. This is really creepy, Bug. I can't believe you like this place."

"It's part of who we are." She shrugged.

"These wall vaults remind me of hospital morgue drawers." He visibly fought off a chill.

They walked to the center of the cemetery where the nicely maintained crypts were located. One crypt stood erect on a large marble slab and appeared as large and inviting as an entryway to a home. Clara imagined a spouse who had been left behind or a child seeking the guidance of a parent sitting under the eaves and speaking to their deceased loved ones as the rain fell around the cemetery.

The intricate wrought iron gate wrapped around the structure and culminated in sinister looking finials. The entire structure was carved from marble. The top was comprised of five turrets each crowned with a massive cross.

"This is a family crypt." Jackson pointed and Clara walked up to stand next to him. "See the angel statues? The torches are pointed down indicating the death of a child." Jackson scanned the area with his eyes. "It makes you realize how hard life was."

"It does and you're right, this place is creepy. I want to see the voodoo queen."

"Piggy back." He lowered and she climbed on.

Jackson skipped a little too fast and Clara squealed.

He stopped in front of the vastly decorated mausoleum of Marie Laveau. The tomb was tall and Clara wondered if the queen's body stood upright. She imagined Marie watching all the visitors who came to see her to leave coins, beads, and flowers. Hers was the most decorated tomb in the cemetery. However, her resting place wasn't as well kept as Clara thought it would be given the attention it garnered. Layers of paint peeled due to years of extreme weather conditions.

"Here lies the body of Marie Laveau. All those who trespass will be damned."

Clara gasped. "It does not say that."

Jackson laughed. "Why is it decorated with Mardis Gras beads?"

"Put me down," Clara whispered in his ear. She stood in front of the crypt that towered above her. "The beads are offerings."

"Offerings?"

"If your desire is met you must return and leave an offering."

"Oh, I see."

"Do you have a quarter?" She took the coin and drew an X on the tomb. Then she turned three times, knocked on the grave and yelled, "I wish for love to prevail."

"What, pray tell, are you doing?"

"Don't you know the legend of Marie Laveau?"

"I'm afraid I don't." His arms wrapped around her from behind and he rested his head on her shoulder.

"She was a hair dresser by trade and she was good at her job. So good in fact that she was popular with society women."

"That is some talent." He chuckled. Clara swatted his hand that rested on her stomach.

"She knew everyone and everything. She was also very gifted. Her powers could heal the sick and she spent a lot of her time doing just that."

"So kind of like a doctor then, only I'll bet she didn't have to pay for malpractice insurance."

Clara ignored his insolence. "Her gris-gris bags had magical powers that could bring luck or protect the keeper from evil. To this day, her power transcends the grave, but first one must believe."

"Shh, listen," his lips whispered and then he was gone. Footsteps crunched around her on the gravel as people meandered up and down the footpaths.

She turned in a circle but had lost sight of Jackson. She whispered his name, but he didn't show.

Suddenly hands landed on her ribs encircling her from behind. He growled in her ear. "Gotcha."

She leaned into his side and he kissed her lips.

Behind them a man cleared his throat, a man with a deep voice. She knew it would be Clay. They turned as one unit, Jackson's arm around her waist and her body resting at his side. "Somebody want to fill me in here?"

Eve pulled Clay's arm. "I think we should go back to the hotel. We can go down to the pool, sit in the hot tub." She tried really hard to distract him and it almost worked. Especially when she mentioned she'd brought the white bikini. Clay's hand cupped her cheek.

Clara wanted everything out in the open, wanted to stop hiding her love for Jackson, or being afraid to touch him, or kiss him. "We're together."

Eve's hand went to cover her mouth before she moved it. "Clara, no. Not here."

"Why not here? I don't want to hide it anymore."

Clay wasn't talking, wasn't moving. "I wanted you to know that I love him. And he loves me."

His face turned into a storm with raging veins pulsing at the sides of his temples. His snarl was the first sound he'd made in a matter of minutes. "What the fuck do you mean he loves you? You love him?" His arms were soaring violently through the air as he expressed his thoughts. Next to him Eve tried to grab one and still it. "And you knew about this, Eve? You knew and you kept it from me?" Her face turned grave as her jaw dropped and her lips moved, but no sound came out.

"I just have one question." His head scanned from Jackson to Clara. "Have you been intimate?"

Clara looked down to her shoes, but she heard Jackson. "Yes, we have. It's my intention to marry her."

His certifiable laughter sent chills racing up and down her spine. "Oh, well that intent makes it okay for you to fuck my nineteen-year-old sister!"

Jackson winced at the ear splitting yell.

Clay leaned into Jackson until they were nose to nose. Eve tried to pull him away, but it was like she didn't even exist. Clay's focus was white hot, and it was all aimed at Jackson. "How long has this been going on?"

Oh, God. Not that question. Jackson would answer it truthfully, she knew it as sure as she knew her name. "Two years." Clay's hands scrubbed his face. His nostrils flared as he ran his fingers through his hair, ripping out several pieces.

She watched his hand form a fist down at his side as his chest reared back to gain leverage. His meaty hand went soaring through the air. She opened her mouth to scream, but no sound escaped. She told her arms to lift, but they wouldn't. The sound of flesh colliding with flesh was unmistakable. The blow was so strong it knocked Jackson to the ground. Clay's hand fisted in Jackson's hair, pulling him to his knees and then he threw another punch while Eve and Clara screamed.

"You are dead to me!" Clay bellowed.

He punched him again and Clara shrieked as she jumped onto his back. "Stop it! You'll kill him!" He gingerly slid Clara from his back.

He turned to Eve. "You lied to me. I deliberately asked you if something was going on between them and you lied to me."

Eve had to run to keep up with his retreating strides.

Ice Water

13

Down on her knees, Clara looked into the mess that was Jackson's beautiful face. "Cracker Jack," she whispered.

He squinted at her. "Not quite the reaction we'd hoped." He spit blood out onto the ground.

Around them people had given them a wide birth but watched and whispered, as they observed the destruction unfold.

"Do you think he broke any bones?"

He tested the motion of his jaw, moving it from side to side and spit out more blood. "I don't think so. My eye feels swollen shut. Is my eyelid cut?"

"It's swollen shut, but I don't see a cut. What can I do, Jackson?"

"Help me up." She put her head beneath his arm and he stood on shaky legs. "There's a drugstore on Canal Street. We'll pass it before we reach our hotel. I'm going to need a few things."

He put his sunglasses on, but they hardly hid the brutal beating Clay had unleashed on his face. As he turned his head from side to side the subsequent ripping and wrenching sound made her cringe. Large salty droplets made their way down her cheeks and plopped onto her arm.

She'd never seen Clay act in that way before and could hardly believe he had levied such brutality against another human being. They'd been friends for their entire lives. Jackson was a brother, but all that would change. What had Clay said? Jackson was dead to him now. The tears kept flowing and she was certain that her emotions had never been so strained—not even after her accident. She'd been hurt, but she'd also been in shock for several weeks. It was Jackson who'd been there when she'd needed him most.

Through her tears she asked, "Why didn't you hit him back?"

"Christ, Clara. In his mind I'm the guy that had sex with his seventeen-year-old sister. I deserve his wrath and abandonment."

Her head shook vigorously. "No."

"Let's just focus on the drugstore."

She sniffled and cried until she could no longer breathe from her nose. They walked in silence except for occasional snorting and spitting from Jackson. Inside the drugstore he picked up a handheld basket and then removed his sunglasses. Clara gasped at the amount of swelling around his eye. She followed behind him as he went straight to first aid and started throwing things into the basket: gauze, butterfly bandages, antiseptic cleanser, peroxide, skin adhesive, aspirin, anti-inflammatory pills, and water.

As they made their way to the front of the store, people stared at his beaten face. He looked a fright with his bloodied shirt and neck. She crossed her arms over her chest, rubbing her arms. She wished he would let her do something to help, but he seemed intent on handling the purchase. When she attempted to take the sack from the clerk, he snatched it from her hands.

As they walked from the drug store to their hotel, she had to jog to keep up with him. He opened the door to their room and threw the bag down on the bed. "Plug the sink and fill it with water." He pulled his shirt over his head and threw it in the trash. While the water slowly filled the basin, she grabbed the bag and laid out the items on the countertop. She heard the door open and went to see what was going on. She peered out into the hallway to see his retreating back, the ice bucket dangling from his fingertips. "Jackson?" Nothing. There again, she could have gone to get the ice for him.

Frustrated, she returned to the bathroom to ensure the job he'd given her was completed to perfection. Once the sink was filled she turned off the faucet and waited for him.

He walked in with the bucket of ice and dumped it into the sink, stirring it with his fingers. Her brow furrowed. She didn't under-stand anything that was going on, but who was she to argue with a doctor?

He waved his hand over the counter. "Move all of this stuff so I don't get it wet."

She fished the plastic sack out of the garbage and reloaded it with the purchased items. She gasped when she watched him plunge his face into the ice water bath. Thinking he should come right up she began to get nervous, especially when he started to moan. She retrieved a clean towel from the rack and waited for him to surface. He must have held his head down for close to two minutes. When he rose he let out a low, raspy groan. She placed the opened towel across his arms and he patted his face.

"Where's my stuff?"

"I put it on the bed."

"Get it, will you please."

She guessed the pain was causing his agitation, but even still he'd said please and she held on tight to that one simple kindness. Swiftly, she retrieved the bag and brought it into the bathroom. She carefully laid out each item on the countertop just as before.

He pushed the plunger down to drain the water and grabbed the red antiseptic soap out of her hands. "I've got this." He leaned over the sink, snorted, and spit. "Clara, please go into the other room."

"What? No, let me take care of you."

"I can take care of myself. Go into the bedroom." Her body experienced a deep ache at his stinging words. In one dramatic sweep of her arm, she had all of the items back in the bag as she walked from the bathroom.

"Clara, this isn't helping." He followed behind her. With the handles of the sack laced through her fingers she sat on the bed. "Clara, you know I need that stuff. What's with this childish behavior?"

And now she was childish. "Jackson, I love you and want to take care of you. I'm part of this too. I didn't take the pain, but I am now. I *need* to take care of you. I need to know you will be okay. I can't do that from the bedroom and I refuse to let you doctor yourself. Call it selfish, but I need to help get you back to rights to get past what happened today. I don't know why you can't understand that."

"My head feels like a basketball. I can't really discuss this right now. Please, I need the pills and that water fast." She jumped down off the bed and opened the water bottle, placing it in his hands.

"Which pills? Aspirin, inflammatory, or both?"

"Two of each."

She placed the pills in his palm and headed straight into the bathroom. "Come sit on the toilet seat."

While he got situated, she scrubbed her hands with the disinfecting soap. She pulled a piece of gauze from the box and squirted it with the vibrant red liquid until it was saturated. She delicately swabbed his face ridding it of blood and dirt. She completed this process several more times. "What's next?"

"Peroxide."

She cleansed each scratch and gash. "There are a few lacerations on your cheek and above your brow."

"The skin adhesive."

"How does it work?"

"Pull the skin together and dab it across. Hold it until it dries. Don't blow on it."

She followed his instructions exactly as he'd dictated them. She was careful not to breathe her germs on the wounds while she waited for them to seal.

"Now you can apply a butterfly bandage to the others. Just make sure they're not set so tight it pulls the skin."

When she finished, he stood and grabbed the ice bucket. "Do you need more ice?" She took the container from him and was gone before he could protest. On her way back to the room, she found an unattended housekeeping cart and grabbed additional washcloths and hand towels. She placed several cubes of ice in a towel and wrapped it so that it was as flat as possible. Jackson reclined on the bed with his eyes closed. She held the icepack gently to the swollen tissues of his face. "Jackson?"

His hand slid over hers. "Bug, I more than love you."

"Jackson, I'm sorry." Her eyes filled with tears yet again.

"Hey, it's what we wanted, right? To share our love with the world, to finally come out of hiding. Things will start to get better now."

She tried to pull away, but he wouldn't release her hand. "Don't go."

"I'm just going to climb up next to you." She slid into bed next to him, on the side that wasn't so bruised and rested her head on his shoulder.

Her eyes closed and she exhaled into the quiet room. The calm ocean-like movement of his breathing lulled her toward sleep.

When she woke, it was two and a half hours later. Next to her, Jackson's swallow made a hollow thud in his throat. "You know that song? About the cars and your perfect eyes?" His voice was gravelly and deep.

"The one about chasing cars?"

He nodded. "That's our perfect song." The swelling around his eye had gone down considerably and was almost altogether unnoticeable. However, the bruises had gotten a little darker.

"It doesn't matter where we are, or what we're doing, or what everyone is going to tell us we should be doing. And trust me, that's going to happen. What we're doing is not acceptable in modern society. They're going to try to break us apart, but in the end, it's got to be you and me together, not focused on the swirling vortex around us, but focused on each other. We'll have to shut out everyone and what's being said. We know our intentions are true and pure. No matter what's going to be said, we know what's real."

His words scared her. It's like they were preparing to go to war. The two of them and their great love against the world. "I'm prepared to do all of those things. I don't know how, but if you're with me I can do anything."

"Your family may never forgive us. I hope they will eventually forgive you, but you need to know they could be lost to you forever. I want you more than my next breath, but you need to know this could be it. It's because I love you that I could let you go, if you wanted, though it would utterly kill me. This could be your last chance to bail before permanent repercussions open a chasm between you and your family. Essentially, you would be giving up your family for me."

His revelations always had the ability to render her speechless. Like now, she felt her mouth moving, trying to make sound, but she couldn't. She closed her eyes tight and reopened them to push back the tears. She'd cried enough. The one thing she was ultimately sure of in her life was Jackson. She could not survive without him.

"I can't live without you. Even if it means I won't see any of my family again, I don't care. I would rather be dead than to try to figure out how to live without you."

"I'm a selfish man, Bug. I shouldn't let you give up your family for me, but I'm too weak to stop you."

"I don't like this conversation."

"It's reality. We've got to talk about it."

"How about we talk about the fact that you were the only one there for me when I had my accident?"

"We can talk about that too."

She flipped onto her stomach next to him in the bed. "You were there when it happened. You saved me. And you were there again after. You saved me a second time." He wiped away a lone tear that tracked down her face.

"I sometimes dream that I'm being dragged by the horse. In the dream, the pecan grove at the estate is always on fire and I can actually feel the burning on my shoulder and back where my scars are. I wake up from the dream when I've become buried under a pile of rocks and can't breathe. In reality, when I wake up you're always there either standing over me with coffee or sleeping next to me."

"Why haven't you told me about these dreams?"

She traced the lock of hair that fell across his forehead. "You have so much to worry about: school, work, money, me. I don't want to burden you with more. I'll be fine. I just have the dream every now and then. Mostly, I think about what would have happened if you'd not been at the estate that day. I would have been alone."

" I would drop everything, I would burn my degrees, I would forfeit school for you. Clara, I. Would. Die. For. You. You're what matters, everything else can be replaced. And you know it was Clay that asked me to be there. I had planned on coming up for Easter weekend to be with the family, but when he'd told me you'd be the only one home, I reconsidered because I'd had feelings for you even then. I thought maybe it wasn't a good idea to be alone with you at the estate, but Clay insisted that I go. Said he'd feel better if you weren't alone during the holiday weekend. I thought that was a legitimate reason." He shrugged. "I'd planned to grill us some steaks for the occasion." He inhaled so deeply his chest and ribs expanded to their max position. "In the back of my mind I kept thinking I could get into real trouble with you. I'd devised several ways to divert my attention when you were around."

She smirked. "Yes, I know. You were very closed off. Reserved. Almost rude. I didn't like you so much."

"But I thought you wanted to marry me?"

"Please." She rolled her eyes. "Seven-year-old Clara didn't know anything."

"I beg to differ. I have a framed, one-of-a-kind original drawing that says she did."

"I can't believe you have that hanging in our living room."

"It's my most prized possession."

She closed her eyes and recalled their first time. After the stitches had been removed, her scars were hideous. She'd wanted to hide, wanted the ground to open up and swallow her. She'd wanted to die rather than go on trying to figure out how to live in a body she no longer recognized as her own. They'd told her that skin grafting was an option, but it was a horrendous procedure that would require extraction of the skin from her inner thigh. Recovery time was long, and scarring was absolutely certain, but her shoulder and back would heal with a better appearance.

It was Jackson who had convinced her not to do the graft. He'd been there when the stitches came out. Once she saw her back she'd been upset at him for convincing her not to go ahead with the procedure to lessen the appearance of the scars. He'd pointed out that she'd be creating more scars and it wouldn't be worth it. He held her while she cried at the hospital, waiting for her parents to come back from their cruise. Waited for Clay to get done fighting the refinery fire.

That night at the estate Jackson came into her room to check on her and she'd been crying. She'd asked him who would find her desirable now. He'd told her to show him her back. She remembered not wanting to. It had taken quite a few minutes, maybe thirty, to drop her robe and stand naked before him. And then she'd turned and let him have his fill of her unsightly body. He'd said she was a beautiful woman and she'd snorted in that way she did when she found something ridiculous.

She was about to cover herself back up with the robe when his hands draped over her body to rest on that spot just where the shoulder meets the arm. He was behind her and dipped his head to kiss around her scars.

Throat clearing in her ear forced her from the beloved memories. She opened her eyes to see deep blue pools simmering at her. "What exactly are you thinking about so intently, Bug?"

The blush spread across her face as quickly as fire spreads across dry grass. She lowered her head to her chin, but he turned onto his side and lifted beneath her chin with his finger.

"I was just thinking about my first time. *Our* first time. In my room."

He drew circles on her arm. "Do you remember what you asked me?"

"I asked if you wanted me, even with the scars."

"That's right, and what was my reply?"

"More than my next breath."

"Exactly. That's how it always was, and is, and will be with you." He kissed her lips. "Tell me, what happened next?"

These were her private memories, and she didn't know if she wanted Jackson in her head. She looked at his beaten, beautiful face. Her brother was twice his size almost. And yet he'd taken Clay's wrath, thought he'd deserved it even. Who was she kidding? She wanted Jackson everywhere, knew he would never use her precious thoughts against her.

"You kissed the scars. It was the first time I'd felt wanted in that way"—she swallowed the lump in her throat and closed her eyes— "the first time I felt needed."

"What'd I say next?"

"You said I was the most beautiful thing you had ever seen. And then I turned and was rewarded with my first kiss. It was spectacular. Your breath was mint flavored and your tongue wicked. I can still feel my heart beating as if it would leap from my chest, grow wings, and fly away."

Jackson's face erupted in a full face-splitting smile and sadly a wince. "I love you. What I did next was very bad, but it's always been complete consumption with you. I couldn't even stop at gunpoint. You standing before me naked and sweetly innocent was paradise. I was no longer living in hell. Some might say that I took your innocence that night. But no, you stand before me like that every time, and I swear it's as if I'm seeing you for the very first time all over again."

"I was hoping you were going to say, two years later, I fulfill your every dark desire and sexual fantasies."

"God, you do that and so much more."

"That makes me feel better. I'd like to think I'd learned something in my promiscuous two years."

His poor beaten face frowned at her and she felt her eyes widen at the implication.

"Jackson, what's wrong?"

"You're not promiscuous," he whispered, leaning away from her. "I need to make an honest woman of you. Should have already. I'm not a very good person. I'm extremely selfish."

"I didn't mean—" She leaned closer to him.

"I know what you meant, but if I were inherently good I would have stopped after the first time."

It was her turn to frown. "The first time was no fun for me." She smiled, unable to prevent it. "The second and third times were unbelievable." She took in a deep breath. "And before you get all upset about my first time, it's not that it wasn't special, because it was. I just don't think any woman has ever thought the first time was as good as the second and third times."

His fingers enclosed her earlobe. "I'm sorry I hurt you at the tender age of seventeen."

"Jackson, you didn't hurt me. You were helping me. I felt undesirable. I didn't think any man would ever want me but you proved that not to be true. I needed everything you had to give me in that moment."

His fingers massaged where they rested. "I know. And trust me, it was incredible. I'll never forget how you fully gave yourself to me, unselfishly. Your trust, your purity . . ." he couldn't finish his statement because he gasped and choked.

"Jackson?"

"Tell me what *you* remember about the first time."

Why did he want to know? It was erotic, painful, scary, wonderful. He'd think she was crazy.

His fingers traced a line down her arm from her shoulder to her knuckles. "Please, tell me."

At his pleading she was helpless. "I remember being scared, but I trusted you with every part of myself. I knew you wouldn't take and not give."

"I could never hurt you. It kills me to think I did that night."

"You didn't. Joy and pleasure are the only memories I've ever had of that night because my heart stopped bleeding."

"Tell me in detail."

She exhaled on a sigh. This was tough. "Well, you carried a naked me to my pink princess canopied bed. Then you caressed and kiss every inch of my body. Your tongue licked from my hip to my knee. I was drowning in your attentiveness. I became lost in you and I still haven't recovered."

He pulled her palm to his lips and kissed, followed by a wince. "And I reap all the benefits." He smiled contentedly. "Continue."

"So bossy. Where was I?"

"I licked from your hip to your knee."

"Oh right, then I think it was about discovering how to make me . . ." She coughed into a closed fist.

His eyes simmered at her, and he grabbed her hand to kiss the tips of her fingers. "It was the first time I tasted you."

She thought she had died during her accident or sometime after at the hospital and then gone to heaven. His mouth on her felt so good. "Then I experienced my first orgasm and fell in love with you and your wicked tongue all over again."

He chuckled and kissed her, his wicked tongue sliding into her mouth and tangling with hers. At the end of their kiss, he held her face in his palms. "The gifts you've given me are more precious than anything I could ever give you in return, but I'm resolved to spend the rest of my life trying to be worthy."

"Jackson." Her voice came out whispered.

"Don't argue here, Clara. It's true you gave me everything and continue to do so."

She didn't know what exactly he was talking about. Her innocence, the fact that she'd only ever had sex with him, loved him, kissed him. She'd trusted him that night that seemed so long ago. Not just with her body, but her mind, spirit, soul, everything. He'd been so gentle with her, whispering the sweetest things in her ear about how wonderful she felt wrapped around him. As far as first times go she'd had a great one. She'd hold tightly to those memories for a lifetime.

Her cell phone buzzed beside her on the bed. She checked the screen. "It's Eve." She pressed to answer the call.

"Hey, how's Clay?"

"Things are a little bumpy. How's Jackson?"

"He's better."

"Please tell him I'm so sorry about all this."

"It's not your fault."

"I know, but I should have told Clay about your relationship with Jackson when I found out the day of the wedding. He could have cooled down during the honeymoon and maybe this would have never happened."

"Eve, please don't blame yourself. You don't know that. It could have ruined your honeymoon."

"I guess that's true."

"Can I please speak with Clay?"

"He's not here. He went for a walk, said he'd be back much later." She exhaled dejectedly into the phone.

"Awe, Eve, I'm sorry. Please let me know if I can do anything."

"Goodbye, Clara."

She sniffled and darn it all, a tear fell. She didn't want to cry anymore. At nineteen years of age why should she feel guilty about her relationship with Jackson?

"Bug, what is it?"

"I'm just sorry Eve got dragged into the fray. They're newly-weds. Their only concern should be if they've eaten and showered in the last two days.

He laughed. "You're such a funny thing and the only person who can make me laugh."

"I know."

"What's that?"

"You hardly ever smile and you laugh even less unless it's the occasional laugh at me."

"Not at you, because of you."

"I don't understand the difference."

"You're my reason for living, Bug. There's a huge difference."

I Don't Want To Try That

14

The morning after his beating, Jackson looked at himself in the mirror and realized he was the monster that stared back. The swelling had diminished, but the bruises and cuts were nasty.

Clay had called. He wanted to take Clara to breakfast. From what he could glean of the conversation Clara had with him, he'd made it clear Jackson was not to attend. Martyr that she was, she refused to go without him. It caused another ripple when he tried to convince her to go alone. She'd cried and they'd become frustrated with one another. He was willing to drop her off and wait while she spoke with her brother. Then she'd gone and made perfect sense with her amazing insight—they had to stand together or they'd be torn apart.

How had he thought Clay was going to react when they'd told him of their lies? The reality was worse than anything he could have imagined. Knowing Clay, the physical blows had been expected to some extent, but his voice had taken on the characteristics of an animal when he'd screamed the words Jackson never wanted to hear. Now the thing he feared the most had happened. Clara was stuck somewhere between the two—between Jackson and her family. It wasn't fair to her.

Clara had fretted all night long about Eve. She felt guilty about bringing dishonesty to the newlyweds. She'd cried herself to sleep in Jackson's arms as she mourned for her relationship with Clay. She might not understand it, but he knew that's why she cried.

He thought about the situation in reverse—if he'd had a baby sister and some older guy had taken advantage of her. How would he handle it? Just exactly the same way Clay had. He wouldn't believe a guy his age would have honest intentions with a girl of nineteen.

He cringed when he thought of what he'd done with her when she was seventeen. What was wrong with him? What he'd done was considered statutory rape in some states. That thought had been eating away at him. What they had wasn't born of a crime. It was honest and pure. Always had been. He knew it all those years ago when he himself was seventeen. She'd been the only one he could talk to about his parents.

Over the years their connection had become intense. When she'd turned fifteen he backed off because she was beautiful and he'd been attracted to her then. But then she'd needed him after her accident. When she'd stood there naked, revealing all of her vulner-abilities, all he'd meant to do was reassure her and make her confident of her beauty.

Their lives grew entwined like vines. Once they came together in that carnal way their fates sealed, and it became impossible to untangle himself from her—they'd become one root. Their physical and emotional connection grew, nourished by the love and need they fulfilled in one another.

With the first touch of his lips to her silky skin he knew he would never be able to pull away without a taste. A taste led to a touch that led to a need for them both. He'd needed to be connected to her on an innate primal level and she'd needed the same. When they came together it was like he'd been reborn. He had her and everything she brought with her—purity, innocence, and truth. He no longer felt alone, but part of something huge that grew from a tiny seed into an all-encompassing tree of life that he needed to survive. She needed the shelter and shade that tree offered just as much as he did.

"Let's go get some beignets." She sidled up to him in the bathroom and made eye contact through the mirror. He'd been so deep in thought her bright morning demeanor had startled him a little.

"Okay so no beignets. What would you like?"

He wanted to not be the albatross around her neck. He was the source of all the problems in her life. "Beignets are good." His voice was unsteady.

She frowned at him. He tugged her out of the bathroom and gathered his wallet and the hotel keycard.

"Ready?"

She nodded.

They walked to the familiar green and white striped awning. It was early so the lines weren't long just yet. At the window he placed their order.

"Two orders: one no sugar. Two coffees, au lait."

He heard Clara's deflating sigh and turned to see the source of her discomfort. Clay and Eve appeared under the awning. She gripped his arm firmly and said, "Wait here."

He watched Clara approach as if she were a deer and her brother a lion. Every move she made deliberate. Every move he made stilted. While he waited for his order he watched them. Not much was happening, but then he saw Eve look at Clay anxiously and then she worried her bottom lip in her teeth. Clara's hands fisted at her sides as Clay shook his head in disdain.

Jackson was sore and he felt it when he tensed. He carried their coffees in to-go cups stacked one on top of the other in one hand, and two bags of beignets in the other. There was a free table not far from where they stood, so he set his course for it. After he set down the breakfast items he took his stand next to Clara.

"Good morning." He extended the olive branch. "Won't you please join us?" He gestured indicating his table.

"We were just leaving." Clay broke the branch in half. He tugged Eve's arm, pulling her in front of him and urging her forward with a hand to the small of her back. He turned to Clara. "I meant what I said."

Clara ran after him. "No. Please." She tugged on his meaty hand. "Please stay." He pulled his hand free and moved forward with purpose. She watched his retreating back for a while. When she turned, her face was a mess—red and blotchy from tears and frustration.

Jackson placed his arm around her and she leaned into his side as they slowly made their way back to the table. She blew her nose with a napkin and sipped her coffee. "What did he say, Bug?"

Her eyes, large and luminous, stared at him without blinking.

"Tell me."

Biting her lip she shook her head, resolved to leave him in the dark.

"I need to know what I'm up against here. I need you to tell me."

She closed her eyes tight and spoke. "He said he wasn't going to sit idly by and watch me make a mistake that could ruin my life."

Jackson's breath hitched and his skin prickled. He'd thought of Clay as a brother, a friend. He knew Clay would be mad about their deception, but he never thought he'd think of Jackson as a mistake. The thing of it was, Clay was absolutely right. Jackson knew he would be Clara's biggest mistake.

***

They spent the rest of that weekend taking in the sights, sounds, and smells of New Orleans. Clara changed the subject whenever Jackson mentioned Clay, but her brother's words were singed onto his brain. Jackson couldn't remember New Orleans ever feeling so drab. His demeanor was anything but festive and at odds with the environment surrounding him—no matter what was going on in his private life, the city's pulse didn't cease. It had become as irritating as an ingrown hair. He breathed a sigh of relief when they'd finally loaded up the car and were headed back home.

"Do you remember when you started calling me Bug?"

"There are many reasons. But I remember the first time. You said it was because I was like a gnat."

"At the time you were. You'd hover around me constantly, making sure I'd come down for meals, and you forced me to interact. I couldn't get rid of you no matter what I did."

"You were so mean. I thought you hated me."

"I could never hate you. I loved you even when I was mad at you because you never gave up on me."

"And you were there for me when no one else was."

He stroked her head. "They wanted to be there."

She smiled and looked down, shielding her eyes from his view. "I know, but it was you. *You* saved my life. It's always been you Jackson. Since I was seven years old. "

Seven and seventeen. His life stopped the day his parents died. It restarted the day he and Clara came together. Would anybody believe she'd saved him and he unreservedly loved her? Would they listen as they told their story? Or would their future be destroyed by anger and hate?

"I think if Clay and the rest of my family knew how deep our connection ran they'd understand."

He disagreed. In fact, he thought they'd respond just as Clay had. The evidence was quite damning: He'd had sex with their baby sister when she was seventeen and he twenty-seven. That's all anyone would see when they looked at them. And he shouldn't be forgiven for what he'd done.

To make matters worse, he was attempting to cling to her for the rest of his life. He wanted to bind her to him so deeply that there would be no way to sever their connection, but it wasn't fair to her.

It wasn't fair to her!

She hadn't lived her life. She hadn't discovered who she wanted to be, what she wanted to be. She'd sacrificed, put off her hopes and desires to stay with him as he pursued his medical degree. If he truly loved her wouldn't he want her to pursue culinary school and maintain a strong connection to her family? If he loved her he would set her free. The more he thought about it, the more he knew what his next move had to be. And he wasn't sure he'd survive it.

. . .

***

JACKSON SPENT the rest of the ride home going over different scenarios in his head trying to come up with something that didn't make him out as the bad guy. He imagined himself as a thirty-five-year old brother of six with a nineteen-year-old sister. Then his mind conjured up a faceless twenty-nine-year old man, a man that was living with his sister and wanted to propose marriage. A man that had taken her innocence at the age of seventeen. Every scenario had the same ending—he was a gangrenous limb that needed to be severed in order to save her future.

"You've been awfully quiet, Cracker Jack. What's going through that head of yours?" Clara reached across the gearshift and clasped his hand in hers.

He was a mistake that could ruin her life. *You are dead to me.*

Clay's words had never been clearer. Jackson wouldn't come between Clara and her family. There would be nothing he could say to make her understand why they had to break up, but he'd save her from herself. She could find a thousand guys to marry her—most of them better off than he was, but she only had one family.

Family was irreplaceable. No one knew as well as Jackson just how true that statement was. If they were to stay together she'd grow to hate him for taking her family away from her. He'd be the reason she hadn't attempted to make her dreams a reality. She should be at cooking school. What he had to do was going to hurt them both, but he couldn't stand the thought of her growing to hate him one day. It would kill him.

"I was just thinking."

"About what?"

He exhaled long and loud. "I was thinking you should attend that culinary school in Texas." The words sounded hollow. *How would he survive if she was so far away?*

"We've been over this before. I would do it only if I could still sleep in your bed every night. Since that's not possible, I'm not interested. Besides, I have new goals. One day I hope to open my very own artisan cheese shop. I'm going to have cheeses that people can only find at my shop."

The cheese shop idea was a good one for her. She was filled with knowledge of all things cheese. He loved how passionate she became when she regaled him with the history of the cheese they consumed. She'd get a little wrinkle on her forehead while she deliberated over flavor and made her judgments.

It would kill him to let her go.

"Jackson?"

"Hmm?"

"You're different. I've seen you moody, but that usually fades away once we're together."

He pulled their clasped hands to his lips and kissed her thumb. For the life of him he couldn't figure out what she saw in him. He was a moody difficult bastard. In spite of all that he was she'd loved him

"It's complicated. Your brother, my former friend and brother, my link to the only family I've got, is no longer part of who I am. It's only a matter of time before you're issued the same ultimatum."

"What ultimatum?"

"He said I was dead to him."

"Yes, but in time he will come to see our love for one another."

A cynical laugh started soft in his throat and deepened, but he couldn't stop it, even when he saw the hurt look on her face. She turned away from him to look out the window as his laughter became intermittent giggling and then slowly subsided. "It's never going to happen. But I do appreciate your naiveté."

Nothing was said after that. They drove in silence for forty-five minutes. He pulled into their complex and followed her into the apartment. He closed the door and said, "I think we should take a break from each other."

She turned swiftly and stared, unblinking, into his eyes. Her face slowly contorted into a frown. "I don't want to try that."

"I need some space so I'm asking you to stay at your apartment for a while." His jaw clenched so hard he gave himself a toothache.

"You need space?" She sighed. "From me?" Her words came out in a tortured whisper.

No Bug. Never from you. His thumb scratched across his brow. "I need distance from . . . everything."

"Everything?" Her voice cracked.

He closed his eyes and nodded. "Life is out of control. This relationship is much harder than I thought it would be. Managing work, school, and us . . . I just can't keep up with the pace." As much as it killed him he felt his resolve take hold and clamp down, turning his face and body to stone. It was the same feeling he got when he dug in to save a dying man in the emergency room, or when he pedaled his bike with all his might to overtake a car on top of the Horace Wilkinson Bridge.

She gulped air through unshed tears. "It's been hard, but the one thing I've remained sure about in all of this is *you . . . us . . .* you'll never convince me that you haven't felt the same."

"I can't do this anymore . . . I don't want to do it anymore." If he looked at her he'd crumble. The life was leaving his body; his fingertips had already gone numb. He vigorously rubbed his fingers through his hair. "You have an apartment much nicer than this one. I think you should go to it."

"I-I don't want to go. *I love you.* Every decision I've made for the last two years has been made with you in mind. I thought it was the same for you." She choked through her staccato breathing.

How could she be questioning anything? He lived to serve at her feet. Knew he was nothing without her. He let out a gasp just so he could take in some air. Her grief was twisting his insides like a pretzel. It felt like he'd ingested hot glass.

"My every move has been calculated to include you in my life, the life we have already taken a dazzling bite out of. You're my reason for getting up in the morning, for breathing. You're the reason I have been able to go on living. I would have given up on life if it hadn't been for you.

Gah! He could not do this.

He needed to do this.

For her, he would do this.

He put his head down, not making eye contact, but listening to her impassioned pleas.

"You work so hard all the time and I want you to accomplish your goals, your dreams. But most of all I want you to be happy because you've made me happier than I'd ever imagined being. I thought I was in your dreams, your goals, your future." She frantically shook her head. "No! I know for a fact I was in your dreams. You can't feign a love like ours. All our emotion, our love and need is greater than any one bad or negative moment."

That's right, Bug. You know the true me. I'm in your heart so deep. Don't forget me.

"You've always said you need my love and happiness to help you find your own. One can't exist without the other."

He did need her around to feel happy and content. Without her he'd succumb to the darkness and suffer bone-crippling nightmares. She alone kept his demons away and now she'd be gone.

She whispered and choked, "You said you'd stand by me forever."

The room became eerily quiet. She looked down at her clasped hands. "You wanted to be married so badly you were grumpy for two weeks after the wedding." Her gaze found his. "Has that all changed for you?"

No, Bug. It hasn't. I love you and this is killing me. I'd rather be dead than to try to figure out how to survive without you.

His eyes narrowed and his brow curled in pain. He would sacrifice his wants and needs for her to have a shot at a full and complete life—a life with all her brothers, and her parents' support of love and encouragement. There was no room for him in that picture. He saw the great room at Christmas, full of St. Martins, Clara and her mom in the center. All of the brothers holding babies and sitting shoulder-to-shoulder with their wives. He wasn't part of their family. He was a stain that needed to be lifted.

He looked at her shoulder because he could never bear to see the pain he caused reflected in her eyes. "It's changed for me." He pointed from her to himself. "This is just taking too much energy. It's become difficult."

"If this is all true then why won't you look me in the eye when you say it?"

His eyes closed tightly and his jaw locked. His teeth might shatter but he didn't care. Time hung in the air. When he finally opened his eyes he knew his expression was banked, lost, hollow. The only way he'd be able to look at her was to look through her. "It is all true. We're holding each other back. This isn't healthy. You can go do all the things you want, like culinary school, without me here to keep you down. This obsession we have with one another needs to end."

"I don't believe you." She gasped and her eyes pleaded with him and demanded the truth.

What could he tell her? What would she believe? He'd have to hurt her, but didn't want to. Only it wasn't to hurt her, it was to help her and give her the future she deserved. He inhaled deeply. "Given everything that's happened—the secrets, New Orleans, your accident, my parents' death—I think it would be better if we broke up. A clean break can mean a fresh start. You're not good for me. I need something . . . different."

"Jackson." Huge salty bullets streamed down her face. She looked down at her hands clenched tight. "Don't do this," she whispered.

"I won't return until I know you've gone."

"Jackson, our future is weeping because you're about to erase it."

His hand hovered in the air before her, reaching, but then it dropped and he shook his head and turned to make his exit.

Oh, God. He wanted to turn back around and pull her tightly to him.

Don't turn around.
Let her go.
Don't turn around.
Set her free.
Don't turn around.

But I need her to survive.

Don't turn around.

Bug, stop me, reach out and stop me.

If she stopped him from walking out the door he'd cave.

His hand rested on the cold steel doorknob. He waited a beat, hoping she would stop him or that he would be too weak and stop himself. Instead he growled in his throat and then gasped, almost sobbed, as he opened the door and walked slowly through it, listening for her footsteps. The only thing that could be heard was a huge gaping vacuum of silence. It was so vast he could hear his own heartbeat.

He opened the car door, every action so painful it was almost impossible to move. Huge tears fell from his eyes; he was so disoriented he couldn't see. His head swan and he was dizzy. He felt the pull of gravity deep in his bones. He folded into his car and landed heavily in the seat.

With every imaginable regret he'd had in his life permeating the atmosphere, he slowly inserted the key into the ignition and started the car. His throat burned and tears flowed down his cheeks. After he shifted the car into reverse he backed out and drove away. In the rearview mirror he saw her flailing her arms, screaming his name. And then she fell to her knees.

His fingers tensed around the steering wheel.

Let her go.

He watched as the image of her on her knees in the street became smaller and smaller in the mirror.

Choking out a cough he said, "Oh, Bug. I'm dying."

His foot punched the accelerator.

He felt as he had the day his parents had passed.

The world had become dark, cold, and impossible to navigate.

Code Jackson

15

Numbness settled into Clara's limbs. She knew she needed to get out of the street, but she couldn't move. A car behind her stopped. She heard the commotion, but everything slowed to a crawl. A hand on her shoulder startled her and she looked up into the face of Mr. Porter.

"Clara? Are you hurt?"

"Yes," she wailed and gasped. The look of worry on his face sobered her. "No, not physically anyway." She put her hand to the ground to push herself up.

"Can I help you with anything?"

"No, Mr. Porter, but thank you."

"You sure you're okay?"

"No, I'm not sure at all. Jackson just broke up with me."

His brow curled into a pronounced frown. "That's not something I would have ever expected." He stared at her with a quizzical look on his face. "I'm sure it's just temporary."

"I don't know . . . it sure seemed final." She shuddered.

She walked toward the door. "See you around Mr. Porter."

Standing in the foyer she wrapped her arms around herself and rubbed her arms. On the console table by the door sat an electronic frame that cycled through images of them.

She cried as she watched two years of their life play in loops on a five by seven square. They had so many memories to bury. One of him in a red sweater she'd knitted him. The right sleeve protruded past his fingertips and the left ended at his elbow. One of her with frosting on her face from a cupcake he'd dabbed on her nose.

There was the one they took together at the Baton Rouge State Fair on the Ferris wheel, their heads together. He'd taken some candid photos of her too. He liked catching her just waking up or when she was yawning, eating, or laughing uncontrollably. She'd done the same.

There was a shot of him in his paramedic uniform just home from an eighteen-hour day. He'd been so exhausted. Another one of him in nothing but hospital scrub bottoms looking like sex on a stick . Another scrolled by of him in a lab coat with a stethoscope draped around his neck.

She wanted the frame, but knew it would rip her heart out to play it. Plus to remove anything from the apartment seemed sacrilegious. There was no way to separate any of it. The items couldn't be divided because they'd discovered and explored them together. Everything they owned existed because they were together. To remove any one item would be too much like admitting they were done and she couldn't force herself to do it.

She could only manage to gather some of her clothes, her laptop, and the fluted pie dish he'd given her. She also grabbed a few of his worn T-shirts and his pillow. She wanted his scent all around her until it faded away.

Car loaded with the items, she attempted to back out, but an imaginary tether connected her to the space. Her foot wouldn't cooperate and allow her to hit the gas because once she left this place, Cracker Jack and Bug would formally be over.

"Jackson." Tears streamed down her face.

She dug in her school bag and removed a Post-it note. She wrote an important message she needed Jackson to read before he went into his apartment.

***

Jackson pulled into the complex. Immediately he saw that her car was gone. He didn't want it to be true. He'd half thought she wouldn't leave, but she'd believed the lies he'd told her about needing more. He'd hate himself to the grave for the hurt he'd caused her.

At the door, he pulled off a post it.

Code Jackson

He removed a pen from his pocket and wrote

Code Clara

beneath her print. He stuck the sticky note on the foyer table. Tears fell for the past and for the future that had been erased.

She should forget him and it should be easy. He was too old, too poor, and too shattered to be with her. Given her tendency to be introverted, she'd easily fallen beside him and they'd rocked to a rhythm set by the tune of their hearts. But she needed to find her own rhythm, a young pulsing beat that would love eternally.

The apartment was just as he'd left it. His heart seized when his gaze landed on the electronic frame. A picture of Clara running through the halls at the hospital was currently displayed. He kicked the door shut behind him and took the frame off the base. He walked to the couch and plopped down, his limbs numb. His blood slowly pulsed through his body as silence surrounded him.

A new set of pixels molded into a picture of Clara on her stomach, legs bent behind her, smiling under a beach hat at the apartment pool. A cracked sob escaped his chest.

To say he couldn't live without her was modest. Without her he'd surely suffer. Death was preferable to the torture he'd endure without her light in his life.

After an hour had passed, he realized his body was in a state of shock at the loss.

Two hours.

The clock screamed the time. He'd been home for . . .

Three hours.

Provocative shades of orange and red mocked him into a lull between sleep and alertness. The sun slowly set.

Why had his parents died?

He wished they were here to help him navigate the unknown ahead of him. In fact, the only thing he knew about the future was that it would be dark and he'd be alone.

At least once a day he asked himself about his parents.

One decision had changed the course of all their lives. Dad had won flying lessons at a fundraising event he'd almost not attended. Mom had been sick the night of the event, but she'd told Dad to go without her. He recalled Dad not wanting to leave, but then Jackson had told him he'd take care of her.

He scrubbed his face with his hand while he stared into the darkness of the apartment, the gloom settled in his chest. All that he'd lost left him existing in a void, a palpable absence that was present in every moment, every breath. If Dad had stayed home, he never would have won the tickets that led to their eventual death.

If Jackson hadn't said he'd take care of her, his Dad and Mom would still be here. He'd been the kindling that lit the fire. It was crazy to think like this and he knew it. Replaying the events of that dreaded day made clear what could have been changed to avoid the loss of his beloved parents. He couldn't push the thoughts from his mind.

When he was twenty-six, he'd told sixteen-year-old Clara those words. She'd quoted Helen Keller to him: "'What we once enjoyed and deeply loved we can never lose, for all that we love deeply becomes a part of us.'" She'd gone on to say that the cherished experiences and loved ones remain a part of you even after they're gone. That grief is strong because the love we had was so strong. Grief is love in absence, love that has no physical outlet but still yearns to be expressed. At sixteen, she'd known what others never learn in a lifetime. She was born older. He was emotionally stuck at seventeen.

Still, he'd carved his own meaning into his parents' deaths and it included Clara. When he'd made love to Clara the first time, he'd found the answer to his destiny. If he lost her, they had died for nothing.

Four hours.

Dusk was a time he'd always hated. He'd sit and wait for his parents to return from work. He was alone, like he was now. Eventually he'd realized they were never coming to relieve the darkness.

Five hours.

Just as Bug was never coming back.

He yelled. For how long he didn't know. A knock at the door interrupted his plummet into the burning hot center of the earth.

He opened the door.

"Oh, hey, Mr. Porter."

"Hey, kiddo." He rubbed his bulbous nose. "Looks like you've joined an underground fighting ring. Thought you might want some company. I've got a pizza coming. Not on my diet I know, but I always say if we give up what we love we may as well be dead."

Mr. Porter nervously chuckled and turned toward the sounds of a car motor. "Oh, there's the boy now."

Mr. Porter was wise and had known great pain as he'd struggled, along with his wife, as she lost her battle with cancer. He'd spent one of his lives and was back to live out the second without the woman he loved by his side. Jackson wondered how many lives the guy had.

Mr. Porter met the pizza guy at the car. Soon he stood before Jackson, holding a hot sausage pizza in the air.

They sat on the couch and ate while watching sports news. Three pieces of pie later Mr. Porter spoke about the weather.

"If Camille were around she'd be gearing up to plant her bulbs in the ground." He cleared his throat. "I may have to give it a go myself and see if I can get them to grow in her little garden on the patio. She loved caladiums."

He wiped his face with a napkin. "I saw Clara this morning." Mr. Porter didn't look at Jackson as he spoke, but stared at the TV.

"Seemed pretty upset. Said you'd broken up with her. For what it's worth, when I watch you two together, it reminds me of Camille and me, when we were much younger of course. I loved her fervidly and was just glad she let me."

"How do you survive without her?" Jackson's voice cracked.

"She's all around me. I even find myself speaking aloud to her. If I'm lucky I'll have a dream-filled sleep. We're together again only she's not sick. In the dreams we're just doing mundane things like folding laundry, but the love and laughter we share make the task full of passion." He scrubbed his face and sighed. "Some days are easier than others."

"I'm sorry for your loss." Jackson knew Clara had taken several meals over to Mr. Porter's apartment after his wife had passed.

"My great love is gone, yours isn't. Whatever it is that's keeping you apart isn't greater than the love you have for one another. You cling to that and it just may give you something to hold onto as you make your way through the shifting sand."

Jackson nodded. The old coot was crazy. He went to the fridge and retrieved two beers, handing one to Mr. Porter on his way back to the couch.

Jackson remembered closing the door behind Mr. Porter. He didn't remember much after that. He was sprawled on his stomach across the couch; drool leaked from his lips and created a puddle beneath his cheek. Early morning light from the window pierced his skull. He groaned and rolled to a sitting position. Five empty beer bottles cluttered the floor around him. The clock read seven o'clock. Damn, he was late for work at the firehouse.

He quickly showered and changed clothes. At least he hoped he was late for work. Clay may have had him terminated. He stuffed a change of clothes for the hospital in his backpack and gathered his keys, locking the door behind him.

Sitting behind the wheel of his Honda, he turned the key in the ignition. Nothing. He pulled out the key and then tried again.

"Perfect!" The Honda had been eating through batteries lately. A buddy had told him he needed a new alternator, but he had neither the time nor the money for such a luxury.

He hopped on his bicycle. Given the hour, he'd probably get to the station faster by bike than car anyway. As he pedaled, he thought about Clara. She always hated when he took his bike over the bridge that crossed the Mississippi River. He missed her fretting over him and squeezing him tightly before he set off. Thoughts of *shifting sand* and *clinging to a great love* made their way through his brain and he wondered where they'd come from.

His great love was gone. And now he was completely alone with no love, no family, no Bug. Hell, he hadn't even had time for friends. He was closer to Clay and Auggie than he was to anyone except Clara. He'd lost them all when he'd lost her.

On the bridge, traffic moved swiftly and more than once he felt a car crowd him as it passed. He could have sworn a Buick had connected with the right pedal on his bike, but maybe it was just the wind and noise. After all, he hadn't crashed. Recalling last week's wreck he refocused and rode defensively.

He was relieved to pull his bike into the station bay. He rolled it to a stop and looked up only to lock eyes with Clay. They both froze and then squared off. Jackson lamenting loss in his corner, and Clay pawing like a bull in his. Jackson had no strength left in him to fight. He hoped they could speak civilly, but if Clay wanted to attack him, Jackson wouldn't put up a fight. He'd actually welcome the pain. His body had been numb since he'd watched Clara fall to her knees as he'd driven away.

Jackson held his palms in the air surrender style. "We broke up."

"That doesn't make any of this okay."

"You're right, it doesn't." Jackson looked off to the side before bringing his gaze back to Clay. "I can't tell you how sorry I am, but I do love her, more than my own life. I would have died trying to make her happy."

Clay's arms almost couldn't cross against his broad chest. "Spare me the details. And that's bullshit. If you loved her and wanted to keep her happy you would have never touched her."

"I wanted to marry her."

Clay's enormous deep laugh filled the space. "Over my dead body."

Jackson swallowed the thick rope of saliva in his mouth. There was nothing he could say that would make Clay understand why he needed Clara. "Do I still have a job here?"

"I can't fire you for raping my sister."

Jackson winced. "It wasn't like that."

"It was exactly fucking like that." Clay's yell was so loud it hurt Jackson's ears and he wanted to cover them, but he fought the instinct. "Just stay out of my fucking way."

Clay turned and walked out, leaving Jackson standing between the trucks. Firemen and paramedics currently on duty had come out to the garage to see what caused the commotion. Jackson glanced around, but nobody would make eye contact or even speak to him.

He spent the morning of his shift inspecting gear and completing inventory of the rig.

Around one-thirty a call came through of an explosion at one of the refineries. Jackson hopped onto the fire truck and Clay drove the crew to the site. It was strange to Jackson that he felt an innate need to be near Clay. The man hated him, but Jackson felt closer to Clara by being near Clay. He could also hope that one day his supplemental family would once again acknowledge him. He didn't relish the idea of being cut off and utterly alone in life. It wasn't healthy.

The fire had long been put out. Jackson and Clay worked side by side treating workers with minor burns and smoke inhalation. They worked as a duo with efficiency afforded by years of emergency experience together. After the last victim had been treated, they worked diligently to clear the area of all bio-hazardous material.

Jackson loaded the last red trash bag into the truck while Clay stowed equipment next to him. "Clay, I need to ask you something."

"If it's about work, go ahead."

It wasn't, but Jackson chose to ignore the warning in his tone. "Has anyone been over to check on her since yesterday?"

"What's yesterday?"

"We broke up yesterday."

Clay slammed a metal storage door closed on the truck and turned to Jackson. "She has her family now. Don't worry about it."

Jackson frowned. "Can you just ask Eve to go check on her? Please."

Clay harrumphed all the way to the driver's side, but pulled his phone out and called Eve.

When he hung up, Jackson asked expectantly, "Well?"

Clay exhaled through his teeth. "She's on her way over."

Jackson's shoulders sagged in relief. He knew Clara had left her best friend behind at Tulane and would ultimately be alone with her pain. The thought of her suffering in her little apartment all alone caused acid to burn in his throat. He wanted to gather her in his arms so they could mourn the loss of Bug and Cracker Jack together.

Oh Vomit!

16

Clara sat on her couch surrounded by wadded up tissues. She was supposed to be working, but she'd called in sick because she couldn't stop crying. Luckily, she was off for the next few days.

She'd checked her social media, email, phone, and instant messenger accounts relentlessly. She'd heard nothing from Jackson. Not even a status update.

As soon as she'd updated her status to *feeling heartbroken* a lot of her friends messaged her to find out why. She couldn't very well tell them. No one had known about their relationship. Yet she had a strong desire to speak to someone. Maybe she needed to see a counselor. Or maybe a psychiatrist was more what she needed. She felt utterly devastated and depressed.

You're not good for me . . . I need something different.

Those words haunted her. They'd taken root inside her and were starting to grow into something ugly.

"It's going to get rough before it gets better. Don't give up even when he does." She recalled the words Claudia the psychic had spoken.

She'd come up with a list of reasons why she wasn't good for him. Even wrote them down. The scar on her back burned as she contemplated it as one of the reasons. An image of Veronica formed in her mind. What could she do to act more like Veronica, to look more like her?

A knock at her door had her scrambling to scoop all of the tissues into her arms. She dumped them in an empty planter behind the TV. Shoot! Her place was a mess and so was she. Whoever it was, now pressed on the buzzer. She went to the peephole and looked through. Just Eve.

Clara opened the door.

Eve's wide eyes settled on Clara. "Oh my God. Clara." She offered a sympathetic smile.

Clara frowned and rubbed her hand through her hair to mat it down while Eve walked into the living room and took a seat on the couch.

"Your face is so swollen. Are you okay?"

"I've been upset. I think I cried for twelve hours straight."

Eve looked around the space. "Have you never unpacked?"

Her stuff was still in boxes and her framed pictures leaned against the wall, stacked against one another.

"Um . . . I don't really . . . I kind of lived with Jackson."

Eve leaned forward and touched her knee. "Tell you what will make you feel better. How about I order Chinese food and we hang your pictures."

Clara leaned her cheek against the back of the couch. "I don't want to stay here."

"All right, then you can come stay with Clay and me."

She pulled her knees to her chest. "You know you're twelve years younger than Clay."

"Yes, but I was twenty-three, not seventeen, when I met him."

"That doesn't matter. We're only ten years apart. You're twelve."

Eve placed her palm on her forehead. "Clara, I don't think that's the issue."

"Well it should be," Clara screamed through her tears.

"No, it shouldn't. Clay loves you. Jackson took advantage of the St. Martins' generosity when he had sex with you at the estate when you were seventeen. That betrayal is what has upset Clay so much."

"But it wasn't like that. Please, Eve. You're the only one who can talk to him. You're the only one he has patience with." Clara stopped, not really wanting to spill the next words because they were so intimate, but she needed to make Eve understand. "I needed Jackson's touch that day. He sensed that. He has a way of always knowing what I need. Sometimes even before I know."

She removed her old baggy T-shirt and turned. Eve's gasp for breath was sharp against the quiet of the living room. "I had a bad accident. If he hadn't been there, I would have died. I was left with horrid scars. I thought it would have been better if I'd died because at least I wouldn't have to see the scars every day for the rest of my life. Scars that I wanted to make disappear, anyway that I could. Sometimes, I still don't recognize my own body."

She put her shirt back on and turned around to face Eve. "I almost had some really painful surgeries, but Jackson talked me out of it. As a teenager, I thought the mutilation of my back was the end of everything. Thought no one would ever take a second glance at me. But that night Jackson made me feel beautiful and wanted and sexy and loved."

Eve swallowed. "Clay hadn't told me about your accident. I'm sorry."

"Sorry for my accident or sorry about me and Jackson?"

"Both."

Clara grasped Eve's hands in hers. "I can't exist without him, Eve. Please, you've got to help me. Be my ally against Clay. Help me make him understand. I've known Jackson for twelve years and during those twelve years I always knew he was the only man for me. Always knew we'd live our lives together. He's not just a phase, he is life to me."

"You seem so much older than nineteen."

Clara nodded. "I know. I've always been kind of strange. It's hard living under a microscope. I was the youngest of six. Five older brothers who would move entire mountain ranges if I needed them to. And that part of it is wonderful. But it's the meddling they do in my personal life that's not so wonderful. I used to wish I'd been born first or as a boy because then they wouldn't overly protect me as they all do. Don't get me wrong, I love every last one of them. But I need to be able to make my own decisions and mistakes and to live my life the way I want to."

"I'm glad you weren't born as a boy." Eve smiled at Clara, her gray eyes sincere. "I believe in you, Clara Grace. I understand what you want. I'll be your faithful ally. But I won't lie to Clay. I won't keep things from him either."

"I understand and I'm sorry about New Orleans. I hope everything is okay now. I can talk to him if you want."

"Oh, honey I took care of him. Don't you worry. He can't stay upset at me."

Clara wanted to be happy for them but she couldn't quite fake it. "Can you please ask Clay to check on Jackson. He's all alone now."

"I'll push him in that direction, you don't have to worry."

But worry she would.

***

That night Clara helped Eve with dinner. They prepared lasagna with salad and garlic bread. When Clay walked through the door, Eve wrapped herself around him like she hadn't seen him in six months. Like those soldiers' wives at the airport gates when their men come home. They engaged in an intimate embrace and kissed for several minutes. Sighs and moans could be heard as Clara walked toward her room to give them the privacy they clearly needed. It was like they'd forgotten she was even in the room. Cookie, the Papillon mix they'd acquired during the hurricane, trotted behind Clara.

She crawled into bed and let the blue feeling take her where it wanted. She cried. Not the gut wrenching, can-barely-breathe-through-the-tears crying she'd done all day and night, but steady slow-moving tears. Eve and Clay's intimacy made her ache for Jackson's embrace and the light scent of his cologne mixed with the mint of his breath. Her eyelids became heavy and she let them close.

"Clara Bear."

Clay stood over her next to the bed. "Time for dinner." He patted her head and then leaned in and kissed her hair. "Glad you're here."

She followed him to the kitchen, stewing in her anger at him and his hypocrisy.

As they ate Eve and Clay spoke about their plans to purchase a vehicle for Eve.

"I don't really need a car. I like to walk."

"It's not safe for you to walk everywhere."

"If safety requires loss of my freedom then I'd rather take my chances."

"No. You can't just think about how the danger affects you. If something were to happen to you, I'd be devastated."

Eve huffed. "Fine, Clay, I'll drive everywhere. But promise me you'll take me for long walks as soon as you get home."

His hand covered hers. "I promise to walk with you to the ends of the earth."

"Oh vomit!" Clara pushed hard against the table causing the dishes to clang loudly.

They both turned to Clara. "Er . . . sorry . . . I'm just really missing Jackson. Did you see him? At the station today, did you see him?"

"I did."

"And?"

"And what?"

"And how was he?"

"He was fine."

"Did he say anything about me?"

"Clara, I don't think this is the best road to go down."

She stood and threw down her napkin. "Oh, you don't? Well, what if I'd meddled in your relationship with Eve? Would you have let me tear you apart? Sometimes I hate you so much I just want to punch you!" Drops were steadily streaming down her face as she ran to her room and slammed the door. She plopped down on the bed.

The shadows on the wall moved and she turned into the face of Clay kneeling at her bedside.

"Just leave me alone."

"I know it's hard, but it will be better this way."

"It won't be better. He was everything to me and you pushed him away with your you-are-dead-to-me macho bullshit. Not to mention beating him to a bloody pulp."

"He took your youth and innocence. You were seventeen."

"He didn't take it. I gave it to him."

Clay clicked his tongue and exhaled sharply. "He asked me to check on you."

"Is that all he said?"

Clay looked down, shielding her eyes from him. She sat up in the bed. He was keeping something from her. "Tell me."

"I don't know, he said you guys broke up."

"He broke up with me," she screamed and bawled.

Clay's forehead furrowed.

"What?" She placed her hands on his shoulders. "Tell me. God, please tell me."

"I got the impression, from what he said . . . how he was acting, that it was a mutual breakup."

"How was he acting?"

"Intense, low energy, brooding. But then he's always like that."

"He's not always like that." Her tears slowed and she sniffled. "Is that all he said?"

"Hmm?"

"Did he say anything else about the breakup or about me?"

"No." He stood and walked out of her room.

Clara was skeptical, but she wouldn't press her brother anymore. She pulled Jackson's shirt from her bag and laid it across her pillow. Inhaling deeply, she smiled for the first time in over twenty-four hours.

Zip Block Bags

17

It was eleven-thirty. He'd been working hard for over sixteen hours and now Jackson returned to a Clara-less apartment. Had she been there she would have greeted him at the door, taken everything from his hands, kissed him, massaged him, showered with him, made love to him. Tears filled his eyes. It had been ingrained in him that men should not cry so much. But now that he was a man without hope he let the tears flow.

Sighing, Jackson sat down to read the mail. He opened an envelope labeled: *Time Sensitive Document.* He'd been approved for a loan he'd applied for before the breakup. He'd had an idea, but now it seemed it would never culminate in the happily ever after he'd been so sure of. He'd not thought it possible, but with that realization his world became even darker.

He tossed the envelopes on top of the coffee table and then walked slowly through the apartment, as if he thought something sinister was waiting for him around each corner. He pulled fresh clothes from the dresser and pressed play on the iPod speaker. When the sounds of Clara's music hit his ears, he turned to see her iPod in the dock. She hadn't taken it with her. In fact, it appeared that she hadn't taken any of her things and for the first time in over twenty-four hours he smiled. He knew his girl and he knew her lack of finality meant she refused to give up on them. Still, he'd hurt her and her family. He couldn't see a way for them to be together that wouldn't require her to choose between him and them, a decision he would not allow her to make. He knew what it was to go through life without the support of family, and he wouldn't force her to choose. He thought of her happy, surrounded by her loving brothers and father and mother.

Hoping a hot shower would soothe his sore muscles he turned on the water and let it heat. He stepped into the tub and saw all of her bath products including the loofa she used on him when he came home from a long day and night. His throat burned and his tears mixed with water from the shower spray.

When he finished his shower, he pulled on the clothes he'd set aside and then plopped down onto the bed. He was immediately surrounded by her fresh, clean scent. He hugged a pillow and closed his eyes tight imagining it was her body his arms were wrapped around. For a few moments he could pretend that none of it was true. Her scent was so strong he imagined she was in the bed next to him, giggling the way she did when he couldn't even keep his eyes open.

Minutes later her scent was dissipating, blending with his own. Franticly he paced to the kitchen and retrieved a zip lock bag from beneath the counter. He stuffed the cases from her pillows into it and zipped it up tight. When he spotted two of her worn shirts on the floor he grabbed those and placed them in the bag with the cases.

He set the bag next to him on the bed and rested his head in his hands. He was losing it. He needed an endorphin release to get rid of his pain. A vigorous bike ride would do the job. He gathered his keys and wallet and shut the door behind him. He jumped on the bike and raced away, peddling as fast as his legs would allow, enjoying the wind in his hair and the burn in his thighs. Gaining speed, he adjusted the gears to allow for maximum torque. Her face, her body, her sighs filled his brain. The love they'd shared for two incredibly glorious years was now broken and he had to find a way to let go.

He took the bridge with more speed than he ever had before. When he hit the top he sat straight and left only one hand on the bars. Lifting his head to the sky he let the moist warm air beat against his face. He'd remember her as an angel, as he did his parents. A phantom memory that could make him happy, and sad, and calm, and anxious all at the same time. He'd remember that at one moment in his life he'd been part of a love so great it could carry a man through a lifetime. Two years was all he'd been given, but it was enough. Her vitality for life would carry him through his.

His front tire locked on some tire tread in the road. Vibrations shook his bike hard and the back tire fishtailed. Using his weight he tried to apply more pressure on the front handlebars to counter the effects, but he was no longer in control. The bike went to the left, his body went to the right and his head collided hard with the ground. Skidding vehicles could be heard all around him. His senses slowed and he couldn't hear things as clearly as before. His vision went spotty and his eyes closed. She was there. Clara, talking him through the pain, telling him he'd be okay and speaking about cheese and what the cows had eaten.

Then she was seven and her bright honest eyes stared into his:

"You will be part of our family forever because marriage, don't you know, is an unbreakable bond."

"But we're not married."

"But we will be. I'll marry you into the family so you won't feel lost."

"I'm not lost."

"You are lost. Like the time I got left at Macy's because I was hiding in a rounder. I was lost. I didn't have any family. I was scared and alone. But they never stopped reaching for me. That'll be you and me," she said as she pointed to herself and then to him.

"I don't know."

"Don't you want to marry me?"

"If it means I won't be lost, scared, and alone, and that you'll always be reaching for me, then I'll marry you today."

She giggled. "I can't marry you today I'm only seven."
She held up seven fingers.

***

Jackson's body ached worse than the time he had a bad case of influenza. A faint humming funneled around the wisps of fog in his head. People mumbled about fractures and cracked bones. He managed to force one eyelid open. The vision before him was blurry, but he'd spent so much time in this place he'd recognize it even if seeing it through a thick sludge: Baton Rouge General Hospital. Those were *his* fractures and cracked bones the doctors and nurses spoke about.

He recalled his bike ride and the tire gator that caused him to go out of control, but nothing after that. The brain shuts down when it's in trauma. Knowing the signs and symptoms of concussion, he knew he had one before they discussed it. A CAT scan had already ruled out traumatic brain injury. That was a good prognosis. Or was it? If he could lose his memories things wouldn't hurt so much. But he couldn't wish for that if it meant never knowing Clara's existence.

He'd be alone in his recovery, and rehabilitation was long and hard. He'd witnessed it when he did orthopedic rotation. He'd never seen anyone do it alone. Family supported the patients' efforts and motivated them to premorbid status. He was alone. He wouldn't be motivated or supported. No one would be coming to worry for his life or to bring him cards and teddy bears. No one would cry for him. At least if he'd died he wouldn't have to figure out how to survive and recover without Clara.

With those thoughts he depressed the button on the patient-controlled morphine drip and closed his eyes.

How About Five?

18

Soft knocking at Clara's bedroom door disturbed her light sleep.

"Yeah?"

The door opened to reveal Clay disheveled and standing in a pair of sweat pants. Not having bothered to change for bed, Clara still wore her day clothes. When had she fallen asleep? After their argument? Maybe he couldn't sleep.

"Clay?"

He walked to her bedside table. Soft light filtered from the shade of the lamp beside her bed.

"Clara."

His face was gaunt. Prominent ridges outlined his lips and eyes.

"Something's happened." His voice cracked. "I need you to get up and get ready to go."

He turned to walk away.

Frantic, she jumped to her feet and reached for his arm. "Clay." Her hair stood on end, electrified by fear. "It's Jackson."

"There was an accident. He was on his bicycle. . . the bridge—" His whispered words were lost.

Her vision blurred, not from tears, something else. One million thoughts peppered her brain until something in her temple snapped like a rubber band. She'd gone numb. She stood frozen. The one thing she knew for certain was that one could not turn back time. She felt an overwhelming sense of hopelessness wash over her. She should have fought for them, for *him*. Now she might never get the chance.

They rode to the hospital in silence. She didn't recall getting into the car. Fireflies of light flickered through her window as cars passed with beaming headlights. Eventually the lights blurred into one solid ray, like those skewed photos that she used to enjoy of nighttime cityscapes with light trails. She wouldn't like them anymore because the photos would forever remind her of this night.

Suddenly the car door opened and a hand pulled her out. She hadn't been aware they'd stopped. Clay guided her into the E.R. She felt her legs about to give out, but knew all she had to do was follow him. Differences aside, he'd lead her to Jackson because he knew, even if only subconsciously, they needed each other in order to survive. One could not exist without the other.

She stood behind her brother at the counter and waited for him to make a move. It was the first time she'd noticed Eve at his side.

"He's already in a room," Clay said.

They walked down a corridor and stopped in front of an elevator. Logan and Jessie were in front of them. Their son carried a plush Hedwig owl and held Logan's hand. She wondered how they'd arrived ahead of her. Then she remembered Logan was a doctor. He didn't actively work as one, but he'd completed his residency here at this very same hospital.

She cleared her throat, "Logan, do you have any information about Jackson?"

"No, I just got a call from Dad that there had been an accident and came as soon as possible."

"Guys!"

Behind them St. Martins abounded including her mother and father. She ran to her mom and hugged her.

"Oh, honey." Her mother rubbed reassuring circles on her back.

When she pulled away her gaze connected with Cash. Isa was there too.

They all migrated to the third floor waiting area. Briggs and Lacie, Finn and Brook were already there. Seated and waiting.

"How did you get here before us?" Clara asked, dumbfounded because they lived in Whiskey Cove.

Cory answered, "We got the call from Dad and came as soon as we heard."

Clay leaned into her and whispered in her ear so only she could hear, "I may have given them a head start so that you'd have the support you would need when we got here." He kissed the top of her head.

She didn't know if she should be mad at him for not telling her as soon as he got the call or pleased that he thought of her needs.

"I want to see Jackson."

"Doors are locked. We're waiting on a doctor," Logan said.

Camp, Jenny, and Andrew exited the elevator. Her entire family had come to support Jackson. Clara wanted Jackson to see how much family and love he had. Energy sizzled through her spine. She was finding it difficult to wait. Why weren't they allowed into his room? How badly was he hurt? Unconscious? She wouldn't contemplate any more questions, and instead focused on all of the support before her. She watched as her brothers doted on the women in their lives.

Auggie and Mia arrived, hand in hand. Clara was overcome with emotion at the sight in front of her—family and friends all here because they cared about Jackson. Even Clay.

A man in green scrubs burst through the set of locked double doors. Clara gasped at the blood, *Jackson's blood*, on his scrubs, but kept her eyes intent on the doctor, hoping for any shred of information.

Dr. Weaver greeted her parents. Given their greeting it became apparent to Clara that they knew each other relatively well. She was grateful for that small granule of hope. Dr. Weaver seemed to be purposely speaking low so Clara walked over to stand shoulder to shoulder with her mother. Logan stood next to their father.

" . . . fractured ulna in the right arm"—he traced fingertips across his arm—"grade two ankle sprain with complete tearing of some, but not all of the ligaments, grade three concussion due to closed head injury. CAT scan, as you know, revealed no long lasting trauma. However, he's been in and out but has been unconscious for a while. When he wakes we'll downgrade the injury and move him from ICU."

Medical questions went through her head that she didn't know how to put into words. He wasn't brain injured, but he was in ICU and unconscious. Instead she asked, "Can we see him?"

"What are there, twenty of you?" Dr. Weaver's eyes scanned the clan. "How about five?" He held up his palm to display five fingers.

She accompanied her mother and father beyond the double doors. Clay and Logan followed, rounding out a group of five.

The ICU rooms formed a circle around a nurses' station. Dr. Weaver walked to room three. Clara followed her parents through the door.

First thing she noticed were deep abrasions along his shoulder and neck. Deep abrasive wounds that seemed to ooze in the low light. She gasped as her hand instinctively went to cover her mouth. Slowly, she made her way to the bedside and stood next to his head.

"Cracker Jack," she whispered.

His left arm was casted and his right foot was encased in a red puffy bag. She leaned over and kissed his temple. "I'm here, Jackson." She whispered low in his ear. "Everybody's here. Your family has come to take care of you."

Her mother and father took up the space next to her. "His face is all bruised and he has a black eye. The doctor didn't mention that," her mother said.

Clara's anger at Clay immediately sizzled in her veins as she recalled how the bruises got there. "That's because those bruises were put there by Clay, not the bike accident." She glowered at him.

"Clara," Clay hissed. "I don't think that's something you want to bring up right now."

"Son, why on earth would you hit him?" her father asked.

"I didn't do anything that you wouldn't have."

Clay and Clara glared at one another as the other eyes in the room observed their exchange.

Clay spoke. "Let's just focus on Jackson right now."

"Fine." Clara turned her attention away from Clay. She clasped Jackson's hand in hers and gave it a gentle squeeze.

As the hours passed she waited, never leaving his side, her eyes intent on him, willing him to wake up. Various members of her family had trickled in and out. A lot of his colleagues from the department came, as well as medical peers he worked with. Mr. Potter stopped by and dropped off a pot of tulip bulbs he'd harvested from his yard. Veronica even came to check on Jackson. Clara smiled at her when she'd squeezed her shoulder and gave her a soda.

By late morning, Jackson was mumbling in his sleep. Something that sounded a lot like he was calling for Bug over and over. Clara reassured him by whispering of her love in his ear. More than anything, she was relieved he was coming around.

As morning turned to afternoon, more friends popped in. Jackson was amassing quite a bit of get well paraphernalia. Teddy bears, plants, flowers, and cards dotted the small room. Clara was sure the nurses were tiring of the St. Martins' overly abundant presence, but because they loved Jackson they tolerated his expansive family and network of friends.

"Bug?" Jackson moaned in his sleep.

"I'm here, Cracker Jack." She whispered into his ear. His eyes rolled beneath the thin skin of his lids, but he didn't open them. The doctor said he would soon and she continued to pray for that.

The hours wore on and she passed the time by enjoying her family. In one corner of the room she observed Parker, a family friend, speaking with Brook while Finn sat broodily observing the exchange his wife was having with the friendly guy.

"Hey, babe, we're going to get some coffee. You want anything?" Brook signed to Finn.

"No. I'm good." He signed back and then rubbed her huge round pregnant belly and smiled. "Hurry back."

"Clara, you need anything?"

"No, thank you."

Once they were gone, Clara asked Finn, "What's your problem?"

Finn's brow hitched. "What's Parker doing here anyway?" he signed. "I didn't know they were friends."

Clara giggled. Finn's intensity could always be counted on for a laugh. "You're utterly ridiculous. Brook only has eyes for you." She knew Parker was still pining after Brook, but it was useless. The woman was over the moon for Finn and pregnant with his child.

The corner of Finn's mouth curled. "I know, but I still get jealous."

"Please." Clara rolled her eyes. "She's about to give birth to your child."

Finn smiled widely. "Yes, she is."

"Parker and Jackson do some fantasy football league together." Jackson didn't have much time for that kind of thing anymore, but occasionally they'd go to Logan's pub and, while the guys played the game, she'd hang out in the kitchen with Brook. Clara knew Parker from Moretti's. His family had a huge seafood business that supplied orders all over the south. Moretti's bought all of their shrimp and fish from David Seafood. Parker was a great guy, but the poor man had been in love with Brook since she first set foot on Louisiana soil. Brook had only wanted to be friends.

"Isn't it time you married her? Maybe then Parker could move on."

"I asked but she won't," he signed with downturned eyes. Clara hadn't known he'd asked. She knew Finn was self-conscious about not being able to speak and thought his hesitance stemmed from that one detail. "The stuff she had to go through with her mom really fucked her in the head."

Clara nodded. "I'm sorry, Finn. I didn't know you'd asked her."

"It's okay, I'm not done trying. I'm gearing up for the grand gesture. It'll be so spectacular she won't be able to say no."

Clara's smile spread to large proportions. "Let me know if you need any help. I can't resist a good proposal story.'

Clay and their parents came back into the room. That's when she felt a squeeze from the hand wrapped in hers.

"Jackson."

"Bug?"

"I'm here, Cracker Jack."

His eyes opened, unfocused at first, but slowly taking her into his gaze. He smiled and then his brow crinkled and he groaned.

"What is it? Do you want the nurse?"

"No, I just need you." He struggled, but finally swallowed. "Bug, I love you." His hand moved haphazardly around wires and splints but finally reached her hair and stroked there.

"I love you, Jackson."

She leaned in and placed a kiss on his lips, lingering there for several seconds. Behind her vigorous throat clearing occurred. It was from Clay's large thorax. She'd be able to decipher that sound at a sold-out hard rock concert.

She turned. Mom, Dad, Logan, Finn, even Clay, regarded her curiously. The rest of her family filed in, sensing the seriousness in the room. For the moment she'd completely forgotten anyone else existed.

Her dad stepped forward. "Is there something you want to tell us?"

Her eyes cut back to Jackson. His face contorted into a deep frown.

"We . . . we're together." Clara said.

Silence pervaded as she scanned from her dad to her mom to Clay. Finn and Logan had slipped out.

Dad spoke. "You're only nineteen, and Jackson, you're almost thirty. It's a little Don Johnson of you." He grimaced.

Jackson groaned.

"He's twelve years older than Eve." Clara pointed to Clay.

"Yes, but Eve's not nineteen." Dad countered. Clara couldn't listen to this same, tired reasoning.

Her mother sighed. "I don't think you two give Clara enough credit. She was born older. I trust her."

"Would you say that if I told you that their intimate relationship began two years ago?" Clay's brow hitched.

Clara's lips tightened. Her parents gasped.

Her fingers trembled and she couldn't bring herself to look directly at any of them so she looked at Jackson, looking so small in the hospital bed. The lights felt too bright, exposing everything she'd kept hidden. "I don't want to stand here in front of all of you and tell you the most personal details about mine and Jackson's intimate relationship. None of you had to live through that kind of scrutiny. But if it means I can save our future, then I'll do it."

Cash stepped forward. "You don't have to do this, Clara Bear."

She nodded. "Oh yes I do so please listen." She took a deep breath. "The day Jackson arrived at our home, rain pounded against the windows, and he stood in our entryway with shoulders hunched like a frightened bird, his duffel bag dripping onto our welcome mat. When our eyes met, something electric passed between us—recognition, maybe. Or fate. We had an immediate connection."

She reached for his warm hand. "I could feel the darkness in him—not just sadness, but something heavier. It lived in the hollows beneath his eyes, in the way his smile never quite reached them. I'd hear him at night sometimes, pacing, or worse, completely silent. That silence terrified me more than anything.

"I checked on him every day until he moved into the dorms to start college. Two years and four months, to be exact. I counted every single one of those mornings like treasures."

She looked up, finally meeting their eyes, her chest so tight it hurt to breathe. "I'm telling you this because before you hear the rest, you need to understand how it began—not with romance, but with a child recognizing something essential in another soul. Something that has never, not for one moment in all these years, dimmed or faltered.

"A few days before my seventeenth birthday, you know I had my accident. Jackson was twenty-seven and had already been through med school. He was the only one home. He used his skills to save my life that day. He saved me again at the hospital where he had called ahead so that the team was ready to treat me when I landed, saving precious time. Following surgery, he came into my room and spoke with me after the med team told me my options for scarring. I was determined to do skin grafting." She shuddered at the memory of it all.

"Skin grafting is a horrible process that would have involved removing the skin of my inner thighs and attaching it to my back and neck. It would have resulted in even more scarring and would have been very traumatic and painful. He asked me to wait. I was determined to have it done that day. To start the process of making myself pretty. He again asked me to wait. He explained that I could make the decision at a later date and it wouldn't change anything. There was no rush. He said there were other less invasive options that I might try first."

She swallowed hard, trying to clear the heaviness in her throat. "I had to come to terms with the new person that I was and that person to me was ugly. Unfamiliar. I got rid of mirrors because I couldn't stand to see my reflection. I didn't recognize myself. The thought of putting in the work to overcome the skin tears was too much to comprehend and I didn't want to be on this earth anymore. Jackson stayed at home and spent long hours with me the days and months following my accident. He knew I had changed into some-thing that could hurt me."

She held her chin high, proud of their devotion to one another and ready to fight anyone who opposed their love. "A few months after the wounds healed and closed up he had come up to my room. He saw me hiding, as I do, with my hair and my clothes. Only he wouldn't let me cover up. He wanted to make me feel beautiful. I needed to feel beautiful. I needed to feel wanted. He gave me that. And I gave him something too. Losing everything at seventeen had left him emotionally frozen in time, to that place where the pain lived. He had yet to move past it. Jackson, even at seventeen, was more mature than any one of you now.

"He and I were drawn together in this space of utter loss. He gathered my hair and moved it to rest over my shoulder, started placing kisses on the scars on my back. I asked him to make me feel wanted and beautiful. And he did. And there is nothing shameful about what we did.

"I'm only going to say this once, and then you're going to stop or what needs to be will just be. I love you all very much and it kills me to say this but I will walk out of that door today with you or without you. If you choose to accept me then you will accept him. You will stop treating him like he's a stain on the family and you will embrace him with open arms, just as you dome, because he's part of me. He's in my bone marrow and there's no separating the two of us."

Clara gathered her book and placed her bag over her shoulder.

"Clara, you aren't thinking straight and you never do when it comes to Jackson," Clay said. "The whole thing is way too intense for you at such a young age."

She turned angry eyes on him. "Clay, I don't want to hear it. You've done the big brother thing. You've beat him down, made him pay for what you believe is dishonoring your little sister. You've gotten inside his head. So much so that he was distracted when he was driving across the bridge and he may never be the same because of it. If he doesn't have a full recovery, I will never forgive you because I begged you to stop but you wouldn't."

She walked toward the door and then turned around not finished with them yet. "For the life of me I don't understand how you don't see that I could search the world ten times over and never find anyone as special as he is. I would never find anyone who loves me more than he does. Who would do anything to give me what I want or need. He breaks his back working because he wants to give me the world. I won't even look at anything in the stores when he's with me because if I do it will end up on my counter. He will find a way to provide it.

"It's not just monetary things that he gives. He gives me everything that he has to give. And I'll say it again . . . no one could treat me as well as he does. He's never even cursed in front of me which is less than I can say of all of you. He respects me so much.

"And Clay, believe me or don't, I don't really care, but you want to know the most ironic thing about this whole ordeal? Jackson is so much like you sometimes it drives me crazy. It's almost ridiculous how I've fallen hard for someone who mirrors your every trait. He is always considerate, constantly shielding me against life's harsh realities, his influence is everywhere and his loyalty is unyielding. These aren't weaknesses exactly, but they remind me so much of you that it stirs up anger within me because you won't accept him. Don't make me hate what I see in the mirror."

A warning beep resounded from Jackson's bed. A nurse entered, waving her hands in the air. "Everybody out now. And from now on it's two at a time. You all are lucky I don't ban you from visiting altogether."

Clara didn't move, just stood quietly and watched as the nurse pressed several buttons.

"Is he okay?"

"Blood pressure is up. We can attribute that to the conversation, but he needs to recover if he's going to get better."

Clara nodded. Jackson was oblivious, fast asleep.

Break Up Better

19

Jackson seemed to be underwater as he heard the muffled voices reverberate around the room. He could make out a word here and there. He must surely be dreaming because it sounded like somebody whispered "Cracker Jack" into his ear. But no, he was definitely hearing Clara now. She just said, "I'm here, Jackson. Everybody's here. Your family's come to take care of you."

On second thought, he must be dreaming because he had no family. He desperately wanted to open his eyes, but as much as he willed them to open they wouldn't. His mouth wouldn't work either, or he would have said, "Don't leave me."

His brain wasn't making connections. It sounded like people were arguing all around him, but he still couldn't get his eyes to open. And he heard Bug again, but surely the morphine was playing tricks on his mind. "Bug?"

"I'm here Cracker Jack. I love you."

He said her name again. And she answered once more. How long could he keep this up? He didn't know, but he'd do it for an eternity just to hear her sweet voice in his ear.

A giggle, *her* giggle. The playful one. And he felt something warm in his hand. Another hand maybe. *Her* hand.

He squeezed with all the strength he could muster.

"Bug?"

"I'm here, Cracker Jack."

He felt his eyes roll around in their sockets and slowly open. Blurred images were all around him in varying shades of light and dark.

"What is it? Do you want the nurse?"

"No, I just need you." He struggled, but finally swallowed. "Bug, I love you." Despite the pain, his hand reached for her cheek caressing its softness.

"I love you, Jackson."

Warm honeyed lips pressed to his and finally he was able to open his eyes. She was more breathtaking than ever—like finding an angel in the ninth circle of hell. He heard her father's voice. He was asking about them. Clay was there too, and Mrs. St. Martin. They were questioning her about the extent of her relationship with Jackson. He wanted to help her answer, but the words wouldn't come.

She'd told them they were together. Her mother and father didn't seem so upset about her admission. That was promising.

Clay's booming voice wasn't as accommodating. In fact, he'd just ratted them out. Jackson thought he heard gasps.

I'm so sorry, Bug. I should have been the one to tell your family. He could no longer focus on the conversation as dreams overtook his consciousness.

Mrs. St. Martin was upset. She usually smiled as they talked about books and movies when he came to the library. Today she was different. Grave and serious. She patted the seat of the chair next to her.

"Come sit by me."

He dropped his backpack on the floor and sat, precariously perched on the edge. He'd known instantly something was wrong—had read it in her odd, board-stiff demeanor that was so unlike her usual warm and inviting nature.

He didn't want to sit back all the way in the chair. He sensed something bad and thought he may need to flee at any moment.

She told him Dad's plane had crashed. "Your parents were killed on impact."

The words hit him like a physical blow. The room tilted beneath him, the edges of his vision darkening to pinpricks. His mouth went desert-dry as a high-pitched ringing filled his ears. Mrs. St. Martin's voice seemed to come from underwater, distorted and far away.

She had sobbed and wheezed, clutching him to her bosom. His own body remained wooden, unable to process the command to cry, to scream, to do anything but sit there, suspended in a moment that would forever divide his life into before and after.

And then she'd offered him a second chance.

"Don't you worry, Jackson. You're going to come home with me. You'll be my son now. You will always have family."

His eyes fluttered open. He scanned the room and then his gaze settled on the window ledge stuffed to overflowing with cards, plush animals, and flowers.

Sitting in a corner chair Clay read the newspaper. Jackson searched the room, but it seemed to be just Clay in the room with him. He pressed the button on the bed to raise the head. Clay immediately folded the paper and stood. He hovered over Jackson, his gaze piercing.

"I'm sorry about your accident. Please let me know what I can do to help. Time off from the station, money, what do you need?"

He was sincere and it made Jackson's throat burn all the more. "Thanks." His voice was raspy. "I plan to start back at the station as soon as possible. Probably next week."

Clay scoffed. "Jackson, if you show up at the station next week I won't let you work."

"I'll bring a work release."

"You need to take some time and think about what it is you really want to do. Don't you think?"

Jackson didn't miss his intent look that said he meant something more.

"What?"

"You've got your graduation coming up. It's time to look for a job. Logan has some hospital connections. We could help you apply at various institutions around the state."

"As in away from Baton Rouge."

"I just think it would do everybody some good."

Clay's hands squeezed the railing as he leaned in. "She's my baby sister. I'll never give up fighting for what I believe is in her best interest. As long as she's with you I'll fight it, the entire family will fight it because you fail to see what everyone else does."

"And what is that?"

"That you and her are way too intense and obsessive together. It's not healthy for her. She can't even function without you."

Jackson swallowed back the heavy lump in his throat. Everything Clay said was true. However, his body was not in tune with his mind. He needed her but he couldn't have her. That's all he knew.

"You're going to have to force it. I can't get her to leave the hospital. She's napping right now in your office."

Immediately Jackson recalled their last romp in that space. His heart broke all over again for the loss that was imminent.

"I'll end it."

"She said you broke up with her."

"I did."

"Break up better this time. I'll send her in."

Chocolate And Caffeine

20

Bathed in the dim glow, Clara's senses were invaded by the clinical aroma of antiseptic mingling with the musty scent of aged books. This peculiar fragrance was a stark echo of her temporary dwelling within Jackson's office. The faint murmur of the hospital outside the door provided a constant soundtrack, punctuated by the distant symphony of monitors like the ones keeping vigil on his health—a haunting nightly serenade that had become all too familiar.

She stretched out on the rigid cot, her body rebelling against its unyielding surface. His residual scent hung heavy in the air, adding weight to her senses. His absence echoed loudly in the room, filling it with an emptiness that was almost tangible.

The need to be at his side again tugged at her relentlessly, compelling as a magnet's pull. With this urgency nipping at her heels, she hastily slid into her sandals and moved towards the door. As she did so, a lone prescription pad caught a glint from the scant overhead light.

She grabbed a pen and wrote the words they'd always promised to one another. Promises that she never could imagine they would break but had.

*I love you and I know
you love me too.
My brother is wrong.
It's always been us.
You and me.
Together.
Forever.
Against the world.*

She held the pad to her heart before placing it back on the desk. "Come back to me, Cracker Jack," she whispered.

A light knock at the door had her moving. Clay stood on the other side.

"Jackson's awake."

"I'm coming." She grabbed her sweater and closed the door behind her. They rode the elevator to the third floor in silence. She followed him, but at the door he stood aside and gestured for her to go in. She turned back to Clay to catch him closing the door, leaving her alone with Jackson.

Approaching the bed cautiously, she cleared her throat. "Jackson."

Dark blue irises pierced her heart. "Clara."

"How do you feel?"

"Better."

"You look better."

His gaze never broke from hers. The intensity was too much for her to process and she didn't want to think about what his behavior could mean. Anxious, she picked at her fingernails.

"Clara, I want you to go home." His voice cracked under the strain of his injuries, each word landing like shattered glass between them.

The blood beneath her skin seemed to simmer, then boil at his words. Her throat constricted, making it hard to swallow as the familiar acid of rejection corroded her from the inside out. The persistent beep of his heart monitor punctuated the silence between them—steady, unlike her own pulse hammering in her ears. She couldn't do this again. Be dismissed like they were nothing, like they had been nothing more than mere acquaintances.

"I want to help. You'll need someone here to help you recover." Her fingers unconsciously smoothed a wrinkle in his blanket, betraying the caretaker instinct she couldn't suppress.

"Clara, the staff here will see to that. I'm being transferred to rehab this afternoon." He inhaled sharply, as if gathering strength. "I won't have time to worry about you." He choked out the words, the last sentence said on the breath of a tortured whisper.

His wincing eyes lied as his gaze penetrated her. Behind the hardened exterior he tried to maintain, she caught a flicker of something else—a momentary softening, a flash of longing quickly submerged beneath his resolve.

Clara turned her face away from his because she didn't want him to see her eyes filled with tears, how they transformed the antiseptic white room into a watery blur. There was nothing left for her to say. A half-finished sentence hung in the air between them, heavy with all they wouldn't acknowledge.

She gathered her paperback—the dog-eared copy of poems he'd given her on their second anniversary, the one she'd been rereading in the waiting room for courage—and collected the wrapper from her snack earlier. Her fingers clutched the chair's edge for a moment, her body reluctant to obey the command to leave. Finally she moved to the door and fumbled it open.

She crossed the threshold without looking back. Just focused on walking forward, though each step felt like moving through hardening concrete. The hallway stretched before her, impossibly long, each footfall echoing with finality. Clay and Eve were there to escort her out of the hospital, their hands gentle on her shoulders as they guided her away from the man who kept choosing to let her go.

At Clay's house, she showered and donned her best sundress, fixed her hair, and applied a little makeup. Looking at her appearance in the mirror her spirits lifted a little. She'd always loved the feminine white dress with delicate pastel-pink flowers. However, she

could definitely see her panty line and swapped her current underwear for a sheer thong. She decided to focus on work since it was
something she enjoyed. Mr. Moretti was more than happy to allow
her to work long hours to make up for her time off.

By the afternoon she'd completed a double batch of mozzarella.
As she rolled the curds through her hands the bell sounded,
announcing the arrival of a delivery at the backdoor. Wiping her
hands on her apron, she walked toward the back to accept the
delivery.

"Oh, hey Parker."

"Hey yourself."

"I've got fifty pounds of shrimp for you. Here's the invoice."
The yellow receipt crinkled at her touch and because she was such a
mess she started to cry.

"Thanks, Parker. Let me get you a check." She wiped the tears
from her cheek.

His hand at her shoulder guided her to a stool in the kitchen.
"Clara, forget it. I can get the check next time."

She nodded.

"Hey, what's going on?"

"I just . . . I just want to . . . I don't know." She started crying.

When she shook her head in a hopeless gesture, he said, "Wait
here. Don't get up, okay? I'll be right back."

He returned several minutes later with two cappuccinos and a
tartufo ice cream ball. He took the stool next to her at the stainless
steel prep station. "All right, now we've got what we need to get
through this."

"What?"

"Chocolate and caffeine."

He was such a nice guy. She couldn't believe he was still so gone
on Brook. He was extremely handsome. He deserved a shot at real
love.

Clara sipped the rich, smoky coffee, the contrast of cool chocolate with hot liquid satisfied her senses and actually made her
happy. She relaxed as they sampled the ice cream together in
silence.

"I'm gonna go out on a limb here and say that your crying has something to do with Jackson."

Clara moaned around a spoonful of crunchy chocolate shell and cold melting cream. "You'd be correct."

Parker crunched on a hazelnut from the center of the ice cream ball. "It's a hell of a thing, isn't it?"

"What's that?"

"Trying to figure out love without losing your mind."

"You speak like you know a little bit about it."

He chuckled as he wiped chocolate from his bottom lip. "Yeah, you could say that."

"Who broke your heart?" She already knew, of course.

He cocked his head at her. "I think everybody but Brook knows I was in love with her."

"*Was?*"

Parker's expression shifted. "Yeah, well I'm not going to admit to still loving her when she carries another man's child in her belly."

She closed her fingers around his wrist. "Hey, you're a super nice guy. In comparison, my brother is an ass. But I think it may help you to know that Finn loves Brook like no man has ever loved a woman before. It's intense. He's changed. He would never hurt her."

"First of all, that's not entirely accurate, but that does help so thanks." He had one of the best smiles around, he'd rebound fine, but first he had to get over Brook. She looked away and sipped her coffee.

"What's not accurate about it?"

"The greatest love of all time is without a doubt you and Jackson."

Clara stirred her melting ice cream. "How do you know there is a me and Jackson?"

Parker leaned forward. "Are you kidding me? I'm not blind."

"Is it that obvious?"

"Yes, it's that obvious. Plus Clay sent me to check on Jackson which means—I know you guys broke up. So what's going on there?"

"At the moment, there is no me and Jackson. He doesn't want me anymore"

Parker's head shook vigorously. "I happen to know that's not true. He's hurting.

"I don't believe that. He's the one who broke us up." She winced at the thought of that dreaded day.

"Sometimes the greatest profession of love is to let someone go."

Clara licked her spoon, her mind toying with Parker's words. "I don't know. Sometimes I think fighting for love is the greater profession because you have to stick your neck out for the one you love."

Parker tilted his head like he was intently thinking about her words. "Letting go quietly involves great suffering. Please tell me you know the difference. Jackson may have spoken the words to break up, but that's not the message in his heart." Parker's palm rested over his chest.

"Whenever you're around, his eyes and thoughts are on you. Trust me. You know that Father's Day golf scramble when he and I partnered ?" Clara nodded. "Came in dead last. In previous years we'd placed in the top. However, this year, you were there handing out refreshments with the Junior League. He couldn't stay away from you. Kept going back for pimento cheese sandwiches."

Clara laughed despite herself. "I had no idea." She remembered that day as if it were just a few weeks ago. She'd made the sandwiches he kept coming back for.

"I told him we should claim you as a handicap, but he tried to play innocent. I knew better. He ate nine of those sandwiches. Counted them myself. Finn called him the 'pimento cheese bandit' by the end of the day."

"That's ridiculous. Nobody could eat nine sandwiches."

"The man was determined. Said something about how the secret ingredient must be crack cocaine because he couldn't stop eating them." Parker leaned forward. "What was your secret ingredient anyway?"

Clara stirred her ice cream until it became soupy. "A touch of cayenne pepper. Adds a little kick that most people can't identify."

"Diabolical. I like it." Parker tapped his spoon against the bowl. "So what are you going to do about Jackson?"

"Nothing. He wanted space, so I'm giving him space. An entire galaxy of it."

"I don't know what's going on with him right now, but give it time. I think he'll find his way through it and back to you."

She took a deep breath. God, she hoped that was true. "Thank you, Parker."

He nodded and then wiped his mouth with a napkin. "I'm gonna unload that shrimp and then I've got to get moving. Got some deliveries to make, but if you want to hang out or talk just text me."

"I definitely will text you to hang out."

They stood together and he hugged her. She felt comforted by his presence and a little sad when he walked out the door.

She squared her shoulders and stood up straight. Time to push past her self-indulgent pity party. Or at least try a little harder.

It was time for her to head to the hospital to pay a visit to Jackson.

Behind the wheel of her car, she thought about what Clay had said was his greatest worry about her relationship with Jackson: the way they obsessed over one another. She would go so far as to agree that together, the two of them created an intensity born of pain and loss so great that it caused them to take comfort in one another at extremely intimate levels. However, she failed to see how that could be a negative thing.

At the hospital gift shop, she grabbed two coffees and an angler magazine. Maybe she could convince him to give up cycling and try kayaking. That seemed much more tame.

Entering Jackson's room, her eyes fell on Briggs and Lacie.

"Hey, Clara Bear." Briggs leaned over and squeezed her tight.

Lacie reached over and kissed her cheek. "Good to see you, Clara. Mmm, that coffee smells good."

"I would offer you one, but I accidentally drank out of both of them." She giggled.

Lacie smiled and whispered, "I'll make Briggs take me to PJ's. Give you guys some time to catch up."

"Come on, Briggs." Lacie linked her arm in his.

"Well guys, that's my cue. Be seeing you." He shook Jackson's hand and they exited the room.

She walked up to Jackson, kissed his cheek, and sat in the chair next to his bed. Gone were the days where she could be comfortable around him. This new space they existed in cradled them in not only physical pain and loss, but mental as well. Not knowing how he would respond to her made her nervous around him, something she'd never been.

In the end it was *her* Jackson and the harder he pushed her away, the harder she'd push toward him. As long as he still wanted her because no one decided their future but them.

"I got you a caramel macchiato and this." She set the coffee on the table and handed him the magazine.

"*Sportsman's Paradise.*"

"Mmm hmm. And this month is all about angling."

"I don't enjoy fishing." He tossed the magazine on the tabletop.

"I know, but I thought you might read about it and drum up an interest."

His brow quirked at her. "Clara, we've talked about this. Why are you here?"

She shrugged, her shoulders moving in a small, helpless motion. "Jackson, please don't push me away again. I can't... just please... let me sit here. I need to be next to you." Her voice trembled, pleading with him. "I can't just quit you cold turkey. I need to let go a little at a time." She huffed out a breath, her lungs heavy with emotion. "I was hoping we could remain friends. I could use one."

He winced at her words, his features clouding over momentarily before he regained his composure. She watched him closely, trying to decipher the pain hidden behind those dark eyes of his. "Do you hurt?" she asked softly.

"No, I'm on pain meds," he replied curtly, turning away from her gaze.

"So you don't want to be friends or what?" she challenged, unable to accept his rejection so easily.

"Since we were lovers..." He trailed off, his voice rough with emotion. "I think it will be hard for us to now just be friends."

"It's going to get rough before it gets better. Don't give up even when he does." Code Claudia the Psychic.

She swallowed hard, feeling as if a knife had just been driven into her heart. "Hmm," was all she could manage to say in reply.

The silence between them grew heavier with every passing moment, weighing on Clara's already burdened soul. She felt like she was drowning in an ocean of unspoken words and unrequited feelings. The nurse returned to check on Jackson, dutifully taking his vitals before leaving them alone once more in the dimly lit room. Clara closed her eyes tightly, willing herself not to break down completely.

Finally, Jackson spoke up again, his voice barely above a whisper in the stillness that surrounded them. "Clara." Her name on his lips was like a caress on her ears, sending shivers down her spine despite the circumstances.

"Mmm?" she replied softly, not daring to open her eyes for fear of what she might see in his face.

"What are you doing?" he asked tentatively after a moment's silence passed between them.

"Shh," she soothed him gently, feeling the weight of their shared history pressing down upon them both like a suffocating blanket. "Please... I haven't slept in days." Her words were little more than a rasped whisper as exhaustion threatened to overwhelm her at last.

She reclined the chair all the way back. She felt a pillow land on her chest. She took it and arranged it to suit. Then he passed her a warm blanket that smelled like him. She inhaled deeply and closed her eyes.

The Salad Is Mine

21

God, he was three seconds from losing his mind. She'd asked him point blank if he was pushing her away because of what her brother had said. He'd never lied to her before and it was one of the hardest things he'd ever done. She'd tried to stand strong, but he'd heard the whimper escape her throat.

He'd wanted to tell her then that it was all bullshit. That he loved her with everything he had. But what she didn't know was that Clay had threatened him, more than once, to end it. What Clay said was hurtful, but Jackson knew he was only trying to protect his baby sister. Jackson couldn't deny the truth in the words he had spoken. He'd said Jackson had used Clara to divert his attention away from the pain of losing his parents.

Yes, she'd diverted his attention, but she also carried his heart in her hands. His chest grew dark and hollow when she wasn't around. Together they'd walked through the desert enduring conditions of bottomless burning and thirst. He followed her smile, she followed his voice, and they'd emerged hand in hand with hearts entwined. The emotions they'd felt were honest and pure. That was their story.

She was so close to his bed. If he stretched out his arm he could touch her, and dammit, he needed her touch like he needed air to breathe. He could smell her fresh clean scent and hear the little sighs she made when she slept.

He hated Clay in that moment. Hated him for not recognizing what they had. Hated him for not accepting his love for Clara. Hell, maybe he'd never been good enough to be one of them. He would die with this weight on his chest, a heavy boulder that bruised and held him in his rightful place. He loved her, probably could never love another after experiencing her pure and honest affection. When he was with her he was a whole man, a king. Without her he was a peasant begging for crumbs.

Letting her go was the hardest thing he'd ever done. And he'd done a lot of difficult things over the years, like maintaining medical school and his job as a paramedic. And of course, the loss of his parents was high on that list. But she trumped them all. Every time she came around and forced him to deny their love he died a little inside. He didn't think he was strong enough to keep up the charade. It would be one thing if he only had to tell her once, but she kept coming back, refusing to give up on their love.

He wanted her next to him one last time in bed. She was dead to the world. He could just scoop her up and bring her to the bed. He'd return her before she woke.

And that's exactly what he did. Soreness be damned. He maneuvered using his good leg. As he stared down at her sleeping form he knew that for her he would sacrifice his needs. She would have her family even at the cost of his heart—without her he didn't need it anyway.

Since the chair was close to the bed, all he had to do was lift her and then pivot. He positioned her so that he could slide in behind her and spoon—their favorite position to fall asleep. He needed to feel her skin so he slid her dress up. *Shit*! He'd forgotten she wore those tiny panties with this particular dress. He thought about the hard journey he had ahead of him and willed his erection to go down.

Day turned into night and his eyes became heavy.

They were in a flowering meadow. The flowers on Clara's dress mirrored the flowers that made up the crown on her head. She ran from him and he caught her as she swung around a maypole. They fell down to the ground and lay on a bed made of colorful flowers and ribbons. His hand slid up her dress and palmed her butt, full and warm. She moaned and arched into him. He squeezed her breast that fit his hand so perfectly.

His fingers found her wet channel and slid inside her cozy heat. Wet with desire he fingered her until she writhed for more. He pulled from her and his fingers glistened with her juices. He licked each one and savored the sweet taste of her he'd been denied for too long.

He fisted his cock and moved aside the slender ribbon of material that concealed her secrets. As he slid Shis erection through her wetness, she moaned low in her throat and used her hips in an erotic dance, spurring his desire. As she pushed back he slowly entered her from behind until her warmth hugged him fully. He held onto her tightly as one hand kneaded her breasts and the other pressed her closely to him.

Their intimate connection was no longer a desire but a necessity. His pace quickened and his hand traveled down between her legs as his fingers caressed her gently. He applied delicate pressure to the tender spot between her folds, increasing the pressure when the knot grew hard. He knew her body better than his own and with the increased wetness he pumped faster from behind sending both of them soaring over the edge.

It was a wonderful dream and he hoped he never woke.

However, a nurse entered the room, making adjustments to the equipment beside his bed. Slowly his senses awoke. He inhaled and was rewarded with the scent of their lovemaking. Then he felt the warmth of her body as she pulsed on him, riding out the wave of ecstasy they'd created.

"Don't move. We're covered by the sheets. Pretend to be asleep." He whispered in her ear.

The nurse stood by and added something to his IV bag. "You know she's not supposed to be in that bed."

I didn't know this nurse that well since she worked in ortho and I was in emergency but something on my face must have communicated the necessity of breaching the rules. She gave me a look that said she'd retreat on the issue.

It hadn't been a dream. His body had reached for her even when unconscious. And hers had responded the way it always had.

Once the nurse left the room, Jackson pulled from the warmth of Clara's body. She rolled over so that they were face to face.

"Cracker Jack, I love you." She kissed his nose.

"Clara, I . . . I thought I was dreaming. I didn't intend to . . ." He rubbed his eyes with the palms of his hands. "I'm on pain medication right now. I should have made you leave before. I wasn't even consciously aware that we were doing it. I was asleep. I don't know how it happened." He shook his head in disbelief. "This is so messed up. I can't think clearly. I'm sorry. I shouldn't have touched you, but I needed to sleep next to you one last time."

"One last time . . . *one last time.*" Her voice was strained. She stood and pierced him with her blue eyes. "Our bodies speak the truth—too bad your mouth only spews lies."

She walked to the bathroom and gently closed the door. Chiding himself all over again for what he'd let happen, he stilled when Clay walked through the door.

"Where is she?"

Jackson's eyes scanned the bathroom door.

Clay closed the door to the room and then knocked on the bathroom door. "Get out here, young lady."

Clara returned and huffed when she met the brick wall of her brother. "Really, Clay? I'm a little old for the *young lady* speech."

"How many times do I have to tell you that I worry about you? You didn't come home last night so I called your phone and it rang for a while and then went to voicemail. Eve and I drove over to your apartment, but you weren't there. Then we went to the deli and Lucian told us you'd been off for an hour. It's not until I texted you, frantic with worry, that I finally heard from you and it's that you're going to spend the night with Jackson at the hospital." Clay ran his hand forcefully through his hair.

Jackson's stomach burned with acid as he witnessed their exchange.

"What would you have me do, Clay?" Clara's hands rested on her hips. "You meddle in my life like you have some kind of claim over me. You can't tell me who I can and cannot be with. I'm an adult. And I meant what I said. Leave me alone, or I'll never speak to you again."

"You weren't an adult when this started and I'm your older brother."

"But I am an adult now and you refuse to recognize it." Clara showed the palm of her hand to Clay. "I don't want to argue. It's not worth it." She set intense blue eyes on Jackson. He watched as her chin quivered and her eyes churned like a liquid storm. "I can't be the only one willing to fight for what we have. We're done." She grabbed her things and swiftly walked out.

Clay turned to Jackson. "I'll deal with you later."

"I'll look forward to that," Jackson replied with a sarcastic lilt in his voice. Truth told, he would like Clay to lay into him. He wanted someone to beat him bloody for what he'd done. He deserved to be in pain for the anguish he'd brought into Clara's life.

***

Four days post-crash Jackson's body was feeling much improved. His heart, however, was far from okay.

He'd started therapy three days ago and that had gone much easier than he'd expected. He didn't even have to wear the air splint on his ankle anymore since none of his ligaments were torn, just sprained. Additionally, it seemed his ulna bone was only splintered, not broken. That would speed up his recovery time and the cast would be coming off within a few weeks. The worst of it was the bruising and road rash caused from hitting and then sliding on the pavement. Muscle and bone on his right side were badly bruised and he felt as if he'd been tumbled dry on high heat. Every breath and step he took hurt like hell.

He'd be discharged today and that was all well and good, but he didn't want to go home to nurse his injuries in a Clara-less apartment.

He thought about staying at the station, but ruled that out when he thought of Clay's icy stare piercing him. Nurse Higgins handed Jackson a clipboard and waited for him to sign his discharge papers. When he finished he looked up to see his buddy Parker.

He nodded. "What's up?"

"Cash and I fought over who had to take care of your sad ass. Since he's got Daria, I lost. You ready?"

Parker's hitched brow said he sought a response. Jackson shrugged, "We're not gonna stay on a shrimp boat, are we?"

"Hey, you'd be surprised how impressed the ladies are when I take them back to my boat."

"Spare me." Jackson rolled his eyes.

"You'll be putting me up at your apartment. I'll expect white glove service."

Jackson's head tilted, "I'm afraid you're in for a letdown."

"Just have to make do with the couch then."

Jackson slowly ambled to the door, hissing here and there when his body seized in pain.

"Easy does it." Parker freed him from carrying a bag filled with his clothes.

They made it into the hall and Nurse Higgins greeted them with a wheelchair. She patted the seat with her hand and Jackson obeyed.

"Parker, here's his prescription." As she spoke they walked and Parker pushed the chair.

"He can have one pill every four hours for the pain. Make sure he stays away from work. He's been given the next four weeks off from his residency and I know Clay isn't expecting him at the station during that time either."

"Will do, nurse. Thanks."

At the apartment, Parker set him up on the couch and left to fill the prescription and pick up food. With work and school Jackson hadn't really had much time for Parker since Clara had moved back to Baton Rouge. However, Jackson had nursed Parker back from a few severe hangovers. One especially bad episode had left him face down in a pool of his own vomit. Jackson had found him on his boat. The poor bastard had been obsessing hard over Brook.

Sounds of the door opening came from the entry. He supposed it was just Parker returning, but what if it was someone else? *Bug.* With wide eyes he searched and Parker appeared, gesturing a hello with full hands.

Jackson felt his hopeful expression deflate.

"I know I'm not exactly your type but I think if we try we can make things work out between us."

Jackson scoffed.

"Expecting someone else, were you?"

"No, I didn't expect anyone else."

"Because it seems like you were." Parker talked as he walked into the kitchen and returned with plates, sodas, and utensils.

He set a pie dish down on the coffee table. The fluted pie dish he'd given to her. "You saw Clara."

"I did. She said chicken pot pie is the only thing you'll eat when you're down. She hooked us up. Also got tiramisu and this salad."

A caprese with Clara's handmade mozzarella. "The salad is mine." Jackson reached out a hand to take the pass off from Parker.

"Fine by me," Parker tore the lid from the pot pie and dug into the pie plate with a fork. Jackson grumbled. The bastard was lucky the Wüsthof chef knife he'd bought Clara wasn't nearby.

Along with the iPod, she'd left all of her kitchen stuff here. What did it mean?

"You wanna talk about it?"

"There's nothing to talk about," Jackson replied around a mouthful of food.

"Okay but I'm not engaging in any more drive-by's so you can spy on her apartment." Parker forked another huge bite of chicken pot pie into his mouth.

"I'm not spying on her apartment. I'm spying on her."

"That's not messed up at all. Guess you don't want to hear about my delivery yesterday at Moretti's."

Jackson sat up and placed his clean plate on the coffee table. Parker had his full attention. "Tell me."

"She broke down crying. I think she was trying to be strong. She was all smiles when I got there but then, out of nowhere, she broke down."

Jackson's heart ached from the yearning to hold her and not being able to. "Why was she crying?"

Parker took a swig of cola. "She said you broke up with her."

"What did you say?"

"I didn't really *say* anything. I got us coffee and ice cream and I sat with her."

"How did you leave her?"

"Better than I found her."

Jackson grunted.

"Damn, I like chicken pot pie, but this is on a whole other level."

Parker had already eaten a quarter of the dish and reached for more. "Don't eat any more. It's mine."

Parker held his palms in the air surrender style. "Fine. I'll focus on the dessert." He held up a huge slice of tiramisu and quirked a brow at Jackson. "Want some?"

"I'm good."

Parker was a great guy. His easygoing nature and quick wit made him fun to be around. Hell, he had even been able to get a smile out of Sister Timber—one particular sadistic nun at Sacred Heart who liked to take a ruler to the palm of little hands. Jackson's memory conjured up the phantom sting from his years at school.

Parker sighed. "If you want to spy on her, I'll take you but you need to work on this obsession you have with her. Maybe dial it down a notch."

"I can't dial it down because I have a huge Clara-shaped hole in my chest and it hurts."

"Dude that's insane."

While they ate they watched *Swamp Life* and Jackson was left pondering the Clara-status update Parker had given him. He hated to hear that she was hurting.

"That's at least a twelve-footer."

"Hmm?"

"That gator—twelve-footer, don't you think?"

"I missed it."

"How could you miss it? You're staring at the TV.

Or was he staring through it? "My mind was somewhere else."

Parker paused the television. "I think you mean *with* someone else."

"Yeah, whatever."

"Dude, I'm not gonna rat you out. Talk to me."

Jackson exhaled through clenched teeth. "I love her, but sometimes love is not enough."

"You know, it's not exactly a secret. Whenever she's around, you're only focused on her. She's the same way. You guys are like those pesky love bugs that surge in the spring."

Jackson smiled widely. They were exactly like those bugs that stayed connected for a long time before and after lovemaking.

"You're right, though. Sometimes love is not enough. At least she loves you back. If Brook had returned my love I wouldn't have let anything keep us apart."

"Not even family?"

"Brook doesn't have family. Or she didn't. I guess she has the St. Martins now."

"What I mean is, if she'd had family and they opposed your relationship would you have pursued it knowing she'd have to make a choice?"

"If we'd loved one another we'd work through it. Might take some time, but family is family. Once they realized the love was pure I think they'd come around."

Jackson didn't think that was true in his case. For starters, Parker and Brook hadn't started their relationship while she was a minor. It didn't matter how beautiful his and Clara's relationship was because he'd broken an unspoken pact. As far as bro code goes, Clay would never let him live it down, not that he should.

***

As the days passed Jackson's bruises and bones healed. However, his heart was another matter. He was still on medical leave from the station but he was determined to get a shift in at the hospital. He was suffering from a broken heart and sheer boredom. Two things that didn't mix well especially when his heart had been full and his time had been limited before the accident. And yes, he still sat at her curb every night and watch the shadows behind the curtains. It was the only thing he looked forward to every day.

He strolled into the emergency room dressed in scrubs and ready to tackle the evening when Nurse Higgins approached.

"Doctor Olivier, you still have three weeks of recovery left. I want you to take care of yourself," she ordered.

Jackson felt bad for not pulling his weight with his peers. No one said much of anything, but he knew how hectic their schedules were, even when fully staffed. He'd been given several independent study assignments to complete during his medical leave. "Mrs. Higgins, I assure you I'm quite capable of performing my duties. Check it out, no cast." He held his arm toward her for inspection.

She patted his back. "Dr. Olivier, I have no doubt about your capabilities. I want you healthy and happy and you're still looking peaked. You need to take a vacation. But since you refuse to take care of yourself I'm prepared to see that you don't return until you've been given a work release."

"That's three weeks from now."

"Well, I guess you better go find something to do with yourself. I still have that timeshare in Florida. Strolling along the white sand beaches can clear a person's mind."

"Thank you, Mrs. Higgins. I think I'll just hang around here."

"Let me know if you change your mind."

"Will do."

At least while he was here he would grab some journals to read while he lazed around the apartment. Making his way to his office he paused to check his mailbox.

On top of his desk he made a pile of things to take home. Looking around for a duffle bag his eyes landed on his prescription pad atop the table.

A chuckle emerged from his throat as he read.

"Clara." He ripped the note from the pad and placed it in his pocket. As he stuffed the duffle with books and journals he scanned the room to ensure she hadn't left any more tidbits.

In his mind a plan formed.

Blue Fish House

22

Clara piled into Eve's new car. Excited, Eve took the driver's seat with Clay beside her while Cookie jumped onto Clara's lap.

They headed home to the estate in Whiskey Cove. Dad was grilling up a side of beef from a cow he'd had butchered. Clara frowned at the thought. She knew how the food chain worked, but she'd rather be far removed from the process.

Before they left downtown Baton Rouge they stopped at Clay's favorite sandwich place to grab lunch.

"I'll just wait here with Cookie," Clara volunteered. She could use the solitude.

"You want a shrimp po'boy?" Clay asked.

"Yes, please."

Eve left the car running so Clara and the dog wouldn't suffocate in the oppressive heat. Parkway was a statewide favorite for po'boys and the place was packed. She knew they'd be in there for at least twenty minutes waiting for their to-go order. Bored, Clara scrolled through her email. She leaned into Cookie and the dog's tongue swiped her neck and face at the exact time she depressed the camera button on her phone. She uploaded the picture to one of her social media accounts and added a caption: *The new love in my life.*

Glancing across the street Clara identified Jackson's old Honda hatchback. Then she watched as he unfolded from the car. A sleek black BMW pulled in behind his car and a woman with long shapely legs, full hips and breasts, and long slinky black hair exited the vehicle. She wore tall black pumps that made her long legs even longer and more toned. Her pencil skirt hugged her hips as she slithered toward Jackson with sultry flair. The loose silk shirt she wore was low cut and she could imagine the view Jackson had as he stood several inches taller.

Clara's jaw dropped as she watched them lean into one another for a hug. Jackson's arms wrapped around her. The beautiful woman raked her hands over his back. When they pulled apart she kissed his cheek.

They walked, his hand on the small of her back. She laughed at something he'd said and then he stopped in front of Blue Fish House and opened the door for her.

"Blue Fish House," Clara whispered. That place had not been in their everyday budget—the sushi restaurant was *their* special hangout. They'd been there for the last two Valentine's Days, once on her birthday, once on his.

Her world turned blue. She felt sick. She'd often wondered why he seemed to need her so intensely. When they'd made love he'd be inside of her for so long, holding himself back at times just to stay connected longer. It was extreme, but she hadn't minded. She'd reveled in it and she'd missed it. Some part of her needed that fierce connection, even if he no longer did.

Cookie emitted an impatient whine at Clara's side before jumping into her lap. Hot tears slid silently down her face. Did dogs prefer one mate to another? She didn't think they did. And wouldn't it be a perfect world if humans didn't? Delirium had settled in. Was she actively contemplating the positive aspects of dog life?

The doors opened and Eve and Clay entered the car. Clay removed his sunglasses and regarded her with a raised brow. "Clara?"

In that moment she hated him. What he'd said to Jackson that day had set the wrecking ball in motion.

"Clara, are you okay?"

"No, I'm pretty far from okay."

"What's wrong?" He seemed genuinely concerned and wasn't that rich?

"What's wrong is *you*."

He shared a frown with Eve. "*You* are the reason I'm not happy. *You* are the reason Jackson broke up with me. *You* are the reason he's with someone else. I think I hate you."

Two sets of eyes stared at her. Three if she included Cookie's. "Your macho bullshit speech to Jackson was the knife that sliced our relationship in two and now I have something to say to you." She closed her eyes as tears threatened to fall, but then anger eviscerated the tears and she only felt white-hot rage.

"*You* are *dead* to me."

"Clara, I had just found out about you and Jackson and was angry."

"It doesn't matter. You don't say that to someone who considers you his only family. You pushed him away from me!"

"What did you think my response would be when you decided to tell me? He fucked you when you were seventeen!"

Eve and Clara winced at his harsh words and tone.

"He betrayed our family. Tell me, Clara, was the deed completed on your childhood bed, the pink one with the princess canopy?"

She opened the door and jumped from the car as fast as her feet would let her. She cried and wailed and then she thought she heard a bark. She was sure she heard it a second time. She turned to follow the sound just as a van struck Cookie. A yelp filled the air, followed by Cookie's complete stillness. Clara ran to the van along with Clay and Eve. Clay bent down and picked up the dog. "His neck is broken."

***

Eve held Cookie while Clay drove. Clara watched Eve as she

cried, her tears trailing down her cheeks and chin to drop onto Cookie's fur.

Clara cleared her throat. "Eve, I'm sorry."

She just sniffed and cried some more as she stared down at the lifeless dog.

"I never wanted—"

"Enough, Clara," Clay grumbled. "This thing with you and Jackson has hurt enough people. It's over."

They drove the rest of the way in silence to Whiskey Cove. The family referred to it as the estate, but her childhood home was much more than that. Whiskey Cove was where she felt peace and contentment. She knew she could always find her balance down the dusty roads that held all the answers to life's questions.

Once Clay parked the car in front of the large home, Clara jumped out and ran toward the fields. Using the phone in her hand she punched up Brigg's number.

"Hey, Clara." Their family vet's voice always soothed Clara's worries.

"Mr. Zelenski." She couldn't get out more than that before a huge wailing fit of tears hit.

"Clara? Are you hurt?"

"I'm okay, but Cookie is dead. And it's my fault . . . I left the car door open and I . . . I don't know. She followed me and then . . . and then . . . a van hit her. Eve's devastated and I feel horrible."

"I'm coming."

"Okay."

The open space cleared her mind. She knew the retired Mr. Zelenski would come. His home wasn't very far from the estate and though he was retired, he still came to treat their horses, cows, and other livestock. She walked out until she could no longer see the house and stood at the highest peak of the property that expanded over a few square miles. Walking toward the fence that Dancer had attempted to jump caused the scars on her back to tingle.

At first, Clara had thought the horse had gone mad or gotten spooked as she took off in an erratic canter and then a full gallop.

Later she'd realized Dancer's foot had been in a fire ant bed. The ants had viciously stung her hind legs. She'd bolted and attempted to jump a fence but her legs collided with a wire and Clara had been thrown from the horse. Her upper body landed along the rusted out balusters and rods of the iron fence. Clara's feet were tangled in the stirrups as Dancer ran along the fence line. As a result, Clara's back had been sliced open repeatedly on the jagged iron.

She'd passed out due to the trauma and loss of blood. If Jackson had not been at the estate, she would have bled to death right there on the ground she loved so much. The experience he'd gained as a paramedic and his training as a doctor saved her from prolonged infection. While waiting for emergency transportation he'd treated her back, cleansing the area with saline, dressing what wounds could be dressed, and cutting away tissue that had been irreparably damaged. The surgeons said his diligent care had sped the healing process.

After that day, when Jackson wasn't in class or working he was by her side. They were close before, but they'd become inseparable. They were two beings that embodied one space. Love bug season took on an entirely new meaning. She'd often wondered about the bothersome pests that seemed to be connected on some evolutionary level. Turns out, when the bug's mated they remained conjoined for several days afterward. The bugs just couldn't bear to part.

Thunder rumbled in the background and dark gray clouds hung heavily in the sky. The metallic smell of rain hit her senses and she inhaled. She loved a rainstorm and today it certainly matched her mood.

She walked back toward the estate. The breeze picked up and was cooled by the cloud cover. She tried to imagine looking at the world through Jackson's eyes—through the lens of complete and utter loneliness. She hoped he realized that he had family and friends, but deep inside she knew things would never be like they were.

Inside, she headed to the kitchen where Clay, Eve, and Mom were all seated around the breakfast table. Her body stiffened as they eyed her with purpose. She sat on the one remaining chair at the table.

"Eve, I'm sorry. Will you be able to forgive me?"

She grasped Clara's hand. "It's not you I blame." She looked at Clay.

He pointed to his chest. "*Me?*"

"Don't act so surprised. You're too stubborn for your own good. If you would open your mind you'd be able to see the facts."

"What facts?"

"Clara and Jackson have been together for two years and as I understand it were close several years before that. They love each other and want to get married. Clara's living her life as an adult. She has an apartment and a job. You may not want her to grow up, but she has. I love you Clay, but you're not her father and yet you're the only one making such a huge spectacle. The man in question is not some drifter, it's Jackson she's chosen to share her life with. He's a hard worker, he's a doctor, and they love each other. It could be much worse. Besides, I know you love Jackson. Instead of dictating how you want things to go you should listen when people tell you what they want."

Clay stood and huffed out to the backyard.

Eve worried her lip in her teeth. Clara felt bad once again for involving her. "Eve, I'm sorry you've been sucked into this."

She shook her head. "It needed to be said."

Mom placed a hand on each of them, "It did."

Dark blue boxes with envelopes and cards cluttered the tabletop.

"What's all this?" Clara asked.

"These are Jackson's invitations." Mom lifted one from the box and passed it to Clara.

"Invitations?"

"For completion of his residency and becoming a fully-fledged doctor. Help me address them, will you?"

Clara sipped from her mom's coffee and said, "I can't believe he's finally finished all that training."

Clara ran her fingers across the embossed Rod of Asclepius

symbol. She'd learned in philosophy the name for the medical symbol of a rod entwined with a serpent. Some Greek god and healer had wielded a similar cane and now it had become associated with healing.

Announcing
Doctor Jackson Read Olivier
A graduate of Louisiana State University
School of Medicine
&
Completion of Medical Residency
Please join us in celebrating Jackson's accomplishments
on the seventeenth day of May
five o'clock in the evening
1 St. Martin Place, Whiskey Cove
Proudly hosted by Clifton & Catherine St. Martin

"What's with all the prescription bottles?"

Her mother picked up a party invitation that looked more like a prescription for medication, rolled it, and stuck it in a bottle. "You put the invitation inside."

Clara picked up an invitation and read:

Five out of five doctors recommend
You come celebrate with
Dr. Jackson Reid Olivier.

"It's the cutest thing I've ever seen. You really have a knack for this, Mrs. St. Martin," Eve said while she rolled another invitation into a bottle.

"Well, I can't take all the credit. I saw it on the Pinterest. And when are you going to start calling me Kat?"

Clara studied her mom's face. "Do Clay and Dad want to throw Jackson a party?"

"Of course they do. Jackson is part of the family and he's celebrating a great accomplishment."

Eve stuffed bottles as quickly as her fingers would allow. "Eve, tell me. I know you know Clay's true feelings."

Eve sighed. "He said he did not understand why you felt you had to deceive him. He wished you would have told him two years ago."

Her mother's hand touched her arm. "It's okay, honey."

"Mom, you're not mad about me and Jackson?"

"I would have been upset, but you said it's been two years. It seems my emotional reaction is not a factor here." She cleared her throat and cut her eyes to Eve. "*Our* emotional reaction is not a factor. I knew you and Jackson had a connection. I could sense it was deep. It always was. You've always been emotionally mature and responsible. You never follow the masses nor is your course led by what's expected. You're guided by your heart. In return you require an accepting, giving, and complex individual. Jackson makes sense because he possesses those traits."

"And Dad is on board with this?"

Eve nodded. "This morning he said that you could do much worse than Jackson Olivier."

Hmm. Despite what they said, she couldn't have gone to them when she was only seventeen and said: *Hey, I like this guy—he's ten years older than me and we're having sex. By the way, it's Jackson.*

Eve's hand grabbed hers. "Don't you worry, Clara, your brother will come around. I'm slowly working on him."

Her mother put the lid on a full box of addressed invitations. "Clay loves you very much. Ever since the day you had the accident he's felt responsible for what happened. Says he should have been there. In the aftermath, he's been overly solicitous of you. He wants to protect you now since he wasn't able to before. Your brother loves you and wants to make sure you're safe."

"He loves his sense of duty more. Never let it be said that Clayton James St. Martin didn't honor his role as brother to his baby sister or fireman to his city." She folded her arms across her chest and stewed in her anger. "Besides, the damage has already been done. Jackson broke up with me and apparently he's moved on."

"Yes, Clay is driven by his honor. But that's not a bad thing. No matter what he says he'll never turn his back on you or Jackson. Give it some time, he'll come around. And don't you worry about Jackson. He can't stay away from you. He never could. Again, give it time."

Her mother was right. Clay hadn't completely turned his back on Jackson and that meant the world to her. It was one of the reasons she couldn't stay mad at Clay. Jackson though, she wasn't so sure about. He'd broken her heart again and again breaking up with her. She didn't have it in her to make it through another break up with him. Her heart was so full of holes as it was, she found it hard to take a deep breath lately.

The door opened and in walked Dad, followed by Mr. Zelenski who was carrying a puppy in his arms that looked exactly like Cookie must have in her first few weeks of life. Cooing immediately ensued. Eve leaped from her chair and darted up to Dad.

"She looks just like Cookie." Really they could be from the same litter Clara thought.

Eve took the pup into her arms. They rubbed noses. "Well, she's not Cookie, but it's a good start. She'll have big shoes to fill."

"One of my workers was only too happy to have me take this little fella off his hands. Their dog had a litter of five." Dad gave Clara a sympathetic smile. She mouthed a 'thank you' across the table to her Dad. "Where's Clay?" he asked.

"Backyard." Clara answered.

***

That night Clara lounged in bed staring at her phone. It had become her nemesis. She wanted to use it to text Jackson, or better still, to call him and hear his voice in her ear. She exhaled on a sigh. She'd avoided Facebook because she didn't want more sympathy from her friends regarding her depressing status update. More than once, she considered Twitter since Jackson used that platform more than any other because it was quick.

Somewhere she had stored a password to her account. She downloaded the app and ran through a list of possibilities in her head. She tried *Jacksonnbug4ever* . . . *Clara-n-Jackson* . . . *CrackerJ@ck1!* —that worked. She was logged on. She typed his handle in the search bar and accessed his page. On his wall was a tweet from two days prior.

> Big changes on the horizon. Congrats, Jack! See you
> soon.

Jack! How could she. Clara placed her cool hands on her hot cheeks.

It was the woman from before. She clicked on the profile of the woman who'd left the message. Samantha Boyd. Southwest Louisiana Realtor. Clara had to admit she was certainly beautiful in her sophisticated attire. Her age was also much closer to Jackson's than Clara's. Numbness settled deep into her bones as she stared at the image of the cultured woman. A woman who actually looked like the wife of a doctor.

See you soon.

She winced as she read the words again. . .

SEE YOU SOON.

Many questions tried to pierce her brain and her subconscious just couldn't wait to make her feel inferior, but she wouldn't let any of it percolate. Evil penetrating vines of deceit would reach out and strangle her.

She cued up his number and let it ring.

She was desperate to hear him reassure her that it would always be him and her together forever.

It went to voicemail. She let his low masculine voice cascade over her, warming her from the inside out.

"Jackson, I . . ." She couldn't very well ask him how his date with Samantha had gone. "I just wanted . . . *needed* to hear your voice." Seconds passed. She exhaled into the phone. "I miss you. Hope you are healing well. I wish I could have helped you more, or just sat with you. Helped you pass the time." More seconds ticked by. "Um . . . goodnight Jackson."

Totally lame, but she had to leave a message because she always did. It was expected. Just like it was expected that without her he would have been in turmoil so great that he'd barely be able to face another waking day, let alone consider dating someone new.

The Cowbell

23

Jackson retrieved the mail and a small package. On second look he realized the package was a pill bottle with an address label on it. Strange. There seemed to be something inside of it. He twisted the cap off and pulled out a piece of paper.

The St. Martins were throwing him a party. Celebrating his accomplishment just as any family would do for their son. He knew the proverbial shit had hit the fan that day at the hospital when they'd found out about him and Clara and yet they still supported him.

His heart stopped beating, frozen for a moment as the disbelief settled into his spine. A grin stretched across his face. A thick card fell from the stack of mail in his hands, hitting the ground with a thud. He bent and picked it up. The feel of the textured envelope and padded thickness overwhelming his already excited senses. He ripped it open to reveal a party invitation. *His* party invitation.

He unfolded a handwritten note:

Jackson,
We love you and are extremely proud of your accom-

plishments. Your achievements need to be celebrated. We have big plans. See you soon.
Catherine & Cliff

He placed a hand on his chest and inhaled around the sting in his throat. He loved the St. Martins and he thought if he could make them understand just how much their daughter and sister meant to him they would have been encouraging of his relationship with her.

As it was, he knew he wouldn't do anything further to jeopardize Clara's relationship with her brothers and parents, or to further alienate himself from their good graces.

Inside the apartment, he changed into tattered and faded jeans and a snug white T-shirt with paint stains.

He grabbed his keys, wallet, phone, and his favorite of Clara's journals. Sliding into the driver's seat of his old Honda, he held his breath as he turned the key. When he felt the thrum of the motor vibrate through the dash his lips curved into a smile.

As he drove, he thought about the progress he'd made on the little place he'd taken out a loan to purchase before he and Clara had split. It was intended to be her birthday present. He'd thought about selling it but he wanted her to have the shop even if he wasn't in her life to watch her enjoy it. So he'd kept it and he'd been sanding and painting the walls, trying to make it look a little presentable before he let Clara set eyes on it. The place had been a coffee shop so the plumbing and the kitchen were good for Clara's cheese shop needs.

Endeavoring to keep himself busy during his hiatus from work and school, he'd laid new laminate floors. He supposed he'd pushed himself too far but truth told, he'd welcomed the steady throb of pain in his forearm. It meant he was doing something that might ultimately make her happy. He owed her this for the friction he'd caused between her and her family.

He parked against the curb and walked up to the little shop. Inside, he inhaled the strong smell of glue and paint. As he looked around at his work he smiled. He could see Clara in here as clearly as he could see himself in emergency. Her bubbly personality would attract and develop repeat customers. At the Italian bistro, she raked in the tip money. She'd told him it was one of the reasons she continued to work there. He'd tried explaining the tips were good because she was a delight and people would follow and support her wherever she served.

Working on this place for her and concentrating on recovery saved him when he'd needed it most. How many times had he driven by her apartment? How many hours had he lain awake at night, staring at the photo frame of pictures? Out of nowhere he'd break down with anxiety at not being able to put his arms around her and pull her close. His mind played tricks on him at night. In his apartment, he'd see her walk by in his peripheral vision only to turn and see the image vanish into thin air.

His phone vibrated from his pocket and he pulled it out to answer.

"Hello."

"Hey, it's Keith. I'll be there in about ten minutes with the sign.

"Great. I'm here."

He slid his phone into his pocket and grabbed a sanding block. The cabinets were almost done. He wondered about letting her pick colors but he knew her favorite color was purple. A deep amethyst had caught his eye and he thought black accents would make a chic pallet for an artisan cheese shop.

As he painted the first cabinet deep purple, the door opened to admit Keith. Short and squatty, he was sincere about his work. "Howdy."

"Hey."

"Floors look good."

"Thanks. Finally got them all down."

"I've got the sign out on the trailer if you want to come take a look."

"Great."

Jackson followed him outside. When he untied and pulled the blue tarp away he was amazed.

"It's more perfect than I could have visualized."

"Yeah, I think it will fill the space nicely." Keith made a span with his hands, the width of the mantle where the sign would hang outside above the door.

Jackson nodded. The architectural style of the cheese shop was primarily Georgian, characterized by a symmetrical facade, large sash windows, and use of bluestone. The dark stone was inlayed in wood that was painted a satin black.

Keith had cut the letters in all caps with perfect spacing into easy to read yet sophisticated letters that read: THE COWBELL. The Veranda font stood out in gold and beneath the titular were the words: Artisan Cheeses. The gold color made it so that it could be easily read against the black satin color of the building.

"It's perfect."

"And did you need it to be hung?"

"Definitely. Do you have an estimate for the job?"

"Since you bought the sign . . . figure another grand."

Jackson nodded. "That'll work. Would it be possible to hold off hanging it until next week?"

"Sure, I've got some time on Thursday."

"Perfect. Let me get you a check."

Walking inside to write the check Jackson couldn't think of a better way to spend seventy-eight hundred dollars. He'd also ordered a couple display cases to house cheese, but he'd let her determine the rest. He recalled how they'd spent countless hours roaming Ikea as she dreamed of everything she wanted to purchase for her shop.

He wanted to be the one to make her dreams come true.

Fate was a funny thing. As Jackson made his way back out to the sidewalk, he saw Clay speaking to Keith as he re-tarped the sign.

"Gonna be a cheese shop." When Keith saw Jackson he hitched a thumb over his shoulder and said, "Here's the man who can tell you all about it."

Jackson passed Keith a check for the additional charges. "Thanks, Keith. See you Thursday."

Clay and Jackson stared each other down. When he'd had

enough, Jackson gave up and went inside the shop and resumed painting on the cabinets. Eventually Clay walked inside.

Clay's heavy footsteps gave away his nervous pacing but Jackson was done with placating Clay. He had no reason to tread lightly with the fireman. Not anymore.

"What's all this."

Jackson didn't turn but kept painting. "I'm fixing up this shop."

"I can see that. As if you didn't have enough to do with your residency and EMT job."

"It's just something to do."

"According to the sign guy, you're the owner of a cheese shop."

Jackson's brush stopped. What was it to Clay anyway? He leaned the brush across the tray of paint and stood. "I am now." He decided to come clean with Clay. "The truth is, I had taken out a loan for this building and was in the process of buying it as a gift for Clara. I know we have broken up but I still plan to offer it to her."

"You can't be serious." Clay's eyes narrowed. "Is this some roundabout way to win her back?"

Jackson sighed. "It tore my fucking guts out to break up with her. This is the most contented I've been in weeks. I actually wake up and don't wish I'd died in that plane right along with my parents. This has given me a way to grieve the two of us. I owe her this. I can do this for her. She's nineteen. No one will give her the loans she'd need to get her own shop, but she needs her own shop. She deserves this. I can have an investment. I don't have to see her to make that happen. You have no say in this. I'm sorry for all the harm I've done."

Jackson used his finger to wipe at a small drop of purple paint. "I can't say I should have never done it because I know whatever we had will have to be enough to last me a lifetime. There is no one else for me. And that's fine. I've got my work and the memories of us. I can make it on that. I'll be a bystander in her life, someone watching her succeed from afar. All I've ever wanted is for her to be happy. I can still make that happen. Even if I'm not the one with her. Even if her family hates the actions of me and their only daughter. I can give her the things that make her happy in spite of that." He lifted the paintbrush and resumed working on the cabinets.

It was several minutes before Clay spoke. When he finally did, Jackson realized Clay didn't really know the things that made Clara tick. "I'm listening to you, Jackson. I know you don't think I am. I keep getting stuck on the fact that she is nineteen. What in the world does she know about running a successful business? What does she even know about cheese? Mozzarella sure, but a whole business based on the sale of cheese? I can't help but think you are not being rational. She doesn't know how to keep books or fulfill inventory. What's she going to do with a place like this? It's too much. You and her have always been too much for one another."

Jackson closed his eyes and inhaled, getting madder at every word Clay spoke. He set the brush down yet again. Standing up, he pulled the purple journal from the built-in shelves, opening it to his favorite passage. Before he read he decided to give Clay a piece of his mind.

"You don't know anything about her. You've used what little knowledge you have of her to ruin her life. I used to think of you as a brother. Now I hate you. I hate you for not seeing how special she is." With that, he read from the journal.

"The Cowbell: Artisan Cheese Shop.

"I've started on my CCP, it's the road to becoming a Certified Cheese Professional. To take the exam I need four-thousand hours of experience in the cheese industry. I'm two-thirds of the way there. It turns out cheese is much more high maintenance than I could have ever imagined. Many things must be considered. Cheese ripening is a science that has a lot of moving parts.

"A whole ripe Flora will have some give to it; probe it gently in its paper wrap and it should feel a bit squishy, like a ripe peach. If it feels hard, the cheese got too dry somewhere en route—most likely in the retail cheese case. These cheeses want humidity to keep that mold progressing on the rind. To avoid improper ripening, buy from the source or your most-trusted cheese monger. That will one day be me . . . Clara at The Cowbell.

A thought: arrange the cheeses by regions, or use a map. Map wax paper!"

Clay sat on the floor with his back against the windows. "She never said anything about this."

"She said it all to me!"!" He couldn't help the anger and the tears that fell from his eyes. He passed the journal to Clay so he could read how she created inventory information.

"The Cowbell: Artisan Cheese Shop," Clay read aloud. "What's this?"

"Keep reading."

"I've started on my CCP, it's the road to becoming a Certified Cheese Professional. To take the exam I need four-thousand hours of experience in the cheese industry. I'm two-thirds of the way there. It turns out cheese is much more high maintenance than I could have ever imagined. Many things must be considered. Cheese ripening is a science that has a lot of moving parts.

"A whole ripe Flora will have some give to it; probe it gently in its paper wrap and it should feel a bit squishy, like a ripe peach. If it feels hard, the cheese got too dry somewhere en route—most likely in the retail cheese case. These cheeses want humidity to keep that mold progressing on the rind. To avoid improper ripening, buy from the source or your most-trusted cheese monger. That will one day be me . . Clara at The Cowbell.

"A thought: arrange the cheeses by regions, or use a map. Map wax paper!"

Clay sat on the floor with his back against the windows. "She never said anything about this."

"She said it all to me!" He couldn't help the anger and the tears that fell from his eyes. He passed the journal to Clay so he could read how she created inventory information.

Bayley Hazen Blue:
MILK TYPE: Raw Cow Milk
STYLE: Natural Rind Blue

.

MILK SOURCE: Jasper Hill Farm's Andersonville Herd

FORMAT: 7 lb Wheel

AFFINAGE: 3-4 Months

SHELF LIFE: 12 Days

TYPICAL PROFILE: Peppery, Anise, Grassy, With An Umami Roast Beef Backbone.

THE STORY: Bayley Hazen Blue is a Jasper Hill Farm original, and is made from high-quality whole raw milk. It is named for an old military road commissioned by George Washington during the Revolutionary War. Though no major battle ever took place, the road brought Greensboro, Vermont its first settlers and continues to be used today.

SENSORY: Bayley has developed a loyal following because of its fudge-like texture, toasted-nut sweetness, and anise spice character. The paste is dense and creamy, with well-distributed blue veins. The usual peppery character of blue cheese is subdued, giving way to the grassy, nutty flavors in the milk.

PAIRING AND SERVICE: The texture and flavor make Bayley an ideal choice for any lover of blue cheese, but with a balance of flavors that renders it accessible to those new to the style. Try pairing with a fruity red dessert wine, toasty Imperial Stout, or a hunk of dark chocolate. Bayley is also ideal for crumbling over a juicy burger or adding to a salad with spinach, walnuts, and dried tart cherries.

1

When Clay finished reading, he passed the journal back and Jackson saw that his jaw had dropped. Maybe he was finally getting through his thick skull. "This is journal number three of dozens, and it's my favorite. She talks about her dream for the store. I've read it hundreds of times. It's what I read right before I go to bed, and again upon waking up. She must have a hundred write-ups about specific cheeses. She asked Moretti to let her do inventory, so she could learn. She's enrolled in online courses for business. Clara's not like us. It isn't going to take her an entire lifetime to figure it out. She understands who she is. She may be nineteen but she was born older than you or me. I'm still a toddler fumbling around blindly finding my way through this life, and you're. . . I don't know what you are Clay." The big guy grumbled next to him.

"Clara though, she knew what she was born to do. I had hoped what she wanted to do would include a place for me but it's out of our hands. That's okay though. I can support her still. There are no rules. Not anymore. Not now that she is an adult."

Jackson snapped the journal shut. "I'm unwilling to discuss anything further about the past and our relationship. She's your beloved sister and I trust you to forgive her for past transgressions. She loves you so much. Try to find it in your heart to understand her. She's not seven years old anymore. Learn who she is."

With that he resumed painting.

After a time, Clay picked up an unused brush and painted next to him late into the night. No words were exchanged but the emotion in her big brother's actions were not lost on Jackson. He hoped these actions meant that Clay was finally moving on.

Moving on was the only way the healing process could start.

Jackson and Clara needed to heal.

Samantha Boyd

24

Rolling around on her pink-canopied bed, Clara contemplated readying for Jackson's graduation day. Her phone beckoned to her from the nightstand and she realized he'd returned her call sometime during the night.

"Clara, if I asked you to trust me I would expect you to laugh given our circumstances. I can't say much now. I've actually got to go but I will tell you that things are not always what they seem. Thank you for calling."

She couldn't be sure but it sounded like he'd spoken that last bit with a smile on his face. She felt jealous that he would be smiling as she struggled to hold back tears. His extremely strange message left her scratching her head. She tossed her phone into her purse and dressed for the day.

At Jackson's residency graduation, the call of his name reverberated around the assembly hall. He crossed the stage to accept his certificates looking sexy in the tailored navy Hugo Boss suit she'd help him pick out for her mother's fiftieth birthday celebration that had been a fancy affair. Cheers and whistles erupted from the St. Martin section of the auditorium and Jackson waved in their direction.

Outside they waited for him to emerge from the gaggle of graduates. The June air hung thick with perfume, sunscreen, and the particular scent of wet hot concrete from an earlier drizzle. She shifted her weight from one foot to the other, her sandals pressing crescents into the soft grass just off the sidewalk. *What if he walks past without seeing me? What if, after everything, this moment doesn't matter to him the way it does to me?*

As he walked their way, his eyes held steady on hers through the sea of family members young and old. His intensity hollowed her chest, each heartbeat suddenly painful and precious, as if her body had forgotten how to perform its most basic function. A contradictory urge to both run toward him and flee altogether left her rooted in place, trembling slightly.

He reached for her, and the world narrowed to the scrape of the nylon in his suit against her bare arms, the lingering scent of the cologne she'd given him last Christmas, the solid pressure of his chest against her cheek. She could feel his heart hammering as frantically as her own, his fingers pressing into her back with a desperation that told her everything words couldn't. He held her as if she might dissolve into the crowd if he let go too soon.

Behind her, she sensed her mother's knowing gaze, her father's slight clearing of throat. Only then did he release her, the corners of his eyes damp, before he greeted the rest of her family with the polite smiles and handshakes that belonged to a different, more formal universe than the one they had briefly inhabited together.

"We're so proud of you, Jackson." Mom said.

He smiled. Behind him a classmate called his name. "The college has set up a reception for the graduates, but I'll be quick."

"Great. We'll see you back at the estate." Dad hugged Jackson and then Jackson accompanied his peer inside.

As Jackson disappeared into the crowd of well-wishers and fellow graduates, Clara stood there, trying to collect herself. His touch still lingered on her skin, the memory of his closeness a comforting yet agonizing weight in her chest.

Her parents exchanged a glance, wordlessly communicating the unspoken questions that hung in the air. Her mother reached out to squeeze her shoulder, offering silent support as her father cleared his throat once more.

"Are you alright, honey?" her mother finally asked, her voice soft with concern.

She nodded, forcing a smile that felt brittle on her lips. "I'm fine, just... overwhelmed, I guess."

Her father nodded in understanding, his eyes lingering on the spot where Jackson had disappeared from view. "He's become a remarkable man," he said quietly.

"He has," she whispered, her gaze still fixed on the path through which he had left. "He really is."

With a heavy sigh, she finally tore her gaze away and turned to face her parents. The weight of unspoken emotions hung heavy in the air between them, a mix of pride, longing, and uncertainty.

"Let's head back to the estate," her father suggested, breaking the silence. "We can celebrate properly there."

Nodding, she looped her arm through her mother's, drawing strength from the familiar touch. As they made their way back through the crowd to the SUV, the beat of Jackson's heart still reverberated in her, a bittersweet reminder of a moment that felt both fleeting and eternal.

Today marked the beginning of a new chapter for Jackson, one filled with the promise of possibilities, regrets, and the lingering ache of a love that might never find its way back to her again.

***

That evening, adrenaline thrummed through Clara's veins, not just enveloping her body in warmth but making her fingers tremble as she tied the sash around her shorts. Each heartbeat felt too strong, too insistent beneath her ribs, as if warning her this was reckless. She was prepared to fight Jackson, Clay, Samantha, and anyone else who tried to stand in her way of reclaiming the love of her life—even as a small voice whispered: *What if he doesn't want to be reclaimed?*

She was one who preferred to use a precisely organized group of words to translate her feelings but right now the only thing that felt right was *fuck that!* With words, one could lie about the state of their feelings or how nice someone looked in an ill fitted pair of jeans. Actions and body language were where the truth lied. And Jackson's body language said he still loved her with everything he had. She'd focus on that.

In preparation for the party, she wore a pair of dressy beige-colored shorts with a sash around the waist that she tied into a bow, retying it three times until it looked casually perfect. She paired the shorts with a black silky top.

Beneath her blouse she'd donned a tank top that read, *My heart belongs to an E.R. doctor.* Her fingertips traced the words through the silk, like touching a talisman. She finished the look with a pair of black wedge sandals with gold accents, then stood before the mirror, suddenly uncertain. For a moment, her reflection showed everything —the hope, the fear, the years of longing compressed into this fragile moment.

The thump of bass could be heard from the lawn, each beat syncing with her pulse. Kickoff was minutes away. She grabbed Jackson's gift, the weight of it in her hands making everything real. At the threshold to the back door, she hesitated. Thinking about her and Jackson's pain endured at such young ages, she wondered if a person could really rebuild something that had crumbled. Could time heal, or did it just teach one to carry the wounds differently?

When her foot connected with the terra cotta patio tiles, some-thing electric raced up her spine. She could sense Jackson's presence before she saw him, the way prey feels a predator—not with fear, but with an ancient recognition that transcended thought. Her mouth went dry. Yearning, strong and pure, coursed through her, settling as an ache behind her sternum that made it hard to draw a full breath.

She search for the other half of her heart and found it sitting under an umbrella, speaking with her mother, though his gaze— with eyes that had watched her laugh and cry and grow for more than a decade—held hers immediately. Their conversation stopped and both of them smiled at her, but only one smile mattered.

Jackson's wasn't the easy grin she remembered; it was cautious, the corners of his mouth tight with something that might be hope or regret. Time stopped and the wind that formerly caressed her skin ceased. In that suspended moment, she remembered him at twenty-seven, laughing in the rain, pulling her close and whispering, "You're it for me, Clara."

She'd tried to exist without him, filling the spaces with work and friends and the occasional date that never felt right; she couldn't very well invite him to her senior prom. But for eleven years he'd been part of her world, her life—the standard against which she measured every connection. Their bond wasn't only physical, it was cellular, as if somewhere in the formation of who she was, his name had been written into the blueprint.

Collective chatter filtered through the air as she observed additional partygoers trickling in.

Her mother jumped to her feet and approached. "Clara, will you give me a hand with the cake?"

She set her gift on a chair and followed her mom into the kitchen. "What were you and Jackson talking about?"

"Just catching up."

Clara was suspicious, but knew her mom well enough to know that she wouldn't give information if she didn't want to—tight lipped her dad called it.

Grabbing one side of the cake board while her mom held the other, they gingerly carried the cake out to the patio. Three levels comprised the white cake covered with fondant. The top tier displayed an edible stethoscope. A medical cross decorated the middle tier and the bottom boasted Louisiana State University gold and purple stripes. A fleur-de-lis decorated the board the cake sat on, along with an edible ribbon that read *Congratulations Dr. Jackson Reid Olivier.*

"There. I think that looks good." Her mom fussed over the angle while audio feedback had several bystanders clutching their ears.

"I'm going to bring out the appetizer platter I made," Clara said.

"Honey, the whole thing's being catered by Fat Boy's Barbeque."

"I know Mom, but I made something special. It's just a snack tray with some cheeses."

"The cheese you make?"

"Yeah."

"Do you want to set it up next to the cake?" She moved the cake to one side.

"Sounds good."

In the kitchen, Clara opened both doors of the industrial sized refrigerator and pulled a large tray from the shelf. Turning, she almost collided with Jackson. He smiled at her and picked up a bocco cheese ball and popped it into his mouth. The cheese balls were about the size of cherry tomatoes and she'd arranged the platter with heaping mounds of them, along with fresh basil and red and yellow vine tomatoes. The hors d'oeuvres were seasoned with olive oil, Italian seasoning, sea salt, and pepper.

She held the platter as she watched him chew. When he finished, he selected a tomato and another bocco ball and tossed them into his mouth, one behind the other.

"Bug. I'm—"

Annoyed by the interruption of Auggie and Mia, Clara huffed.

"There he is. Dr. Olivier, I was hoping I could get you to take a look at this oozing sore on my ass," Auggie said.

"Gross." Mia's nose scrunched.

"I'm kidding, of course." Auggie took Mia in his arms and passionately kissed her.

Clara's jaw dropped at the sight while Jackson's deep blue gaze burned through her.

Auggie and Mia finally pulled apart. Mia seemed embarrassed as a deep blush settled across her face and neck. "Congratulations, Jackson."

They each took turns hugging and congratulating Jackson and then they all three moved outside.

Jackson looked at her over his shoulder. The words left unsaid sizzled between them.

Once all family and friends had arrived, the party got underway with a chaotic energy that pulsed through the crowd. The DJ, a lanky guy with an infectious laugh, had everyone gathered around a giant version of the classic Operation game. Clara watched as her brother Briggs attempted to extract the "funny bone" with comically unsteady hands, causing the buzzer to shriek and everyone to erupt in laughter.

"Next victim!" the DJ called, his voice booming over the speakers.

The game quickly evolved into a raucous anatomy identification challenge, with guests shouting out increasingly ridiculous names for body parts. Clara found herself laughing despite the knot of tension in her stomach, her gaze constantly scanning the crowd for Jackson.

On the far side of the patio, Cash had set up shop at the outdoor bar, his fingers expertly shuffling a deck of cards. A small crowd had gathered to watch the world champion poker player deal Texas Hold'em, though no one seemed eager to play against him.

"I'll spot you fifty chips," Cash offered to Luca, who shook his head vigorously.

"Not falling for that again," Luca replied, raising his beer in mock salute.

Clara's attention snapped to movement near the pool. Her breath caught in her throat. There he was—Jackson standing with Parker, but they weren't alone. Between them stood the woman Clara had seen Jackson walking with that day he took her to *their* special restaurant. She had her head thrown back in laughter, her hand resting casually on Jackson's forearm. The woman's fingers lingered there, comfortable, familiar. Something cold and sharp twisted in Clara's stomach.

Without consciously deciding to move, Clara found herself walking toward them, her wedge sandals clicking against the terra cotta tiles with each determined step. The woman was still laughing, her perfectly straight teeth gleaming in the late afternoon sun, her body angled toward Jackson in that unmistakable way that screamed interest.

"Hey," Clara said, her voice sounding steadier than she felt. Three heads turned toward her simultaneously.

Parker's face broke into a wide smile. "Clara! Just in time. I was telling Samantha about the time you fell into the crawfish pond."

Jackson's eyes met hers, and for a moment, everything else faded away. She could read nothing in his expression except careful neutrality, which hurt worse than anger would have.

The woman—Samantha—extended her hand. "Samantha Boyd. You must be Clara. I've heard so much about you." Her smile seemed genuine, which somehow made it worse.

"All good things, I hope," Clara replied automatically, the social niceties her mother had drilled into her taking over while her mind raced. Who was this woman? How did she know Jackson? The questions burned in her throat, unasked.

She turned to Jackson, suddenly desperate to get him alone. "Can you meet me in the library in five minutes?"

Something flickered across his face—hesitation? Resignation? But he nodded and said, "I'll be there."

Clara's palms were slick with sweat as she turned away, her heart hammering against her ribs. She grabbed the gift she'd set down earlier, the carefully wrapped package now slightly crushed on one corner from being handled too much. The stairs to the library seemed steeper than she remembered, each step requiring deliberate concentration.

She veered into the restroom, pushing the door open with her shoulder. The cool water she splashed on her face did little to calm the riot of emotions swirling inside her. She stared at her reflection, at the woman looking back with wide, frightened eyes.

"This is stupid," she whispered to herself, gripping the edge of the sink. "It's just Cracker Jack." The childhood nickname felt foreign on her tongue after so long.

But it wasn't just Jackson anymore, was it? It was Jackson and whatever had happened in the weeks they'd been apart. It was

Jackson who might have moved on. It was Jackson who might break her heart for good this time.

In the back of her mind, a cruel voice whispered the truth she'd been avoiding: *because you're afraid this is the last time you'll see him.*

She straightened, squaring her shoulders. The tank top beneath her blouse suddenly felt like armor, its hidden message a declaration she wasn't sure she was brave enough to reveal. With one final glance at her reflection, she turned toward the door. Whatever happened in the library, at least she would know. The uncertainty had been killing her slowly for months.

The hallway stretched before her, the familiar path to the library now feeling like a walk to her own execution. Each step brought her closer to the moment that might change everything—again.

"No," she cried. She'd fight for him, for *them*.

Opening the door, she exited just as Jackson was rounding the top of the stairs.

Her heart lurched violently, a physical pain so acute she nearly gasped. Clara forced her suddenly dry mouth to form words as her pulse throbbed visibly at her wrists. "Hey." The single syllable emerged strangled. What else could she say? I miss you? I love you? I'll fight for you? A thousand confessions crowded her throat, none making it past her lips. "It's really good to see you."

He took her hand, and the familiar callus at the base of his thumb scraped against her skin—that small roughness she used to trace with her fingertip while he slept. The contact sent a current up her arm that settled somewhere beneath her ribs, a warmth both welcome and devastating.

"I couldn't agree more." He kissed her knuckles, his lips lingering a half-second longer than they should have in an act of torture that was so unfair. She stood suspended between wanting to pull away and wanting to fall against him, her body remembering his touch while her mind screamed caution.

"I wanted to congratulate you." She pressed her lips together, biting the inside of her cheek until she tasted copper, physically restraining the words that threatened to spill out—how she wanted to take him home, peel away the formal clothes, celebrate against walls and on floors. Instead, she handed him the bag of gifts she'd collected, her fingers trembling slightly. "You've worked so hard and you're a wonderful doctor. The field of emergency medicine is gaining a hero."

His eyes found hers, and the intensity in his stare pierced through her carefully constructed facade. The same eyes that had once mapped every inch of her face now saw straight through to her vulnerability, to the longing she couldn't disguise. As he always did, he sensed that she needed his touch and so he moved in, pulling her toward his warm strong body. The familiar scent of him—antiseptic soap layered over something distinctly *him*—made her dizzy with memory.

"I couldn't have done it without you, Bug."

"Bug." She whispered, the nickname catching in her throat like a physical thing. That single word transported her instantly to one of their suspended moments together in time, when she'd spent the entire night curled against him on the hood of his car, watching stars and talking until dawn. *You're like a lightning bug*, he'd said, *brightest when everything else is dark.*

His forehead furrowed, that familiar line appearing between his brows—the one she used to smooth away with her thumb when he studied too late. His stare turned curious, head tilting slightly to the right the way it always did when he was trying to read her. "I miss that name," she admitted.

First, she gave him the large binder book that she'd been working on for the better part of a year. She'd stayed up countless nights collecting these letters, her fingers cramping around the pen as she wrote to former patients—the written word a detail she found important since she'd asked for their own responses to be written. She recalled her eyes burning from crying over their responses. The binder felt unnaturally heavy as she passed it to him, her hands reluctant to release something that contained so much of her heart.

He regarded it with a quizzical look as he opened it. He read the first three of dozens of letters his patients had written, about him both as an EMT and an ER doctor, including the last letter, which was from her. He was a wonderful doctor and all of his patients loved him and she felt it important he realize that. Even if he didn't have a blood relative, he had the community that loved him.

"Doctor Olivier, you may not remember me, but I came in with my three-year-old daughter lying unresponsive in my arms. You will never know the desperation of a mother with a sick child whose fever that, no matter what I'd tried, continued to rise to dangerous levels. Your gentle words and assurance helped me through the darkest moment of that night. You are the first time I realized that God puts real angels in our path to help us through our journey here on earth. Thank you for being here with us."

Clara watched his face hungrily as he read, counting his breaths, noting how his left eyebrow lifted slightly—his tell for when something touched him deeply. She held her own breath, suddenly terrified she'd miscalculated, that this gift would seem presumptuous rather than meaningful.

But she needn't worry. For she knew him. Knew what he needed and when he needed it. Tears gathered in the corners of his eyes, clinging to his lashes before spilling onto the plastic binder cover as he closed the book. She remembered how he always cried from the left eye first, how he used to turn away to hide it. Now he let her see.

"Theresa and her daughter Emma. I remember every one of my patients."

Clara nodded, her throat constricting. "I know." She wrung her hands to keep from reaching for him, twisting her fingers until they ached, the physical pain a distraction from the magnetic pull she felt toward him. "And they remember you. You're so special to the people you've helped. You read it. You're an angel from heaven."

Jackson shook his head. "I'm no angel." His eyes found hers, holding her captive in their gaze. "You on the other hand..." He closed his eyes and breathed in deep as if drawing her essence into him. "You definitely fell from heaven." He swallowed thickly, his Adam's apple bobbing in a way that made her remember pressing her lips against his throat. "Thank you for this. I'll cherish it always."

She passed him a gift bag, their fingers brushing in the exchange. She felt the touch everywhere.

"Now what do we have here?" He pulled out the leather messenger bag and admired the brass plate engraved with his initials. "It's just perfect, Bug. I'll use it every day and think of you." He smiled. He dug around in the bag and removed the silly pillow-cases. "E.R. doctors do it stat." He laughed—full belly jiggling laughter that Clara felt like a physical blow to her chest, the sound so achingly familiar it nearly doubled her over. "I think I know just the place for these."

"Our bed. . . er . . . I mean your bed. I'd ordered them before . . ." The words escaped before she could trap them, and heat bloomed across her face and neck. Her shaky hand instinctively clasped her mouth, as if she could physically push the confession back in. The moment hung between them, her accidental truth laid bare, her longing exposed in two simple words: *our bed.*

"Bug." He pulled her into his chest, and for a traitorous moment, she let herself sink into the familiar scent of him—mint and coffee and that indefinable warmth that had once meant home. "I have something for you." He pulled a folded piece of paper from his pocket, the crease worn as if he'd opened and refolded it several times. "Meet me at this address at ten o'clock tonight."

Her throat constricted, each word an effort pushed past the knot of emotion. "I don't want my things. They remind me of you so I'll have to get new things." Even as she said it, she pictured the dog-eared copy of Steinbeck they'd read aloud to each other, his margin notes in her favorite poetry collection, the mug with the chipped rim that had somehow become hers—artifacts of a life that was crumbling away.

Jackson shook his head, the slight tremble in his fingers as he pointed to the paper in her hands betraying something she couldn't quite name. "Be there, Bug."

"Jackson." His name escaped her lips like a prayer, like a plea.

He walked through the door, his footsteps echoing against the library's hardwood floor.

"Jackson." She followed after him, her body moving before her mind could catch up, but he walked with purpose. He waved a friendly hand in the air without looking back, the casual gesture a stark contrast to the earthquake in her chest.

"Tonight, Bug."

The Tux

25

What was she supposed to do now? She stood frozen, the paper clutched in her hand, fingers unconsciously crushing it into her palm as if she could absorb its message through her skin. She assumed he had her things to give back—the final punctuation mark on their story. He didn't even want her to come to his apartment to get them. She couldn't think of better symbolism for the door slamming on their relationship. Each step he took away from her widened the distance between them exponentially.

But she wouldn't go because to do so would be admitting they were through and she just couldn't do that. Yet even as the thought formed, another voice whispered: *What if this is your last chance to see his face?*

Gah! Of course she'd go and pour all of the energy she had left into begging him to come back, reciting all the promises they'd made to each other.

She sat back on the chaise lounge in the library, the leather cool against her heated skin. The tears came without warning, ripped from somewhere deep and primal. She sobbed—not the pretty, cinematic crying of actresses, but the ugly, gasping heaves that bent her double. Each breath felt like inhaling glass. Her ribs ached with the effort of containing the storm inside her. The silence of the library, once a sanctuary they'd shared, now pressed against her ears like an accusation.

Between ragged breaths, she unfolded the paper, smoothing it with trembling hands. His handwriting—the familiar slant of letters she'd seen on grocery lists and love notes—blurred before her eyes.

How would she get through this? She cried until her body could no longer make tears, until her eyes felt like sandpaper and her head pounded with the dull rhythm of aftermath. The shadows in the library lengthened, time sliding away while she remained static, anchored to her grief.

It was getting late. She glanced at her watch—8:47p.m. She had half a mind to go to the stupid address and give Jackson a good swift kick in his balls. She pictured herself doing it, the momentary satisfaction, and then what? The same emptiness, but with one less chance of... of what? Reconciliation? Closure? She didn't know which terrified her more.

She sighed, a sound that contained all the words she hadn't said when she had the chance.

Her mother entered the library and sat next to her on the chaise, patting her hair like she used to when she was a child. "Are you ready?"

"Ready for what?" Her throat was raw from crying.

"To go see Jackson."

"He told you?"

"He told me to ensure you'd go."

"I don't want to go." She snorted because she couldn't breathe. Part of her wanted to go and release the words that pushed against her chest. "It's just too final. I can't do it."

"Honey"—she put her hands on Clara's shoulders—"things aren't always as they appear."

She was dumbfounded because Jackson had spoken those same words to her. "Mom?"

"I can't get into too much of it right now because we need to go. Trust me. You want to go to the address on that paper."

"But Mom—"

"Trust me." Her mother stood and gently guided Clara from the room. "Go and get yourself together. We'll leave at 9:30."

Clara stumbled into the bathroom, her eyes red and swollen from tears. She turned on the cold water, letting it run over her hands before splashing it onto her face, hoping to wash away the traces of her sorrow. As she dabbed her cheeks dry with a towel, she caught sight of herself in the mirror. Puffy eyes and blotchy skin stared back at her. With a deep sigh, she reached for a tube of light foundation and patted it gently onto her face. The cool cream was soothing as it smoothed over her skin, masking the evidence of her crying jag.

Her thoughts wandered back to Jackson, each memory pricking at fresh wounds. She imagined him waiting at that unfamiliar address surrounded by boxes filled with remnants of their shared life: mismatched mugs from weekend flea markets, photos capturing laughter now lost to time, and that silly cactus they had named "Spike."

Shaking off the reverie, Clara applied a soft touch of blush to bring some color back to her cheeks. She uncapped a tube of raspberry lip gloss and swiped it across her mouth—a small armor against vulnerability. The sweet scent lingered in the air as she closed the cap with determination.

With one last glance in the mirror, Clara squared her shoulders. Her heart might be fragile right now, but she'd face whatever awaited at 10 p.m. with as much composure as she could muster.

In the car, Clara's mind short circuited as she tried on different scenarios. If Jackson involved her mother, he must really want her stuff gone. And why meet at this weird address? Maybe Samantha was already living with him. A gasp escaped her throat as she rested her head against the window.

Her mom placed a reassuring hand on her knee. "Easy, Clara. I promise you're creating an impossible situation in your mind."

"What am I supposed to think?"

"I suggest you stop thinking for the time being."

Her mother reached over to turn on the radio. The volume drowned out Clara's thoughts as John Legend's "All of Me" blared through the speakers. The lyrics wrapped around her like a bitter-sweet hug, tugging at memories she'd tried to shelve away—Jackson singing in a cartoonishly high-pitched voice, pulling her into an offbeat slow dance in the middle of their living room. Her throat tightened, the familiar notes winding through her like a siren's song.

She wanted to hear it now, wanted to believe it was a sign they would find their way back to each other, despite it all. She bit her lip and blinked hard, refusing to let the tears fall again. Her mother's hand reached out to change the station. "No, I want to hear it."

The song encompassed exactly what they were to each other. They loved each other unconditionally in spite of all the imperfec-tions, of which there were many—her scars, Jackson's moodiness from never dealing with his loss. But they'd found their way through his unlit paths together, hadn't they? She at least thought they had.

Did he not feel she'd lightened up his dark streets? He certainly had lit hers up. He'd made her confident enough to take the reins at the deli, to confront her father about wanting to switch gears from college to cheese monger. He'd made her feel beautiful again. If she had not instilled in him the same feelings he'd instilled in her then everyone was right . . . they didn't belong together.

However, she refused to believe any of it. She'd felt his need for her time and again. She knew she was his light.

Sometimes the greatest profession of love is to let someone go.

Parker had said that. Could Jackson have pushed her away to save her relationship with her family? She had a sneaking suspicion he had.

However, it didn't mean he had to run to the arms of the first woman he saw. That hurt. She was so confused.

They parked on the curb somewhere in downtown Baton Rouge. The streetlights cast long, flickering shadows, making every-thing look different and yet somehow familiar. She sat in the car, looking left, then right, the buildings holding echoes of memories she couldn't quite pin down. She blinked and realization struck.

"Hey, we're at Bon Mange. What are we doing here?" It was the restaurant where they'd had Jackson's birthday dinner. The sudden rush of recollection made her heart skip.

"I can assure you we're not going to Bon Mange." Her mother's voice held an edge of mystery, but her eyes were gentle with understanding. "We're going across the street." She indicated the direction with a toss of her head, her earrings swinging in the dim light.

Clara followed her gaze to a blank storefront, her confusion deepening. "Mom, you know this place?"

"I do." Her mother's smile was secretive, a conspirator in hopes Clara hadn't dared breathe into being.

They crossed the street, the cool night air nipping at Clara's cheeks and mixing with adrenaline in her veins. Her mother opened the door to the empty building and motioned her inside. Clara hesitated on the threshold, her eyes struggling to adjust to the complete darkness. She took a cautious step in and saw nothing.

"There's no one here." Her voice echoed back to her, uncertainty lacing each word.

But then, suddenly, overhead lights came to life, their brightness stinging her eyes. She blinked into the light, and as the room came into focus, she staggered back in shock. Her entire family stood before her, their smiles wide and welcoming. "Is this some kind of intervention?" she whispered, her voice shaking.

Her mother was behind her now, cupping her shoulders with a reassuring touch. "We're all here, baby, because we love you." The words wrapped around her like a soft, warm blanket. Clara's breath caught in her chest, the sight and sentiment overwhelming and impossible to fully absorb in the moment.

She had imagined Jackson waiting for her with boxes of old things—evidence of a life she thought was over—but she had never imagined this.

Her gaze scanned from brother to brother. Her sisters-in-law were all there as well, filling the room with a happy chaos. In sum, six sets of St. Martins stood before her, along with her mom and dad. Her shock made way for wonder as she took in the scene. Her eyes landed on a large, colorful sign, THE COWBELL: Artisan Cheeses, leaning against three cheese cases. The middle case was operational and packed to the brim with cheese. Her jaw dropped further. It was unbelievable. She observed her brothers. They all smiled at her with mischief and love.

Then something clicked.

Her smile slowly stretched across her face and she let out the breath she'd been holding. "I love it! But what's going on?" This was beyond anything her family could have pulled together on their own. She'd only told one person about her cheese shop dreams. One person who would have remembered THE COWBELL name.

Footsteps thudded across the floor behind her brothers. Her heart raced, each beat loud in her ears. She couldn't see who it was but heard the sound of determined shoe soles hitting the wood floor. She leaned to the side, craning her neck for a glimpse. Then she saw him. Her knees weakened and her smile waned, replaced by shock.

"Jackson," she whispered. He wore a classic black tuxedo complete with bowtie and looked more ravishing than she'd ever remembered.

He stood before her, strikingly formal, and offered a nervous chuckle. She'd been noting every little way he had changed in the few weeks since they had broken up—the slight unruliness in his hair, the way his shoulders drifted forward in a hunch she had never noticed before. He stuffed his hands in his pockets, his gaze falling to the floor for a few seconds.

The room was so quiet she could hear the blood rushing through her ears, everyone holding their breath, every set of eyes fixed on him and her. When his gaze returned to hers, she knew he'd regained his composure. The look he gave her was full of an intense resolve and a strange softness, as though he were about to share something that would change everything.

"Clara." He took a deep breath before speaking, his voice full of sincerity. "I owe you and your family an apology." He took her hands in his—gentle, steady, and sure—and gazed intently into her eyes as though no one else was in the room with them. "What I did was wrong." Clara blinked, her mind racing to make sense of it all. "No matter how much I loved you, I shouldn't have touched you. I should have waited." His voice was thick with emotion, and it quivered like the tension she felt in her heart. "But I was weak." He dropped his gaze to where their hands were linked and then back up to her face. "I needed your innocence and goodness that day"—his voice cracked and broke, and Clara felt it physically as a shiver ran up her spine—"and every day since." The rawness of his words hung in the air between them.

Her brothers exchanged glances, their faces turning from expectant to serious, their usual teasing absent as they watched the scene unfold. Her sisters-in-law all stood silent, the smiles slipping from their faces, replaced by expressions of curiosity and concern. But more than anything, Clara felt the weight of her mother's eyes on her, urging her to listen, to hear.

If she'd had the presence of mind, she might have laughed at the idea of Jackson standing here and saying these things, but instead she was frozen, stunned—her body like lead, her heart beating wildly, and the rest of her unable to move. If she'd had the strength, she might have pulled her hands back in anger or surprise, but his grip was warm and steady, and she couldn't bring herself to let go. He was here. After everything, he was here.

The silence grew heavy, and for a sliver of a moment, Clara worried he might stop talking. But his lips parted, and he spoke again.

"I've loved you since I was seventeen and you were seven." His eyes held steady on hers as moisture collected in them, the words raw, true, and finally out in the open. Clara was completely quiet and overwhelmed as Jackson continued to speak.

"It all started with your breakfast announcements. Night and day flowed with the current. Sorrow in my wake, emptiness ahead with nothing to push against the tide and upset life's disappointing balance. I'd witnessed what happened to my parents when they'd attempted to veer off course and I was afraid to live life. With your calm reassurance and determined spirit, you alone brought me out of the shadows of my nightmares and let me follow at your heels into life. I fell in love with you as you delicately reintroduced me to life and all it had to offer. I want to love you for the rest of my life."

He spoke as if nothing else mattered, his words urgent, raw, and steady. They made Clara's heart miss a beat and then race to catch up. This scene was not one she had ever dared to imagine. "I got a job at Baton Rouge General," he admitted, and Clara felt the room sway around her.

She tried to process his meaning, to make herself understand how he could be here, like this, saying these words. "I used the promise of my salary to get you a line of credit for this space." Clara drew a sharp breath, her senses barely keeping pace with him. "You can order what you need as far as stocking the case and anything else you will need." His gaze was direct and insistent, his voice full of conviction. "I believe in you, Bug." The old nickname was a balm to Clara's heart, softening and healing all at once. "I'll need you to sell some cheese." His smile was tender yet triumphant, a shimmering contrast to the tiredness in his eyes.

While he was like a man transformed, Clara remained utterly still, rooted in place. She was stunned and speechless as Jackson continued.

From the depths of his heart, a plea emerged, whispered with a raw vulnerability that stirred the very air around her. "Bug, you're my greatest love. My greatest hope is for your family, *our* family, to accept us.

Us.

He looked around at all the faces in the room. "I know what it means to lose your family. I wouldn't wish that on anyone." He held her hands in his and looked down at them, rubbing his thumbs over them. "I know I messed up over and over again but please just consider all that we are before making any emotional and hasty decisions about a future with me."

His eyes met hers. "If I haven't lost you, I should send you back to them. Should they not accept me, I should send you back. But I tried that already and it nearly killed me. I'm not strong enough to turn you away. I will crumble under the weight of life without you by my side."

A fleeting smile faded from his lips, replaced by eyes brimming with unspoken sorrows, each line etched on his face telling a tale of silent battles fought alone. "To have them welcome us would be a gift beyond measure, a validation of our bond. But know this, my darling: I cannot bear to walk away from you and I promise to never do it again."

Cue the ugly cry. Huge gasping breaths left her body at his words. She leaned into him and wiped her face on his tux. His strong hands pulled her back so he could look upon her face. "We're better together. Let's tread this path together, navigating the unknown with steadfast resolve. I will continue my work at the station to support us through any trials that may come. You can trust that you will never want for anything as long as I'm alive."

Descending gracefully to one knee, he made his intentions known. "I hope you know I never wanted to breakup but I under-stand the pain of losing family and I never want that for you. I only did what I did out of love for you, even though it killed me a little every day to be without you."

She squeezed him to her body. "Sometimes the greatest profes-sion of love is letting someone go."

He smiled at her as tears made it to his lips. "That's right."

"Parker told me that."

Jackson face took on a look of skepticism. "That's pretty deep for Parker."

Clara scrunched up her nose, thinking of her last memory of Parker while Jackson reached into his pocket and pulled out a silver engagement ring.

"I don't have a lot of spare change right now, but when I do," he held the ring up to the light," this will get better."

She lowered to her knees in front of him, and like he always did, he pulled her into him, resting her on his thighs so she wouldn't be kneeling on the floor. He looked deeply into her eyes, "Clara, I hope one day to regain your trust." He gasped a breath. "The only lie I ever told you was—"

She covered his lips with her finger. "I know why you lied. I know it was your only lie, and I trust you with my life." In the back of her mind, unanswered questions lingered about the woman in the pencil skirt. In her heart she knew Jackson would have never betrayed their love so the answers did not even matter.

In that moment suspended in time, he sealed their fates with the simple ring he delicately placed on her finer, whispering vows that echoed through the walls of their shared sanctuary. "Together, we shall weather any storm that may come our way. My heart is yours forever. Marry me."

Clara's heart swelled with emotion, overwhelmed by the depth of Jackson's love and vulnerability. She reached out a trembling hand to touch his tear-stained cheek, her voice barely above a whisper. "Jackson, your love fills me with strength I never knew I had. I can't imagine my life without you either."

Jackson's eyes searched hers, a mixture of hope and fear reflected in their depths. "I know it won't be easy, Bug. But together, we can face anything that comes our way."

A flicker of determination crossed Clara's face as she met his gaze. "I choose us, Jackson. I choose to walk this path with you, no matter the challenges."

Tears of relief welled up in Jackson's eyes as he enveloped her in a tight embrace. "Bug, God, you're the other half of my heart."

As they stood, locked in each other's arms, a sense of peace settled between them, a silent understanding that they were bound together by a love that could weather any storm.

Jackson nuzzled Clara behind her ear, the curtain of her hair affording them both some privacy. Together they found solace in the knowledge that their love was a force stronger than any obstacle they might face. And as they whispered promises to one another, their souls intertwined in a dance of eternal unity, ready to take on whatever the future held for them.

"Did my family know you were proposing tonight?" Clara whispered in his ear.

"No, I only told them about the store," he whispered back. "I no longer care if they accept me. If you do, that's all that matters."

Together, as one, they faced her family. Jackson spoke first. "I lost my mom and dad. I know what it means to lose your family. It isn't something I want Clara to experience, but I don't think any of you want that either. Can you see a way for us to be together and also be part of your lives?"

Mom came forward with arms extended, followed by Dad. "Of course we can. You're our son. Let's move forward leaving the past in the past. I understand how it happened."

Dad put an arm around Jackson. "It's not a bad thing. You and Clara are destined, but sometimes society doesn't understand the people who live within it. You two survived things some people will never have to face. You don't owe anyone an explanation. I know how much you love Clara. Any father would be lucky to have you as a son-in-law. I'm extra lucky that I get to claim you as a son as well."

They hugged and cried. After a while Jackson looked to his best friend in this world. "Clay, your support would mean everything to me. I can't . . . I don't want to come between you and Clara." His deep, shaky breath spoke of the turmoil inside.

Clay stepped forward and pulled Jackson in for a hug. "I've seen a lot over these past few weeks. You two aren't conventional I'll say that, but you have my support. Anyone who opposes your love will have to do it through me."

Her mom's arms enveloped all three of them. "Honey, you and Jackson always had an intense connection. Your eyes always found one another in a crowded room, even at public venues—if he was there, you'd gravitate toward him. I've watched it play out for years." She turned her attention to Jackson. "I love you, Jackson. I have no doubts in your abilities to take care of my baby girl." She pulled him to her and hugged him tightly for several seconds, maybe minutes. She could hear Jackson's cries.

The door opened and Samantha walked through it. "Sorry I'm late." She handed them a bottle of champagne. "Congratulations."

Jackson took the bottle, "Thank you," he said, and then looked to Clara. "You remember Samantha. She's the Realtor who helped make all of this possible."

Suddenly all of the questions Clara had surrounding the woman standing before her became resolved.

"I can't stay long, but I wanted to pop in and make sure you had everything you needed."

"We're great. Thank you," Jackson said.

"I hope you two will be very happy."

She hugged them and then she was gone. Clara's jealously had been unfounded, and she felt more than a little silly.

All of her brothers and their wives approached and offered their congratulations. And then there was Clay. He pulled her to his mammoth chest. "Clara Bear, I could never leave you, not for anything. Even if you marry this guy." His thumb gestured toward Jackson. "Truth is, Jackson is a great guy. One of the best."

Clay's eyes met Jackson's. "She's my Clara Bear, I had to be sure she wouldn't get hurt. I'll protect her with my life until the day I die." He shrugged. "It is what it is, but I gotta say I'm glad it's you. I know you love her and will stop at nothing to keep her happy. I love you, man."

Clay and Jackson hugged again while huge, salty tears streamed down her face and soaked into her shirt like rivulets of relief and joy. This was the best night she could remember, a night when everything had fallen into place, a beacon of promise heralding the first of many more.

Moments ago, they had stood at the brink of unimagined futures, pledging their lives in a spontaneous act of devotion, without the promise of family. Now, they were here, together, basking in the glow of newfound certainty that included every one of their family members.

Jackson, with an eye for detail and a flair for romance, had set up wine, cheese, olives, crackers, and various other fixings, turning the empty space into a feast fit for celebration. He orchestrated the scene with such thoughtful precision, Clara couldn't help but smile as she watched him seamlessly create a joyful gathering. Their small shop transformed into a haven of love and laughter, a sanctuary where their engagement was celebrated with the very people whose acceptance made it all sweeter. Everyone talked and laughed, toasting to the life they would build together. Clara watched Jackson, love-struck, as the sulky, consistent pout he'd carried in recent days seemed finally to have vanished. For a moment, she missed seeing it on his face, but that was before he caught her eyes and the telltale sparkle in them revealed all of their shared secrets. His sexy smolder was back and stronger than ever. She sat wrapped in his arms, barely able to wait to be in his bed tonight and wake-up in his arms in the morning.

Clara loved her family, but she found herself glad when, around two in the morning, they started to disburse. They had all been there, sharing in the joy that so recently had felt elusive. For years, she and Jackson had behaved like thieves in the night, hiding their bond from the world, but with each passing hour, that weight grew lighter. Her family was finally showing Jackson their love and acceptance as her beloved. Her heart overflowed with gratitude and relief.

She and Jackson accompanied Clay and Eve to the door of the restaurant, the last two left from the night's festivities. Clara noticed how they lingered—either wanting to savor the moment or perhaps to smooth over the rough edges of the past. Clay held Clara's hands in his. "Will you forgive me for being an obstinate asshat?"

She smiled at Clay, her eyes twinkling with genuine affection and humor. "Of course I will. You've been an obstinate asshat for an extended period, but I'm getting used to it. Truly, I just feel sorry for Eve. She has to live with you."

Clay offered a mock-offended gasp, then turned to Eve with laughter in his eyes. "Don't feel sorry for Eve. Not for one second. She has me right where she wants me, and she knows it." His wink was exaggerated and playful, filled more with love than arrogance. Eve yawned against his chest, leaning into him with comfortable familiarity.

Eve cocked one eye open and smirked. "And well-trained."

"Ugh. I don't want to witness that." Clara scrunched her nose and smiled.

"I love you, Clara Bear." Clay placed a loose strand of her hair behind her ear, the affection in the gesture touching Clara deeply.

"I love you back, Clay. Always," she said, embracing him with all the warmth of a sister.

Clay pulled back, looking at Jackson with a measure of newfound respect. "Jackson, I wouldn't trust anyone else with my Clara Bear and you know how overprotective I am. I know you'll treat her well. For what it's worth, there was never a doubt in my mind about that. Really. I'm glad it's you, and I'm sorry about the face punch. I was wrong about you two." He paused, sincerity lacing his words. "I can see you live to give her the world. I'm happy for you both." They hugged, a true brotherly embrace that spoke of forgiveness and a promising tomorrow.

Jackson nodded as the weight of Clay's words settled over him like the support he had craved for so long. "I would have done the same thing for a baby sister of mine, Clay. I'm sorry for my deception." Jackson pulled away, a smile of relief on his lips.

"Hey, I get it." Clay shrugged, a cheeky grin lighting up his face. "Love makes you do crazy shit." He glanced down at his wife, whose head now rested heavily against his chest. "Looks like I better get her home before she starts drooling all over me."

Jackson locked the door behind them. "I'm parked in the back. We can—"

Clara jumped against Jackson's body, wrapping her arms around his neck and her legs around his waist. "Cracker Jack. I love you."

He giggled. "I'm glad because there's like a hundred pounds of cheese to sell."

"Can I see my ring now?" She looked down into his eyes and watched the lines across his forehead become more pronounced. He was embarrassed about the ring.

With her in his arms he walked to one of the stools at the counter and set her gently down. He dug around in his jacket. "As soon as I can, I'm going to make this ring right. This one is only temporary." He placed the ring on her finger. It was very simple with its silver band and small diamond in the center.

"Jackson, I want this ring. Forever. This is the ring I want to peer down at when we're old and gray because when I look at it, I'll recall this moment. It's perfect." She couldn't imagine ever wanting to replace their memories with something else.

His hands cradled her jaw, and his thumbs swirled in her cheeks. "God, I've missed your dimples." He kissed her. His touch was slow, reverent, and sweet. Like he was discovering her all over again, for the first time.

Don't Think, Just Remember

26

Clara and Jackson rode back to the apartment with fingers intertwined. At each red light, they found it impossible to resist the pull of one another, leaning over to kiss with a fervor that left them breathless, even as the impatient honks from other cars made them giggle like giddy teenagers. The urgency of the horns only added to the thrill, a minor distraction from the bliss that enveloped them.

As street lamps flashed by, Clara couldn't stop herself from stealing glances at her hand, mesmerized by the way her ring caught the light, and even more so by what it represented.

"I love the way you look in a tux," she said, her eyes tracing the line of his jaw. It made her heart race, knowing they belonged to each other without reservation.

He arched an eyebrow, a teasing grin curving his lips. "I'm glad, though I think you'd look much better in it." He pulled her in for another quick kiss before a yellow light turned red.

She giggled with a happiness that seemed to reinvent itself with every moment they spent together.

Once home, they barely noticed how hot the apartment was. They bounded across the floor in a flurry of laughter and love's intoxicating warmth, leaving a trail of clothes from the door to their bedroom.

Jackson laid her back onto the bed, careful and tender, his lips brushing her cheek as he moved down the length of her body, igniting a firestorm of anticipation and delight. He removed her sandals and tucked her feet in his lap. As he pressed his thumbs into the arch of her foot, Clara sighed from the indulgent pleasure and sank back into the pillows with languid abandon.

"Jackson, that day Clay brought me to you in the hospital I thought . . . I thought if you didn't make it my life wouldn't be worth living." Clara's voice hitched with the memory of it, the terrible unknown stretching before her in that sterile hallway, terror gripping her so completely she could barely breathe. She ran her fingers through his hair, each touch a desperate reassurance that he was by her side, warm and alive. "I couldn't imagine a world where you didn't exist, where it was just me, alone," she said, her voice breaking. "Those nights when I didn't know if I'd lost you for good, it was—" She stopped, unable to find the words for the nothingness she had felt.

"Clara." Jackson whispered her name, a gentle plea for her not to relive those days.

She shook her head, insistent. "It was hard on me when you gave up on us, you know." Her eyes, glistening with vulnerability, locked onto his as she spoke. "I know it hurt you too, and that you were suffering because you thought you were giving me the gift of family." Her voice softened, the intensity of her words met with the tenderness of her touch. "But you know what?" She paused, wanting him to feel the magnitude of her resilience.

He kissed her lips, a feathery brush that was all love and gratitude, smiling against them as if sealing a promise. "What's that, Bug?" His voice was saturated with hope.

"I'm so tired of everyone telling me what's best for me," she said, a fierce determination breaking through the rawness of her confession. "I know what I need to survive in this life and it's you." Her resolve was unwavering, stronger than even she expected. "I'm really kind of angry about the whole ordeal." She felt the burn of injustice over all they'd lost, over the months spent heartbroken when they could have been together.

He chuckled next to her ear, his breath a soft caress that sent shivers down her spine. "If this is you angry," he teased, his voice a low rumble of amusement, "I'd hate to see you irate. I'd have to fear for my life."

The ache of the past was replaced with tender relief as the sound of her laughter filled the room. He knew now he had under-estimated her, this brilliant and headstrong woman who loved him without condition or restraint. Through the whole relationship ordeal, Clara had managed her family and she had fought against Jackson's decision to push her away, a fact that both thrilled and humbled him. He inhaled, breathing in her presence, and she could hear his slight moan when his lips closed around her earlobe. "I just didn't want to leave you alone, Bug."

She stood and pushed playfully at his chest. "Are you making fun of me?"

"No, Bug, I love your spirit. I've missed you." He caught her hand as she rose, pulling her in close. She didn't resist. He turned her so her back pressed against him and his hands wrapped around her body, clasping her just under her breasts with a possessive tenderness. "You have no idea how much," he said, resting his head on her shoulder as if he could never be close enough to her. "You're right. I've undervalued your opinions and actions when it came to our relationship. I thought you needed the world and family, and I broke us apart to get you that. I know that now." He paused, his words measured and sincere. "I'm hoping you'll give me this one, Clara. I'm sorry."

His embrace tightened. "I know what it is to live without family —the pain of having no one, the soul-crushing absence of a place to call home, the unrelenting pit of loneliness that eats at you every single second. I never wanted that pain for you." She knew how much it hurt him to say those words.

His voice wavered with the weight of what he had survived. "Even if it meant I'd be living in pain at the crushing loss of your love and light from my life." He kissed the curve of her neck, feeling the rhythm of her heart as if syncing himself to it. "But I'm too weak to live without you," he confessed, his voice raw and unguarded. "I thought I was strong, but I'm not. I concede, Bug. I can't do it." There was desperation in the way he clung to her, his every word a plea for her understanding and forgiveness.

"But now we don't have to." He pulled her closer still, every inch of his body enveloping hers, a promise that he would never let her go again. "Please don't be angry with me on our engagement night. Not tonight." The vulnerability in his voice was staggering, and Clara felt the depth of his longing down to her core, knowing now how much he had endured to give her what he thought she needed, and how they had both suffered as a result.

"I'm not angry with you. I don't think I've ever been angry with you. I think it's impossible." She pulled from him to turn and gaze into his eyes. "I want to ask you something that I've asked you before, but this time I want you to answer." He grimaced, indicating he knew what was coming. "Will you?"

He swallowed, the action making a hollow thud in his throat. He nodded as he unzipped her shorts and let them fall to her ankles. "I will, but I want you naked. At least give me that."

"I want you naked too." She started on the cummerbund around his waist.

He had her down to her tank top. "My heart belongs to an E.R. doctor." He smiled and kissed her lips.

"It does."

His gaze on her was unyielding, unblinking. "I'm glad." He pulled her shirt off, along with her bra. They stood before one another naked.

"Okay, we're naked." She cleared her throat.

"All right, shoot." He squared his shoulders, prepared for her assault. But her questions weren't meant to hurt him.

She shook her head. "Nah uh."

"Are we done with that line of questioning then?" The lilt in his voice sounded hopeful.

She shook her head, a flutter of uncertainty passing across her face before hardening into resolve. "Get on the bed." She pushed him until he sat against the headboard, her fingers lingering for a moment against his chest, feeling his heartbeat quicken beneath her touch. On her knees, she crawled between his legs, the mattress dipping beneath her weight. His brow hitched as he looked down at her, a question in his eyes that she answered by taking his growing length into her hand and creating a physical bridge to cross the emotional chasm she was about to make him leap.

"I want to know about your parents," she said, her voice softer than she intended. "I barely remember them. I can't even recall what they looked like, but I remember them coming to the estate for a barbecue." A fragment of memory surfaced—his mother's perfume, something like jasmine and rain, and how it had mingled with the smoke from the grill. Her thumb traced small circles against his thigh as she spoke, a subtle reassurance.

Her tongue swirled against his heat as he inhaled through clenched teeth, his stomach muscles tightening, not just from pleasure but from the sudden intrusion of the past into this intimate moment. His fingers tangled in her hair, neither pulling her closer nor pushing her away—suspended in indecision.

"Why would you want to know about that? They're dead." His voice cracked on the last word, and she noticed how his breathing shortened, how his jaw worked against emotions he rarely displayed.

Awe, Cracker Jack. The childhood nickname slipped through her mind with a tenderness that surprised her. She was instantly sad for him—not the performative sympathy of adulthood, but the raw, helpless sadness of recognizing a wound that would never fully heal. She paused her movements, resting her cheek against his thigh and looking up to catch his gaze, really catch it, until he couldn't look away.

"They created you," she whispered, "and their spirit lives on in you." Her free hand found his, their fingers interlacing in a grip that felt more naked than anything else they were doing. "Of course I want to know about the people responsible for bringing you into the world." The unspoken thought hung between them: *I want to understand every part that made you, especially the broken pieces.*

He inhaled deeply, the air catching slightly in his throat. "My father was a civil engineer, educated at Stanford. Eventually he became the city manager for Baton Rouge. My mother was a non-profit lawyer, educated at NYU." The facts flowed easily—credentials and titles—the safe territory of public achievement rather than private truth.

She looked up, releasing him from her lips, her eyes holding his with a gentle insistence that made his pulse quicken with something adjacent to fear. "I don't want to know about their resumes. I want to know the intimate details of their day-to-day lives. What did they like? What did they not like?" Grasping him in her hands, her touch both tender and commanding, she said, "I'm going to make love to you with my mouth while you talk. Don't think, just remember."

As she took him into her mouth he groaned—a sound rising from a place deeper than desire, from that vault where he'd locked away the memories of his parents as people rather than positions. His shoulders tensed as he placed his hands on her back, massaging her skin, his fingertips betraying a slight tremor. The physical intimacy was familiar territory; the emotional excavation she requested was not. She understood that talking about his parents was difficult for him. Nonetheless, he knew she believed it was crucial for him to confront those memories, so she encouraged him to open up about them.

"My father," he began, his breathing shallow against the dual sensations of pleasure and exposure, "he collected vintage fountain pens but never used them. Just displayed them. Afraid to actually put ink to paper." The irony of this detail—this first real truth he'd offered—wasn't lost on him as her warmth enveloped him, drawing out more than just physical response.

"I guess one of the earliest memories I have is taking one of those Mexican serape Saltillo blankets down to the park on the Fourth of July. We walked from the house hand in hand." His fingers feathered through her hair. "We left early; Mom had packed a picnic lunch. Dad loved her fried chicken, so did I for that matter. It was delicious and she had this little secret she made us swear not to tell anyone . . . she put an entire bottle of Tabasco in buttermilk and marinated her chicken in that. I became privileged to that information as a teen. Anyway, I guess I was about five years old around the time of the picnic. We made a day of it. Dad brought a Frisbee and a baseball, and mitts and we just hung out at the park. We'd claimed a great piece of real estate from which to watch the fireworks show and were content to relax there all day."

This was the most she'd ever heard about his parents or his childhood. She didn't want him to stop talking, but she felt a pressing need to hold him, so she straddled his legs, wrapped her arms around his neck, and kissed him. In return his lips were punishing in their rhythm. He needed her. She broke the kiss and said, "What else do you remember?"

He closed his eyes and shuddered in her arms. "The moment I found out they were gone. I remember like it happened yesterday." His voice broke. "I prayed and prayed that night. I prayed on my knees until my legs went numb." The intensity of his voice was erratic, loud and soft. "I honestly thought I would wake up and they'd be there. They weren't of course. But you were there. Your mother and father were there. Hell, your whole family was there. After the first few months I began to resent all of you. What you had. But it became so easy to love you."

Forehead to forehead, she caressed his jaw in her hands and gently kissed him. "I love you, Jackson."

"I don't know what else to say." His voice was dry and raspy. Tears rested on his lower eyelids.

"You don't have to say anything more." Now that he'd broken through the barrier, she knew in time he'd tell her more, but for now she needed him inside of her as much as he needed to be inside of her.

Slowly, she rotated her hips so that her core rubbed his hardness, bathing it in her moisture. The familiar rhythm came back to her body like muscle memory, though it had been weeks since they'd been together. Three months of empty sheets and one-sided conversations with his ghost. He fisted the root, holding it in place so that she could take him in.

As she lowered herself his tears fell from the ledge where they'd perched. She hadn't expected his vulnerability – Jackson, who had always been so careful to keep his emotions locked away. Something had broken open in him. She kissed the tears away, tasting the salt on her lips.

"Bug, I need you. Thank you for this and for never once giving up on me."

The nickname squeezed her heart—he'd called her that since the first morning when she'd appeared in his room, nagging him to come down to breakfast. His voice cracked on the words, and she saw the utter devotion in his eyes. The way he loved her was intense and deep but now it was also honest. They'd been accepted.

"No thanks needed. I will always be your lighthouse. We will guide each other through every storm, never ceasing to shine light onto the path."

His warm lips molded to hers and then he took her bottom lip between his teeth and moaned like he tasted the finest wine. He smelled like that sandalwood soap she'd bought him for his birthday —he'd kept using it even after she left. The thought made her throat tighten. Masculine hands at her hips gripped her hard and turned her so that she was now beneath him. A strand of her hair caught between them, pulling slightly, but neither stopped to fix it, the small pain a reminder that this was real, not another of her desperate dreams.

He pumped into her deeply and sucked a nipple into his mouth. Her fingers found the small scar on his shoulder – from the bicycle accident that had first made her realize how, in an instant, all of this could end. It made silly things they'd argued about like money and schedules seem superficial. The only thing that really mattered was life.

Normally she could hold out and wait for him, but the intensity of his possession of her body had her ready to lose her mind. It had been too long since he'd been inside of her, and she needed the release only he could bring – needed to feel whole again, to know that despite everything that had happened between them, this connection remained the one constant.

"Jackson, I need to come," she whispered.

"Are you saying you want this to be quick?"

"How about we do it quick now, take a break for a slice of left-over cake from the party and then we explore each other until noon?"

He growled on top of her. Then he thrust into her hard and pushed her legs toward her chest. His need was voracious and for the first time in their two-year relationship he let himself go. Lost in their ecstasy he moaned, pounding repeatedly into her body. Energized by his actions, she met him thrust for thrust moving her hips to allow him to go as deep as possible. Her hands raked down his back and he cried out her name as he emptied into her. Her back arched as she spiraled out of control around him.

A surge of emotion washed over her, overwhelming her with a profound sense of gratitude and love for the man lying beside her. She leaned in to kiss him, a sweet and lingering connection that spoke volumes without words.

In that moment, they knew their bond was accepted, as it had been forged through trials and tribulations that only deepened their love for each other. As they lay there, basking in the warmth of their shared love, it felt as if their journey was just beginning because they'd finally be able to show off their bond to the world.

With a contented sigh, Clara nestled closer to Jackson, their hearts beating in perfect harmony. In each other's arms, they found solace, comfort, and unwavering devotion.

As the world outside continued to spin, they remained entwined, two souls bound together in a love that would withstand any storm.

Together, they faced the future, knowing that as long as they had each other, they were unstoppable. And with that thought, they drifted back into a peaceful slumber, wrapped up in the safety and security of their love.

Epilogue

They didn't want a long engagement, so they'd placed their names on a waiting list. Amazingly, a date became available in December.

Today—she—would—be—his.

So many changes had occurred for them over the past few months. Jackson had started his job as an E.R. physician. Clara hadn't thought much would change when he took his full doctor position in emergency medicine because he'd been a resident there, but she was wrong. The section chief was in a hurry to mentor Jackson into the director of clinical services position and his hours were long and tedious, but he loved what he was doing, and they loved their newfound freedom as a couple in love. Every day she'd pop in for a visit with him and was content to wait however long was needed for a window of time when they could be together, even if only for a moment.

Her little cheese shop was holding its own as well. By the third month in operation, she was able to pay her own overhead and food costs and even put a little money away. She loved talking to people and getting them passionate about cheese, olives, jams, and honey. The strangest thing about her gig was that she paired wine with cheese and made recommendations. At the age of nineteen she was allowed to sell wine, but she wasn't allowed to drink it. Consequently, she wasn't moving too much wine. She was relieved they hadn't stocked much of the stuff.

On top of her new business and his new role as E.R. doctor, they also were in the process of moving. Her father had purchased a home for them in Auggie and Mia's neighborhood. Jackson was adamant that he be the one to provide for all of her needs, but she knew her dad had always dreamed of giving his little girl her first home. He finally had to agree to let Jackson pay him back when he was in a position to do so.

With work and moving, Clara was happy that the wedding plans came together seamlessly. Jackson gave in to tradition and let her parents pay for most of the wedding. She had the perfect dress, the perfect setting, and the perfect man.

Her mom and all of her sisters-in-law were sitting in the parlor of the church. Clara's dream was about to come true. In an hour she would walk down the aisle of the St. Louis Cathedral and marry Jackson. She'd asked Eve to be her maid of honor and as she stood in her silky white dress, she scanned the room. She couldn't imagine this day without a single one of her sisters-in-law or her mother. In that moment she knew Jackson had been right—she needed her family. He had selflessly sacrificed his need of her to give her back to her family. She shuddered at the memory of living without him. She would never have to again. And best of all, her family had given their blessing and shown their love and support for the union.

Women hovered all around her. Brook and Isa were busy steaming wrinkles she couldn't even see out of her gown. Jenny and Lacie pinned her hair, and her mother touched up her lip gloss. Jessie, Eve, and Mia were busy fluffing all the bouquets and discussing the processional.

The hour passed quickly, and they all lined up at the door leading to the sanctuary. She stood to the side and watched the processional line get shorter and shorter. Excitement flitted in her stomach, and she knew she'd never been this happy before. "First Day of My Life" by Bright Eyes drifted through the speakers. Her father walked her to the doorway arch leading from the foyer into the sanctuary. She told him to stand there with her until the first verse was complete. No one expected the quirky song. She guessed they were listening for Mendelssohn's Wedding March, but she'd saved this little surprise for this moment.

Jackson turned the moment she and her father filled the arch. He always knew when she was in a room. This knowledge caused a large smile to break across her face and she thought her skin might split. He threw her an equally big smile.

"You ready to march?"

Her dad kissed her hand and placed her arm in his. "Yeah, Daddy."

"I love you, Clara Bear."

"I love you, Dad."

They marched slowly, her gaze locked with Jackson's. Her song for him blasted through the large speakers. When her father gave her to Jackson the room fell away, along with all the people. There were no walls, nothing existed to confine them. Together they would face the world as one.

The covenant they entered into meant more to her than the house, the cheese shop, or his title as doctor because it meant they were accepted. They were acknowledged as equals. She'd been allowed to make the decision to love him for the rest of her life and the fact that her family supported her in that decision was humbling. They'd support her and Jackson through anything now, no matter how difficult the circumstance, or high the hill to climb, her family would be there, pushing behind them.

They exchanged vows and rings—her wedding ring boasting a big shiny sapphire that he said was the same shade of blue as her eyes during climax. The sweetest words she ever heard were spoken by the priest, "Ladies and gentlemen, may I present Mr. and Mrs. Jackson Reid Olivier." Old fashioned yes, but she was made to be Mrs. Olivier, and she knew he needed her to be as well.

The wedding ceremony started at seven o'clock. It was seven forty-five when they walked, hands joined, through the front door. A New Orleans brass band waited for the wedding party to exit, and then the trumpets and rich saxophone sounds swelled into the night air, vibrating through Clara's chest with each note. "When the Saints Go Marching In"—the song's message wasn't romantic, but the brass notes pulsed through her veins like a second heartbeat, making it impossible to stand still. They marched down Bourbon Street through the French Quarter with her family and friends in tow. She'd never seen Jackson so happy and carefree; his face transformed in the golden light of street lamps.

Her dress dragged along the filthy streets, collecting memories in its hem. Clara glanced down at the gathering grime and felt a fleeting pang—her mother had fussed so much over that pristine white—but she smiled at the thought that perfection had never been their story anyway. Love was messy, real, and infinitely more beautiful for its imperfections. This dirty dress would tell the truth of their beginning far better than any preserved gown in an attic box.

People from hotels, apartments, and nightclubs joined their festive parade. Those who didn't whooped and hollered as they passed. On a wrought-iron balcony, Clara spotted an elderly couple watching, the woman's weathered hand resting on her husband's shoulder, their eyes reflecting decades of shared sunrises. Something caught in Clara's throat at the sight—a glimpse of what she and Jackson might become.

She tugged at his arm, and he bent his head toward her ear. "Cracker Jack, this is the best day of my life," she whispered, her voice cracking slightly, tears making the street lights blur into stars.

"Bug, it's also the best day of mine. Thanks for giving me back my life." His fingers tightened around hers, a silent acknowledgment of the darkness they'd both crawled through to reach this light.

"Hey, you stole my line." Her smile ached in her cheeks, almost painful in its fullness.

"Mrs. Olivier, you saved me that day I arrived in your home.

Her throat burned with unshed tears. "Mr. Olivier, you saved me right back." The accident at sixteen, an unspoken memory between them, her pills lined up on her nightstand, his gentle care coaxing her to sit up and take them with the cool water he always brought her.

They kissed, holding up the march, but no one seemed to mind.

As their lips met, Clara felt a strange, fleeting awareness of time's passage—this perfect moment precious precisely because it couldn't last forever, each second slipping away even as she tried to memorize it. Their hearts were truly entwined and could now beat together as one. Nothing would ever be more perfect. Clara turned to her family and smiled as she rested her sleepy head on Jackson's shoulder, finding that familiar hollow where her temple had always fit, breathing in the scent of his skin that had meant home long before they had one together.

Their eyes locked for a moment, a lifetime of understanding passing between them before they spoke.

"Together forever," they said in unison, words that felt less like a promise and more like a recognition of what had always been true.

Notes

The Cowbell

1. The Bayley Hazen Blue Cheese information comes from Jasper Hill Farm, an artisan cheesemaker in Greensboro, Vermont, owned and operated by Andy and Mateo Kehler. The Bayley Hazen Blue information can be found on their website: jasperhillfarm.com/bayley.

Hate To Love You
Excerpt

A Whiskey Cove Novel

━━

Chapter 1 (Lacie)

I looked down at the letter in my hands. I'd walked back and forth in front of the mailbox five times now. To any onlooker I was engaged in a game of one-player tennis.

Lacie Ryan,
Please sign and return
to confirm your spot in the cohort for the
Louisiana State University
Speech-Language Pathology
program by the 30th of March.

If the mailbox in front of me would offer the additional service of reaching out and shoving this acceptance letter into the envelope, I'd pay good money for it. I willed it to grow anthropomorphic features for a few more seconds.

"It's official, I'm losing it. Not that I ever had *it*," I muttered, and stuffed the letter down deep into the bottom of my bag.

Despite the early morning hour, my grumbling stomach, and the mailbox dilemma, I forced myself to experience real joy at the wind blowing through the drapery of flower vines at the big wooden arched doors and stained glass that greeted you at the entrance of Acadian Kitchen, a little boutique grocery store this side of the Mississippi—make that the west side—in the little haven of Whiskey Cove.

Acadian Kitchen was just one of the family-owned shops on

River Street in a town so cute I sometimes felt like an imposter. On the cuteness scale, I was somewhere in the middle. That meant that every day, I spent time putting on my face and tried to place my best foot forward. At five foot one inch, I was awkwardly short, and several times per day, I caught myself making faces that were anything but cute—mostly because I only wore my glasses when my eyes were tired, otherwise, I preferred to squint.

And then there were people like my friend Kenzie who greeted me with hair as red- orange as a three-alarm fire, but who could rock a potato sack and a head full of tangles like she was dressed as the queen and ready to attend her jubilee.

"Sakes alive, Lacie, did you do your damn hair this morning?" Kenzie placed her palms on the sides of my face and pulled me in for a close inspection. "Hells bells, you've got makeup on too, and there's no doubt in my mind that this is a freshly pressed shirt." She pinched my silk top through her fingers. "My BFF is fifty years old, but that's okay, I still love you."

Kenzie could be the Town of Cute's mayor. We'd been up for hours on end cramming for finals and preparing for college gradua-tion and everything else in between. I had no doubt she'd rolled out of bed, ran fingers through her orange curls, and then came to work in last night's attire, looking like every badass thing you'd want in your own personal pixie with wings.

I, on the other hand, took the time to wash my face, body, and hair. I applied makeup, and to confirm Kenzie's suspicion, yes, I'd put on freshly ironed clothes and finished the whole thing with a lip gloss that promised to enhance my lips by twenty-five percent. In a word, I was anal, but I respected routine and felt that I could use every bit of confidence gained when I wore a well put together outfit and was freshly scrubbed and put together.

Whiskey Cove and its inhabitants were as sweet as Southern tea. However, surrounding myself with cuteness had its perks, TMJ for instance. But it was hard to hate cute people, and my ride-or-die homegirl was all kinds of cute. Besides, Acadian Kitchen wasn't a bad place to work, especially since I could stop on the front veranda and pick a flower for my hair before every shift, including this funky one that promised to get funkier.

Something just felt off, though it could have been the out-of-date chicken salad I'd scarfed down around one this morning.

The wind blew over my face and arms. I closed my eyes and inhaled the scent of honeysuckle mixed with manure, and well, that was the smell of home. Once summer settled in deep, you could even smell the heat. It smelled like rubber and heated concrete which, believe it or not, also smells like manure.

Inside the boutique grocery store, my footsteps made a satisfying thud against rustic wood flooring that always looked freshly sanded. I inhaled the smell of cured beef, shrimp, black pepper, and dried flowers that was signature boardwalk of a southeast Louisiana small town.

Kenzie scream-yawned while she restocked fruity truffles next to the register.

"Take a look at this," Kenzie passed me a folded square of paper she pulled from her apron pocket and I knew exactly what was on it, and *she* knew *I* knew exactly what was on it, so I was not shocked when her art was staring back at me.

She looked at me with that one-eyed squint she used when she knew she'd hear something she didn't want to hear. It was super sweet for her to design a heart from our thumbprints with our graduation year flanking the right side, but she knew how I feel about tattoos, and there was nothing she could say that would make me change my mind.

Nodding I said, "You know I think your art is amazing and you should make a big book of classy tattoos and self-publish it and retire on a yacht you buy from all your sales, but I can't get a tattoo."

Kenzie did a great impression of a twelve-year-old who just found out there is a passcode on the streaming services for R-rated movies.

"I really don't think I deserve the hard eye roll, but I promise the first tattoo I get will be this heart," I said, holding the fingerprint art in the air between us.

"That one is mine. I didn't bother sketching yours because I knew there was nothing I could say that would change your mind, and I'm a little pissed that I picked you all those years ago to be my BF forever."

I took a second look at the drawing. "Wouldn't matching tattoos be exactly the same?"

The truth was, I might get a tattoo, but I can't tell that to Kenzie because she would take the might and turn it into a 'right now' and within the hour I'd be sitting in a tattoo artist's chair with a needle in my arm? Ass? Thigh? Back? And we are back at the problem that has plagued me all along—where should I put the tattoo? How big should it be? What colors should be used? There is a lot to think about before putting something on my body that will be there forever.

Kenzie snatched the square out of my hand like the nuns at school used to snatch away a chorus book when they knew you had the latest copy of Cosmo hiding behind the book flap. "Did you even listen when I explained the significance of the thumbprints? I get the heart that's made from *your* thumbprint, and you get the one made from *mine*. Otherwise, it's just dumb."

She shoved it down into her apron and returned to restocking chocolate. I had been a crappy friend lately and I promised to get even crappier which hurt my heart. Kenzie thinks we are going to college together, that we are enrolled in all the same classes, that we will be able to carpool, and I don't know how to tell her I'm not going when I can't even tell myself.

I needed to make a decision soon. It wasn't a decision really. I frowned. I don't see how I can take Gramps and Mom's money for school when they work so hard for it, and I'm not even sure I'm smart enough to get through a program where only half make it out.

I needed sugar, stat. I pulled a grape Tootsie Pop from my bag and then stuffed the fraying canvas bag beneath the counter while my mind filled with thoughts about Gramps handing me a lollipop bouquet in the car on the way home from church on Sunday afternoon. He'd say *for the road;* it was something he had always done.

Sniffles were annoying plus they were a dead giveaway of a person's emotional state. When you were thinking about the day your Gramps would no longer be around, sniffles were okay. I pulled the wrapper off the lollipop, the tears in my eyes distorted my vision so it looked like I was holding a small purple sea between my fingers.

"Honey, don't sweat it, I'll never give up on you. We'll get our tats one day. . . we may be ninety years old, but they'll still tat us up right nice," Kenzie's warm hug was like melted chocolate, and I wondered how my mascara would ever hold up.

"It's not that." I wiped a tear away before it could run down my face and ruin my makeup. "I was up at four to help Gramps clean the plantation grounds and set up for an anniversary reception. His memory is not long for this world, and I'm worried someone's going to find out that he can't do his job." I put the sucker in my mouth and mumbled around it. "Mom didn't even tell me about Gramps until this morning when she couldn't figure out how she would be able to help him with the graduation breakfast reception set up in time for the guests to arrive."

"Can he retire?"

"Mom said if he waits five more years his income will be thirty percent more and you know he doesn't make much, so that bump is everything."

And if he did retire, where the hell will we all live? I was kind of hoping he'd retire *after* I graduate with my degree and could get a decent paying job. One of those jobs where you can go to a bank and qualify for a home loan. Mom has never qualified for any loans. Makes sense, who would give a self-employed house cleaner a hundred thousand dollars to be repaid over twenty-five years?

"Too bad Mr. Landry is gone."

Nostalgia pains hit deep in my core. I still remembered Mr. Landry's enthusiasm on opening day of the pool for summer. He'd man the grill with enough hot dogs and hamburgers to feed the entire town. We'd swim all day and by the end of the day could barely keep our eyes open from exhaustion. "Mr. Landry's kids run things differently. If something is costing them money, it's gone."

"Tell me about it. I still remember that cow they slaughtered when it went cross eyed," Kenzie said while chasing away a chill.

I cringed thinking about them finding out about Gramps. Mr. Landry and Gramps had been friends. They'd been on the USS Vincennes together during the Gulf War. When Mr. Landry's parents died, he was called back home and inherited the plantation, but it hadn't been kept up. Mr. Landry threw himself into renovating the place, and when Gramps was discharged from the Navy, there was no question he'd find Mr. Landry, or Skip as he called him, and together they licked their war wounds and created a place that is still around almost forty years later.

So many people had celebrated at the Landry Plantation. It was the place people went for weddings, graduations, anniversary celebrations, baby showers, birthdays—if you could think of a reason to celebrate, Landry Plantation was where you came to get your party on.

When Mr. Landry died three years ago, Gramps started his decline. First his memory and then his physical stamina diminished. "Memory is something that can be exercised, right?" Like muscles. I learned something about the memory centers of the brain when I took an undergraduate neurology course for speech therapists, but we just learned about the brain, not the therapy.

Kenzie's mouth twisted to one side in thought. "I don't know but we'll find out in the Neurogenic Disorders course."

The letter in my bag beneath the counter that needed to be mailed was screaming at me, and I imagined it sprouting wings and flying itself into the mailbox slot. I had my doubts that obtaining a degree in speech-language pathology was the quickest way to help Gramps, but it was all I had at the moment that offered any relief to my anxiety, so I'd hold tight to it, but it meant that I had to mail that acceptance letter.

My thoughts were interrupted when Frannie Faraday Fontenot tripped into the store and knocked over the daffodils I'd set out yesterday. The whole thing was a massacre of yellow petals and a release of pollen that had Kenzie simultaneously sneezing and assisting Mrs. Frannie.

"Oh, would you look at that . . . I've just ruined a nice flower."

"You ruined quite a few," *achoo*, "nice flowers, Mrs. Frannie, but," *achoo*, "it's okay because I don't like daffodils anyway," *achoo*, "they seem to have a hangdog expression that gives off a rather needy vibe."

After Frannie greeted me, Kenzie helped her understand and find clarified butter for whatever dish she was cooking from The French Chef cookbook. She'd watched a movie about a lady who cooked everything in the cookbook. Since then, Mrs. Frannie started her own version of the movie just after her grown son, and my Sunday School teacher since I can remember, became sick with ALS. The only problem was that Mrs. Frannie was great at making sweets but bad at making food. Her son, Steve, and my grandfather had started to decline around the same time.

I suppose that was the nature of progressive, degenerative diseases. Yet another thing I learned in the undergrad survey course on acquired neurogenic disease. And I believe that was reason number three to set my letter free. The decision wasn't an easy one to make. My mind wouldn't let me forget that this grad school was super hard—only fifty percent made it through. Mom and Gramps wouldn't let me go on my own either. They insisted on helping me with money they didn't have.

Kenzie continued sneezing while she swept up the flowers in front of the register, while Mrs. Fontenot eyed the massacred flowers with a frown. She plopped the butter on the counter, along with a pint of cream. "You can put the daffodils on my tab too, Lexie."

Achoo. "No, Mrs. Fontenot, the store can write off a few broken stems. You know Dad would never approve of charging you for broken products, or in this case, stems."

"Well, okay, darling, but don't go getting in no trouble because of me."

Kenzie shook her head. "No trouble, ma'am," and then sneezed her way to the back of the store, her *achoos* getting fainter and fainter.

"Watcha making today, Miss Frannie?"

"It's a be-your blank sauce today."

"Buerre blanc," I corrected. Languages were an interest of mine. I had not taken French, but living in Louisiana and especially working in a gourmet food store had taught me how to pronounce French food items. In fact, Frannie would do better buying a tub of the sauce we sell in the store.

"Oh, honey, you don't need to go getting all fancy with me and that French stuff. I never could get the hang of French, too many silent letters and all that."

"How's Steve doing?"

Her face had more lines than the last time I'd seen her, and the heavy makeup didn't quite cover all the darkness beneath her eyes. "He's got his good days and bad." She sniffled. "You know he's having more bad days than good ones lately. Can't really swallow too well. I'm having to chop up his food in the Cuisinart. Still, he chokes it down." She wiped away a tear. "I'm sorry."

I placed my hand on her arm. "Mrs. Frannie, don't apologize. Do you want me to come over and sit with Steve so you can go to bridge night at church?"

"Oh, honey, I know he'd love to see you."

I bagged her two items and then made her change. "Second Tuesday of the month, right?"

"That's it." She picked up her bag. "And we will see you at the blessing of the graduates' breakfast."

Before Mrs. Frannie made it out of the door, Kenzie came running up with a box of Benadryl and a cup of tap water. "Ring me up quick. Between the Aquanet holding up Frannie's beehive and the flower slaughter incident, I'm about to put that *orgasm on the tenth sneeze* hypothesis to the test."

My eyebrows hit my hairline at the thought of actualizing Kenzie's theory about *snexing* as she called it. I rang her up and watched her down two pink pills. She was a master at taking those things and then chugging coffee or Red Bull and, on occasion, both. "Ugh, can you believe this? Are my eyes puffy?"

I shook my head no, but inside, I was keeping a big fat *yes* under wraps. In the South, we liked to use little white lies to pretend the bank accounts were in good shape, the kids weren't driving us crazy, and that we looked better than we did on any given day. Jesus forgave white lies. It was the *black* ones that could get you kicked out of a Sunday singin' with a BBQ chaser.

"I think it's time for some beignets and a café au lait." Kenzie's words sounded as lazy as the stretch she made over the countertop. "I'm going to Bishop's, want anything? Do not say Dr Pepper."

Kenzie came up close behind me to tie the apron that I held to my chest. A Dr Pepper did sound good. "You know I don't drink chicory."

"And you call yourself Cajun."

Once the apron was secure, I turned to face her. "I've never once referred to myself as Cajun."

Kenzie reached across the register table to grab her wallet that rested beneath the counter. "Hmm, it may be time to rethink this friendship." With a quick motion she flipped the top up on the counter and walked through, letting it flop back down with her signature-style bang. I'd been around her long enough to pre-wince. "I'll be back, and then you can go on break." Her gum cracked like rapid-fire bullets.

Back at my job of picking through buckets of flowers, I detected Lawson's walk on the wood planks. Ba-dump. Ba-dump. If you paid attention, you could identify anyone from their walk.

Lawson was Kenzie's cousin. He also sported a head full of copper penny red wavy hair and was the cutest sixteen-year-old I'd ever seen. No acne, no awkward tooth-straightening braces, no BO. The Thibodeauxs knew how to grow them.

"If you wanna take a leak you'll have to do it at Bishop's or Heather's. Toilet's overflowing again." Lawson snorted and pulled his phone from the pocket of his rubber hunter green apron.

I watched red spots pop up on the apples of his cheeks.

"What did you do, Lawson?" I teased.

"It wasn't me," he said as he shot green daggers at me. "For all we know it's one of those feminine hygiene products again. Grandpa Jack's got Roto Rooter on the way."

"It's a great time to be alive, isn't it?"

He raised a brow as he watched me before giving up and shaking his head. "You're so weird." He walked toward the back of the store all while looking at his phone.

Meanwhile, I refilled and trimmed the dried eucalyptus and hydrangea bins that were all around the register, making everything fresh and floral. As places of work go, it wasn't a bad gig. For starters, it was impossible not to smile in this place as the Beach Boys' brand of syncopated rhythm drifted from the speakers in the ceiling. And if the Beach Boys didn't do it for you, there were individual pieces of Belgian milk chocolate available at the register. Three dollars could get you five pieces to gorge on.

. . . but sometimes . . .

The song would change, and my mood right along with it.

I set fire to the rain. . .

Suddenly, I was right back in the place I didn't want to be.

And I threw us into the flames . . .

I wondered how much it would cost to telephone the United Kingdom and how hard it would be to reach the singer, Adele. I wanted to do the impossible too . . . to throw all of the lies, the hurt, and the memories into a barrel and set it on fire.

But then, if I knew how to set the rain on fire, I would have already done that and moved on with my life. As painful as it all could be, I was still a realist. I wouldn't lie to myself and say things like *I'm over him,* because I wasn't, and this song proved it in so many ways.

A chill ran down my spine despite the eighty-degree temps we'd hit by 8:00 a.m. The hair on my arm stood up. With every millisecond that ticked by, my chest got tighter and tighter until there was no air left inside to expel.

Tell me what has to be wrong with the universe, my karma, the alignment of the stars, for Adele to play overhead at the same time *HE* would decide to waltz back into my life looking even sexier than he did four years ago. God in heaven, the man could sell a pitchfork to the devil. Even his muscles had muscles, but it was the white collared shirt with the sleeves rolled up that revealed arm veins for days that made the bottom fall out of my vagina.

Lucky for me, most people didn't come into Acadian Kitchen to buy condoms and beer as those things could be gotten cheaper at Walmart.

Unlucky for me, Caleb Dean St. Martin didn't have to worry about money.

Enjoy this book? You can make a big difference. Reviews are the most powerful tools in my arsenal when it comes to getting attention for my books. Much as I'd like to, I don't have the financial muscle of a New York publisher. I can't take out full page ads in the newspaper or put posters on the subway.

(Not yet, anyway).

But I do have something much more powerful and effective than that, and it's something that those publishers would kill to get their hands on.

A committed and loyal bunch of readers.

Honest reviews of my books help bring them to the attention of other readers.

If you've enjoyed this book I would be very grateful if you could spend just five minutes leaving a review (it can be as short as you like).

Thank you very much.

Keep in touch: Join Gina Watson's email list at ginawatson.net to receive alerts regarding sweepstakes, contests, giveaways, and upcoming book releases.

About the Author

Gina Watson writes steamy, small town romance novels with lovable characters. She published her first novella in 2014. Since then, she has published over twenty romance novels and novellas in many sub genres including small-town, forbidden love, new adult, and action-adventure.

Gina makes her home in Vermont with her husband, Brian. They married on Valentine's day and celebrate Valeversary every year while trying hard to live out their very own HEA ending. With hot cocoa and snowy picture windows it is practically perfect.

For more information:
ginawatson.net/
ginawatson@mac.com

Follow Gina Watson's BookBub for new release info and sales: https://www.bookbub.com/authors/gina-watson

News

Want a LITTLE more: Subscribe to **Gina's Newsletter**, which announces her biggest news, like book releases or sales readers won't want to miss. This is an infrequent mailing—**one to three times per year**—and is *different from GinaWatson.net News, which requires a separate subscription.*

Want a LOT more: Subscribe to **GinaWatson.net News** to be notified when there is news about books, brand new excerpts, cover reveals, event details, fun reader book-related extras, updated FAQ, great press, etc. Whenever news on the home page is updated, you will be too.